JP

SERIES

BOOK TWO

BY RICHARD LAWS

First published 2024 by Five Furlongs

ISBN 978-1-7397026-4-9 (Paperback)

'The Shake'

An American racing term. Possibly the source of the widely used phrase, 'In the shake up' that describes those horses involved in a close finish.

In the USA, claiming races are popular. For an amount of money (stated pre-race), you can make a 'claim' for any of the runners once the race has been run. In the event of more than one owner claiming the same horse, the racing official in charge of claims, the claims clerk, will conduct a 'shake' to determine who will become the new owner.

'The shake' involves putting numbered pills, one representing each owner, in a pill bottle and giving it a shake. The racing official randomly pulls out a winning pill relating to the successful new owner.

One

September 30th

Graham Dent lifted his binoculars to his eyes and concentrated on the small group of youngsters being led up the gallop by one of his older horses. Beside him, his son and assistant trainer, Hugo, was standing in the long grass smoking a cigarette.

'I tell you, the filly's got bags of speed,' said Hugo, between drags.

Dent didn't reply, watching the filly's knee action, calculating how long her stride was, the way in which she covered the ground. The lead horse eased up the incline and the filly, under hands and heels, broke clear of the other yearlings. By the time the crest of the hill was reached, she had caught up with the older horse.

Lowering his binoculars, Dent turned to his son.

'Put that out carefully, Hugo,' he ordered gruffly, 'You'll start a grass fire, knowing you.'

Hugo threw the butt to the ground, and ground it gleefully into the soft earth with his heel, whilst petulantly breathing out blue smoke that swirled over his father.

'What about the filly?'

Dent rubbed his chin for a couple of seconds before replying.

'You were right. She's decent.'

Two

October 15th

Horse flesh versus horse power. They were markedly different, but the thrill was the same for Geena. It was that surge of strength. Whether it came from riding a racehorse or a motorbike, both were exhilarating. And she was lucky enough to enjoy both, every single day.

Charging up the Yorkshire Wolds on the back of a thoroughbred colt, delighting in its ability, human and horse as one. It was intoxicating. Similarly, the throb of a motorbike, the sound of its engine as it engaged a higher gear, and the sudden, easy surge of power. That was just as satisfying. It gave her a sense of freedom.

But not tonight. Tonight the motorbike beneath her felt sluggish. In this sort of mood, she was demanding more. She required increased power and greater speed. Her heart was pounding. It felt like she was in sync with the motorbike's pistons, but it simply wasn't good enough. She twisted the throttle, discharging more fuel, and the engine responded.

Geena normally relished this stretch of road from Malton to Beverley, its undulations, the constant swinging from one apex to the next. But not tonight. Being well into the evening, the road was empty. Even so, she knew she was driving erratically. She was angry, upset, and disappointed, a dangerous combination that was clouding her mind. And it showed. The bike weaved, its single headlight dashing across verge and road, before the harsh white beam momentarily cut into woodland as the beast in the machine took over. She would never normally allow the metal monster to control her, but these weren't normal circumstances. A spike of fright dulled her anger and, cursing her own stupidity, she wrestled the motorbike back under control.

Steadying herself, she slowed, taking the next two corners of the A1428 Beverley Road in a lower gear, forcing herself to breathe evenly upon reaching the crest of the hill on the edge of the Yorkshire Wolds. She slowed to an eventual halt and flicked up her visor. Moonlight played on the virtually straight piece of road beneath her, lighting it up and making the tarmac shimmer as it wound its way downwards to the crossroads, a roundabout at its centre, lying at the bottom of the valley.

A mechanical noise behind her. The flash of a headlight on a nearby hedgerow. Now two headlights strafed the road. A car was approaching, and by the note of the engine it was arriving at speed. Her heartrate leapt again. She recognised that engine, that car. It was unmistakable, and it spurred her back onto action.

She engaged a gear, twisted her throttle and shot forwards down the hill, towards the crossroads, and the roundabout with its single lamppost at the centre of its raised circular plinth. Fifty miles an hour easily achieved, sixty, touching seventy…

Behind her, the car shot over the brow of the hill, its headlights bouncing as it picked out its quarry clearly for the first time. Thirty yards, twenty yards, then a mere five yards behind, its horsepower swamping the bike.

The car rushed up alongside, dwarfing the rider, short bursts of shouting and hand waving emanating from the passenger seat window. She gritted her teeth and twisted her throttle as far as it would go, edging ahead, the road beginning to flatten out. The car matched her, diving in, making her wobble, staying level, challenging her. The roundabout approached. There was a scream from the car window. It suddenly veered away with a screech of rubber on tarmac, the scream quickly lost in the darkness. Geena looked back to the road and gasped, immediately engaging her brakes, skidding and squirreling through the junction and onwards to an inevitable meeting with the raised centre of the roundabout marked with black and white chevrons.

The motorbike struck the band of black and white tiles that edged the roundabout, catapulting Geena over the handlebars in a cartwheeling arc through the cool night air. It was an awkward landing, the sort that made one of her chasers wince, the rain-softened ground allowing her arms and legs to dig a furrow, scarring the grass.

When the two companions left their car and approached the motorbike rider's unmoving, mud-encrusted body, one of their number recoiled at the sight of her arm, bent at an unnatural angle. Presently, the second man ventured forward, turned the young woman over, lifting her visor. At first, a pair of glassy, unfocused eyes stared into the cloudless sky studded with stars, but with a single blink, the spirit in the previously lifeless body returned.

Kneeling over her, he spoke quickly, with harsh words, quiet and insistent. A moment later Geena was staggering to her feet, holding her limp, aching arm. She stared defiantly at her pursuers, trembling from a mixture of anger and fear. The first man held no fear for her. It was the other man who held the greatest threat.

The two figures watched Geena lower her visor over narrowed eyes and stumble over to her stricken motorbike. No one helped the young woman right the vehicle, or kick start it. Geena set off on the heavily compromised motorbike, but not to her original destination of Beverley, instead, she did as they'd demanded, and took the road east.

Retracing their steps, careful not to step on the glass fragments of her wrecked headlight, the two figures returned to their car. The driver gunned the engine and they departed, heading back over the Wolds. Back to Malton.

Three

March 4th

The female presenter of Look North produced a benign smile as the weatherman passed the television audience back to her on the other side of the studio.

'Thanks *a lot* for that George,' Margo Steele said, careful to keep her sneering contempt for the man fractionally on the right side of acceptable, 'Our viewers aren't going to thank you for *that* forecast.'

'I can only report the facts, Margo,' George grumbled

rather stiffly.

Perfectly positioned to show off her long, newly fake-tanned legs to the camera, Margo Steele ignored the weatherman's reply, instead producing a soft, condescending chuckle for the viewers, 'And now, something to warm our hearts after that dreadful weather forecast. It's an uplifting story of recovery and hope in our region.'

She clasped her bare knee between knitted fingers, pulling it towards her and rocking slightly, 'I visited York earlier this week to meet a young woman who has had to battle with the effects of a terrible brain injury, but is now bringing a smile to the faces of every single visitor and resident of York she meets.'

Margo produced one of her well-practiced smiles, the warm, but slightly earnest one that told the audience to expect their heart-strings to be plucked.

Robert Farley scrambled down the side of his tatty armchair for his remote control. He hated these sort of sycophantic interviews that served the television station's thirst for a tearful local story, rather than what it did for the poor soul being asked the questions.

His one-bedroom flat was lit by an old lamp that, like most of his belongings, he'd picked up at a local charity shop. The remote control remained unfound, winning the game of hide and seek and thus the television channel stayed on the local news.

A short set of images of the River Ouse in York set the scene, but it was when the picture cut to Margo and her interviewee standing beside the river, appearing black and oily in the background, that Robert's fumbling for his remote control was forgotten.

Margo was doing one of her long-winded, self-satisfied introductions. But it was the small, wiry-framed woman in her mid-twenties standing beside her, a golden retriever sitting at her heel, that held Robert's attention. It was her… *his* good morning girl.

'Brooklyn Hartley was a promising young jockey,' Margo said, her face looking pinched as she spoke into her hand-held microphone. Despite the icy breeze whipping a strand of hair across her face, Margo ignored the distraction and turned to face the young woman and her canine companion.

'So Brooklyn, working for the Graham Dent yard in Malton, you rode dozens of winners for your stable as an apprentice and a career as a professional jockey was beckoning, wasn't it?'

The girl nodded and broke into a smile.

A shiver ran down Robert's spine. That smile was unlike any other he'd ever encountered. And every morning he made sure he received its wonderfully life-affirming radiance.

Margo's tone altered, she turned to face the camera, becoming serious, 'However, a horrific accident at the stables in October last year saw Brooklyn sustain a serious brain injury. Emerging from a coma after a month in intensive care at York General Hospital, her accident left Brooklyn unable to maintain her balance, read, write, or talk properly, leaving her dreams of pursuing a riding career in tatters.'

'So you might be wondering what we're doing on this footpath that follows the River Ouse all the way through York?' said Margo with a knowing smile.

'Well, because Brooklyn can still only say a few words, her injury having affected the speech centre of her brain, then *I'll* tell you,' Margo continued, grinning at her interviewee and then back at her audience once more, 'Brooklyn has become something of a star attraction on the banks of the Ouse. In order to aid her rehabilitation she was told to keep active, and that's what she's done, along with the help of her Labrador, Titan. They started to walk the banks of the Ouse every day. Six miles, twice a day, every day of the week for the last five months.'

Margo put her arm around the young woman, who

pursed her lips, appearing slightly uncomfortable with the enforced close contact.

'And every person she meets gets a smile and Brooklyn says the one phrase that she has always been able to say since she woke in her hospital bed.'

As if on cue, Brooklyn smiled. Robert shivered. It was a radiant smile, a smile displaying a youthful innocence, filled with warmth, trust and a touch of hope. A perfect set of teeth were set into a face that bunched up into glorious radiance and was complimented with light blue eyes that seemed to shimmer.

'Good morning,' said Brooklyn.

'Good morning,' Robert whispered to the two-dimensional woman on the screen. A rare smile had worked its way onto his face.

'Isn't that an absolutely amazing smile?' Margo told her audience with a shake of her head, 'And Brooklyn says 'good morning' to *everyone* she meets on her walks. Every single one!'

'Good morning,' added Brooklyn.

Margo smiled down at the girl.

'Brooklyn has become well-known along this part of the river and is now something of a local celebrity, with residents and tourists commenting online, wanting to know more about this enigmatic young woman with her Labrador, her two words, and her big smile. So much so, she has caught the attention of York's tourist board...'

The camera panned out to reveal a mousey, middle-aged woman wrapped up against the cold. Margo introduced her and started a conversation. It emerged that Brooklyn was to become the face of the city's latest set of adverts promoting York to tourists.

Robert zoned out of the banal banter between the two women, concentrating instead on Brooklyn. She had a hand on Titan's head, idly scratching the dog's ear, but was looking off-camera. She smiled again, and another woman, older this time, came into the camera shot and gave Brooklyn's hand a squeeze and she received a kiss on her cheek from the girl.

'And we're joined by Brooklyn's mother, Janice,' said Margo, going on to ask her a question that started with 'What does it feel like to have a daughter who...'

Janice Hartley was small, like her daughter and clearly not from York. Her Liverpool accent cut through the interview like a knife.

The fawning Margo asked her second question of Janice, but the camera had picked up on Brooklyn and panned out slightly to catch it. She was smiling once more, lighting up the screen.

'Good morning!' called out Brooklyn to someone unseen, effectively cutting through Margo's interview with her mother. Margo and Janice both paused to look at the young woman, Janice smiling, Margo irked at being interrupted.

Brooklyn turned back to them, still smiling. Robert smiled too - he couldn't help it. A moment later a man's voice shouted from off-screen, 'And a good morning to you young 'un!'

The camera panned away from Margo and landed on an elderly man walking along the riverside footpath with the aid of a stick. He wiggled it in the direction of the camera for a moment, smiled, and passed on by.

'Well, you can see for yourself the affect this young woman has had on the people in York,' said Margo as the camera returned to provide her with a close-up, 'And as she continues to recover from what was a life-threatening injury, Brooklyn Hartley and her Labrador, Titan, are doing their best to bring a bit of old-fashioned Yorkshire warmth to this city, one person at a time.'

Four

March 6th

It had been two years since Robert Farley had felt the warmth of fresh blood on his hands.

Fighting the revulsion created by the touch of the slick red ooze between his fingers, he carried on regardless, until tears of frustration, then desperation, and finally, desolation, fell freely from his cheeks. With knees and back aching, his shirt collar and armpits damp with sweat, he ceased working on her and with the little strength he had left, he made sure, by pounding on her chest.

Exhausted, Robert fell back from the body to sit panting on the footpath, legs apart, head bowed. A few feet away Titan padded forward and sniffed at his mistress's hair. Lying on her back, the girl's head was cocked to one side, her big, beautiful blue eyes staring vacantly through him, shoulder-length fair hair only minutes before being a neat bob, was now strewn messily across her face. He absently rubbed his face and then examined his hands. Slamming his eyes shut, disgusted by the blood, nausea swiftly built within him.

Spinning his body over, Robert noisily regurgitated his poached egg-on-toast breakfast onto the dark green stems of a group of newly sprouted Himalayan Balsam. He didn't mind so much, the ugly plant plagued this section of the riverside footpath and he felt far better for having emptied his stomach.

Someone else disagreed, if their shocked gasp was anything to go by.

Robert twisted his head up and around and discovered he wasn't alone on the riverside path. A pock-marked young man, barely out of his teens, was staring down at him wide-eyed. Cowering behind him, a heavily made-up younger woman was holding her hand to her mouth, displaying a set of false nails and was obviously the source of the gasp. The man was holding a phone in a classic video-making stance, its many camera lenses twinkling at Robert.

'The blood. You've stabbed her… Is she…' the girl said hoarsely, her voice trailing away, unable to utter the word.

'No. Yes… she's dead. I tried… I mean, yes. Stabbed. I…'

As Robert began to push himself up from his knees, a glint of early morning sun percolated through the overhead branches of a tree and bounced off something metallic beside the bloody body. Without thinking, Robert grasped the shiny object. Immediately aware of what he was holding, he examined the knife. He was overcome with a need to explain to the two teenagers.

'I think…'

Both the youngsters stepped back at the sight of the knife in his hand. Robert thrust his hands out, but this only made them both cower further away down the leafy path.

'She was… I couldn't help…'

Robert stopped speaking, aware he wasn't making much sense. He stood up… and immediately regretted having done so. Standing at six foot three inches, and muscle-bound from his time in the forces, he towered over his audience. Having accidentally stepped into the growing pool of rapidly congealing blood beside the young woman's corpse, and still holding onto the bloodied knife, it wasn't a surprise that the boy and girl had become terror-stricken and backed away even further. The boy still held the phone out, videoing him.

'No, no. You don't understand… I just…'

A piercing scream from behind Robert drowned out the rest of his sentence. He whipped around and was puzzled to find a small, besuited middle-aged man astride a bicycle, sunlight bouncing off the orange helmet fastened to his head. The scream had been so high pitched… As if to provide confirmation, the man stopped staring at the bloodied body blocking the footpath and looked up into Robert's eyes, then at the knife in his right hand, and screamed again. Behind Robert, the boy and girl started to angrily shout something about the police at him.

Robert's mind swam, only moments before being consumed with the young woman at his feet, Robert was now experiencing a confused, gut-wrenching panic attack. Fighting for breath, he held up both his hands in a vain attempt to bring hush and some semblance of order to his situation, Robert noticed the middle-aged man's helmet again. A camera bobbed around as the man's garbled threats were interspersed with a third round of scared, high-pitched screams. The man's bicycle was leaning invitingly against his hip.

Robert cast a sad gaze down at the body, his chest still heaving. He pocketed the knife, muttered an apology to the deceased girl, and in one swift movement, lunged forward, and grabbed for the man's bicycle. It was easily torn from the older man's grasp and Robert set off at a run, eventually mounting the bike and pedalling furiously. Careful to avoid the overhanging and encroaching foliage that surrounded the riverside footpath on both sides, Robert pumped his knees up and down. The bike thudded over a cattle grid and he weaved past three dog walkers. The last voice Robert heard behind him came from the irate cyclist.

Among the many words of rage shouted after him was the one accusation Robert had spent the last two years of his life wishing he could forget.

'Murderer!'

Five

'That went well.'

'You think so?' Bain replied, surprise in his voice.

'No!' Holly said through a long sigh.

'Ah, sarcasm. I should have known,' he groaned, still staring blankly at the laptop screen that until a few moments ago had held a video image of his father with whom he'd shared a largely stilted and perplexing conversation.

'At least he didn't demand we pay back the money we owe him,' said Holly in a tone meant to sound positive, 'Perhaps he's forgotten about it?'

Bain appreciated this was an attempt by his friend, business partner, and currently his landlord's daughter, to cheer him up. She was probably embarrassed for him. Anyone would be after witnessing the way his father had spoken to him. From his workstation at the other side of the attic room he lifted his eyes from the laptop, straightened, and flashed Holly a weak, but positive smile.

'A nice thought, but my father never forgets. Not where money is concerned.'

He shivered. It was half past five on a Tuesday in early March and, noticing it had already dropped dark outside, Bain got up to draw the curtains. The temperature in their office at the top of the house always fell sharply as soon as the sun moved to the back of the house in the afternoon. As he returned to his desk he glanced over at the open fire that had been roaring earlier in the day; it was now reduced to burnt-out embers.

Leaning back and pushing her chair away from her desk, Holly yawned theatrically, arms held straight out, hands open, palms up and fingers splayed. Bain sullenly watched her and was reminded of a Mickey Mouse alarm clock his mother had sent him as an eight-year-old child at boarding school. The time according to the position of Holly's arms was a quarter past eight.

'I'll get downstairs and check on my very own family millstone,' she said, continuing to stretch whilst getting to her feet.

From under Bain's desk emerged Daisy, his three-year-old Jack-a-something. She sat down and looked up expectantly at Holly, betraying her outwardly patient demeanour by thumping her tail excitedly on the carpet. A visit downstairs to the kitchen could result in some sort of treat, usually care of Ronnie, Holly's mother.

'I'd quite happily trade your mother for my father,' Bain admitted.

'You can have her,' Holly muttered on her way to the attic door, 'I doubt your father hangs his washing out, leaves your sopping wet jeans out overnight in sub-zero temperatures which forces you to defrost them the next morning.'

Bain smiled to himself as Holly left with Daisy at her heel. He could still hear their footfalls as they descended the two flights of creaky stairs belonging to the large detached Victorian house in Northallerton he'd called home for the past seven months.

As their footsteps faded away, Bain returned his attention to his laptop and clicked hopefully into his emails. And after discovering, surprise, surprise, there was nothing new, he moved onto the internet and began flicking through various news websites, searching for anything that might lead to some half decent, paying work.

Managing to delay paying his father back only gave him a few weeks leeway. His father was a successful businessman and close friend of right-wing politicians. Owing a man like him money - despite being his son - meant living in a permanent purgatory. The debt was the perfect excuse for his increasingly determined father to insist Bain ceased writing nonsense about sports (his father's words) and return to London. A management role had been earmarked for Bain alongside his elder brother in his family's property company. He couldn't think of anything worse; a boring desk job combined with having his constantly critical father as his boss.

What he and Holly needed was a story, a *proper* story that would generate actual, real revenue. Hard cash in the bank would clear their debts and give them the freedom to pursue more interesting, powerful stories, rather than living hand to mouth. But surviving together as investigative journalists was proving more difficult than either of them had imagined. Earning a living from writing about skullduggery in sport was tough, despite having broken one of the biggest sports crime stories of recent times.

It had been six months since he and Holly had written their feature on the attempted theft of one of the top stallions in the country and exposed a race-fixing scandal. It had been picked up by The Sunday Times, and for a time afterwards they'd been busy as other work was pushed their way, but that interest had dried up. Bain was back to covering minor league football matches and writing the odd two-hundred-word feature for sports magazines, whilst Holly was helping them scrape a living by picking up small human interest stories for the local newspapers and their websites in North Yorkshire.

He'd assumed publishers would be beating a path to their door to publish their book, huge advances being thrown at them from every direction, but it turned out that the consensus was that race fixing didn't sell. The Sunday Times had been gracious enough to pay them eighteen thousand pounds for their feature, and they'd been lucky to get that. There had been no bidding war, and their book hadn't sold anything like the anticipated volume. It left them with a dwindling bank account and Bain having to grovel to his father for an extension to his initial loan, and now, a second loan… that had been refused.

Bain grimaced at his computer screen. Monitoring news feeds from all over the internet, the same few stories appeared on every website, from the Oban Times to the Brighton Argus. Each report was essentially the same, using the same facts, only framed slightly differently depending on the politics of the site, or how desperate they were to attract readers. The lead story was the same everywhere; the manhunt, now into its third day, for the York riverside murderer.

Headlines ranged from 'Hunt for York Riverside Murder Suspect Widened,' on the Guardian website, to 'Viral Video Shows Farley's Fatal Knife Frenzy,' courtesy of The Sun. Along with thirty million other people, Bain had watched the video, and thankfully, there was nothing frenzied about it. The footage shot by a pair of students who had stumbled across Farley kneeling over the body with a bloody knife in his hand, was marred by the two of them screaming at him, and some extremely jerky camera shots. They'd managed to catch Farley pounding on the poor girl's body, being sick, getting to his feet, the flash of a blurred knife in his hand, and him running off. His protests were inaudible above the students and a cyclist's screams, whose bicycle Farley was seen to steal.

A lively discussion was raging online as to why the students hadn't done more, as they filmed Farley stabbing the girl, and whether Farley had been trying to calm the youngsters down afterwards, rather than threatening to attack them. A studious Facebook user had noted that in one swift panning shot showing the cyclist, he had a camera on his helmet. This had set off a whole new set of discussion threads. Why wasn't this footage available online? Was it a conspiracy by the police to withhold it, was it too gruesome for public display? Was the aged cyclist the real killer, or was the deep state involved?

Under growing pressure, the police had quietly announced the cyclist with the strangely high-pitched scream had forgotten to switch the camera on when he left home. The condemnation for the man's lack of diligence, and his odd scream that made him sound like a teenage girl, had filled social media for the next forty-eight hours.

Bain was listening to a tearful interview with Brooklyn Hartley's mother, Janice, when Holly came back into the room. She wore a distinctly disgruntled look, so Bain paused the video.

'What's up?'

Holly bared her teeth and shook her head wearily, 'Mother.'

Bain considered his response for a long moment. He'd never met anyone quite like Holly's mother. Ronnie was one of the most intelligent and forceful people he'd ever met, and yet she was also forgetful, easily distracted, and in the right mood, could be downright argumentative.

'What's Ronnie done now?'

Holly sat down heavily in her swivel chair, 'I found her on her knees on the kitchen floor covering it in those little dog biscuits shaped like bones. She's making a montage called 'The cry of the forgotten' with them, apparently inspired by Banksy.'

'Sounds arty.'

'She'd been watching a documentary on him,' Holly explained with a shrug.

Bain considered this for a few seconds.

'Where's Daisy?' he ventured.

'My mother was allowing her to eat some of her creation,' Holly griped, 'She said it was something Banksy would appreciate, as he liked to shred his art. She doubted Banksy has considered actually eating it. So I left her to it.'

Bain had a vision of Daisy with her stomach the size of a volleyball. But he told himself that Ronnie would know better than to allow her to eat the entire box of gravy bones.

As Bain and Holly returned their attention to work, the room fell silent, apart from the tapping of fingers on keyboards. The door to the attic opened a crack two minutes later. Daisy trotted in and curled up in her worn, flat basket at Bain's feet, stretching herself out to soak up the last of the warmth from the fire.

It was thirty minutes later when the doorbell rang. Daisy sprang to her feet and gave a low woof. A minute later, Ronnie called up the stairs.

'Bain! Holly! You've got a visitor.'

Holly caught Bain's gaze and recognised the same spark of hopeful desperation in him she was experiencing. It couldn't be a proper job could it?

Daisy was off like a shot through the open attic door. As Bain and Holly made their way downstairs the sound of a male voice telling Daisy, 'What a good girl she was', travelled up the stairs. Holly led, and as they reached the final landing she was met by the sight of her mother standing beside a well-built, muscled man with short straight hair who was balanced easily on his haunches, petting a delighted, tail-wagging Daisy. The visitor looked up at Holly as she descended the last few stairs, and smiled. Early thirties, with a lived-in face, and an air of diffidence about him, he straightened and said in an accent difficult to pinpoint in terms of region, 'Good evening, Miss Grant.'

Ronnie glanced up at her daughter and Bain behind her and said, 'This is Mr…'

She turned back to the man, 'Sorry my dear, what did you say your name was?'

'I'm afraid I didn't,' replied the stranger apologetically, adding a warm smile to his statement, 'It's probably best that I don't saddle you with my surname. What friends I have call me Robert.'

Behind the visitor, a large rucksack, almost the size of Bain was leaning up against the hallway wall. A thick hat and gloves lay on top, but when Ronnie offered to take his heavy-duty all-weather coat, he politely refused. He then thought better of it, removing the coat to reveal a thick wool jumper, but insisted on keeping the arctic grade coat hooked over his arm. Taking in his steel-toed boots, he had the look of a man professionally kitted out for the worst of the weather.

Holly shook the man's hand first, a tentative, quick shake. She was surprised to find Bain keen to pump the man's muscular arm up and down at length before escorting him straight into the dining room, just off the hallway, the last place they would normally take a visitor.

Have I underestimated how bored Bain has become over the last few months? Why else would he be acting like this, wondered Holly as she followed the two men into the dining room. Or was it simply desperation? Anything for a chunky new case? Either way, she decided, he's acting oddly.

She stood opposite their visitor, the dining table between them. He made no move to take a seat.

Bain doubled back into the hallway to have a quiet word with Ronnie out of Holly and Robert's earshot. She watched through the open door to the hallway as her mother's eyes widened in reaction to something Bain had told her. Ronnie gave her a worried glance, then disappeared in the direction of the kitchen. When Bain rejoined Holly and their visitor in the dining room he made sure to click the door shut behind him.

'I'll get straight to the point. We don't have too much time,' stated Robert before Bain's hand had time to leave the doorknob.

Careful to address himself equally to both Bain and Holly, he added, 'I'm Robert Farley. I imagine Mr Bainbridge has advised Mrs Grant to call the police, so forgive me if I cut straight to the chase.'

As Bain joined Holly on the other side of the table, Farley paused a moment to cast an experienced, searching eye over the two journalists. When he spoke again, it was with striking certainty.

'I did not kill the Good Morning Girl.'

Six

It was icy cold in the dining room. The only room on the ground floor that wasn't heated, it was rarely used, and yet the air still held a stale tang of Pledge. Even so, when Holly shivered, she put it down to the words Robert Farley had just uttered, rather than any nip in the air.

Farley eyed Bain suspiciously as he pulled out a dining chair. Thoughtfully pursing his lips, Farley hung his jacket on the chair back and sat down. His hosts remained standing. He pushed both sleeves of his thick woollen jumper up his forearms and tapped on the face of his watch. Satisfied with whatever the watch was displaying, he looked up at Bain and Holly, standing rigid behind their chairs on the other side of the table.

'You must know who I am,' he stated, his breath condensing in the freezing air, momentarily giving his craggy face a worryingly ghostly appearance.

Bain nodded, strategically standing a fair distance around the dining table from the man, but for safety's sake remaining close enough to Holly to be of some use if something untoward were to happen. He caught himself, and a swift re-examination of this logic made him shiver. His protective response, whilst honourable, was a fantasy. He'd be useless should Farley leap at them. It was more likely his athletically talented business partner would be the one doing the protecting. Bain edged a little closer to Holly.

'And from your reaction, I can tell you *did* ask Mrs Grant to call the police,' Farley said assumptively, casting his hard blue eyes over to the closed dining room door before allowing them to come back and rest on Bain.

'You're Robert Farley, currently the focus of a huge manhunt,' Bain stated levelly.

Farley didn't appear unduly concerned. Instead, he crossed his arms and leaning back in his chair, studied the two of them with unguarded satisfaction.

It took Holly a couple of seconds to place him. Holly froze once his identity registered fully. Farley was the man in that horrible video that was currently infesting every corner of social media and the news channels. A sudden awareness of the triangle of mistrust that she, Bain, and Farley now shared made her heart lurch, then drum out a loud, thumping beat in her chest. She edged a little closer to Bain.

Robert Farley didn't move. With arms still crossed, the sleeves of his thick woollen jumper were bunching up to his elbows. Holly cocked her head to one side, noticing the bottom half of an aging tattoo on Farley's right forearm. Although difficult to make out, it looked like a crest with planet earth at its centre, finished off with scrolls above and below.

'I've got a chance with you two,' Farley said, pointing a finger at them both in turn, 'I don't fancy my odds, but still, it's a chance. You're both quick on the uptake. I'll need that.'

'Mr Farley, you need to explain why you're here,' said Bain, resting a hand lightly on the back of a dining chair, torn between learning more from Farley, and grabbing Holly's hand and bolting for the dining room door.

Farley placed has large hands palms down on the table, 'I'm here because I need your help. Please, sit down... and call me Robert.'

Holly didn't know why, but she again edged her feet towards Bain. It felt like the right thing to do. Conversely, Bain slid into a seat directly opposite Farley, his inquisitive nature finally conquering his fear.

'This is the man the police have been looking for in connection with the murder of Brooklyn Hartley,' Bain told Holly, his gaze never leaving Farley, 'The girl stabbed to death on the riverside path in York.'

'She's already worked that out,' Farley countered, having noted how Holly was sticking to Bain like a limpet, 'Look, I have no more than ten minutes before the police get here, perhaps less. I need you both to listen.'

Bain eyeballed Farley, 'You didn't kill her?'

Farley shook his head, 'The girl was dying when I came across her. I tried to save her.'

'I knew it!' Bain exclaimed, slapping the table with his palm and beaming triumphantly up over his shoulder at the still standing Holly.

The tension in the room should have broken, but Holly saw to it that it remained taut.

She scowled at Bain, 'The news reports seem pretty damning. The police say they're not looking for anyone else in connection with the case.'

Farley leaned forward towards Bain, his chair making a

scraping noise, 'How did you work out it wasn't me?'

He sounded genuinely interested.

'Too messy. Far too messy,' admitted Bain, 'Also, I've been analysing that video those teenagers took. Something about it that wasn't right.'

This was news to Holly, 'What do you mean?'

'Murderers don't tend to examine the murder weapon and show it to the people who are videoing him. There was one particular moment, where you held the blade, then realised your prints would be all over the... what was it? A scalpel, or something similar?'

Farley didn't reply for a long moment, he was hardly moving, staring at Bain wearing a stunned expression. A moment later he snapped back. Very slowly, telegraphing every deliberate movement to his intimate audience, Farley dipped into the pocket of his coat he'd hung on his chair.

'It was this,' he said quietly, placing a small knife onto the shiny teak dining table top. It was about five inches long with a wooden handle and a short, sharp blade. He slid it carefully towards Bain.

Farley seemed only too happy to rid himself of the murder weapon. He withdrew his hand and eyed the blood tarnished knife with a look of disgust.

Holly leaned across the table to inspect the knife, careful not to touch it. Bain did the same. The two inch blade looked worryingly sharp. The entire length of the object was smeared with congealed blood and Holly could make out a number of bloodied palm prints on the wooden handle.

'Most of the prints will be mine,' Farley explained, 'But I didn't wipe it, just in case some of the killer's prints are still on there.'

Holly shivered. The girl's upper body and especially her face and throat had been cut to ribbons, but some of the wounds hadn't made sense on the video, until you saw the weapon. The knife's blade hadn't been long enough to kill her with one or two lunges. The killer had been forced to slash away at his victim. Holly found herself imagining the surgically sharp blade doing its work and had to look away. Brooklyn must have been in excruciating pain until blood loss saw her lose conciousness.

'I had to run,' said Farley, a hint of desperation seeping into his words, 'You understand why, don't you?'

'I checked your background,' Bain replied immediately, nodding at the man's arm, 'You're ex-forces, and based on that tattoo on your forearm, you were in the navy.'

'Marines,' Holly broke in, taking a seat for the first time.

Bain's eyes widened and he gave her a questioning stare.

'He was a commando,' she added with a shrug, 'It's the Latin in the scrollwork underneath his tattoo, *Per Mare, Per Terram* – By Sea, By Land. It's the motto of the Royal Marines.'

A thought struck Holly.

'That's why you think it was too messy!' she said directly to Bain almost forgetting Farley was there, 'He's a trained, professional killer, why would he stab the girl so many times when he could have…'

Holly watched Bain's face curl up with acute embarrassment and after rolling her eyes at him, she turned to Farley. But before she could issue any apology, he was waving a dismissive hand at her.

'Great, you've got it. I knew you were the right people,' said Farley in a businesslike manner, 'I don't blame you for calling the police, but I need to leave. They won't believe me. I doubt they're even looking for anyone else. Take a look at my forces record, I'm sure one of the newspapers will have dredged it up by now. Then you'll understand why I had to run.'

Farley's watch made an electronic beep.

He got to his feet and pulled on his coat, 'All you need to know is that I didn't kill the girl. In fact… I really liked her, I used to set off to work early just to make sure I would pass her walking her dog and get a 'Good Morning' from her. I know how that sounds, but seriously, I would *never* hurt her. That's why I'm here. I want you to catch whoever did this. Not for me, for the girl.'

He drifted off for a second, standing with his muscular shoulders slack, his eyes focusing blankly on them. Holly was suddenly aware of the tiredness emanating from Farley.

'There was something deep in her eyes,' breathed Farley, 'And that smile was... special.'

'You want us to investigate Brooklyn Hartley's murder for you?' asked Holly, unable to hide her incredulity, 'You? The number one suspect?'

'You're... what do you call yourselves? Detective journalists?'

'Investigative journalists,' Bain corrected.

'Then investigate this!' Farley exclaimed, his rugged features becoming animated, 'It should be right up your alley!'

'You were caught red-handed. Literally,' Holly pointed out in exasperation, 'You had Brooklyn's blood all over you on that video. Is there any wonder the police are after you?'

Farley turned to regard Bain, trying to judge whose side he was on. Recognizing the same dubious look Holly had given him, his eyes narrowed. Bain sensed the first sign of frustration in their visitor. Farley needed them. He'd been a forces professional, so he could evade the police, as he had done for the last three days, but he couldn't investigate a murder. He couldn't clear himself. He needed Grant Bainbridge to do that for him.

The lines on Farley's forehead knitted themselves together and he gave a small sigh. Opening the dining room door he located his backpack and slung it over his shoulders in one easy movement.

'I'm asking for you to investigate,' he said, pulling on his hat and gloves, 'That sweet young girl needs someone to find her killer. And I need... '

Farley's voice trailed away and the big man paused in the middle of the hallway.

'I'm going out the back,' he told the two of them gruffly, 'You need to look at where she worked, where she got that awful head injury. I read your stuff on that race-fixing ring a while back and thought you'd at least understand. I reckon this has something to do with that racing yard in Malton where she used to work.'

Bain and Holly shared a sidelong glance.

'Wasn't Brooklyn an apprentice jockey?' Holly whispered to him.

As one, they hurried after Farley as he set off down the hallway and through the kitchen. He slowed for a moment in the conservatory, passing the seated Ronnie, apologising for the intrusion and the hassle he imagined the police were about to cause her. She crossed her arms and gave him a curt nod in return and told him the conservatory door to the garden was unlocked. Farley pressed his lips together and gave her a small nod of acknowledgement before stepping out into the cold evening air.

'Why us, Robert? Why are *we* the right people to investigate this?' Bain called out after him as he, Holly and Ronnie spilled out onto the back lawn to watch as Farley retreated down the garden.

Farley faltered, then stopped half-way across the back lawn. He lifted his face and looked up into the clear, moonlit sky and sighed, as if angry with himself. Spinning around, he lifted his gaze to meet Bain and cleared his throat.

'I forgot to mention… I've heard the news reports,' he said in a quiet, apologetic tone, 'They say the girl never said anything after her accident in the stables apart from 'Good morning'. But that's not true. She said something else to me before she died. It's why I thought of you.'

In the distance, the wail of a police siren had Farley cocking his head and peering in its direction like a nervous deer.

'What did she say?' Holly demanded over Bain's shoulder, scared Farley might flee before giving up Brooklyn

Hartley's last words.

'Snowdrop,' replied Farley without hesitation, 'She said snowdrop.'

'Are you sure?' Bain queried.

Farley stared at him, 'She was dying. She had to cough up blood to get it out for Christ's sake. I know what I heard. I reckoned it was the killer's nickname or something.'

'The full name of her killer would have been better,' said Bain quietly.

Farley's eyes fell to the grass and he grimaced for a moment, 'I asked her. I pleaded with her to tell me his name. But the words just... wouldn't come. Perhaps she didn't know who it was... And then she... went, I couldn't bring her back.'

'The blood on you...' said Bain.

'I tried to resuscitate her,' Farley replied sullenly, 'I was at it for four, maybe five minutes. It's why... I don't look good in that video.'

Holly hugged herself, partly from the chilly breeze whipping around the fruit trees, but mostly to fight the urge to rush forward to console Farley. The man was hurting. For a few seconds, his whole body seemed to sag, weighed down by the memory of Brooklyn's final few moments.

Another police siren rang out, closer this time, and Farley snapped out of his funk, alert once again.

'That knife. I reckoned it's used on horses. That means horses or racing is involved somehow. That's why I'm here. You're supposed to be the experts,' he barked, staring at Holly and Bain with accusing eyes.

'Find out what Snowdrop means,' he growled.

Farley stumped another ten yards down the garden before snapping, 'I'll be in touch,' over his shoulder.

Holly turned her head and gave Bain another sideways look to see what he thought, but he wasn't even aware she was there. A dreamy, almost vacant smile now graced his face. Holly knew what that look meant; Bain was already hooked on this story. Slightly irked, she turned back and caught a last glimpse of Farley, athletically scaling the seven-foot ivy-covered brick wall at the bottom of her mother's garden. Their unexpected visitor dropped over and disappeared from view.

'That man must have spring-loaded feet,' remarked an impressed Ronnie.

Seven

'So you let him go?' DI Golden said coldly, not for one minute expecting an answer from Holly or Bain, 'The most wanted man in Britain pitches up at your house, and despite being the nosiest investigative journalists I've ever come across, you couldn't keep him talking for the twenty-five minutes it took me to get here?'

Kirsty Golden, standing with her hands on trouser-suited hips in front of the empty fireplace in the dining room, surveyed the seated audience she'd been interviewing for the past forty minutes. Ronnie, Bain, and Holly were all avoiding catching her eye, but to be fair, Ronnie had her eyes closed. Golden half wondered whether the woman had nodded off. She imagined it was probably past Ronnie's bedtime and it *had* been an eventful evening.

Bain and the Grants had already proved they had the knack of being drawn into this sort of pickle. The race fixing and horse-knapping scandal last year was proof enough that they'd happily involve themselves in all sorts of scrapes for the sake of a good story.

Golden had received Ronnie's phone call on her way home to Northallerton from York. Aware the lady was an eccentric, she'd made the decision not to call it into the York office, not until she'd spoken with the trio face to face. While Ronnie had been adamant that the highest profile fugitive in Britain was standing in her dining room, Golden hadn't been about to mobilise half of North Yorkshire's finest without getting the facts straight first. She was finding her working life tough enough as it was, and her new boss was the sort who'd revel in her making a mistake.

She'd been called into Sayer's office two days ago, three days after Brooklyn Hartley had been murdered, to listen to a colleague, a seasoned detective called Frank Kirby, label the Farley case a, 'slam dunk' and suitable for a fresh-faced new kid like her. It had made her blood boil.

Kirby believed the pursuit of Robert Farley wasn't worth his time as he'd unearthed a new lead in a drugs case. Both of them had been working separately on this same case from different locations because it affected the whole of Yorkshire. Golden had recognised Kirby's actions for what they were; a way to sideline her, now they were based in the same office.

Sayer had promptly allocated her to the Brooklyn Hartley murder investigation, leaving Kirby to pursue his hot lead at Hull docks. Kirby was sure the drugs were being imported, whilst she was sure the gang were wholly based in Yorkshire.

'Get investigating and find Farley, fast!' had been Sayer's only instruction. Golden winced inside. Investigating was the very last thing Sayer had in mind. He just wanted the suspect, no, the *killer* caught. With Farley's workmates in York and one or two of his army pals already interviewed by Kirby, she'd started by talking with the girl's mother, then Brooklyn's friends and work colleagues over in Malton. But Sayer had made it crystal clear, the prerogative was to catch and charge Robert Farley with murder.

'This is a simple track, trace, and charge,' he'd advised the team, 'We have the evidence given by the three eye witnesses at the crime scene, as well as the video, and Farley's career history and subsequent expulsion from the navy only adds to that already damning evidence. Go get Farley!'

All the evidence pointed to Farley's guilt, but contrary to Kirby's slam dunk theory, a team consisting of over twenty officers, including three officers of Golden's grade, had failed to bring the man into custody for the past three days.

Golden's move to the York office from Northallerton had caused ripples of disgruntlement, not least with Sayer. He was proving to be a difficult man to please. On allocating her to the Brooklyn Hartley murder team Sayer had announced in a voice loud enough for the rest of the team to hear through the Plexiglas wall, that, 'Even she couldn't cock this one up.'

The team's failure to immediately locate Robert Farley and charge him with Brooklyn Hartley's murder had Sayer on their backs noon and night. She had next to no space to operate and half expected Sayer was privately delighted with her lack of a positive result. Claiming he was under immense pressure to curb the media's hawkish attention, he was still demanding a swift arrest despite Farley being as elusive as 'Willo The Wisp'.

Despite pointing out a number of anomalies with the video, Sayer's response had been unequivocal. Find the prime suspect, charge him, and worry about the details once the media interest wanes.

'This job is about managing public perception,' Sayers had hollered at her only this morning, 'The residents and tourists visiting York need to feel safe enough to walk the streets again! That's what matters right now.'

Golden had gritted her teeth, agreed with her boss, and hated herself for doing so ever since. She'd endured three days of badly broken sleep, building pressure to get a result, and a growing realisation that the situation was becoming intolerable. Farley had gone to ground and was no closer to being located. Then as if by magic, she gets a call on her way home. Farley has magically popped up at the Grant's house, back in her home town of Northallerton!

The Grant's dining room was suddenly bathed in a strong white light for a few seconds, dragging Golden's thoughts away from her problems. The noise made by a police helicopter buzzing above the house made Ronnie wrinkle her nose, although her eyes remained closed. This was the first sign that Golden had called in the sighting of Farley.

'So, you enjoyed a friendly little chat,' said Golden, returning to business, raising her voice to a pitch loud enough to rouse Ronnie from her doze. She came to life with a slight jerk and much blinking, 'And during this... *chat*, Robert Farley claimed he wasn't Brooklyn Hartley's killer, and before scaling a seven foot wall wearing a heavy army issue backpack, he handed over his murder weapon to you. Now why would he do that?'

'We've *told* you,' groaned Holly miserably, 'Robert was trying to prove to us he didn't kill Brooklyn. He said he was trying to revive her, not kill her. He insisted someone else was involved.'

'Mmm... ' Golden hummed, setting off on a slow circuit of the dining table, 'It's *Robert* is it?'

'He wanted us to call him Robert,' Bain murmured.

'Calling him by his first name makes him less of a monster, eh?' Golden suggested.

No one answered as Golden continued to perambulate around the large oval dining table.

'But you'd had no contact with him before tonight?'

'None,' answered Holly, 'And we're not sure how he found us. It's not as if we advertise where we live.'

'Which begs another question. Why you three?' Golden wondered aloud, 'What brought an ex-soldier...'

'Commando,' Holly interrupted.

This comment was received with a moment of silent contemplation from Golden as she digested this new information. Her briefing on Farley had him described as a dishonourably discharged seaman.

Holly got a warning flash of Bain's eyebrows which she acknowledged, vowing to keep her mouth shut for the rest of the interview.

'Thank you, Holly, ...what brought an *ex-marine commando* to this house do you think?'

'He didn't trust your lot,' Ronnie remarked sleepily but still managing to inject sharpness in her tone, 'And from the way you're treating us, young lady, I can see why.'

Golden stopped her slow walk and allowed her head and shoulders to droop, 'Okay. Listen up you three. I know you're hiding something, I can smell it.'

Holly almost voiced the opinion that the smell was her mother's liberal use of Pledge, but managed to swallow the urge to share this with the policewoman.

Golden pulled out a chair and sat down, careful not to catch the flares of her trouser suit on the legs. The chair felt hard and cold as her backside landed. Golden was suddenly impressed that none of her interviewees had complained about the length of time she'd had them sitting down. She carefully crossed her legs and leaned into the dining table, lowering her voice conspiratorially.

'Look, I'm guessing that Farley asked for your help. And if he did that, he probably told you some information that is pertinent to…'

'We haven't withheld any information that would help you catch him,' Bain insisted, 'We've told you everything, including Brooklyn's last word.'

'Snow… ' Golden said, rolling the word around her mouth, 'dr…op. What's that mean to you?'

Bain shrugged, a sour expression twisting his mouth downwards, 'I really haven't the foggiest.'

Golden stared disbelievingly at him.

He returned Golden's penetrating stare with one of his own. The stand-off only lasted a few seconds but when Golden finally broke eye contact, Bain was struck with the weariness and deep-seated frustration he'd seen lying behind those tired eyes. Checking his phone he found himself striking a more compromising tone.

'It's late, and I… *we* are probably not at our best,' Bain suggested, his eyes somehow larger, brighter than before, 'Perhaps we should revisit this conversation tomorrow, or actually, later today, given its past midnight? We might come up with something for you after a few hours of sleep. Things always look better the next day.'

Golden gave a sharp sniff of disapproval, and for a fleeting moment considered ignoring his request, but it was impossible to stay so belligerent when Bain was gazing at her in... *that way* of his.

Leaning back in her chair, Golden considered her options. Bullying the withheld information out of the three of them hadn't worked, and she doubted a night's sleep would change that. They were investigative journalists, and whilst she was desperate to catch Farley, they would be equally desperate to follow their story. With a bit of luck, Farley might still be caught by the battery of policemen scouring the Northallerton area, but based on past experience of this man, it was unlikely. He'd now had several hours to make good his escape. Besides, if he'd been a commando, surviving excruciating conditions and evading capture by the enemy was part of basic training. North Yorkshire would seem like a walk in the park compared to the war torn locations in which Farley had served his country. But there *was* that dishonourable discharge...

Bain and Holly probably wouldn't know about that, and Golden doubted Farley had mentioned it to them... Who would? Especially when the boy had died in an eerily similar way...

A new thought struck Golden. A cheeky, almost scurrilous thought... perhaps she could turn Holly and Bain's involvement to her advantage.

'I tend to agree,' she announced whilst still gazing thoughtfully at Holly and then back at Bain, 'Mr Bainbridge-Hall is right. I think our minds will be sharper after a good night's sleep. Thanks for your help the three of you. Be assured, I will be back.'

With relief showing in all three faces, Golden made her way out of the dining room and into the hallway, thoughtfully swinging the knife in a plastic evidence bag. Golden stopped and backtracked a couple of yards, coming to a halt in the door frame and pausing for a calculated few seconds with her back to Bain and Holly, before turned around.

'Whatever it is that you're keeping from me, I assume it isn't information that could place a member of the public in danger,' she stated, 'That being the case, if any of you subsequently came into possession of *further* information that would have relevance to my inquiries, I'm sure you would report it to me immediately?'

Holly and Bain shared a furtive glance.

'Without a shadow of a doubt, DI Golden,' Holly replied firmly.

'Bain?' Golden queried, seeking further confirmation.

He stared at her. She was being back-lit by the hallway light and her outline had him fascinated.

'Oh! Er… yes of course. I… um, or rather we, will be straight to touch. I mean, in touch… We'll be straight in touch with you should anything… come up.'

Satisfied, but only just, Golden gave them a perfunctory nod and stepped into the hallway, only to return and frame herself once again in the dining room door a moment later.

'There's just one more thing.'

Bain pressed his lips together to stifle a smile. He had an image of TV detective, Columbo, standing there, his glass eye sparkling as he delivered his killer question to a suspect caught unawares. After all, he did own the entire DVD collection of the show. He wondered if Golden was aware she'd not only used the hackneyed old catchphrase, she'd also adopted Peter Falk's manner. He decided not. She was too young, and more importantly, unlike him, she wasn't a nerd.

'This knife. The short-bladed knife covered in Brooklyn's blood. I don't suppose any of you would know what a blade like that would be used for?' asked Golden.

Holly and Bain shook their heads. However, Ronnie, unusually quiet for the last hour, now smiled.

'Of course I do!' she exclaimed, 'It's a whittling knife, or a farm hands' knife for cutting baling string. However, it could also be a farrier's knife. I would watch them working with those sorts of knives when I was a girl. All sorts of uses, but I'd have my money on whittling or farrier…'

Holly gave her mother a penetrating stare. Ronnie pursed her lips together, thought about what she'd said, and the smile fell from her face.

Golden sniffed and looked away, secure in the knowledge that Holly and Bain would be all over this case. A stable lass had been murdered with a farrier's knife after sustaining a major head trauma in the yard several months before. If that didn't get their investigative juices going, nothing would. She'd have to try and make Sayer see sense regarding Farley, but in the meantime, having Bain and Holly turning over a few choice rocks on her behalf could be beneficial. Besides, keeping them close to her might lead her to Farley.

'I'm dedicating all my time to finding Mr Farley. Come to think of it, I don't know whether returning here tomorrow will be necessary anymore,' Golden quipped, 'I have a feeling you might be busy finding leads for another one of those stories in your chosen field of expertise.'

There was a short pause. No one answered the detective. Golden raised an expectant eyebrow.

Bain's frown flattened out and he quickly cleared his throat, 'Yes, we will be following up on Robert Farley's visit tomorrow, um.. doing our job...'

'Good. I hope your investigations are fruitful. Unfortunately, I will have my hands full searching for the elusive Mr Farley, as instructed by my Chief Constable.'

'That's a shame,' Bain agreed, meeting Golden's gaze with all the guile of a cat who's already got its paw firmly in the cream.

'I'll let you get on then,' Golden said, and fluttered her eye-lashes in what could have been a blink, or the most surreptitious of winks, 'I'll see myself out.'

Her heels sounded on the parquet floor and the front door creaked open, then clicked closed.

Holly asked, 'What on earth was all that about?'

'That… was our free pass!' Bain exclaimed.

'Free pass? For what?'

'A free pass to investigate the murder of Brooklyn Hartley!'

Holly pondered this for a moment, 'So all those looks between you and Golden wasn't some sort of weird romantic signalling system? She was asking for our help with the case?'

'Yep! She wants our help,' Bain replied brightly, trying to ignore the warm feeling in his stomach he'd been experiencing ever since Golden had batted her eyes at him.

Ronnie had been listening to the conversation with heavy-lidded eyes. She now yawned expressively, her arms stiffly stuck out at odd angles.

'I'm off to bed,' she told the two of them sleepily, 'And for the record Bain, maybe my daughter was right. In my day, getting a free pass had nothing to do with investigating a murder.'

Eight

It was a Thursday evening when Gregory Blunt's wife left him. Blunt had the day etched into his memory. It was definitely a Thursday. He always ate chicken on Thursdays, and that evening, after his midweek shower, he'd been forced to get himself a bowl of cornflakes for his supper.

Miriam had become a woman of few words, but that evening she'd found her voice. And for only the third time in twenty years of marriage, Miriam had dared to raise her voice to him. And for no good reason! Her inexplicable tirade had touched on a wide variety of his so-called failings, however, there were two recurring themes; that he was a skinflint, and worse, that he was boring. She'd also mentioned him being overbearing and downright creepy, but Blunt had chosen to ignore this part of her rant – the woman had clearly lost her marbles by that point. Once her flood of complaints had become a trickle she'd closed the rather one-sided conversation by throwing his evening meal at him.

And without another word, Miriam had taken his car and gone to Whitby, on the northern coast. Blunt was horrified. Not so much that his wife had left, but that as far as he was aware, Miriam hadn't passed her driving test and what was worse, she'd known full well that he hadn't insured her for his car.

Miriam knew to have his tea on the table ten minutes after he arrived home from work and when he'd pointed out, quite rightly, her timing that evening was tardy, she had poured his plate of chicken in a cream and chive sauce into his lap and ruined his favourite pair of wine coloured corduroy trousers.

Rather than being broken hearted by Miriam's sudden and rather explosive exit from his life, Blunt was left bewildered. After all, hadn't he been the perfect husband? His successful career as an accountant combined with his conservative approach to their household expenditure had secured them a three bedroom seventies built semi-detached house, with car port. In comparison, Miriam only had to work four days a week – each a ten-hour shift at the local laundrette, which left her three days to do the housekeeping and cook the meals. Wasn't that fair?

Not forgetting their annual week-long holiday in Cleethorpes, and as if that wasn't enough, there was the fact that he'd attended grammar school, and so was able to educate his wife in all matters, and on all subjects. She'd had to persevere with a dreadful comprehensive education and it was only right that he set her straight when her views were wrong…

Blunts' pearls of wisdom were now lost to the world.

With Miriam gone, Blunt was unable to regurgitate his pontifications to his mostly silent, downtrodden audience of one. In her absence, it became his habit to sit in front of his old boxy television of an evening, eating a microwaved baked potato, and telling a photo of Miriam and himself on holiday in Cleethorpes in 2004 that she would eventually realise what a big mistake she'd made, see sense, and come back home with her tail between her legs. After all, she'd had it good! What more could a wife expect from a husband?

Blunt's puzzlement continued for another month, his confusion lasting long enough for a divorce request to be issued by Miriam's solicitor, citing irreconcilable differences. Blunt set it aside, unable to bring himself to sign. It was two weeks later when a chance meeting turned his life on its head. On that fateful day, Blunt was accosted by one of Miriam's detestable friends.

Since Miriam had always done all the food shopping, learning to navigate his way around the dozens of aisles at the local Co-op had become a necessary weekly evil. Blunt hated his food shop with a vengeance and tended to scurry around the supermarket as quickly as possible ensuring he maintained a constant scowl on his face. This tended to ward off unwanted conversations, so it was a shock when a podgy woman bustled up to him, eyeballed the contents of his trolley contemptuously, and announced, 'Why are you bothering with all those value brands?'

Blunt hadn't answered, hoping his withering stare would be enough to make the objectionable woman depart.

'Surely you can at least afford Heinz Beans now?' the woman had scoffed, a strange, expectant look creeping across her face.

'And why would I waste money on such an extravagance?' Blunt had spat back angrily.

The woman's pasty face had contorted into a deep frown that slowly melted into a huge grin as realisation dawned.

'Oh, my days! You don't know, do you?' she barked between guffaws, 'Your wife won the lottery! Six million quid... and *you* don't know!'

She'd laughed even louder, clasping her hands to her stomach, as if bracing herself against a hernia. The noise prompting shoppers to look down the aisle at the two of them, to either gawp, or grin at the braying woman who was now pointing a finger at Blunt.

'Miriam won the lottery and...' the woman had said, forced to pause to take a breath, '...left you without telling you she'd won!'

Mouth open, embarrassed, and confused, Blunt had frozen in the dry goods aisle. He'd stared at the woman, unable to respond. Eventually the woman's mocking shrieks were lost on him as he came to his senses, dropped his basket and hurried out of the supermarket without making a purchase.

The question of Blunt sharing in the tax free winnings never troubled a courtroom. Miriam freely admitted she had won the prize on the midweek lottery, the day before she had tipped his supper onto his trousers and walked out. To his dismay, Blunt discovered she'd been playing the lottery online, as well as betting on horses each Saturday, using a secret personal bank account she'd kept from him. His wife had been a closet gambler and he'd never known!

He had been advised by a free Citizen's Advice solicitor that a court case could cost hundreds of thousands of pounds, and despite being her husband, he only had a small chance of any court forcing Miriam to share the windfall equally. It was clear she had bought the ticket for herself, with her own money. Being loathe to spend his own money on anything as expensive as professional representation, Blunt had agreed to Miriam's terms... and although it ate away at him, he kept telling himself it wasn't as bad as paying out money to a pompous, overpaid lawyer... but only just.

In early March, Blunt invited his wife to his house, and

with her solicitor in attendance, Miriam made her one-time, take-it or leave-it offer. She would pay him one million pounds if he agreed to a quick, uncontested divorce.

Blunt signed all the paperwork in front of her, trying his best to withhold the anger that was festering within him. Miriam had waited until she held the signed documents in her hand before letting go of twenty years-worth of pent up rage. Having had time to reflect on her previous life, Miriam had advised her ex-husband to stay well away from her, and to take a long, hard look at himself. To emphasise how much she wanted him to stay out of her new life, Miriam had delivered this speech incredibly forcefully, and in language so colourful Blunt had to look up a few words in his dictionary after she'd left.

Her tongue-lashing left the solicitor trying hard to stem his laughter, and Blunt so stunned he was unable to respond. By the time he'd found his voice and started bellowing an expletive-ridden repost through the glass of his lounge window, Miriam had left the premises and was being driven away, a huge smile lighting up her face.

Blunt had continued to go to work for a full two weeks after the money landed in his bank account. But when another Monday rolled around again, he'd woken up in a strange mood. He'd slouched around the house, unable to gain the enthusiasm to get dressed, and ended up not going to work at all. It was the same on Tuesday. On Wednesday, after twenty-five years in the same job, he phoned the owner of the accountancy firm and gave his notice. Blunt found it odd that his boss accepted his resignation with such alacrity. He could have sworn that he'd heard the man cry, 'Get in!' before ending the call whilst he was in mid-sentence.

Blunt mooched around his house for the next few weeks, unable to conjure up very much enthusiasm for anything. Even his model building, that usually ate up most of his spare time, didn't have the same allure. The novelty of daytime TV, take-aways being delivered to his door, and never washing or cleaning anything, soon wore off. Feeling bereft of purpose, Blunt's bewilderment over Miriam's departure was slowly, but surely, eating into his soul.

Over the next few days Gregory Blunt found himself spending long minutes inspecting that photo of himself and Miriam on the beach at Cleethorpes. It was his wife's dismal expression that both fascinated and enraged him in equal measure. Every time he glanced at the photo it seemed to Blunt that his ex-wife's half-smile worsened, going from a grin, to a grimace, a leer, until finally, she was mocking him with a sneer. One evening, worried he was losing his mind, he wrenched the photo from the wall and threw it against their mock stone fireplace, retrieving the photo from its smashed frame only to tear his wife's side of the picture into pieces.

He turned the television on and watched the local news in a daze, then went for a walk to try and calm down. Blunt returned, closed all the curtains and with tears of frustration painting thin stripes down his face, he sat down at the kitchen table. And there, in the detritus of several half-eaten takeaway cartons and pizza boxes, Blunt reached a decision.

Inspecting the scattered pieces of their holiday photo, he told a torn image of Miriam, 'I'll put my million pounds to the best possible use. I'll show you the sort of man I am… *Boring* am I? A skinflint? Creepy? Well, get ready to eat your words, Miriam!'

He began straight away. With a renewed outlook, a single objective, and blood singing in his ears, Blunt set about planning how he would wreak his revenge for Miriam's cruel treatment of him. And if possible, he would make it happen in the most public and embarrassing way he could conceive. His money would be put to good use; to teach Miriam a thing or two she still didn't know about Gregory Blunt.

It wasn't as easy as he'd imagined, after all, his goal was simple, but achieving it annoyingly complex. Killing her would be straightforward compared to what he had in store for her! He wanted Miriam to suffer. He wanted everything she ate to be bitter, every experience her money brought her to disappoint, everything she loved to wither and die…

Blunt spent days, then weeks trying determine how he could make all this happen before realising something was missing, something imperative to ensure his success. It slowly dawned on Blunt that despite sharing a life with her for over twenty years, he didn't know what Miriam loved. Without this information, how could he take it from her? In short, he didn't know his wife well enough to exact the depth of revenge he had in mind for her.

This epiphany hit Blunt hard. And the solution stung, as it involved spending money. Blunt set about employing a private detective to track Miriam's every move. To his horror, he quickly discovered that over the few months it had taken for the divorce to become official she had become something of a social butterfly.

His wife was living in Beverley, East Yorkshire. She'd got a new hairstyle, new clothes, and after attending several night-school courses at the local college, she had new friends. He was disgusted to discover Miriam had also started to waste money on make-up and scent! He'd forbade her from such extravagances during their marriage, but once Blunt examined the photos provided by his private detective, he had to admit Miriam did look *different*. He studied the pictures in minute detail, assuring himself that despite the fact Miriam looked attractive, the layers of slap it must have taken could never hide the woman's hateful nature.

The final page of the detective's report delivered a shock, at least to Blunt. He found himself staring at the new focus of Miriam's life. Blunt had photos of them together, Miriam looking... happy. The replacement for his own love and devotion was almost seven feet tall, had long brown hair and was noticeably much younger than Blunt. This is lunacy, Blunt thought bitterly… she's bought a bloody racehorse!

Blunt had stewed on the photos of Miriam for days. They fuelled his anger, and his lust for retribution. Most of them had been taken, of all places, at horseracing venues. There were several different tracks across multiple days. His detective had reported she would travel on her own, but often struck up conversations with other racegoers. She was at Beverley one day, York the next. Catterick, Redcar, and Ripon, as well as visits to racecourses further afield like Ascot and Newmarket. However, it appeared that the Yorkshire courses were her favourites. He had a particularly large quantity of photos of Miriam at Beverley and Ripon.

His detective also reported that Miriam's racehorse, unnamed so far, and referred to in the information as a 'filly', was trained in Malton by an established trainer called Graham Dent.

Consumed with thoughts of his ex-wife rubbing shoulders with the gentry, Blunt reached a conclusion. Miriam had replaced him with a racehorse!

Nine

April 2nd

Blinded by his inner rage and scarred by rejection, Gregory Blunt drew up his plans, set his budget, fired his private detective, and began to research the trainer of Miriam's racehorse. Then, he put his plan in motion.

This was why Blunt could currently be found hiding in the trees on a steep incline above a frost-covered stabling complex up in the wilds of the East Yorkshire Wolds. Blunt had already been awake for six hours, despite it being only ten o'clock in the morning. He'd followed his prey from Beverley, first to the Graham Dent stables in Malton, and then to this second set of stables just outside the town of Norton, which had turned out to be a racehorse stud. Graham Dent hadn't come to the second yard. Instead, it was his son, Hugo Dent, who had accompanied Miriam.

Blunt shivered. It had to be close to zero degrees. A dew drop was appearing on the end of his nose every few seconds as he inspected the central area of the stud. He was watching through a pair of cheap, antique binoculars he'd picked up from a second-hand shop and was now realising they had been an ill-advised purchase, being woefully inadequate for perusing what felt like a never-ending array of young racehorses being paraded in front of Miriam. She was standing between Hugo Dent and a man called Adrian Cooper, who according to Blunt's google search, was the stud owner and manager. All three of them had stupid smiles on their faces as they cooed over each new animal that was walked over by a stable lass and made to stand in front of them.

Blunt fiddled with one of the rotating knobs on his binoculars, desperate to get a close-up of his ex-wife's face, but it was constantly blurred from being over forty yards distant. Swearing under his breath, he cocked his head sideways around the tree he was hiding behind and strained his hearing to try and make out what was being said below. Frustrated at being unable to catch everything, he stalked through the long, dead grass on the edge of the wood and scuttled over to the back of a block of a dozen wooden stables. A few seconds later he'd climbed through a glassless window at the back of a random stable and fortuitously found himself in an empty box only a few yards away from where Cooper, Hugo Dent and Miriam were standing. Hunkering down against the bottom half of the stable door, to Blunt's delight, he could just about hear everything that was being said.

Miriam was trying hard to concentrate on the stud manager's words, but it was challenging. Despite being well wrapped up and having hand warmers in her pockets, she was beginning to feel the cold work its way into her joints, starting with her toes. Besides, it didn't matter what he said any more, she'd already made her decision. She was quite taken by this solid, good-looking colt that was currently advertising its youthful arrogance by snorting and throwing his head around. The others had been nice enough, but this colt really took her fancy. Full of fizz and vitality, and desperately good looking, he was the antithesis of her other racehorse, Morgan. At least, at the moment. However, she felt it was only right to allow the two men to continue their pitch.

'Now this is a really nice one,' said Hugo, her assistant trainer.

In his mid-twenties, fit, blonde, and undeniably good-looking with full lips and a delicate nose, Hugo was standing beside her, hands on his hips as he assessed the young horse. Annoyingly, he didn't appear to be feeling the cold and only served as a reminder to Miriam that she was approaching fifty years old. Any youthful good looks she may have had, and benefits derived from a decent circulatory system, were long gone. She dug her hands deeper into her coat pockets and tried to wiggle her toes.

Hugo stepped forward and ran his hands down the colt's neck, back and paid specific attention to the legs, 'He's well bred. Has a neat, sprint shape to him and could be the type you're after.'

A few yards further away, Adrian Cooper, the stud manager agreed with Hugo. Cooper was an energetic, wiry chap of a similar age and height to Miriam, who seemed to find it hard to stand still, always in motion. Miriam had taken an instant liking to the man, as he listened intently and spoke enthusiastically. Besides, it was most endearing to look into a face that was constantly creased up with some sort of a smile. Cooper was an ex-jockey, which didn't surprise Miriam in the least, as the stud manager was only a fraction taller than her. This was in his favour. She'd hated how Gregory, her first husband, had towered over her, especially when teaming Blunt's looming outline with his inability to crack a smile for the last fifteen years of their marriage.

Miriam shuddered as an image of her ex-husband's sour expression flitted through her mind. Then she gave a small smile, having been reminded of something her hairdresser in Pickering had told her when she'd treated herself to her expensive new hairdo.

The rather world weary woman had told her, 'There's always a reason a man is single in his forties, hon,' she had crowed, sending Miriam a knowing look via the mirror, 'And you know, hon, that reason is *rarely* a good one. Keep clear of single men in their late forties, that's my advice!'

As Cooper continued to explain something about the colt's breeding, Miriam reflected how browbeaten and helpless she had been whilst being married to Blunt. Having money had opened up the world to her. And being free of his constant undermining had allowed her confidence to flourish. She was her own woman now… and she had no need to jump into another relationship straight away. That could wait, just at the moment she needed to choose a two-year-old racehorse to buy at the Doncaster breeze-up sales. This young colt would hopefully take her racing through the summer season, as Morgan, the two-year-old filly she had already bought at the August sales, wouldn't be reaching a racetrack any time soon.

Miriam snapped back and tried harder to concentrate on Cooper's words as the stud manager stroked the colt down its neck. He invited her to do the same, telling her that despite his young age, he was broken, ridden away, and impeccably well behaved. When she got closer, Miriam noticed the colt exhibited small flecks of grey in his coat, and Cooper confirmed that although he was dark now, he would soon show the signs of becoming grey.

Me and him both, Miriam thought to herself.

Stroking his silky neck twice in long, lingering sweeps, Miriam stood back, only for the colt to bend his head around, regard her intelligently and touch her arm, softly nudging her. His attention worked, and smiling, she stepped forward and stroked him once more, telling him he was a good boy. This sealed the deal, the colt had won her heart and assuming he breezed well enough she would be bidding for him at the up-coming Doncaster breeze-up auction.

Many of the stud manager's words had gone over Miriam's head, but she nodded sagely nonetheless. Cooper might as well have been discussing what he had for breakfast for the last minute, but Miriam was soon reengaged and being carried along by the man's enthusiasm for the young two-year-old.

Whilst Cooper was entertaining and Hugo Dent full of youthful exuberance, Miriam's trainer, Graham Dent, was somewhat distant. Despite having met him a number of times, she hadn't quite worked the man out yet. However, to her untrained eye he appeared to be a consummate professional. Thanks to his stewardship, Miriam had soon realised she had underestimated the complexities involved in racehorse ownership. Thankfully, Dent had guided her through buying a yearling at the autumn sales and the whole experience had been enthralling.

Dent had a decent record over the last decade, his successes coming thick and fast, with his yard averaging around fifty horses each season recording plenty of wins, a number of them in quality races. Miriam had done her homework, and Dent was a safe, albeit eye-wateringly expensive pair of hands. And with Dent retained as her trainer, she had hoped for some success straight away, but so far, it had been one disappointment after another.

The filly she had fallen in love with at the sales and subsequently bought for fifty-five thousand guineas had arrived at the Dent stables the day after the sale and been broken over the course of the next month. Miriam had given the youngster the stable name of 'Morgan' and Dent had reported that she had gone well on her first few gallops.

A week before Christmas, Miriam had received a phone call from her trainer. Morgan was seriously ill with colic. Miriam had visited her filly every day for a week. The filly had been a shadow of her former self. Thankfully, she had slowly recovered, but not to the extent where she could re-enter full training. Ever since the colic episode, it had been a case of three steps forward and two back. Now officially a two-year-old, it seemed the unfortunate filly was never going to recover enough to make her debut on a racecourse. Hence, on Dent's advice, Miriam was now looking to acquire another two-year-old at the breeze-ups, her last chance to buy a race-ready youngster for the forthcoming flat season. Dent had arranged for her to visit Cooper's stud with his son, Hugo. Cooper, a trusted local breeder, was sending several youngsters to the breeze-ups, affording Miriam the opportunity to view them before they went to the auction.

'I think this could be the one,' said Hugo moving forward to join the stud manager in running a well-practiced hand down the colt's legs once more.

'You're getting first look at this years' crop,' Cooper commented, 'We don't allow just anyone to view our horses before a major sale like the Doncaster Breeze-ups. But with Graham Dent being a personal friend, he gets all the inside knowledge on the best yearlings for the new season before the breeze-ups come along. He's always a step ahead of the competition, which means you are too. Graham says you're going to be an important owner this season…'

Cooper didn't so much ask a question, but allowed his query to trail away, married to an encouraging smile Miriam's way.

'I'm in your hands, Mr Cooper.'

'Please, call me Adrian.'

Half an hour, and another four horses later, Cooper and Hugo waved Miriam off from the stud's small car park.

'She was rather nice,' Cooper said out of the side of his mouth to Hugo as he waved Miriam out of his stud's gates and onto the Malton road.

'And as green as grass,' stated Hugo when the car had disappeared from view, 'Which for our purposes, makes her a perfect buyer for you, and a nice, rookie owner for us.'

Hugo manufactured a chuckle and clapped a large hand onto the smaller man's shoulder.

'Seriously Hugo, you think she's one for us?' Cooper asked as they set off walking back to his farmhouse, placed at the centre of the stud.

Hugo detected reservations in Cooper's query and was careful to reply in a manner brimming with confidence.

'Without a doubt. That's three of our owners we've lined up for your horses. You can look forward to a big payday at the breeze-ups.'

Cooper didn't reply for a few steps. Hugo caught sight of him frowning and judged a little push in the right direction might be required.

'You are right to have reservations about Miriam Blunt, but you shouldn't worry,' he stated stiffly, 'She'll be a push-over. Miriam won't suspect a thing, she's more interested in securing the horse she'd fallen in love with, rather than how much it costs. Besides, she didn't work for her money. I looked her up. She won the lottery and left her husband the day after she collected! She *deserves* to be rolled over for a few grand and what's more, she'll never miss it. And *we'll* never get caught.'

'You keep saying that,' Cooper said with a shake of his head, 'But it's not as straightforward as you and your veterinary friend make out.'

Hugo came to a sudden halt and turned on the stud manager, leaning over the smaller man, '*Daniel*. His name is Daniel. And we've brought in an expert to bid up the horses.'

'Expert!' Cooper said scornfully, 'Conor Moran is as crooked as a nine bob note. I just hope that your father…'

'My father won't have a clue,' Hugo insisted with a tight jaw, 'And he certainly won't notice he's paying over the odds. Besides, he doesn't care. He might be bidding for horses on behalf of his owners, but he isn't paying for them.'

Hugo eyes narrowed as he tried to read Cooper's reaction. He wasn't certain the stud manager was entirely sold on his and Daniel's money-making scheme. Perhaps he needed to push a little harder.

'Are you really going to give up your extra profit on that grey colt?'

Cooper looked away from his partner in crime and cast his gaze around the stud, deep in thought. His father had poured his heart and soul into this place over the last seventy years, and he'd done the same for the past thirty years, not to mention his extended family, who all worked hard just to keep the place going. He rested his gaze upon the large stone-built Cooper family farmhouse tucked away at the end of the complex of stables, barns and walkways. The peeling paint on the window frames, the missing tiles on the roof and the grass and buddleia growing out of the guttering made him grimace. The farmhouse's condition was a stark, and accurate reflection of the stud's finances. Perhaps, by bending the rules he could get ahead.

'Okay, the deal we agreed?'

Hugo's solemn face broke into a plastic grin, 'Yes, sixty-forty on the extra profit.'

'Good,' he added with a nod, 'Don't worry Coops, I've got Miriam worked out. She's the perfect owner, clueless about racing and has deep pockets. Mark my words, if we play our cards right she could turn into an owner who just keeps giving!'

Cooper looked away, disgusted with himself.

'Coops? You *are* okay with this?' inquired Hugo, his tone containing more suspicion than compassion.

Cooper found himself in difficulty when attempting to return Hugo an encouraging smile. The muscles in his face simply wouldn't comply. Was hoodwinking wealthy owners so bad? Could it be a crime when you considered that these owners believed they were getting a very good racehorse for a value price? How was that any different to a retailer advertising a product at an inflated price, then marking it down to its true value and advertising it as a big discount?

'Coops? Seriously, you don't look...'

Cooper excused himself with a flap of his hand and disappeared into the nearest vacant stable. The sound of retching soon reverberated around the line of boxes. Hugo remained outside, waiting impatiently. When Cooper emerged thirty seconds later Hugo was standing confidently, arms crossed, shaking his head.

'Either your breakfast didn't agree with you, or you need to grow a pair,' he remarked, 'Which is it?'

Cooper sucked in a breath through his nose and met his business partner's gaze with a sullen, glassy stare, 'I'll have the three horses ready, you get your owners ready to spend big at the breeze-ups.'

Having directed a satisfied nod Cooper's way, Hugo turned to leave, and set off at a brisk pace down the line of stables.

'And keep that vet of yours, Daniel Croft, out of my way,' Cooper called after him, 'Mark my words, Hugo, he's a dangerous young man.'

Hugo drew to a halt, but didn't turn around. Cooper had sounded... cold, irritated, and bordering on angry! His first genuine smile of the morning creased Hugo's lips. So, Cooper *did* have some fire in his belly after all... Hugo took a moment to consider whether to reply, thought better of it, and continued on his way without looking around.

From the empty stable, Gregory Blunt finished writing in his small notebook. He waited a few minutes until he heard the door to the farmhouse close with a bang, then stole away, back along the line of stables, over the paddock fences, through the wood and sidled around a hedge to where he'd left his car. With every step his mind was racing with ideas. What he'd just learnt could be powerful, in the right hands. And to utilise that power to maximum effect would take some careful planning.

Ten

April 4th

To pass unnoticed was a skill. Not to be seen meant becoming one of the unseen. There are unseen members of every community - in clear view, but invisible. It isn't the homeless person begging for pennies in the shopping precinct, or the lone vagrant pitching his tent in the corner of a farmer's field. The unseen are everyday people. The taxi drivers, office workers, or the road sweepers; quiet, unassuming people who pass by without raising any interest. They are the wallpaper of daily life, too ordinary or too numerous to be worth committing to memory. Robert Farley knew this.

Fifteen years of specialist training in the forces had taught Farley many things. Not being identified as the subject of a nationwide manhunt whilst prowling the streets of a small town was just one of the skills at which he had become adept. Which was why he was making his way to the edge of Malton, North Yorkshire, dressed in beige shorts, hiking boots, thick socks, a short waterproof jacket zipped up to his chin, and a flat cap. He wore spectacles, and a compass and a small pair of binoculars hung from a leather cord around his neck. Striding on, upright and purposeful, Farley continued up the road that according to his map, led to an area of hillside that served as the Malton gallops.

He'd operated behind enemy lines in many countries, leaving his role as a commando behind after six years to become an 'operative' for the last seven. This fact never appeared on his service record.

Following the incident on the riverside path he'd cycled home. After a quick shower, Farley shaved off his beard, cut his hair short at the back and changed into the attire of an average office worker, including cheap white shirt and tie and a nametag attached to a lanyard. Old habits. Always anticipate the worst occurring and be prepared; Baden Powell had the right idea.

Farley had grabbed his survival pack, consisting of a small amount of money, a limited, yet versatile range of clothes, a tent and other essentials such as car keys, knife, medical kit, water tablets etc.. and after locking his flat, left on foot. His survival pack had saved his life on more than one occasion in his professional life, and would do so again, although he hadn't expected to have a need for it quite so quickly on civvy street.

Passing a dog walker coming down Langton Road hill, Farley smiled at the young woman with her whippet and tipped his cap whilst wishing her good morning. She reciprocated his greeting, and walked on. Farley checked. She hadn't looked back at him. He'd been unseen.

It was seven thirty in the morning when he reached a large gate held closed by a thick loop of rope. Beyond lay many acres of grass, schooling hurdles and all-weather tracks; the Malton gallops. Horses and work riders were already in evidence and Farley cursed under his breath. He was at the *top* of the gallops, not the bottom. The map hadn't specifically stated the layout, he'd come out of Malton on the wrong road.

He moved further up the hill, watching horses working in the fields beyond for the next hour. Through the hedge, barely in bud, he pointed his binoculars down the hill and forty minutes later found who he was looking for. The trainer was with his son. They'd driven an old Vauxhall up a dirt track running alongside the all-weather gallop and both left the car to watch their string of horses work. He noted the time, number of horses, riders and whether they cantered more than once up the gallop. Farley watched the riders walk their mounts back down to the start of the gallop and filter into a walkway at the foot of the hill before disappearing behind trees and shrubs.

At eleven o'clock, after watching another Graham Dent trained group of horses work up the gallops, Farley set off back into Malton, pleased with his morning's work. He visited a laundrette and washed everything he owned, then took time to walk the streets as a tourist. This meant frequently looking up. It was a sure giveaway he was a visitor; a local rarely looks upwards at sights they've already seen a hundred times before. Locals also tend to avoid tourists like the plague. Being a tourist made him one of the unseen.

He cased buildings, took photos, and Farley found what he'd been looking for an hour after lunch.

After a visit to the library, he returned to his bed and breakfast in the late afternoon and informed his landlady that with regret, he would be leaving to travel up the coast to sample the delights of Sleights and Seaburn. The next morning Farley woke refreshed, enjoyed a hot shower and a full English breakfast, paid his bill in cash, and left.

Eleven

April 5th

Kirsty Golden was thankful that for once, she was working alone. It meant she could enjoy the silence around her, instead of Duggleby's incessant chatter. Since moving over to the York office she'd been lumbered with the presence of DC Duggleby most days. He wasn't a bad policeman, he just wouldn't shut up. Questions, lots of banal questions; why did sandwiches come in triangles rather than quarters or square halves? Why had everyone forgotten how to indicate at roundabouts? Or facts. He was a veritable font of facts. Unwanted facts that cluttered your brain if you let them. Golden was convinced Duggleby spent his spare time watching and re-watching old episodes of QI. She wondered whether he talked in his sleep. For Kirsty, silence really was Golden.

The last two weeks had been one long nightmare, with long hours spent travelling the northern motorways and byways with little to show for their efforts. Reported sightings of Robert Farley had pulled her from York to North Shields, up to Alnwick, across to Carlisle, back up Kielder Water and back down to Bradford and Huddersfield, and it seemed like every small town in-between. Most had either been mistaken identity, or cases of over-zealous identification driven by misinformation or fear. There hadn't been a single sighting they'd been able to absolutely confirm as being Farley. Since he'd visited the Grant's house in Northallerton, Robert Farley had vanished, despite over thirty police officers joining the daily search.

There had been one breakthrough. Among the blood and other stuff on the bloodied knife provided by Robert Farley, forensics had found a single human hair, wrapped around the neck of the handle. However, there was no match to their database and expanding it to everyone at the scene, and all those interviewed was also unsuccessful. Golden wasn't sure whether the hair would prove anything, even if they got a match. And that meant pressure from above, and a lack of progress on her other cases.

The ecstasy manufacturing case, the one she'd been working on before the Farley manhunt had taken over her life, was a case in point. This is what she'd originally been brought over to York to crack and Golden was thankful to get a few days away from the Farley fiasco to spend a little time policing a different case. Alone.

Over the past five years, tens of thousands of manhours had gone into stemming the flow of the designer drug into Hull, York, Leeds and Teesside, without any tangible progress. It was known that dealers across the North were increasingly being supplied by a home-grown manufacturer, but isolating their location and the group involved had been impossible, simply because no-one out on the streets was privy to that information. There were tantalising snippets about where, or who, was involved, but they rarely amounted to anything solid. But you had to follow them up, which is why she was here in Malton.

She was at work, sitting alone in her unmarked Volkswagen Passat on the outskirts of the town watching the comings and goings at one of the doctor's surgeries in the town, acting on information received from a source. An informant inside one of the dealer gangs in Leeds had said he'd heard the ecstasy supply was from, 'A doctor, over in the Wolds.'

While her boss, Sayers, allowed others in the branch to be off chasing a Hull docks lead, Golden was spending time off from the Farley case sniffing around after the Wolds doctor lead. From a solid source, she reckoned it warranted investigating, so for the last three months, until the Farley murder happened, Golden had checked out virtually every single doctor within all NHS and private clinics in the East of the country… searching for anything that might draw her closer to the gang's manufacturing operation.

There wasn't a great deal to see from her position in the carpark outside the neat, brick-built doctors surgery. It was on the corner of a square parade of shops well away from the town centre. Well-tended shrubs masked the entrance, and fifteen minutes of watching hadn't produced anything suspicious apart from a couple of middle-aged men wearing jogging-bottoms who had come out to smoke cigarettes on the street corner and leer at passing motorists, before re-entering the surgery. She idly wondered whether the objectionable men were being treated for a smoking-related disease.

Golden yawned, scanning the other buildings around her. The shops consisted of a small supermarket, a café, a bookmaker, and a dentist. She examined the dentist's surgery again. Could a dentist be termed, 'a doctor'? She doubted it.

Golden got out, locked her car, and decided to swing by the dentists on her way to doing a circuit around the doctors' premises. If that yielded little excitement, she would head inside the surgery to disrupt their appointment schedule and see whether her presence caused anything more than mild irritation.

For the first time in a few days, it wasn't raining. The budding trees and bushes around the carpark were showing tinges of green and every now and again the sun was managing to find a way to dodge the clouds and cast some warmth onto Golden's back as she walked. With a sense of renewal sparking her enthusiasm, she examined the dentist's window and sized up the reception desk before moving on. There was no reason to investigate further, it was a small, one-man operation.

On a day like this she'd have preferred it to be spent at home, or even better, fishing for trout, alone on the River Ure. Thanks to Duggleby's two-day training course, at least she was alone today. Be thankful for small mercies she told herself as she reached the doctor's surgery and started to check around the building, re-engaging her detective's brain.

At the corner of the street, Robert Farley stopped to pretend to regard a poster in the dentist's window offering a discount on tooth whitening. He glanced back at the woman he'd just passed on his way out of the supermarket. She'd had the whiff of policewoman about her but thankfully hadn't looked up at him. She was enjoying the sun too much. Watching her disappear around the corner of what looked like a doctor's surgery, he made off in the opposite direction, ensuring he retained a mental image of the young woman's face.

Twelve

April 6th

'You've made this room really homely,' Holly noted, whilst waiting for Bain to make his next move.

'Thanks,' he replied absent-mindedly without looking up, his attention remaining with the chess board lying on the small table that was wedged between them.

The two of them were embroiled in one of their evening matches, held in Bain's attic bedroom. It was at the top of the house, but bore little resemblance to most attics, being a long, narrow space that travelled the length of the building with a vaulted ceiling being the only indicator you were at the highest point of the house. At the garden end was a double bed, a large wardrobe and several bookcases. Bain had installed the latter to hold his record, tapes, and DVD collections. Moving down the room, his lounge area consisted of two small sofas angled towards a small, ornately tiled open fire with enough room for a coffee table to be set between the two to hold the chess set. Two tall arched windows bookended his accommodation, shedding light into the long, thin room during the day, but with it being dark outside, the purple velvet curtains were currently drawn.

Holly watched Bain reach out and touch the tip of his rook with an index finger, then withdraw his hand with a grimace, apparently unhappy with this potential choice of move. Casting her gaze around his attic room once more, she noticed Bain had finally got around to hanging the last of his paintings on the walls. He'd placed a favourite of hers, an autumnal landscape full of golden hues, in pride of place over the fireplace.

'Your paintings really brighten the place up. I wish I could paint or draw like you.'

'No you don't, they're not mine,' Bain muttered, still concentrating intently on the board.

'Don't be so modest, they have your initials all over them.'

Bain furrowed his brow. Holly couldn't decide whether it was a reaction to her comment, or he was still finding it difficult to make his mind up about his next move. She didn't know why he was bothering, she was set to win whatever he decided.

'They're my mother's initials,' Bain said into the chess

board, 'Emily Bainbridge-Hall,'.

Holly's eye widened, 'Your mother?' she repeated in an excited whisper to Bain's bowed head.

She waited a moment, hoping for further information. It failed to arrive, her opponent remained obstinately silent. Bain rarely spoke of his family, and despite her fascination with his super-wealthy background, Holly didn't question him too often. She knew he had an elder brother, but had never met him. He worked for Bain's father, with whom Bain shared an increasingly poor relationship.

Bain was always reticent to divulge anything to do with his family, tending to change the subject, and although his father had a lengthy Wikipedia page dedicated to his business, and increasingly political career, it was rather short on family background, simply stating that Bainbridge-Hall was married with two boys. Instead, Holly's curiosity survived off the odd juicy scrap of insight Bain absent-mindedly dropped her way. However, she was now on tenterhooks. And this new information was too succulent to ignore. She had to dig deeper.

'I can see why you'd want the paintings hung properly. Your mother is a fine artist. Do you speak with her often?'

Bain lifted his head and his big hazel eyes flickered with the reflection of the flames in the fire before they dropped to the chess board once more.

'My mother died,' he said, moving his bishop across the diagonal and knocking a pawn over with a flick of his wrist.

'But… she can't…'

'She died when I was six. My father remarried,' Bain cut in. It seemed he'd anticipated her confusion.

'Oh… I'm sorry.'

'It was a long time ago.'

As Holly pretended to ponder her next move, she couldn't help wondering why Bain's father's Wikipedia page hadn't mentioned a former wife. He was wealthy, ran a hugely profitable business empire, and had the ear of the current government. Surely it should at least mention the mother of his two boys?'

She pushed a pawn forward a couple of spaces.

'What did you think of Golden?' asked Bain, the tip of his finger now touching the top of a rook.

Holly, irked by Bain's obvious change of subject, issued a little sigh, but let it go. She had learned to accept this state of affairs. A slow drip feed of information from Bain regarding his family was as much as she could expect. To demand more would only result in him clamming up completely. Besides, this was a revelation. Bain valued those paintings above all his other possessions, although she imagined his wax jacket came a close second.

Bain moved his rook a few spaces and tentatively removed his finger.

Holly responded immediately, pushing her knight into a challenging position.

Golden had returned to the house alone that morning and been unusually profligate with her information about Brooklyn, Robert Farley, and the Dent's racing yard. Without saying anything outright, it had been obvious that Golden was giving Grant Bainbridge, as she referred to the two of them, the green light to investigate Brooklyn Hartley's murder. Although nothing was said, Holly and Bain had both been left with the impression that Golden's pursuit of Robert Farley wasn't exactly whole-hearted.

It had also been obvious to Holly that Bain was rather taken with Kirsty Golden. This amused her. She had no attraction to Bain herself. At least, no physical attraction. It was doubtful Golden had noticed, but Holly had spotted the signs of Bain's interest. In particular, the tips of Bain's ears had gone a warm crimson colour whenever the young, unattached, woman's eyes met his. Holly wasn't so sure his interest was reciprocated. Golden was difficult to read, with her pleasant, but eternally sceptical facial features. Her eyes were a different matter. They radiated intelligence.

'I think we should start by getting over to York and talking to Brooklyn's mother, Janice.'

Holly stared back at Bain aghast. All thoughts of Golden, their game of chess, and Bain's family secrets draining from her mind.

'You're suggesting we question the mother of the murdered girl?'

'Mmm...' said Bain, head bowed, his concentration back on the chess board.

'You've got to be kidding.'

'No, it seems to me like the best place to start.'

'Really? So we're just going to roll up at the grieving woman's door and pump her for information?' Holly asked hotly.

'The great preponderance of murders are committed by family or friends,' said Bain levelly, pinching a knight between thumb and finger and retreating the piece back down the board, 'Something happened. Something changed. And whatever it was, it caused the murderer to act. This wasn't a clever or well-thought out attack. It was in daylight, on a busy footpath, and carried out inexpertly, with a poor weapon that I'm guessing happened to be to hand. It was opportunistic and desperate. Mrs Hartley may be able to help us pinpoint what motivated the murderer to strike.'

Holly gave this some thought and found herself begrudgingly agreeing with Bain. However, the thought of facing the deceased girl's mother only a week after she'd lost her daughter in such dreadful circumstances, left her with a hollow feeling.

'But why would Mrs Hartley speak with us? We're not the police and we didn't know her daughter. And I saw you doing the searches for her. We haven't got an address for Janice Hartley.

'Ah, well, I've got an idea about that,' grinned Bain.

Holly surveyed the chess board, then raised her chin and lifted a questioning eyebrow Bain's way.

'Brooklyn was walking her dog when she was attacked, he explained, 'There was a labrador stood in the background of the video those tourists took of Robert Farley beside Brooklyn's body. We know that Brooklyn lived at home with her mother. It has to be walked. The dog has to be walked each day. All we need to do is look out for that labrador in the same area of York and I'm certain we'll find Mrs Hartley.'

Unimpressed, Holly's gaze returned to the game, 'Well, let's hope this idea of yours surpasses your talent for chess.'

Bain frowned as Holly leaned forward, grasped her queen and took it diagonally across the board and thumped it down beside his king.

'Checkmate,' she declared.

Thirteen

April 7th

It was hard not to be entranced by the sight of the wisps of silvery mist being lifted from the slow moving surface of the River Ouse by the early morning sun. But Holly's attention was wrenched back to the riverside footpath she, Bain, and Daisy were walking along in order to examine the approaching dog walker.

It wasn't her. A pensioner with an unkempt beard and a black and white Jack Russell shuffled towards them and passed without comment or bothering to look either of them in the eye. His attention also failed to be diverted when Daisy met his dog nose to nose to share a quick sniff and an attempted lick. Perhaps it was because the pensioner was having to concentrate on not slipping over, thought Holly, the covering of frost on the bankside path being pretty dicey on this side of the river.

'We could be walking up and down this stretch of river for days and never meet her,' Holly said under her breath once the elderly chap was out of earshot, 'Shouldn't we try Avenue Terrace again?'

Bain gave this suggestion a grudging half-smile. His feet were cold and starting to ache. All he really wanted was a cup of coffee and a bacon sandwich. He was beginning to think his serendipitous plan to locate Janice Hartley had been a bad one.

'Yes, we'll try there again,' he agreed, trying to sound upbeat, 'Maybe she's a late sleeper.'

Holly rolled her eyes. Who was Bain trying to fool? This had been a crazy idea.

Arriving at a little before seven in the morning, they'd spent the last two and a half hours walking the streets around the Clifton area of York and doing a circuit around the eastern bank of the River Ouse to the north of York city centre, crossing over Clifton Bridge and heading back towards the city before crossing again at the Scarborough Rail Bridge.

'She has to walk Brooklyn's dog. That's how we'll meet her,' Bain had been at pains to point out the night before as they'd watched a YouTube posted video of Brooklyn and her mother's interview on the Look North news. Painstakingly freeze-framing and comparing the images with Google Streetview had revealed the starting location of Brooklyn's walk be a terraced road in the Clifton area. The rest of the interview had taken place on the riverside, and with the area being popular with tourists it hadn't taken long to pin down the exact filming locations. With no way of finding out exactly where she lived, and Golden unwilling to supply the address due to data protection issues, the plan was to accidentally bump into Janice Hartley. They would then engage her in conversation and get as much information about her daughter as possible.

They continued walking along the willow tree lined bank of the river where an informal rough path had been formed by the constant flow of dog walkers. A few moments later they emerged from under the trees with the Scarborough

Railway Bridge in front of them, it's crisscross of metal being picked out against the grey sky. They crossed over the pedestrian footbridge and headed back through a maze of streets to stand at the end of The Avenue, a street they'd already traversed several times this morning without spotting Janice Hartley or Brooklyn's labrador.

Bain looked down the deserted street containing two lines of two-story terrace houses that faced each other, then found his attention drawn to Daisy, who was shivering. The two terraces were forming a unnatural corridor that enabled a chill wind to whip unmercifully down the valley of dwellings. He turned to Holly and noticed her cheeks were white and pricked red.

Bain exhaled loudly, 'I'm not happy about what we're doing. This is daft. I don't know what I was thinking. For all we know, she could live miles away from here.'

Holly managed a small smile, 'I saw a café just down there on the main road... coffee?'

'Definitely,' Bain agreed, rubbing his hands together, 'I could *murder* a bacon sandwich!'

They turned their backs on The Avenue and set off across the road with renewed purpose, the promise of hot coffee in a warm café already lifting their spirits. Reaching the footpath on the other side of the street they were forced to a halt by a large golden-haired dog. It was straining on a lead that stretched around the street corner, its owner, presumably on the end was still to round the corner. The dog set off down The Avenue, pulling hard on its tether. A second later a small, round woman wearing a deerstalker, thick coat to her knees, and wellingtons, bowled around the corner. She was struggling with the controls of a retractable lead attached to her dog, who was some ten yards further down the street ahead of her.

'Titan? Titan! You slow down *now*!'

Bain shared a disbelieving look with Holly and the two of them leapt forward to help the poor woman.

'Thank you so much. He's desperate to get home and is such a headstrong boy. He hates the cold and this darned lead has broken,' Janice Hartley told them in a grateful scouse twang as Bain and Holly helped her gain control of Titan.

'No problem, Mrs Hartley,' said Holly with a smile, and introduced herself and Bain, 'Actually, we were hoping to speak with you.'

'Are you another of Brooklyn's friends from Malton?'

Holly paused a beat, but before an answer came to her, Mrs Hartley had fired another query at her.

'And who is this?' she asked, indicating the shivering Daisy standing at Bain's ankle, 'That little love looks frozen stiff.'

'This is Daisy,' Bain said proudly.

'Do you not think she should be wearing a coat in this weather?'

Bain regarded the shivering Jacka-something and was suddenly wracked with guilt.

'So, you two *are* looking for me,' Mrs Hartley confirmed with a smile.

Bain and Holly shared a surprised look that told Janice Hartley that they were indeed looking for her.

'That's okay. Are you press then?'

'We're investigative journalists,' Holly replied. She was about to embroider this with a reason for them wandering the street of York searching for her and her dog, but Mrs Hartley cut her short.

'You come with me, I'm just over there,' she said, indicating a small terraced house with a green door a little way down the street, 'I'll talk to anyone who can help catch the man who killed my Brooklyn. I reckon the longer I can keep my Brooklyn's name in the papers, the better.'

Without further hesitation Mrs Hartley set off down the street with Titan, waving for them to follow.

'And please bring your dog in. She needs to get warmed up!'

Fourteen

Holly had to smile. She'd spent all last night and most of the morning worried that approaching a grieving mother and asking questions about her daughter's work, private life, lifestyle, and her recovery from a brain injury, might be seen as inconsiderate and terribly invasive. It was turning out to be quite the reverse. Mrs Hartley was brimming with information about her daughter and only too happy to discuss any topic that might lead to her killer being found. And in Mrs Hartley's view, that meant finding Robert Farley, or 'that evil creature,' as she referred to him.

Once Daisy and Titan had been formally introduced to each other, Mrs Hartley showed them all into her lounge at the front of the house. Cluttered with mis-matched furniture, Bain and Holly edged sideways into the room whose walls could have been a still from the Beatles Yellow Submarine animation. It was brimming with colour, from the orange carpet decorated with large red and white spirals to the hand painted walls full of huge flowers, each petal being a different, vibrant colour.

Mrs Hartley produced a couple of gravy bone biscuits from her coat pocket and settled the dogs in front of an old but warm fire that quickly boasted four glowing electric bars.

Bain was keen to get straight down to it.

'Are we the first…?'

Mrs Hartley waved away his query.

'Oh now! So impatient!' she scolded playfully with a wag of her finger, 'There's plenty of time for that. I don't know about you, but I'm parched after walking Titan in the freezing cold. And you two look like you could do with something warm inside you.'

She expertly bustled to the lounge door, throwing her midriff left and right to avoid the furniture, 'I'll get the kettle on, and we can wet our whistles. Nothing gets me talking like a cup of tea. Then you can ask as many questions as you like,' she added.

'That would be lovely,' Holly called after her, although she severely doubted Mrs Hartley's vocal chords needed further lubrication.

'You referred to her as Mrs Hartley before she'd introduced herself,' whispered Bain, as they both warmed themselves on the hot orange bars of the electric fire.

'Drat, sorry about that.'

Bain discarded her apology with a quick shake of his head, 'No, don't be. We've learned that someone other than the police has been here before us. We need to find out who.'

Waiting in silence for their host to return, Holly and Bain examined their surroundings. Holly found herself mesmerized by the avalanche of colour.

A minute later Mrs Hartley was back carrying a worn steel serving tray. Over a scratched picture of Frankie Dettori the tray was loaded with three mugs of tea, a bowl of sugar and an array of biscuits. Bain's eyes lit up as he spied a couple of Tunnock's Caramel Wafers in their distinctive red and yellow wrappers.

'So where are you two from?' Mrs Hartley asked as she arranged her small, rotund body into an armchair that blazed with an eye-wateringly colourful leaf pattern.

'Northallerton.'

'No, no my dear, I meant which newspaper?'

'Ah! Oh, no, we're freelance. We write for a number of different publications,' Holly explained, 'We've had our work published in The Sunday Times.'

Mrs Hartley's eyes grew big and she nodded appreciatively.

Spotting an opening, Bain took up the questioning.

'We're working on your daughter's murder…'

'Please, call her Brooklyn,' Mrs Hartley interrupted, an unexpected cutting edge to her voice, 'Since it happened, people have stopped calling her by her name… it's always the grieving widow's daughter, or that murdered 'Good Morning' girl. She had a name. A nice one.'

Bain produced a warm smile of understanding and continued, 'Of course. Brooklyn is why we're here, and any background about her would be very helpful in order to… um, keep the pressure on the police to find Brooklyn's killer.'

Mrs Hartley's bottom lip had begun to quiver as Bain spoke. By the time he'd finished his question her round cheeks had gone an angry red colour and tears were welling in her eyes. Digging into the sleeve of her tight, bright red cardigan she shook out a hankie and dabbed at the corner of her eyes.

Holly gave Bain a meaningful look and got up and joined the distressed woman on her tiny sofa. Bain watched, boggled, as slowly but surely, Holly managed to calm and then gently release everything they needed from Mrs Hartley, and more.

It turned out that Brooklyn had been switched on quite late to riding, but after a short stint working at a local livery yard at the age of eighteen, she'd impressed enough to gain a place at the Doncaster Race Riding School, the top place for aspiring young race riders. From there, she had been apprenticed to Graham Dent in Malton.

'She loved it there in Malton,' Mrs Hartley recounted, 'I've never seen her so happy. It was tough, of course, long hours and all that, but she had bags of friends, and started to get regular rides for Mr Dent.'

'You've met Mr Dent? asked Holly.

'Oh, yes, a lovely man. Brooklyn introduced me at Wetherby races last year. He didn't say a lot as he was busy with his horses. It was his son, Hugo, that spoke with me most. Nothing like his father, and Brooklyn wasn't too fond of him, but I thought Hugo was nice, and ever-so good looking.'

Tears returned to her eyes when Mrs Hartley spoke about the day of Brooklyn's accident at the stables in Malton.

'The twenty-second of October,' Mrs Hartley said, her bottom lip trembling, 'It was a young horse. Just bad luck… the wrong place at the…'

Once again, Holly's skills as a counsellor came to the fore as Mrs Hartley teared up. As Bain watched on he couldn't help thinking that Mrs Hartley's remark about Brooklyn's luck was understated. Being in the wrong place at the wrong time had cost Brooklyn her cognitive facilities the first time, and then, subsequently, her life.

'Brooklyn was kicked so hard in the head she went straight into a coma. Caught her just behind her ear, a whacking great bash from its steel shoe that left a mark like a half-moon. That boy Hugo found her. She'd been lying in the stable for half an hour. They rushed her to hospital in Hull and were still operating on her by the time I got there.'

It took a few gentle prods from Holly to keep Mrs Hartley on track, but the facts around Brooklyn's recuperation were slowly teased out. She had come out of her coma after eight days, but the blow had affected her co-ordination, and left her constantly confused. Her motor skills were badly affected, so writing and typing were impossible, and the speech centre of Brooklyn's brain had been badly damaged. She'd had to learn how to walk and think straight again, and she was mute for several months.

'The consultant said it was, die… dyeserty… something,'

'I think it's called dysarthria,' Bain had offered, 'It's when the muscles you use for speech are weakened by a brain injury.'

Mrs Hartley had nodded her agreement, 'The poor wee lass would get so angry and frustrated she couldn't think straight or talk,' Mrs Hartley told them, 'She would write things, but it was just confusing gobbledygook. I couldn't make head nor tail of it. I don't think she ever remembered the accident, or anything about that day… maybe that was for the best.'

Bain was impressed with Mrs Hartley's fervour when it came to her daughter's more recent recovery.

'Mark my words, Brooklyn was getting better,' she

stated with certainty, 'On the day of the um… attack, she headed out with Titan for her walk beside the river like normal, but turned around at the garden gate and just like that, said, 'Bye, Mum'. It was the first time she'd said anything other than 'Good Morning'. I was so pleased… I just wish I'd stopped her, brought her back inside...'

Forty minutes later they were on the doorstep, Mrs Hartley hugging Holly, thanking her for taking such an interest in her daughter, then shaking Bain's hand. He'd hardly said a word since making her cry the first time. But there was one question he was dying to ask, so he held onto her hand and gazed intently into her eyes.

'Apart from the police, has anyone else dropped in and asked questions about Brooklyn?'

Mrs Hartley retracted her hand, Bain's normally productive puppy-dog gaze having a puzzlingly adverse effect on her. However, after taking a step back, she did answer him.

'There was that nice lady from Look North, and the chap from the local paper came a couple of times in the first week, and of course the police keep popping in, but since that horrible man was last seen in Northallerton there's only been you…'

She crossed her arms and her eyes hardened slightly, 'Didn't you say that's where you're from?'

Holly smiled a little too broadly, 'Yes, just a weird coincidence, I guess.'

Mrs Hartley scanned her face and Holly held her smile as best she could, trying not to imagine the dark thoughts the grieving mother was fighting. However, Mrs Hartley broke into a smile and soon brightened.

'I want justice for my daughter, she said earnestly, 'Brooklyn deserves it. You keep an eye out for that man in Northallerton. And if you see him, you keep well away and call the police!'

They both thanked her again, and buttoning up their

coats against the cold, waved a final goodbye.

'Oh, and there was Brooklyn's friend from the racing yard,' Mrs Hartley called after them.

Bain swung round, 'Really? When was that?'

Mrs Hartley's brow wrinkled as she counted back the days in her head, 'Just last week, Friday I think. Yes, Friday. It was the day I put the bins out.'

'And her name?'

'Oh, it wasn't a girl, it was a boy. Had a funny name. He was foreign, but very nice. I think he said it was Mark, Luke... or it could have been Matthew. He was like you and Brooklyn,' Mrs Hartley recounted with a sad, reflective smile, 'He just loved those Tunnock's caramel biscuits.'

Fifteen

April 23rd

Ronnie peered over the top edge of her newspaper, glared at the Widow Solanki, and crumpled it enough to signal she was irritated.

'Must you?' she asked sharply, eyeing her companion who was sitting on the other side the room.

The Widow Solanki, otherwise known as Vladimir, held up a flat palm from his lounger in the conservatory. He wrote something, placed the quiz book he was working on aside, patiently removed his glasses, and gave Ronnie his full attention. The sixty year old man's steady gaze oozed patient amusement.

Vladimir Solanki had an uncommon mixture of Russian and Indian heritage, providing him with soulful brown eyes and a dusky complexion. He was wearing a fancy white silk shirt, tight black trousers that displayed sockless ankles and a pair of moccasin slippers. And it was the flat sole of one slipper that was rhythmically tapping, or rather, flapping out a regular beat against the ornately laid red bricks of the conservatory floor.

'You're making a noise.'

Vladimir's pure white eyebrows sprang up in surprise and his mouth opened into an 'Oh!' shape, wrinkling his silver beard.

'Really? What sort of noise?' he queried.

'You're still making it!' Ronnie growled, aiming her wide-eyed gaze at her next door neighbour's foot.

'What? Oh, am I tapping?'

Ronnie lowered her newspaper to her lap and gave a harassed sigh, 'Yes, you're tapping that foot of yours, and it's driving me crazy.'

Vladimir reached to his righthand ear and removed something.

'I'm solving a Sudoku, dear. It helps me concentrate if I listen to Bach.'

'You're listening to music?'

Vladimir held up a device, small and black. Ronnie squinted at it.

'What's that then, an earplug?' tutted Ronnie, 'You want wax for that, much better than those sponge things.'

'It's a headphone, darling! Or rather I think they call them earbuds,' he said, removing the second device from his other ear.

'Wonderful invention, they attach to my mobile phone. I can listen to all sorts of things, even audiobooks,' he cooed, 'I can't hear your knitting needles when they're in. You should try them, Ronnie. They might put you in a better mood.'

Had such a suggestion come from anyone else, Ronnie might have blown a fuse. As it was, the Widow Solanki was a dear friend, and wasn't that what dear friends were for? To point out when you were being insufferable?

Ronnie thought about this for a moment. She was pretty sure that pointing out other people's shortcomings *was* her calling, whether the person was friend or foe. It was a calling she actually relished. She did it frequently, often in public, as a kindness to the person consuming their time, or indeed their entire life, doing things badly, or downright wrong. Holly and Vladimir had suggested that because she had a certain way with words, there were occasions where her advice could be construed as criticism. Ronnie rejected this as poppycock. She was convinced she was an absolute delight.

However, it did sting when Ronnie was reminded of the nature of her bipolarism, no matter who was doing the reminding. Since Christmas she had been fighting to master a downward swing, a challenge her disorder made on an all too frequent basis. It mostly manifested itself by making her mooch around the house in a grouch, being short tempered and argumentative with anyone she ran into. That was the best of it. Ronnie preferred not to think about the panic attacks and dark, dangerous dips into a short-lived mania. However, she'd started to feel a little better the last few days with Vlad around to give as good as he got.

'Give those earbuds here then,' Ronnie snapped, 'I've worn similar things before, let's give them a go.'

Twenty minutes later, and halfway through Fugue in G minor, Ronnie jumped from her seat as an unknown hand rested itself on her shoulder and gave it a squeeze. She tore the headphones from her ears and glared at her daughter, who was already in defensive mode with both hands wide, palms pushing out.

'I didn't know you were listening to... something,' Holly blurted out before her mother could take a deep enough breath to start ranting, 'I did call out to you! Twice. I thought you'd nodded off, or... well, I thought you...'

'You were checking whether I was dead?' demanded Ronnie, aghast.

'She thought you'd gone deaf, Ronnie!' Bain called out from the kitchen to the clink of coffee cups, 'We knew you weren't dead because you were tapping your foot.'

At the other side of the room the Widow Solanki

rumbled with a low laugh.

Ronnie harumphed a little, but sat back down without tearing a strip off anyone. Holly smiled inwardly, and shot Vladimir an approving look. This was a positive signal. With a little luck her mother was emerging from her days of melancholia.

'It's been a productive morning and an interesting afternoon,' announced Bain as he entered the warm, leafy atmosphere in the spacious conservatory. He set a tray of coffees down and poured into bone China cups as he updated Ronnie and Vladimir.

Vladimir's penchant for wearing rather tight and on occasion, flamboyant clothes, or his softly feminine gestures didn't bother Bain in the slightest. Vladimir wore his homosexuality well. The Widow Solanki (Ronnie's pet name for him, based on Widow Twanky the cross-dressing dame of pantomime fame) was a very likeable, demure, and wise chap as far as Bain was concerned. Yes, he had a few quirks, but who didn't? And Vladimir was devoted to Ronnie.

'How did it go with the girl's mother? I presume you tracked her down?' asked Ronnie. She took a sip of her coffee, grimaced, cast a disproving glance Bain's way, and added more milk.

Bain and Holly spent the next few minutes bringing Vladimir and Ronnie up to speed on their conversation with Janice Hartley.

'She doesn't seem to have grasped one of the most salient points about the death of her daughter… although Bain and I are quite relieved she hasn't,' Holly admitted.

Bain pressed his lips together, silently reflecting on Mrs Hartley's situation, before muttering his agreement.

'We think Brooklyn was killed because of her appearance on Look North. For some reason, that interview was the catalyst that drove the killer to attack Brooklyn. She was killed the morning after that interview aired on television.'

'What's that got to do with the girl's mother?' queried Vladimir.

'She entered Brooklyn for the 'Face of York' competition and insisted her daughter appeared on Look North,' explained Holly, 'Mrs Hartley told us Brooklyn wasn't too happy about being plastered all over the city's tourism advertising. She eventually agreed to do the interview when her mother became upset with her.'

'So far, Mrs Hartley hasn't linked her daughter's appearance on TV to her subsequent attack. Perhaps she doesn't want to... But the fact remains that her insistence on making Brooklyn into a local celebrity may have prompted the killer to act.'

Bain added, 'The interview gave her killer the route she would take every morning with her dog, and to some extent, the timing. The killer chose a densely overgrown part of the riverside path and... you know the rest.'

'Quite,' commented Vladimir grimly, 'The mother's actions aside - and I hope you'll *never* reveal your thoughts on that subject to her - all you seem to have done is implicate anyone who watched Look North that evening. That's about a million people isn't it?'

'If you believe her killer targeted Brooklyn out of jealousy, spite, or some other twisted reason, then yes, we're no further forward,' Bain replied with a shrug, 'But Mrs Farley did say that she felt Brooklyn was starting to be more like her old self, she said as much in her television interview. And if you believe Farley about the words Brooklyn spoke before she died, it adds weight to the theory that someone saw the Look North interview, realised Brooklyn was becoming more lucid and wanted to shut her up.'

'You start to wonder,' Ronnie breathed, 'Whether the accident the girl had in the stables...'

Holly smiled at her mother and nodded, 'May not have been an accident?'

'Let's not get carried away,' Bain said, trying to contain

the excitement that was building in the conservatory, 'Brooklyn was kicked by a horse in a stable. Everyone says it was a pure accident. I doubt anyone was to blame.'

'But it's a possibility!' Ronnie exclaimed in Bain's direction, a little irked.

Quietly pleased with her mother's contribution, Holly nonetheless moved on quickly to avoid a full-blown argument.

'With the knife Robert Farley gave us looking equine in origin we need to understand more about Brooklyn's time at the Graham Dent stables.'

'What about Farley? Are we ruling him out?' asked Vladimir.

Bain glanced at Holly and they shook their heads in unison, 'We can't,' replied Bain, 'He was at the murder scene, covered in blood. Even though we're inclined to believe his story that he was only trying to resuscitate Brooklyn, we can't rule him out.'

'The online video of him is pretty damning. Even so, he'd either have to be an amazing actor or completely deluded to have come here and put up a performance like he did,' said Holly, 'And if Farley is the killer, how would he benefit from involving us?'

'Unless he's got serious mental issues and can't, or won't remember what he did…' Vladimir postulated.

The conservatory went quiet as everyone considered this possibility. It was Ronnie who spoke up.

'Why would Farley tell us about a random word like Snowdrop? It would be a strange thing to make up. Do we have any idea why Brooklyn would be so desperate to tell Farley about a flower?'

Her question was greeted with another contemplative silence. Bain grimaced, 'I've come up blank on that one. I've tried horses, dogs, local places in York and Malton, all sorts, nothing seems to link Brooklyn to the name 'Snowdrop'. It's a good reason to get into the Dent yard and talk to everyone who knew Brooklyn. Hopefully Snowdrop will mean something to one of them and point us in the direction of the killer.'

'So, when do we interview the staff at Graham Dent's yard?' asked Ronnie.

Bain shared a meaningful look with Holly, 'Yeah... we've been thinking about that over the last few days. We can't just pitch up at the Dent's yard and demand to interview everyone. We need to collect our evidence via... other means.'

A smile tugged at the corner of Ronnie's mouth, grew across her face and soon became a broad grin.

'So you want me to buy a racehorse and infiltrate the Dent's yard in Malton, becoming an owner again, just like last time?'

'Oh, heavens no, Mother!' Holly scolded, 'We can't afford that. Besides, last time you ended up needing Vladimir to whack a crazed criminal over the head with your jam pan. It will be Bain or myself going into the yard to find out what's going on.'

Ronnie's grin vanished, replaced with a rather forlorn look her daughter's way, 'You don't need me at all then?'

Bain jumped in, 'Actually Hol, I think we do need Ronnie, but just for tomorrow. If we're at the breeze-ups, and the Dents are at the breeze-ups, wouldn't it be the perfect time for someone to visit their yard, you know, while the cats are away...?'

Holly bit her lip, fearing where this was heading.

'I wondered whether Vladimir might be up for helping you Ronnie. I reckon your joint talents will be well suited to the *sleuthing* that is required. The two of you could visit the yard posing as *potential* owners, rather than actually buying a racehorse.'

The grin returned to Ronnie's face. Vladimir smiled.

Holly shot Bain a dark look and rolled her eyes up to the glass ceiling of the conservatory.

Sixteen

April 24th

The veterinary surgery was busier than usual. It was unlikely he'd be able to make it over to the Graham Dent stables. Alone in his consulting room, Daniel Croft looked down the rest of his appointments for the morning on his tablet and counted them up. Four cats, six dogs, one rabbit and a guinea pig. Twelve consultations in the next three hours, each at an average of a hundred and thirty pounds per quarter hour consultation. Daniel did the math. He always did the math, that was his thing, he liked to think about money. He'd already given a cat a booster jab and seen a dog with a smoking problem (his owner was a twenty a day man and the dog was suffering for it). Well over one and a half thousand pounds for a morning's work, he calculated. Far more than the forty pounds an hour his father paid him as a newly qualified vet. What was worse, he had to stand throughout the entire clinic!

Leaning his elbows onto the rubberised consulting table, Daniel massaged his face with both hands. Smiling at clients was starting to make his cheek muscles sing with pain. Daniel sighed heavily, when your resting face was a sallow grimace, putting on a winning smile all day was pure torture. He glimpsed at the time on his tablet. He had another two minutes before he had to call in Mrs Wild with her Great Dane, Arthur.

Without warning, the private door at the back of his consulting room opened and the owner of Croft Veterinary Services entered abruptly. Daniel's father, Leslie Croft, looked his son up and down. Out of habit, and because he knew it fluffed his father's ego, Daniel straightened, faced him and tried to look attentive. His father closed the door and without a word, slowly turned full circle to inspect the room. Daniel didn't know why, as there wasn't much to see. The consulting room consisted of bare white walls and ceiling tiles, with grey lino, chosen because it didn't show the various hair, liquids, and on occasion, solids, animals might leave behind. Finally, he took in his son once again, dressed in a white lab coat with dark blue jeans showing from the knees down, ending with a pair of ancient Adidas trainers.

Leslie Croft took on an air of mild disapproval. At twenty-six, Daniel was exactly half his own age. Perhaps that was why he couldn't fathom why his son wanted to wear twenty-year-old Nike plimsoles that cost a small fortune.

'Your plans for tonight?' his father inquired, still perusing his son's well-worn but much-loved footwear.

'Dropping in on the Dent's this evening. Got some business there. I won't be too late home. Want me to bring in a take-away?'

Despite being four inches taller than his father, Daniel had never felt he dominated him physically. Leslie Croft resembled an inverted triangle, broad, and full of muscle across his shoulders, drawn inwards to a thin waist and short, stubby legs. A full head of blonde hair masked the first flush of grey above his father's ears and gave Leslie Croft the look of a man a decade younger.

'I know you've got some sort of deal going on with that Dent boy, but be careful. What we have going on here dwarfs anything you'll get from him. Besides, we're onto a good thing here and I don't want any complications…'

Daniel rolled his eyes, 'I know. You keep telling me.'

'Keep it low-key,' his father insisted, 'I want no loose ends. It's taken time to recruit and mould a very useful asset at the Dents. I've entrusted the asset to you and I could do without you blowing it. Understand?'

'I've told you,' Daniel replied grimly, 'Don't worry about the Dents.'

Leslie Croft slowly cocked his head back, his eyes never leaving Daniel's. He regarded his son with a cold judgement that sent a shiver through Daniel.

'Mmm... okay,' his father eventually murmured, seemingly satisfied.

Turning his attention to the shelves on the back wall, Daniel watched his father begin to idly straighten up boxes of tissues, wipes, and disposable gloves.

'I've the latest order planned to ship at the end of the month, so I'll be working in the cellar after hours from tonight,' his father stated casually, 'I want the product off the premises as soon as each batch is ready. Is the pick-up point still secure? Storing it around here is dangerous and will...'

Daniel had been nodding his agreement throughout. He waited for the right moment and chimed in with his father so they both said, '...undermine our contingency,' in unison.

Leslie Croft grinned at his son, a smile almost breaking out around the edges of his mouth, 'It's good to have you on-side. Just... don't get too cocky. I'll tell you when to take the product up there.'

Daniel remained poker-faced. His father spun round, opened the door, and sniffed, 'Get this room washed out with antiseptic. There's an odour of dog in here. Clients like to smell the phenol, it reminds them of TCP. It's a trust thing.'

'Sure. Oh, you know I'm out of the clinic on Wednesday?'

His father puckered his lips in thought, 'It rings a distant bell.'

'The breeze-up sale at Doncaster.'

'Hmm. Horses again, eh? Give me a cat or a dog any day. They're far more straightforward,' his father commented as he stepped out of the room, 'Although I admit, horses are far more profitable.'

'And don't forget,' he added, flicking his gaze to the floor, 'Antiseptic.'

Daniel's shoulders relaxed as the door clicked closed. He detested the smell of antiseptic wash. That was his father's thing; chemicals. He was always messing around with different compounds, which is why the cellar was out of bounds to every member of staff. He doubted anyone beyond the two of them even knew there *was* a cellar under the building, it was so well hidden. The only way in was a hatch accessed from outside in the private yard at the back of the clinic, itself protected by a ten foot brick wall smeared with anti-climb grease and topped with razor wire. A tall gate equipped with steel spikes and a heavy padlock was the only way in.

Back in the day, the surgery had been a coaching inn, and the cellar was used to store the beer and wine. The cellar now had a very different use. Inside the windowless, soundless room, his father produced ecstasy of the highest quality. It had taken Leslie Croft years to build up his veterinary supply chain in order to acquire the right volume of chemicals that allowed him to regularly produce large quantities of the product, which to his father, meant large amounts of cash.

His phone rang. Checking he still had a minute before his next client appointment, Daniel slipped his phone out of his jeans pocket and peered at the small screen. It was Hugo Dent. He accepted the call, ensuring he answered in a friendly tone.

Forty seconds later he rang off having learnt he'd been let down. The breeze-ups were a two day sale. The first day saw the young horses breezing, the second was the selling day. Hugo could no longer attend the breezing day, having to stay behind at the yard to cover for his father. Daniel remained silent as Hugo explained his predicament. After a well-judged delay Daniel told the assistant trainer he was disappointed, but that he understood.

Proud of himself for taking the news so stoically, Daniel told himself that missing the first day of the sale didn't really matter. The second day was the important one. What mattered most was that Hugo had been incredibly apologetic. A pliant Hugo was a useful Hugo.

Daniel grinned, then noticed his tablet was flashing a reminder. He tapped the appointment time and an audio connection was made to the receptionist in the waiting room.

'Okay Phylis,' Daniel sang out with renewed energy, 'You can send in Mrs Wild and Arthur.'

Seventeen

April 25th - Day one of the breeze-up sale, Doncaster

'I still wish you hadn't involved my mother,' Holly complained as she slid her crash helmet up over her ears and handed it to Bain. She checked her phone and shrugged at the lack of missed calls or messages from Ronnie.

'Yep. You've reminded me about your reservations on a daily basis. But what else could I do? You said yourself that Ronnie needed something to give her a lift. This is that lift! You've seen how she's been the last few days. It was a perfect solution, especially with Vlad there to oversee things.'

Bain took the two bike helmets and slotted a solid bar through them both, then attached the D-locking mechanism to the wheel of his Kawasaki Ninja 750 motorcycle. There was a squelch as a heavy SUV drew up a few yards away on the wet grass. The earth was soaking. A fortnight of near-constant rainfall had led to race meetings being abandoned all over the country. Even so, Doncaster had managed to hold its Lincoln flat meeting and apparently the course was fit enough today for close to two hundred young horses to breeze up the straight.

The white rails, representing the last few furlongs of the racetrack, stretched out barely forty yards away from their parking place. Doncaster sales adopted the field as a car park on sale days. Once used as common land grazing for farm animals, the area was currently busy being filled with lines of cars and people, all of whom were carefully navigating the puddles on the waterlogged ground.

Beyond the makeshift car park lay a mess of buildings and stables belonging to Goffs, the major sales house for racehorses in the north of England. Bain was still messing with his motorbike, so Holly studied the small groups of people heading for the entrance to the Goffs railed compound. Most of them fell into a category she would later describe to Ronnie as being, 'countrified, with money'.

Unlocking a panier, Bain removed a dark blue flat cap and put it on, but continued to rummage around until he pulled out something woolly.

'You want this?' he asked, holding up a black bobble hat, 'Ideally, we don't want to be recognised.'

Holly took it. There was still a cool nip apparent in the air. She pulled it on, her short blonde hair being completely hidden, and tried, but failed to ignore the Newcastle United logo emblazoned on the front of the hat.

'You're a Newcastle United fan?'

'Yeah. Couldn't help it living in Blaydon for eight years. Black and white runs through the veins of anyone within twenty-five miles of St James' Park.'

Holly gave him a watery smile, none the wiser, and not much bothered about a further explanation. Football wasn't of much interest to her, that was Bain's thing. With a fair breeze and a chance of rain, as long as the hat kept her head dry and her ears warm, she didn't mind which team her headgear supported.

As they made their way through the lines of shiny, expensive cars and giant SUV's with personalised plates, Holly took a sidelong glance at her business partner. Bain was wearing his wax jacket. The shabby green coat was never off his back, winter or summer. But to be fair, his choice in headgear rounded off his gentrified look nicely.

'The flat cap suits you,' she commented as they walked through the gates and into the Goffs complex, 'You look like a gamekeeper.'

'Drat. I was trying for gentleman poacher,' he muttered dryly in reply, whilst checking his watch, 'Come on, the breezing will start in ten minutes. Let's grab a catalogue and look like we're here to buy, then we'll see if we can spot Dent.'

They set off for the sales office with renewed vigour. The Doncaster breeze-ups were a chance to study Graham Dent up close, without raising any suspicion. Bain was sure the trainer would be here for the two day sale, as he'd bought a couple of horses at this sale in every one of the last five years.

Bain severely doubted he would be able to link Dent to Brooklyn's murder simply by attending the breeze-ups. As he'd told Holly, studying the trainer at close quarters was primarily a chance to get to know the man and the people around him before they initiated the next part of the plan. Besides, Bain always enjoyed a day at the sales, and reckoned both he and Holly needed a day out of the office after being stuck in Northallerton for the last fortnight.

The continuing manhunt for Farley remained a hot topic in the media. Golden's boss, Sayer, had recently come over as a harassed figure when interviewed on TV about the police's failure to turn up any leads. With little to go on, he'd been reduced to using his public appearance to plead for any sightings of Farley to be reported. However, when the Sun newspaper published the contents of Farley's armed services record there had been a second wave of interest.

The revelation that Farley had recently been discharged after serving a number of months in military prison propelled his image back into the limelight. The details were sketchy; having pleaded guilty to disobeying direct orders and threatening his commanding officer with actual bodily harm, Farley had then produced a knife, although he hadn't inflicted any injury. These revelations had ensured extra coverage, and temporarily intensified the search for his whereabouts, and caused Bain to re-evaluate his view of Farley.

A hum of anticipation hung in the air as Holly and Bain

joined a crowd of around three hundred people spread out on the inside of Doncaster's racetrack. Bain explained that Goffs had relocated their sales ground from a dilapidated site opposite the racecourse, to be beside the home straight, at around four hundred yards from the entrance to the racecourse. This meant that they could use the track to breeze the young horses the day before the sale itself. Holly wasn't too sure what 'breezing' meant, but it soon became apparent that it consisted of unraced two-year-old horses being galloped over a distance of about two and a half furlongs, one after another, or sometimes in twos.

'The horses that go through this breeze-up sale tend to command a higher price than at the yearling sales because their potential speed is on show. At the yearling sales they aren't broken, so buyers are basing their decision solely on looks and pedigree,' Bain explained, 'They all breeze today and then go under the hammer tomorrow. The idea is that you get a ready-made racehorse that's been taught the basics and provided the buyers with a taste of their ability. Ideally the horses should be all set to go racing straight away… although it doesn't always work out that way.'

Standing on a raised area of ground that turned out to be the concrete base to a long-forgotten grandstand on the inside of the racecourse, Bain had taken Holly away from other groups of watchers and to the highest point, giving the two of them the best possible view over the rest of the crowd.

'This isn't like a race-day,' said Bain pointing over at the vast, empty grandstands, parade rings, and windswept betting concourse on the opposite side of the track, 'For one thing, no-one gets to watch races from here.'

He continued, 'Sixty years ago the inside of the track would be awash with people when the races were run. We're standing on an old vantage point from the days when the racecourse would attract seventy or a hundred thousand racegoers, rather than the eight to ten thousand that turn up for a standard race meeting now.'

A public address system crackled into life once again and Holly watched as in ones and twos, more young, inexperienced horses were announced by lot number and cajoled by their riders to jump off from a starting point in the distance and raise a gallop down the last few furlongs of what Bain explained was the winter jumps course, minus the fences.

They watched the first few youngsters dash past their position opposite the last furlong in silence, listening to a Goffs commentator extolling the virtues of each of the thoroughbreds' pedigrees. This narrator commented on the way the horse was moving, or the ease with which the colt or filly covered the ground, but Holly was soon casting her gaze further afield, away from the young racehorses, all of whom appeared much the same to her inexperienced eye. It didn't take her long to spot what she was looking for.

Nudging Bain softly in his ribs she whispered, 'I think that's Graham Dent over there,' she said, pulling out a grainy photo she'd lifted from the internet, 'What do you think?'

Bain followed her gaze and sure enough, he confirmed that the trainer he had anticipated would be attending the sale, was indeed standing about thirty yards away from them. He was entertaining a small entourage that Bain presumed were Dent's owners.

A dominating presence, Graham Dent stood straight and tall, a good three inches above every person around him, even without his trilby. With a pair of rimless spectacles balanced on the tip of his nose, Dent switched between consulting his sales catalogue, and peering with studious intent over to the gallop as each youngster approached, making short comments about each as they finished their breeze and sometimes writing notes on the youngsters page in his sales catalogue.

Pulling the brim of his cap down, Bain told her, 'Good spot, Hol. Come on, let's get closer. I want to take a few photos.'

Holly followed Bain as he wandered between the

trainers, buyers, nervous stud managers, and pinhookers to take up a new position, as close to the Dent group as they could get without attracting any attention.

Holly took out her mobile phone and sent a text off to her mother.

'You've let them know?' Bain checked.

Rather pensively, Holly nodded.

'Don't worry,' Bain assured her, 'With Dent here in Doncaster, what could *possibly* go wrong at the yard?'

Holly grimaced, 'You have met my mother, haven't you?'

Eighteen

'Are you *sure* we can't be ourselves?' Vladimir asked for the third time since Holly's text message about Graham Dent had arrived. He rubbed his palm down the driver's side window of his steamed up car and stared at what he'd decided was an unnecessarily grand and somewhat gawdy entrance to the Beverley Hill training stables.

Ronnie squeezed her eyes shut, shook her head and sighed theatrically, 'No! Where's the fun in that? Dent's not here, and we don't want anyone linking me back to Holly.'

'Yes, but surely I could be myself, after all...'

'Just pull the car up to the gate and let me do the talking,' said Ronnie in a friendly, but stiff tone that made it clear that further discussion was pointless.

She patted Vladimir's hand and gave him an indulgent smile. He placed the car in gear and they moved forward. Try as he might, he couldn't help grinning back at his friend.

'Ronnie, you will be the death of me.'

'And not having fun will be the death of me. Drive on!'

Vladimir pulled up to an elaborate steel gate painted black and highlighted in gold. Attached to the front of the gate in steel plate was an artsy depiction of a grey racehorse in full flight, sporting a ridiculously long mane.

Ronnie pushed open the passenger door and went around to stand in front of a large steel box she imagined was an intercom. Attached to one of the stone columns bookending the entrance, she pressed various parts of the device until landing on a button that buzzed. Expecting a voice to demand who she was, Ronnie cleared her throat and rehearsed her introductory speech in her head. To her surprise, the gate made a clanging sound and started to slide open. She turned, raised both eyebrows at Vladimir and shot back into the car.

Trundling along a yellow stone lane, they passed paddocks on both sides with small groups of horses contained within sturdy wooden fences. The road skirted the back of a couple of block built barns and they were soon pulling onto a rough area of hardcore and reversed into a space alongside half a dozen other cars. Vladimir killed the engine and they sat in silence for a moment, taking in their view of the Graham Dent yard through the windscreen. It was dominated by four huge open-ended barns and they could just make out the first few stable doors inside the entrance to each barn before they descended into darkness.

A stable lass wearing riding apparel and pushing a wheelbarrow brimming with soiled woodchips emerged from the gloom inside the nearest barn. She glanced up, but didn't register the newly parked car or its inhabitants.

'Looks like we're not expected, so we may as well do our own introductions,' said Ronnie, pushing her door open and stalking over to where the girl was tipping her load into a brick bay containing a mound of used equine bedding.

Vladimir caught up with Ronnie in mid-conversation. She was busily introducing herself, speaking so quickly Vladimir was sure the girl wasn't following. Ronnie finally asked where she could find Graham Dent. The girl was young, in her mid-teens, and stared at Ronnie with large, round, uncomprehending eyes. Vladimir was about to speak but his nostrils unexpectedly flared. A potent smell was grabbing the back of his throat and trying to throttle him. He coughed and screwed his nose up whilst inspecting the huge pile of horse dung currently wafting its odour over the three of them.

'We're looking for Mr Dent. Is he here?' repeated Ronnie, trying but failing to keep her impatience from her tone.

The girl didn't answer immediately. There was an awkward silence, but presently there was a lightbulb moment of understanding in her eyes and she shook her head, 'The Guv'nor is out at the sales in…'

'Hello there! Can I help at all?' called out a male voice.

Ronnie and Vladimir turned. The voice belonged to a ruggedly handsome young man in polo shirt, jeans, and riding boots. He produced a healthy, white toothed smile as he approached them. Of average height with thick blonde hair, he moved with long, slightly out-turned strides which along with his ungainly arms, gave him a willowy effect. Ronnie pursed her lips disapprovingly upon noticing Vladimir glowing with interest and already smiling back at the lad. She'd have to have a word with him about that.

'It's okay, Amber. You can get on with your work,' the lad instructed the girl. Blushing slightly and looking relieved, Amber disappeared back into her barn with the empty wheelbarrow bouncing along in front of her.

'I'm Hugo Dent, the assistant trainer,' the young man announced, brushing his fringe from his eyes and offering a handshake to both his visitors, 'I'm guessing someone in the office buzzed you through the gate?'

'Tamsin Brayne and my husband, Arthur,' said Ronnie with a smile. She ran the names through her head and was already regretting the non-de-plumes she'd chosen. They were based on a woman she'd met at her local municipal swimming pool and locked in conversation during an aqua aerobics session. She could sense Vladimir bristling beside her. Arthur

Brayne. Mmm… she should have given that more thought.

'My apologies for landing without warning, Hugo,' Ronnie added quickly, 'We're interested in owning a racehorse and wished to discuss the possibility of buying one and having it trained by Graham Dent. Is he not here?'

'I'm afraid my father is away on business, buying young horses at the sales,' Hugo replied, casting his gaze over to where Vladimir's unwashed and unloved twelve-year-old Ford Focus was parked.

He smiled again, but this time there was a definite increase in the amount of effort he employed, making his gracious manner appear a little ungenuine.

'You do realise it's rather an… expensive hobby?' he ventured, looking Ronnie up and down without making any effort to hide the fact he was judging her suitability for racehorse ownership on looks alone.

'Please don't bother your pretty young head about that,' assured Ronnie with her steely blue eyes locked on his, 'We recently sold our villa in the Algarve. We're completely new to horse racing, but would like to get involved with maybe… two horses to start off with?'

Hugo sniffed. What the hell, he thought, he'd give them the ten bob tour and then get rid of them. He had the feeling they were tyre kickers, but he'd take a chance on them for the sake of twenty minutes.

Nineteen

Bain recognised most racehorse trainers by sight. It was the same with football managers and to a lesser extent, coaching staff. He regularly trained himself to recognise names, faces, and even racing silks, doing his best to know at least a little of their working and personal history. It was a mammoth task, constantly keeping up to date with the movers and shakers in both sports, but that was the job, and it was worth doing. His diligence had paid off several times in the past.

He'd once parked up at a racecourse and recognised Harry Glenridding, a young, aspiring trainer who it was rumoured would soon be training for one of the Saudi Sheiks. Harry was getting out of the car beside him. By the time he'd reached the Owners and Trainers entrance to the racecourse, Bain had secured a great little interview with the trainer that confirmed horses from a lesser known sheik were on their way, and the piece had sold well. But just at the moment, Bain was wishing he hadn't recognised the face of the man standing alone at the far side of the breeze-up crowd.

Like Bain, Conor Moran was a man who had one foot in football and the other in horse racing. And as far as Bain was concerned, Conor Moran poisoned everything he touched in both sports.

'I recognise Dent. He's the tall one. But who are the people with him?' asked Holly.

Bain didn't respond. He was staring intently beyond Dent and the group of six people surrounding him. Holly gave him a poke.

'Hey! What's wrong?'

'Conor Moran is here,' Bain whispered with a hand half-covering his mouth.

It took a moment for Holly's brain to kick into gear and understand why Bain had lost all his focus on Graham Dent's group. Conor Moran, architect of Bain's past loss of reputation as a sports journalist, was an itch Bain scratched far too often. Holly always tried to play down Moran's importance, but Bain wasn't the type to forgive and forget. Conor Moran had taken on the role of Bain's nemesis.

Following Bain's gaze she scanned the small groups of potential buyers dotted around them. She had no trouble locating Moran. Despite his collar being turned up on his expensive overcoat, he was smoking, and as he took a draw from his cigarette the orange tip momentarily lit up his face.

Moran exhaled a large cloud of blue smoke that enveloped dozens of people as it caught the breeze after being expelled from deep inside his lungs. Holly narrowed her eyes as the blue wisps rushed at her, followed by the foul smell of burnt tobacco.

'What's he doing here?'

Still solely focussed on the man who had pulverised his writing career four years ago, Bain didn't answer. Moran was currently consumed with his breeze-up catalogue, but when lot twenty-three was announced, a good-looking colt by Mehmas out of a Red Ransom mare, he didn't even look up to watch as it lengthened impressively in front of its potential buyers.

'That's a good question,' Bain said quietly, then, as if coming to his senses, he added, 'Come on, we should make sure he doesn't spot us.'

They were just about to move when Bain grabbed a handful of Holly's coat, rooting her to the spot.

'Did you see that?' he asked excitedly.

Holly shrugged, 'Moran looked over his shoulder. So what? And let go of my coat, will you?'

'He's trying to catch Dent's eye… Look, there he goes again.'

Holly softly slapped Bain's hand and he absent-mindedly let go of her. Turning her attention back to Moran, she watched for a few seconds and sure enough, the football agent waited until the next lot was thumping up the Doncaster straight and then took a sidelong glance Dent's way. As the crowd's attention concentrated on the young horse, Moran turned to eyeball Dent's little group, all his attention on them. There could be no questioning his intentions, it was laughably obvious if you were studying him. He was definitely trying to catch the eye of someone amongst the group of six.

'It's not Graham Dent,' said Holly.

'It's the other chap,' Bain said over her.

They turned to each other.

'You first,' said Holly.

'You saw it too? The older chap definitely nodded back to Moran, didn't he?'

'Definitely. But what does it mean?'

Bain studied the small man at Graham Dent's side. After careful thought, he replied, 'That's Adrian Cooper.'

Holly eyeballed Bain, impatience writ large across her face.

'He owns a stud. Stands a couple of low-level stallions. I'm guessing it's in or around Malton or Norton,' Bain explained, flicking to a page in his catalogue that listed the sellers. He traced a his index finger in a line down the page, 'There he is. Cooper's got four two-year-olds going through the ring tomorrow. The dark grey colt that has just breezed was one of his, and I'm guessing he's trying to get Dent and his owners to buy it.'

'So Moran could just know this Cooper. And perhaps he was just being friendly… or, is something fishy going on?'

Bain compressed his lips, staring over at Dent's entourage.

'There was nothing friendly about that look Cooper returned Moran. It seemed cagey to me, like Cooper was acknowledging Moran, but only to get rid of him. He showed no interest in going over to speak with him. It'll be interesting to see what Moran does next.'

Bain and Holly switched their viewpoint to regard Moran again, but he'd disappeared.

'Where the hell…' Bain exclaimed, lifting himself onto his toes to try and spot Moran, 'Can you see him?'

'I've got him,' Holly said calmly, having put her extra foot in height to good use, 'He's gone down to the edge of the crowd and heading for the gate to the racecourse. It looks like he's leaving. Yep, he's crossing the racetrack.'

'He was only interested in Cooper's horse,' muttered Bain, shifting his attention back to the Dent group.

'At least he didn't recognise you.'

Bain produced a forced chuckle, 'Huh. No worries on that score, Moran doesn't know I exist.'

They watched as Moran jogged across the racecourse, keeping an eye on him until he entered the Goffs sales complex.

'Come on. With me,' said Bain purposefully, 'Let's get closer to Dent and his guests. We might overhear what they're discussing and find out who some of them are.'

Twenty

Ronnie had quickly tired of Hugo Dent. Beneath the thin veneer of a perfectly symmetrical face and healthy, athletic body, laid nothing more than an arrogant ass. For the last few minutes she'd been trying to work out how she would describe the odious creature to Bain and Holly, but was struggling to be as concise, and spikey as she wished. How did you describe a self-obsessed, ill-tempered, thoroughly self-absorbed, and creepy young man? She settled for 'vainglorious twerp' as a tagline for the twenty-two year old, but still didn't feel it effectively plumbed the depths of her dislike for him.

She'd been pleased when Vladimir, initially charmed by Hugo's good looks, had quickly worked the lad out and traded a worried look with her that confirmed he agreed with her own assessment of their tour guide. Any chance the lad might retrieve their goodwill evaporated when she and Vladimir witnessed Hugo's treatment of the stable staff they encountered during their whistlestop tour of the premises.

It was clear the staff at Beverley Hill Stables also found Hugo's manner irritating. The male members of staff were spoken to in curt, and often derogatory language masquerading as friendly banter. Much worse was the misogyny the female staff had to endure, usually served up by

Hugo as dreadful jokes. Vladimir had to force himself to remain silent. In contrast, Ronnie's support of the staff, and her criticism of Hugo became increasingly vocal as the tour progressed.

A casual amble through the first two barns with stops to inspect a stable with a vibrating floor to aid horse's recuperation from injury, and a line of birthing stables, had been interesting enough, but it seemed to Ronnie she wasn't answering Hugo's questions to his satisfaction. The reverse was also true; Hugo had looked through Ronnie on several occasions, only answering Vladimir's queries.

Entering the third barn they bumped into Courtney, a pretty young stable lass who was speaking with a well-built lady in her late fifties called Wendy. A pack of six dachshunds yapped and pawed at Wendy's ankles as she discussed whether the lass could fit in extra shifts. Once introduced, Wendy managed to elicit a raised eyebrow from Ronnie by announcing she was Hugo's mother, Graham Dent's wife.

With black, straw dry hair and a severe fringe framing a working woman's face, Wendy wore an oatmeal tote bag over her shoulder that declared she was a 'Winner at Beverley'. The young lass, with a rake in her hand, was described by Hugo with an amused snort as, 'A crap rider, but at least Courtney knows how to sweep up crap!'

The young girl had blushed furiously and said nothing in reply, never lifting her eyes from the concrete floor. To Ronnie and Vladimir's disappointment, Wendy had been oblivious to the impact her son's comment had on Courtney. It was left to Ronnie to respond.

'I'm sure you're a perfectly fine rider,' she'd told the lass.

'If there's anything around here that needs to be swept up and trashed, it's his jokes,' Ronnie had added whilst glaring purposefully at Hugo.

Five minutes later Hugo and Ronnie crossed swords again. The amble had now become a march, as Hugo had become hellbent on bringing the tour to a close. They'd gone past a stable where a vet was busy bandaging the leg of a gelding. The young vet was fresh-faced, but had an air of worldly experience about him. Ronnie guessed he was in his mid-to-late twenties. When Vladimir said hello to the chap, and started up a conversation about the horse's ailment, Hugo adopted a sour curl to his mouth, but eventually backtracked to the stable door and his impatience dissolved somewhat once the vet's gaze fell on him.

'This is Daniel Croft,' Hugo told them perfunctorily.

'I'm the Dent's hardest working vet,' Daniel offered with a confident smile, coming out of the stable to shake Vladimir's hand, 'There's hardly a day goes by without me being on this yard for one reason or another. Isn't that right Hugo?'

'Daniel is invaluable,' replied Hugo lightly, the two of them sharing an easy smile.

Daniel transferred his attention back to Vladimir, 'Are you owners?'

'Prospective owners,' Vladimir corrected.

'Ah! You'll be attending the breeze-ups tomorrow, I imagine. Looking for a young star racehorse then?'

'Perhaps. We've not decided yet.'

The vet smiled broadly, ignoring Hugo's glare, 'Well, you've chosen the right yard! Hugo here is the brightest young assistant trainer in the country. Combined with the care I give the horses, you've got everything covered.'

Ronnie slowly shook her head, 'Shouldn't you have tied that bandage off?' she said, indicating the gelding behind them who was busy tugging at the swiftly unravelling bandage with its teeth, 'I'm not convinced either of you know what you're doing.'

There was a stunned silence. Hugo stared open-eyed at Daniel. Daniel cocked his head sideways and studied Ronnie with a sudden and unguarded distaste. Eventually the impasse was broken by the vet. His voice had lost the forced jokiness and become cold and edgy.

'My work speaks for itself. Why else would Graham Dent retain me?' he said with a smile that never reached his eyes, 'Choose your trainer carefully. I know Mr Dent chooses his owners with the exact same care.'

Realising that they were in danger of being thrown off the property, Vladimir took hold of Ronnie's elbow and thanking Daniel for his time, set off down the barn before Ronnie could dig the hole any deeper. Daniel traded a scowl with Hugo and watched the prospective owners go without uttering another word.

Reaching the end of the barn, Vladimir took the opportunity to turn and buttonhole Hugo. He asked him the one question to which Holly had insisted they get an answer. Hugo didn't reply immediately, still in something of a haze, glancing back over his shoulder as if he was worried about the vet.

'W… What did you say?' Hugo stammered, looking somewhat confused by Vladimir's query.

'I just wondered if 'Snowdrop' meant anything to you?' Vladimir repeated.

Hugo turned to face the two elderly visitors and placed his hands on his hips, his face hard, and all his attention now focused on Vladimir.

'Why?' he asked suspiciously, 'What have you heard?'

Ronnie and Vladimir were smiling expectantly at him. They could see this was confusing the lad, which made a delighted Ronnie double-down on her wan smile and turn it into a hearty grin.

'Oh, nothing much,' replied Vladimir with a shrug.

'They were all stolen,' said a female voice from inside the nearest stable, 'Some bugger dug 'em all up.'

Ronnie didn't hesitate, she left Hugo and strode off in search of the voice. She found a stable door ajar and inside was a thin young woman in her late twenties with long blonde hair tied back in a ponytail. She was mucking out. Standing patiently against the side wall of the stable was a young filly. It looked in need of a good feed, it's skin pulled tight over its ribs.

The girl looked up, leaned on her rake, and smiled, dirt smudging her cheek and forehead, 'About a year ago,' she said helpfully, 'Some nutter dug up all the snowdrops around Malton. Did it during the night. The grass verges looked like they'd been attacked by a mob of moles. They didn't even bother refilling the holes. You can't find a snowdrop within five miles of here.'

Vladimir and an irate Hugo arrived at the stable door and all of them regarded the tall bay filly. The filly inquisitively turned an intelligent head towards Ronnie, revealing a thick white blaze from her ears to the tip of her nose.

'Always unwell this one, aren't you, you poor thing…' said the girl, running a hand over the horse's withers and down it's shoulder.

'That's enough, Lucy!' hissed Hugo angrily.

The girl gave Hugo a condescending flick of her hand, 'Go ahead and sack me, Hugo,' she called out to him, 'I'm sure the Guv'nor will be delighted, given the number of staff you've upset or scared away recently. If I'm not here, you might have to do some of the work yourself!'

Ronnie immediately took a shine to the woman.

'Did you know Brooklyn Hartley?' she asked.

'Brookie? Yeah. It was awful what happened to her, I mean, the accident and…'

'That's enough,' Hugo interjected, squaring up to Ronnie, 'Who the hell are you two anyway? Press?'

Lucy rolled her eyes at him, 'Who cares if they are? It was awful what that man did to her. I was physically ill, couldn't keep my lunch down when I watched that video online. Brookie didn't deserve that, she didn't deserve any of it.'

'Right. Out you two,' Hugo ordered, trying to herd

Ronnie and Vladimir out of the stable with his arms held out wide.

Ronnie remained standing firm, ignoring Hugo, looking over his shoulder in order to directly address the stable lass, 'Were you her friend?'

'Not really,' the girl admitted, 'If you want to speak with someone who knew Brookie well, then you'll need to find Geena. The two of them were inseparable.'

'Shut your mouth, Lucy!' hollered Hugo.

A woman appeared at the stable door, older and exhibiting an aura of authority, a quality Ronnie felt was sorely lacking in the young Hugo. Lucy's demeanour altered immediately, almost standing to attention, but most importantly, remaining silent. The new entrant to their conversation demanded respect, and possibly engendered a little fear in Lucy, thought Vladimir.

After looking Ronnie and Vladimir up and down, the woman spoke up.

'I'm Lara, the head lass here.'

She spoke in a coarse, Yorkshire accent that went well with her plain, no-nonsense face. She placed a hand on Hugo's shoulder and quietly said something to him. He sagged a little, but deferred, standing back. Lara smiled at him, then turned on her heel, presenting Ronnie and Vladimir with a serious, dead pan look of distain. Lifting an arm to point in the direction of the car park, she spoke with the sort of finality that tells you non-compliance is both unacceptable and would prove fruitless.

'I'd like you both to leave.'

Twenty-One

'...and then she bundled us out of the yard and into the car,' reported Ronnie casting her arm out with a flourish, 'Hugo Dent was livid when we asked about snowdrops.

There's definitely something going on in the Dent stables. I could smell it!'

Sweeping up her mug of tea from the kitchen table, Ronnie leaned back in her chair and swallowed a third of its contents in two big gulps, satisfied with her recounting of their interesting, if short, time at the Beverley Road Stables.

'Is that how it happened?' Holly checked with Vladimir.

Ronnie gave her daughter a disgruntled frown, but waited for her next door neighbour's reply.

'Allowing for a bit of artistic licence here and there, yes, Ronnie's rendition was accurate,' he reported.

Ronnie smirked with satisfaction.

Vladimir continued, 'Despite your mother's tendency to be irascible, she was incredibly restrained in the circumstances. I was all for giving that young upstart Hugo a damn good thrashing for the way he spoke to her and his staff. He's a pretty young boy with a certifiably nasty personality.'

Ronnie beamed across the table at Holly and Bain, 'So, have you got enough to get this written up and published?'

Bain twisted uncomfortably in his seat and looked at Holly, who shrugged back at him.

'Erm… Not really,' he replied, 'We've the bones of a story, but there's not enough meat for a feature, or to get Golden's attention for that matter.'

'Having a young idiot with a foul management style as an assistant trainer doesn't get us any closer to Brooklyn's killer, even if he does have something to hide,' agreed Holly.

Ronnie shook her head, 'I'm telling you, there's something fishy about that yard.'

Holly rolled her eyes, 'I'm sure there is, mother. But the fact remains that in terms of Brooklyn's murder, we're no further forward.'

'Oh, I wouldn't say that,' said Bain, 'The two of you did a great job getting the information about the snowdrops. Then there's this stable lass called Geena to track down. She might be able to tell us more about Brooklyn, like who she was hanging around with, and whether there's someone who might hold a grudge against her or Brooklyn...'

'That might be a challenge,' Vladimir warned, 'The stable lass, Lucy, said Geena had disappeared without a trace.'

'I told you! Fishy,' Ronnie remarked whilst wagging a finger at Holly, 'Definitely fishy. Hugo was very keen for Lucy not to answer questions about snowdrops or that Geena girl.'

'Look, I'm not saying it's not fishy!' sighed Holly, 'But we're only a fraction of the way to understanding what was going on at the Dent's yard when Brooklyn had her accident. But there are more questions than answers. I was thinking that on the way back from Doncaster. Like Conor Moran being at the breeze-ups today. He has something going on with the Dents, but we've no idea what that could be.'

'Then there was that strange man who approached Dent's group and started shouting and screaming. He was arguing with someone called Miriam,' Bain added, 'I've searched for her as an owner, but as far as I can ascertain there's no-one called Miriam on Graham Dent's owner's list.'

'Blunt,' said Holly, 'I'm sure one of them, Graham himself I think, called him Mr Blunt.'

'Hmm, good catch, Hol,' Bain said brightly, 'I'll do a thorough search and see what that surname brings up.'

'What was the argument about?' asked Ronnie, 'I wouldn't be surprised if he was an ex-stable lad!'

Bain shook his head, 'No. I think this was a personal grievance between two people who knew each other well. It got very personal, very quickly. This Blunt character was trying to dish dirt about a woman in Dent's group called Miriam, but Dent was having none of it. Actually, he was quite protective of the woman. A member of the auction house's security staff soon saw to it that this chap…'

'Blunt,' offered Holly.

'Yes, that this Blunt chap was escorted off the premises.'

'I almost felt sorry for him,' added Holly, 'Until he

started getting nasty with Graham Dent and the other chap with him, Adrian Cooper. Up until then, this… Gregory I think the Goff's chap called him, sounded a bit desperate, even… manic. I wouldn't be surprised if he and that Miriam were related.'

'You're hearing and recall of names is phenomenal!' admitted Bain with a shake of his head, writing, 'Gregory Blunt' alongside, 'Miriam Blunt'. He added the name Graham Dent and was struck at how the surnames Blunt and Dent seemed to go together. Holly peered over his shoulder.

'Ha! You'll have to do one of your famous photo boards on that whiteboard in your room!'

'Already started!' said Bain, shooting Holly a grin.

The conversation stalled and the table fell silent apart from the sound of tea and biscuits being consumed, and the ever-present thwapping of Daisy's tail on the floor as she begged, successfully, for the last nibble of Ronnie's bourbons.

'I've been thinking about that poor dead girl,' Vladimir said eventually. He spoke softly, whilst slowly stroking his bearded chin, 'Even with a brain injury she went around calling out, 'Good Morning' and smiling at everyone she met. If this Farley chap didn't do it, that stable lass deserves answers. Virtually every person she met on that riverside walk would smile and say, 'Good morning' back to her, and move on… until one person didn't, they viciously stabbed her a dozen times or more. From what I saw of the girl's body on that video, the killer was frenzied.'

Vladimir scanned the table, 'Even though we've only scraped the surface of what's going on at the Dent stables, Ronnie and I sensed there's something… well, to put it into her words, something *fishy* going on. We should aim to be absolutely certain the Dent yard had nothing to do with her death.'

The kitchen table fell into silence as Vladimir's words impacted on his audience. On the floor at Bain's feet, Daisy sensed the change of atmosphere and gave a low whine and placed her chin on his foot. He bent down and scratched her reassuringly behind one ear. Meanwhile, Brooklyn filled his thoughts.

'We need someone on the inside at the yard,' Ronnie piped up, her tone purposefully bright and bouncy.

'Mother!' scolded Holly, a shade embarrassed, although not too surprised that Ronnie was experiencing Vladimir's observations in a totally different way to the rest of them.

'I'm serious!' Ronnie insisted, giving her daughter a reproachful look, 'We met at least eight stable staff, and we were only there twenty minutes. There has to be talk amongst them! And most of them looked tired and overworked. That vet, Daniel Croft... mark my words, there was something going on between him and that Hugo chump. We just need to find a member of the Dent staff willing to dish the dirt.'

'Lucy wasn't frightened of Hugo. She might help. Then there was that Lara woman. Hugo went pretty quiet when she turned up. I bet she'll know plenty, being the head lass,' added Vladimir.'

'And they *are* short-handed!' exclaimed Ronnie, 'Mary and Courtney said as much. I reckon someone with a bit of experience with horses could walk into a job at the Beverley Road Stables...'

Ronnie's eyes twinkled with unashamed glee as she turned them onto Holly. To her horror, Vladimir did the same.

'Your mother's had worse ideas,' admitted Bain, also resting his gaze on Holly.

Pouting, Holly crossed her arms, 'If it's such a good idea why don't *you* do it?'

'I need to go back to Goffs for tomorrows sale day. Like you said, we haven't got enough information for a feature or to warrant Golden investigating the Dent stables. We need to...' he paused, searching for the right words, '...dig deeper.'

'Oh, please! You're such a whizz with words! Please stop dazzling me with your master wordsmithing,' grumbled Holly, 'Anyway, I can't just walk into a top racing stable like

Graham Dent's and ask for a job!'

'Oh, I think you can,' said a grinning Ronnie.

'You'll make a *wonderful* stable lass,' Bain added with a quick flash of his eyebrows.

Twenty-Two

Daniel placed the well-thumbed Goffs catalogue down on the small Formica table in Hugo's trailer, swung his body around and pitched his crossed legs onto the small sofa that could double as a single bed if required. Hugo's frustrated sigh cut into the perfect silence inside the trailer.

'Daniel! I can't sketch you if you keep moving around!'

Daniel gave his friend an apologetic smile, 'It's a big day for us tomorrow, Hugo, and I need to make that call.'

Hugo, sitting opposite his model, curled one side of his mouth into a disgruntled shape for a moment but was soon reconnected with the portrait currently emerging from the sketching board and art paper resting against his knees.

Daniel took a deep breath and sliding his mobile phone out of his pocket tapped on Adrian Cooper's number. The call connected almost immediately.

'Coops!'

'What do you want Daniel? It's late.'

'It's never too late to talk business.'

The line remained stubbornly silent.

'Hugo will be texting you the lot numbers and what we'll bid for your breezers,' said Daniel.

'You're still using that guy Moran to underbid?'

Daniel momentarily gritted his teeth. Closing his eyes, he pushed his anger down. He needed to keep this call civil.

'Yes, Conor Moran will be the underbidder. He's a seasoned pro. There won't be any issues.'

'Good. Is that it?'

Daniel's voice lowered and became smooth, 'Why so

short tempered, Coops?'

There was a sound of movement, a sigh, a click and silence for a few seconds. Another click, and a short, muffled few words in the background before Daniel heard Cooper's heavy breathing once again.

'For crying out loud, Daniel! I'm in Donny, at the hotel. I've got my wife on hold at the moment! Whatever you've got to say, make it quick.'

'Trust me, you'll want to hear this.'

'Hear what?' said Cooper, his voice suddenly on edge.

'I've been told there was an investigative journalist nosing around at the breezing today.'

'Coops? You still there?' asked Daniel when the anticipated reaction wasn't forthcoming.

'Oh, Christ! Yes, yes. Of course I'm still here!' moaned Cooper, 'We can't go ahead…'

'Coops, Coops, take it easy,' Daniel soothed, 'He's just a freelance hack. There's a thousand reasons for him being there. I doubt he'll be at the sale tomorrow, and if he is, I can deal with him.'

'You bloody better! You and Hugo were supposed to be here today. And Miriam Blunt's ex-husband turning up didn't help matters…'

Daniel listened, asked a few questions about the Blunt fellow. After resurrecting most of Cooper's confidence, he hung up.

Hugo was staring meaningfully at him. He wanted an explanation.

'Everything okay?' Hugo eventually inquired when nothing was forthcoming.

'All good,' Daniel replied confidently, returning to the position he'd previously adopted for the portrait, 'Cooper met Miriam's ex-husband at the breeze-ups today. It's spooked him.'

Hugo's mouth fell open.

'Now don't you start too!' Daniel warned, 'All the chap

did was leer at him and call him and your father a fraud for some reason. It's nothing. Cooper's getting cold feet, that's all. He's getting frightened by his own shadow! It looks like Miriam Blunt has issues with her ex-husband. Nothing to do with us. You've set everything up perfectly for tomorrow.'

Hugo smiled at this platitude. His shoulders relaxed and adopted a contented gaze as his attention returned to his artwork. Daniel was relieved. He'd fluffed up enough egos today and couldn't face doing it again. It was exhausting.

To the sound of Hugo's pencil placing graphite onto the paper, Daniel decided he'd keep a close eye on Adrian Cooper at tomorrows sale. And if this Gregory Blunt, Miriam's ex-husband turned up again, he'd need to deal with him too. Whatever happened, he and Hugo needed Miriam Blunt to buy the grey Mehmas colt for more than he was worth.

***

Miriam Blunt wasn't quite so sleep averse to rate herself an insomniac, but she reckoned five hours a night was all she'd managed for the last fifteen years. Conversely, her ex-husband, Gregory, had gone to bed at nine thirty every night and slept like a log until seven thirty the next morning. A very noisy, snoring log.

As the clock in her hotel room clicked over to midnight, she wondered whether her ex-husband was to blame for her sleep deprivation. Perhaps those three or four hours of Blunt-less time between ten o'clock and one o'clock in the morning had been a subconscious means of keeping her sane?

Being alone in her York living room with just the TV, radio, or if she was lucky, a clandestine copy of The Racing Post, had been the best part of her day. But those five hours of sleep were so ingrained into her body clock she couldn't break the habit, despite not having to listen to the sound of a rutting pig sleeping beside her.

However, her limited sleep did afford her plenty of

time to review her day and plan the next. Having money meant she now possessed time and opportunity in quantities she'd never imagined.

Lying on her queen-sized bed, the television's burbling became tiresome, so Miriam switched it off and lay there a moment, eyes closed, enjoying the silence. Apart from her ex-husband turning up, today had been a good day, and she could easily scrub those few minutes from her memory. She saw him for what he was now; a sad, middle-aged man with control issues. He'd been hurling abuse at Adrian Cooper for some reason she couldn't fathom.

Picking up her Goffs breeze-up catalogue, Miriam flicked to the pages containing the pedigrees of the two hundred and forty unraced 2YO's due to go under the hammer. Graham Dent had earmarked several for her, and two specifically that the stud manager, Adrian Cooper, had been kind enough to show her a week ago. But it was that dark grey colt of Adrian's that she was interested in. She decided to re-examine for the umpteenth time Lot 58, the catalogue page for the grey colt by Mehmas.

Even though she'd been waiting for him to appear, the unnamed colt had caught the eye in a positive way as he made his way up the Doncaster straight earlier that day. She'd liked the way he had stretched out and appeared to be loving the experience. Graham had actually commented on his impressively long stride.

Miriam had always loved a small gamble, and had prided herself in keeping her secret betting bank account nicely in credit without having to resort to regular topping up. Blunt had never known about her secret vice, but she didn't regard her weekly twenty pence Canadians and odd bash at the ITV Seven, Placepot, and the Lottery as serious gambling – it was a bit of covert fun – beating the bookies, even in some small way, had helped bolster her confidence after a week of Blunt chipping away at it. Of course, owning a racehorse was a significantly bigger gamble.

This had been made very clear to her after buying her first racehorse with Graham Dent. She'd paid 55,000 guineas at the August yearling sales for Morgan, and the filly was still battling with an illness that had started with colic way back in October. Things hadn't improved since then, with the vet unable to correct the reoccurring colic problem, it now looked extremely unlikely the filly would see a racecourse this season, if at all.

Graham had been very good about it, keeping her informed as the filly continued to yo-yo between recovery and severe sickness. Confined to light work and with none of the treatments working, when the vet mooted moving the young horse on. Miriam had almost said yes. Instead, she had decided to give the filly until the end of April to show signs of recovery. That was when Graham had suggested she consider an alternative racehorse with which to enjoy a summer season of racing. Which was why she was back in Doncaster, hoping to buy a second racehorse in the breeze-up sale.

Miriam studied the sale catalogue, referring to her laptop to investigate the Racing Post website for breeding information, and then switching back to the Goffs website to study the breeze-up video replays from earlier in the day. At half-past midnight she yawned, and putting her research to one side, padded over to her window and opened the curtains so she could take in the nighttime view.

Standing at the top of the home straight, the Hilton Hotel provided an excellent view of Doncaster's home straight, as well as across the golf course at its centre and onto the back straight, where the white railings were just visible. From her luxury room, high up on the top floor, Miriam took in the dark, empty racecourse concourse below, only barely illuminated by the hotel's lighting. Further along, she could just make out the lights of the Goffs sales ring and stabling complex. All was quiet. Smiling, she crossed her arms and squeezed herself, barely able to believe she was here, at the home of the oldest Group One race in the world.

The sound of scuffling behind her made Miriam twist her head towards the door to the room. The single lamp by her bed only cast a dull light, which meant a horizontal strip of light from under the room door was shining onto the carpet. And a shadow in the corridor was making the light under the door move around. There's no need for concern, she told herself, watching the light flicker. She imagined it would be a hotel porter – it had to be at this time of night - perhaps checking all was well. Had she locked the door behind her? She was sure she had…

A small white envelope shot through the gap at the bottom of the door and skimmed a yard across the carpet. Whoever had caused the shadow, now departed. In her mind's eye Miriam saw the porter walking down the corridor, no doubt he would be slipping little messages of goodwill and thanks under many of the residents' doors.

That's a nice touch, she thought, upon noting that the missive was addressed simply to 'Miriam'.

Instead of the Hilton Hotel headed note she had expected, the few words, written in capitals, were held on a page that appeared to be torn from a lined exercise book. Miriam read the note twice before rushing to the door, opening it, and inspecting an empty corridor.

Cursing, she dived back into her room and made sure the door was locked. She read the note again, becoming increasingly disgusted with its content. Screwing the note up, she threw it forcefully across the room.

'That man is deranged!' she growled quietly through gritted teeth, 'He ruined twenty years of my life. He's not going to ruin the rest of it. This stops now!'

Miriam picked up her laptop and sitting down at the writing desk kindly provided by the Hilton Hotel, she typed out a pointed email to the solicitor who had helped organise her divorce. She sent the email on its way with a vitriolic click of the send button and went for a shower. There was no way her five hours of sleep would come easily to her tonight.

***

Buying this second hand camper van with only a hundred and seventy thousand miles on it had been an excellent purchase, Blunt assured himself as he prepared for bed. Taking one last look out of the window onto the empty B&Q car park he'd chosen as his pitch for his overnight stay in Doncaster, he tugged the little curtain closed on its plastic cord and straightened to walk the two paces to his bed in the dark.

Cracking his knee against something hard and sharp, he swore viciously for a few seconds and collapsed onto his fold-down bed, but remained determined to be upbeat. Blunt zipped up his sleeping bag, pulled his pillow into a more comfortable position, and despite the foam bed in his camper van being woefully inadequate when it came to his sizeable backside, he allowed a smug grin to work its way onto his face.

'Today has been a good day,' he told himself, 'And tomorrow is going to be even better. Miriam won't know what's hit her.'

Blunt fell asleep, only to wake, drenched in sweat an hour later. It was *that* dream again. The stupid, annoying one he'd been having for weeks now. Just for once he'd like the bundles of cash he found in the long grass not to turn into a cohort of small colourful birds that immediately flew away as soon as he touched the money.

***

Daniel had been halfway to falling asleep when his mobile rang. It was Coops again. It had been a long day. Usually asleep by now, he'd not been able to leave Hugo's caravan until after midnight and was tired and irritable as a result. He answered curtly, assuming it would be a short call, but was immediately drowned out by a barrage of abuse from their clandestine business partner.

'Alright, alright, Coops! Calm down and shut up!' he insisted in a soft growl down the line once he'd got the gist of Cooper's complaint. He looked out the window at the stable yard behind the veterinary surgery, and the houses beyond, but not really focusing on them properly. Even though his father would be in the cellar, he needed to keep his voice down. Leslie Croft couldn't hear this conversation.

'Listen, *Dan*!' Cooper replied in an uncharacteristically sarcastic tone, 'How *the hell* can I calm down when I've got people literally popping up in the middle of the night and scaring the life out of me?'

'Tell me what happened, again. Slowly!'

It was that creepy little sod. Miriam's husband…'

'Ex-husband,' corrected Daniel.

The line went worryingly quiet for a second.

'I don't care what he is!' screamed Cooper, 'The creep turned up at my hotel door ten minutes ago, pushed his way into my room, and is insisting I sign over that Mehmas colt to him. You know, Lot 56, the one his wife is wanting to buy!'

'He's clearly got a mental…'

'No! He was there, Daniel!' Cooper cut in forcefully, 'At my yard the day Miriam came to see the colt. He overheard us, after she'd left, talking about inflating the sale price. He even knew what percentages we're splitting the profits!'

Daniel allowed this to settle on him for a moment, annoyingly, to the sound of Cooper's erratic breathing into the mouthpiece. He looked down into the darkness of the back yard and the trapdoor that led to the cellar. For a moment, he imagined what it would be like if all of this was his, and stared even more intently at the trapdoor.

Daniel dragged his thoughts back to the phone call.

'So this Gregory Blunt is blackmailing you. He wants your colt, Lot 56, to go through the sale as if he owns it and he expects to get paid whatever it ends up going for?'

'Yes. He has this crazy idea that he's going to bid his wife up like we were going to. He kept banging on about a vendetta, and how he was going to make her pay by ramping up the price of the colt. He was practically foaming at the mouth. I tell you, Daniel, he's a bloody lunatic!'

'I don't doubt it,' Daniel agreed.

'We have to call tomorrow off,' Cooper continued, 'Deny everything. Pull the colt out of the sale. Let the sale run without our involvement. Then if he goes to the authorities…'

It was Daniel's turn to interrupt, 'That's what he said? He's going to tell this story? What story, and anyway, who's he going to tell it to, Coops? The BHA, Goffs? Neither of them will listen.'

This was greeted with a moments silence. Daniel imagined Cooper standing stock still, wracking his brains.

'He didn't say who he'd tell.'

Cooper waited and after a short pause, Daniel's voice, smooth and authoritative, came through.

'We go ahead with our plans. We all need the profit from that colt. I'll deal with Gregory Blunt and his ex-wife.'

Cooper swallowed hard. This wasn't what he wanted to hear. A voice in his head was telling him he was in too deep, not used to this sort of pressure. He'd had enough. Neither his nerves, nor his physical wellbeing could take much more of this. He wanted out, and if it meant having to sell the stud…

'Daniel! This is getting out of hand. I want out… I don't want any more to do with this double-dealing…'

'Calm down and get a grip,' spat Daniel, 'Blunt is out of his depth. Leave it with me, Coops. Get some sleep, you sound like you need it. I'll deal with Mr Blunt tomorrow.'

Three digital tones indicated Daniel had hung up. Still holding his mobile to his ear, Cooper listened to an automated female voice telling him to please hang up. His plea for sanity had fallen on deaf ears. Daniel was going to sort it… the phrase was all too familiar and Cooper became aware of a churning sensation in his stomach.

Daniel switched his phone off. He'd had enough for one day. Still at his bedroom window, the sudden absence of a light source from his phone made him notice a flicker of light coming up from the cobbles below. Straining his neck, he was able to deduce the reddish glow was coming from around the edge of the cellar trapdoor. He'd have a word with his father in the morning. The last thing he needed was for his father's sideline to be discovered. But first on tomorrow's agenda would be the chopping of Mr Gregory Blunt down to size.

Grumbling under his breath, he drew his curtains shut and crossed his bedroom. Climbing into bed, Daniel Croft made himself comfortable and was fast asleep within seconds, untroubled by any worries.

In his room at the Hilton in Doncaster, Adrian Cooper tossed and turned.

Twenty-Three

April 26th - Breeze-up auction day

Lot 1 stepped into Goff's sales ring at exactly ten o'clock. First up was a bay Ardad colt, who gave a whinny and tossed its head for a moment upon hearing the loud, tinny voice of the auctioneer suddenly boom from the public address system as he made his welcome speech.

The auditorium wasn't full yet by any means, but a smattering of buyers had already bagged their seats, and Bain noticed from his position high up on the first floor balcony that several trainers and a number of agents had started to mass at the entrance to the ring, a favoured area from which to bid.

Beside Bain, Ronnie leaned against the balcony rail and looked down on the auctioneer, amused by what she saw. Immaculately dressed in a pin-striped suit, hair quaffed with a precision she admired, and speaking in received English with a suave nonchalance, the auctioneer brandished his hammer as if he were the conductor of a grand orchestra. She reflected on her own outfit for the day and gave a little sigh - she was hardly dressed to impress.

Bain had insisted they should blend seamlessly into the scene, which to Ronnie, meant she had to wear unflattering clothes, plus a baseball cap advertising a stallion called Showcasing. Even so, she was fascinated by the whole event, and the atmosphere in the sales room was one of increasing anticipation.

'I'm so excited,' Ronnie exclaimed in quick breaths, 'Thanks again for bringing me along, Bain.'

'No problem,' he replied with a tight smile, 'But remember, we're keeping under the radar today. It's a watching brief. Tilt your cap so you hide your face and keep your eyes on Graham Dent and the people around him. We're here to learn as much as we can without raising any suspicion. No speaking to anyone unless you're spoken to, and under no circumstance are you to raise your hand to bid for a horse!'

Ronnie zipped her mouth with thumb and forefinger, then linked her arms behind her back whilst giving him her best impression of a naughty child.

'Good girl,' Bain stated with mock firmness.

He'd hammered the same set of instructions into Ronnie the night before. He glanced at her, trying to determine whether she'd already forgotten them. Ronnie was glassy-eyed, busy drinking in the salesroom. He smiled inwardly. You could rarely work out whether she was being genuinely forgetful, or just mucking around.

Bain had always intended to return for this second day consisting of the sale of close to two hundred two-year-olds, and didn't mind Ronnie tagging along. In contrast, it had taken a good thirty minutes of cajoling and arm-bending in order to get Holly to agree to the other course of action he'd had in mind for her.

Below Bain and Ronnie the bidding on the first lot of

the day began. The Ardad colt started at £5,000 and rose slowly at first, but soon kicked on at a pace once it reached £10,000. It was eventually knocked down four minutes later to a well-heeled lady sitting in the seats on the far side of the ring for £26,000.

'Lady in the second row in the red coat, many thanks and the best of luck with him,' stated the auctioneer, his head down as he spoke, busy examining his notes in preparation for the next upcoming two-year-old.

'I thought they sold racehorses in guineas?' Ronnie queried.

'It's still guineas at Tattersalls, but Goffs take bids in pounds now,' explained Bain, 'The guinea was supposed to be a pound, plus five percent extra for the sales company, but Goffs now charge a six percent commission to the buyer. I guess you can't make a guinea worth one pound and six pence!'

Ronnie watched the sales ring with the fascination of someone new to bloodstock and experiencing it for the first time. As the sold Ardad colt was led away, another lot was brought into the sales ring using a system of gates, the auctioneer introducing the newly arrived horse with just as much enthusiasm about its breeze and pedigree as the one departing. Meanwhile, a smartly dressed young Goffs employee armed with clipboard made a beeline for the winning bidder. Seating himself down beside the lady, he busied himself with paperwork and signatures.

Another three lots went through the ring before Ronnie leaned across again to speak with Bain.

'How much does it cost to have a racehorse in training?'

Bain had to laugh. Holly had warned him this could happen. It was the reason her mother owned a high mileage Fiat 500 and several pieces of furniture, of dubious quality and provenance. Ronnie loved an auction and had the capacity to fall in love with items and then insist she had to have them, whatever the cost. In Holly's words, 'My mother is an auctioneer's dream. She becomes obsessive. Don't let her put her hand up or you'll never get it down again.'

'Owning a racehorse outright is too expensive to even contemplate,' Bain told Ronnie regretfully, hoping this would nip her interest in the bud. It had no such effect.

'No. Seriously,' she insisted, 'How much?'

Bain sighed. Ronnie wasn't going to let this go. It was great to see that gleam of excitement back in her eye, but he had an awful feeling he would be spending the day keeping her on a short lead.

'Based on previous breeze-up sales prices, a two-year old, unraced horse will cost you anything upwards from eight thousand pounds. The average for this sale was forty-two thousand pounds last year. Then it will cost you between thirty and fifty thousand a year for training, feed, shoeing, and vets fees. If you go racing, and it's a big 'if' with a young, inexperienced horse, it will cost you about a thousand pounds per run in entry fees, transport, jockey, and lead-up fees…'

Bain had been encouraged to witness Ronnie's expression slowly losing its childlike zeal during his explanation of the costs. However, she appeared to have lost her concentration and with narrowed eyes was now examining something over his left-hand shoulder.

He was in mid-sentence when Ronnie asked, 'Isn't that Graham Dent down there?'

Bain was about to swing around, but stopped himself. It was imperative that Dent and his entourage didn't become aware they were being watched. Instead, he took Ronnie's hand and led her away into the shadows of the back wall where the balcony hid them from prying eyes below in the main bidding areas.

'Yep, that's Graham Dent alright. And his son, Hugo is there, and two, maybe three of the owners from yesterday, as well as a young girl and boy I don't recognise.'

'One of them is Lucy, a stable lass. I talked with her at the yard,' said Ronnie, remaining with her back to the balcony, 'I think the other one might be called Alan... or maybe Elon?, or am I confusing him with that Musk chappie? Anyway, the one down there is another stable lad at Dent's yard.'

'Two stable staff, eh? Dent must be expecting to return home with a couple of horses today,' Bain reasoned.

'So they can look after the horses Dent buys for his owners?' Ronnie murmured, 'Sounds right enough to me. I can't see that Hugo giving either of those youngsters a day out at the sales for no reason. Not when the yard is so badly in need of staff. That reminds me, I wonder how Holly's getting on, you heard anything yet?'

'No, nothing at the moment,' reported Bain after checking his phone for messages, 'Come on, Ronnie, let's move into the seats so we're not so easy to spot. Keep your head down and your cap on, we don't want Hugo Dent clapping his eyes on you. It sounds like you left an impression on him yesterday.'

'Right back at you,' Ronnie replied, 'We can't let that little horror, Conor Moran, recognise you either.'

Bain caught Ronnie's expectant look, flashed her a smile, and pulled his cap so far down he could only just see out from under its brim.

Twenty-Four

Keeping to his word, Bain had taught Holly how to ride a motorbike.

The deal had been struck when Bain was in no position to argue, and because of this, Holly hadn't expected his promise to be fulfilled. It had been a complete surprise when he had turned up at the house one day with an old 50cc moped. She had mastered the low-powered bike within a month and soon advanced to a newer 125cc model. With Bain's help, they'd managed to find a decent second hand

Honda CB125 with low mileage. And Holly's love affair with her silver machine burst forth from the moment she straddled its mock-leather seat and felt the throb of its engine.

Her ride over to Malton from Northallerton had been hugely enjoyable, taking about fifty minutes. Holly had been on rides with Bain on his bike, but being out on her own provided her with a renewed feeling of freedom and excitement. Her mother had been her usual vocal self when opposing the purchase of a motorbike, but with Bain's reassurances, Ronnie had eventually come around, although she always referred to Holly's Honda as 'the deathtrap'.

After being buzzed into the Beverley Hill Stables, Holly parked up and locking her helmet to the bike, crossed over to where a lone woman was sweeping up.

'I heard you're looking for stable staff?' asked Holly with a smile.

She hardly felt like smiling. It was only the nervous excitement of being undercover that allowed her to stretch the muscles necessary to feign happiness. Inside, she was churned up and asking herself why on earth she'd agreed to Bain's plan to 'bury' her - his words, not hers - in the Graham Dent yard for the next few days. Her objective was to ingratiate herself with as many of the staff as possible and find out whether both Ronnie's, Vladimir's and to a lesser extent, Robert Farley's instincts were right, and there was something underhand going on. So here she was at the Beverley Hill Stables, posing as a stable lass and extending her hand to a small woman who was warily inspecting the proffered hand and failing to shake it.

'I'm all mucked up,' the lass explained, 'You don't want to be shaking my hand, love. And I'm not the one you want to see. You need to talk to Lady Dent. Come on.'

Holly followed the woman, whom she guessed was in her late thirties, and was shown through a long barn and then between several smaller buildings.

'You could get lost around here,' Holly commented,

'Are there horses in all these stables?'

'Not any more,' the woman replied glumly.

'This Lady Dent, do you have any advice for…'

The woman cut her short, 'No, not really.'

Holly tried again a few strides later, 'Have you been here long then?'

'Keep up. It's like a rabbit warren around here,' the woman grinned, 'Not as fancy as you imagined, eh?'

'I've seen worse,' muttered Holly. She doubted the woman had heard, or was interested in her reply.

After another few twists and turns around small wood-built stables with corrugated iron roofs, the concrete path expanded out into a large semi-circle of pock-marked concrete courtyard, clearly the meeting point at the centre of the yard. An ugly grey brick house stood on one side and on the other was a large static caravan. As they crossed the concrete towards the house, Holly noticed it was in fact a row of static caravans, perhaps seven or more, lined up down a thin lane that was backed onto a wood. She modified the description of the caravans to trailers – there was no way any of them were about to be dragged around the country to campsites. By the look of the grass and weeds growing up around them, they'd been in situ here for many years.

The woman stopped abruptly about three paces away from the front door to the house, 'You need somewhere to live then?'

Holly shook her head, 'No. I live with my mother.'

She squirmed at the sound of her own voice delivering such a statement. Surprisingly, this seemed to go down well with the woman.

'Just as well, the accommodation here is in poor shape,' she said, flicking her eyes at the trailers, 'Okay for the young 'uns, but not exactly the Ritz.'

She paused, taking a closer look at Holly, 'I'm Mary by the way. If you still want the job, tell her you're good with a brush and always on time.'

Mary turned towards the house and without warning shouted out loudly, 'Wendy!'

'And don't call her Lady Dent, that's my nickname for her,' Mary advised quietly as she banged on the door with the heel of her hand, 'Just call her Wendy. Makes you think of Peter Pan doesn't it? Silly name if you ask me, but she's okay, Mrs Dent, that is. She'll get you sorted. Oh, and I hope you like dogs.'

Holly boggled at Mary, trying to process her quick-fire round-up of Wendy Dent. Mary must have liked the effect she'd had on her, as the stable lass produced her first smile, but only as she turned her back on Holly to set off in a different direction to the one they'd come in. A short wait later the door opened.

It was dark inside. A figure was standing back and Holly wasn't able to pick out any facial features at first. However, it was definitely a woman. Her short, plump and curvy outline was silhouetted against a rectangle of light coming from an open door at the other end of the hallway.

'Can I help you, my dear?' asked a plummy voice.

Two things happened in quick succession. Firstly, the woman stepped forward and a round, doughy face appeared from the murky depths of the hallway. A splash of daylight revealed Wendy's smile, as well as the rest of her ample proportions. The second was a stampede of small black and tan dogs that spilled out of the house like beans from a can and surrounded Holly's feet, some of them trying in vain to clamber up her legs.

'Don't mind them,' beamed Wendy. She transferred her attention from the pool of writhing fur at Holly's feet and fixed her with an expectant gaze.

'Oh! Er.. they're all good. I um... love dogs. The more the merrier. I'm here to ask if there are any stable lass positions available?' asked Holly as clearly and professionally as possible, whilst bending over to gently persuade one of the more amorous dachshunds to detach itself from her leg.

'Really?' remarked Wendy, as if a little surprised. She looked Holly up and down, 'Can you ride?'

'Yes, I've had experience over in Middleham. I can supply references if you…'

'Oh, no need for that,' Wendy interjected, waving a hand, 'Graham and Hugo will check out your riding ability. And your weight stripped?'

Holly paused a second or two, allowing the question to settle on her. Wendy read her hesitation and blank face.

'Stripped just means without your riding gear, dear. We prefer our riders to be under ten stones, you see,' Wendy explained kindly, extending her arms out from her ample figure and delivering a dramatic wink, 'So that's me ruled out!'

'I'm nine stone two,' Holly answered quickly, keen to move the conversation on.

'That's wonderful, my lovely,' Wendy said in a satisfied tone, 'I thought so. That looks about right. Come on in and we'll get you sorted out.'

'Doggies! Come on in,' Wendy hollered from the passageway, 'Hogarth, Turner, stop pestering Hockney!'

Relieved she was being at least provisionally accepted, Holly attempted to follow Wendy, but had to wait for her gaggle of dachshunds to dash back inside the dark hallway, obeying their mistress's call. Wendy closed the door behind them and trailed the comical little dogs down a hallway, past a set of stairs and into a slightly brighter, but still rather dull and dated kitchen diner at the back of the house. One half of the room looked normal, the other space was a chaotic office consisting of two desks. The first looked unused, but both were buried beneath piles of paperwork, racing magazines, and newspapers. Apart from a space for a flat TV, the walls were covered with a mish-mash of racing photographs of owners, jockeys and staff, and a trio of cupboards against one wall groaned under the weight of what Holly presumed to be thirty years' worth of racing memorabilia.

Holly had ridden as a teenager and thanks to her involvement with Bain, visited a number of racing stables over the last twelve months. She'd also spent a week as a stable lass at the David and Mary Thorne yard in Middleham, a couple who were now good friends of theirs. It had been enormously helpful and meant she had a working understanding of how a racing yard operated day to day. But she was always amazed at how utilitarian and generally underwhelming a trainer's own living arrangements tended to be. She'd discovered that as a breed, the equine community tended to concentrate their time and money on their horses' accommodation, rather than their own. Holly rated the Dent family house as pretty normal - for a racehorse trainer.

Five minutes later, having signed three sets of documents and disclaimers, Holly was following Wendy and three dogs over to the first of the trailers. The trainer's wife had a Tote bag slung over her shoulder that advertised the fact she was a 'Winner at Beverley'. She'd agreed to start immediately, on a two week trial, and as it was only ten o'clock in the morning, Wendy had encouraged her to, 'Get going while the going is good. Hugo and Graham are away at the sales today, so you'll have time to get your bearings, my dear!'

'I won't be needing accommodation,' Holly pointed out as Wendy let out a puff of exertion to lift herself into the first trailer via a free-standing wrought iron step.

'This isn't someone's home,' Wendy assured her as Holly followed her into the trailer, 'We use this caravan as a staff kitchen and break room. The others are for our residential employees and storage of one kind or another.'

'Residential employees?' echoed Holly, and immediately wished she hadn't.

Two girls with their backs to them were busy making coffee from a huge urn at a grubby kitchenette at one end of the caravan, whilst at the other end, three short, thin young Indian men sat at a dining table grinning at her. Beyond them were a group of badly scuffed sofas over which another four women were draped, their feet resting on a coffee table between them. Holly recognised Mary among them, sipping a coffee from the comfort of a two seater sofa. Opposite her a girl of about Holly's age was trying to look small by slumping down in an armchair.

'Your attention please, my dears!' Wendy demanded officiously, waiting until silence pervaded the caravan and all eyes were either on her, or sizing up the new girl, 'This is Holly. She's starting today. Lara, I can see you there, no use hiding, my dear. Look after our new starter will you? Hugo will be back tomorrow to take over her induction.'

'Poor lass,' someone muttered quietly.

It had been said with a certain amount of feeling, but even so, Holly couldn't make out exactly from whose lips the words had emanated. Wendy judiciously ignored the comment.

'Lara? Are we okay with that?'

Lara straightened and offered up a tired, 'Yes, of course, Mrs D,' then looking Holly up and down, added, 'Let's hope she's up to the task.'

Lara spoke in such a rather harsh Yorkshire accent Holly found herself concentrating to make sure she caught every word correctly.

'I don't doubt she will be, my dear,' replied Wendy carefully.

She went on to run through the names of each of the five women and three men in the caravan, Holly desperately trying to commit them all to memory.

With this task completed, Wendy said, 'Lara will put you to work this morning and we'll see you back here at six-thirty tomorrow morning. Okay, my dear?'

Holly answered, but it was unlikely Wendy heard. Already out of the door, she was scrambling back down the caravan step and was soon bustling back to the sanctuary of the house, the three little dogs scampering after her.

One of the girls at the kitchenette was the first to speak.

'You a lesbian, then?' she asked in a forthright manner.

This was greeted with a mixture of giggles and hushed interest from the rest of the staff inside the caravan.

Holly stared into the girl's expectant face for a long moment. She had to be seventeen or eighteen at most. There was no hint of humour or devilment in the girl's demeanour and following a closer assessment of her earnest gaze, Holly was left with the impression the girl wasn't trying to embarrass her. However, before she could shape a reply, the woman in her early twenties by the girl's side jumped in.

'Amber!' she scolded, then turned to Holly to explain, 'I'm Courtney. Sorry about Amber. She's got a head full of social media and trashy magazines and tends to say whatever's on her mind... got no filter, but she means well.'

'Just with the short hair, athletic build. It's a Sporty Spice vibe, ain't it?' said Amber with shrug of her shoulders. The girl appeared a little confused as to why her question had been deemed inappropriate.

'No offence meant, like,' Amber added, her forehead suddenly creased up, worried she'd offended the new girl.

'None taken,' Holly assured her, adding a warm smile for good measure, 'I can't be bothered to spend half my life faffing about with long hair, so I keep it short and easy to sort out.'

'Also, it means I can get my crash helmet on and off easily, she added.'

'Oh, wow!' exclaimed Amber, clearly impressed, her earlier comment immediately forgotten, 'You've got a motorbike? Like, you ride it? That's... super lush! Geena had a bike too. She was cool like you, always buzzing here and there, until she...'

Amber's eyes suddenly teared up. Lois gently took the girl's arm said something quietly in her ear. Amber nodded, dutifully dug a hand into her jeans pocket and began dabbing at her eyes with a grubby looking paper hanky.

At the back of the caravan came the sound of someone loudly clearing their throat.

'Welcome to Beverley Hill Stables, Holly,' Lara announced from the other end of the caravan. In her mid-forties, she delivered her introduction in a grimly ironic tone that raised an equal number of smiles and smirks among the rest of the staff.

Rising from her armchair, Lara added in a lighter voice, 'Come on then, I'll show you the ropes.'

Holly nodded, went over to the sink and turning around, took out her phone, then rapidly framed and took a photo.

'What the hell?' Lara exclaimed, advancing on her.

'I'm so sorry, it's to help me…' apologised Holly swiftly.

'Let's see that,' Lara demanded, attempting to snatch the phone out of her hand, but Holly deftly whipped the device away and maintained a tight grip on it.

'I'm so forgetful,' Holly explained, cringing a little. It had the desired effect, making Lara stand and listen, 'The only way I'd be able to remember everyone's name is to take a photo and learn each name. Isn't that okay?'

'She's got a point,' said Amber, 'It took me months to learn everyone's name.'

'Yeah, let her be,' added a voice from the back of the caravan, 'It must be tough being that old!'

Lara eyed Holly suspiciously for a couple of seconds whilst rolling her tongue around her cheek. Turning on her heel she called out, 'Come on then, let's be having you. There's stables to be cleaned, horses to be walked,' and headed for the caravan door. Holly set off after her.

'That means all of you!' Lara shouted, 'And by the way you lot, if Holly is old, what does that make me?'

No one answered.

'Experienced, and she who must be obeyed!' exclaimed Lara in answer to her own question, 'Come on, work to do.'

To various moans and groans the rest of the Beverley Hill stable staff slowly vacated what Holly was to learn at lunchtime, was the trailer they called the, 'Tea Hut'.

Twenty-Five

A muscle in Graham Dent's cheek twitched. It was the start of a very long day at the sales and his face was already aching with all the forced smiles and false joviality he'd had to dish out to his owners. How different, how easy his life would become without any owners, he thought miserably. Not for the first time in recent months, it occurred to him that training racehorses would be the perfect job if he didn't have to deal with stable staff and owners… or horses come to that. In total, five or six of his owners were guaranteed to be at Doncaster today, some here to buy, others just for the day out, but all of them wanting a piece of him.

He scanned the faces of the three owners he was currently entertaining, and for whom he would hopefully be buying one or two nice horses. There was Miriam Blunt, lottery winner, looking to add another two-year-old to the filly she'd bought at the Yearling Sales back in October. Paul Sanger, self-made multi-millionaire, had his eye on one specific filly that was due up soon. He was another new owner to the yard. And finally, there was the ever-present Betty Poole. Betty's family owned most of the amusement arcades on the east coast and already stabled half a dozen horses with Dent. She was an important owner, and yet Dent loathed her. He couldn't think of a single redeeming quality when it came to Betty Poole. She moaned. Every entry, declaration, run, result, and jockey's performance, was received with negativity. And Betty Poole was more than capable of twisting a good run, or even a winning one into an opportunity to complain. He used to wonder why she bothered owning horses, but experience had taught him that being a racehorse owner offered what Betty *really* wanted; to complain!

Dent could hear her scratchy Hull accent squawking now: 'The horse won too easily', 'It was about time he'd won…', 'Why was the starting price so short, was someone in the yard backing him?', 'Why run him on ground like this?', 'The distance was wrong, that's why he got beat a short head!' The woman was sour to her core.

Just the mention of Betty's name was enough to make Dent wince these days, and although it pained him to be civil to her, he kept on smiling. And Betty Poole kept on sending him horses to train.

Leading his gaggle of owners, plus his son, Hugo, to the seats on the left-hand side of the sales auditorium, the five of them sat down and Dent was immediately bookended by the two ladies. Paul Sanger seemed happy enough seating himself beside Hugo. Plastering a set smile onto his face, Dent opened his sales catalogue and settled in for a thirty minute wait until the first of Adrian Cooper's two-year-olds was due to enter the sales ring. His decision to enter the ring so early was driven by self-preservation. The auctioneer's jabbering as the bids flew in from all sides of the sales ring was highly effective in drowning out Betty Poole's constant moaning monologue.

***

From his position behind a column on the balcony, Conor Moran took in the scene. Lot number six walked clockwise around the ring beneath him as the bids mounted for this powerfully built son of Invincible Spirit. Casting his gaze further afield he could pick out dozens of people he knew. Whether it was Ireland, Britain or even France, he'd been attending horse sales all his life. Born into a racing family in Ireland, he still represented his father's stud between his work representing footballers. There weren't many people in racing he didn't know. But there were two specific groups and three separate individuals drawing his undivided attention this morning and he concentrated on one, then another.

In doing so, Conor caught himself nervously biting the inside of his mouth. This was becoming unnecessarily complex. He'd said as much to Hugo Dent.

Conor's worries receded when he saw Daniel Croft pop up on the opposite balcony. He'd missed him at first, hardly visible as he leaned up against the shadowy back wall. He allowed himself the faintest of grins. He'd heard *things* about this fellow, things that meant he probably didn't have anything to worry about. He'd get his job done, allowing him to do his.

Looking down into his catalogue, Conor shuffled between the pages of Lots 24, 44, and 56, all of them Cooper's breezers. The three young horses represented twelve thousand pounds to Conor, cash in hand. For nothing more than a few minutes of careful bidding. Nice work if you could get it, and Conor found this sort of work at most of the yearling sales each year. There was always a racehorse trainer desperate enough to con a trusting owner.

Twenty-Six

Ronnie slapped Bain's knee, 'Stop jiggling!'

Bain compressed his lips and rubbed at his knees and particularly the leg he'd been bouncing up and down enough to cause Ronnie's irritation. Try as he might, waiting for the Dents to start bidding had him thinking back to their journey to Doncaster. Someone had been following them, he was sure of it. Ronnie hadn't helped. She'd called him a nervous ninny and emitted a long line of frustrated sighs from the passenger seat. Still, the red mini that had become the focus of his attention on the drive down from Northallerton had eventually disappeared from Bain's rearview mirror after he'd doubled back and chosen a circuitous route through

Doncaster. He was feeling better now, but at the time he'd become somewhat flustered. He tried to distract himself by reacquainting himself with the pedigrees of the horses being sold by Adrian Cooper.

'The first of the five Adrian Cooper horses will go through in about five minutes. Lot 24,' Bain told Ronnie, tapping an index finger at his catalogue whilst ensuring his leg didn't jiggle in tandem, 'That's when things will get interesting.'

Licking his lips in anticipation, Bain adjusted his baseball cap and scanned the sales room once again. He and Ronnie were sitting at the very end of the top row. Below him were half a dozen rows that descended in steps to a circular ring in which a young filly was being led around by her young female handler. The rows were padded benches, spotted with potential bidders. Bain was strategically seated to enable him to view the entire sales room, as well as a little way down the passageway leading into the sales arena. The latter was a favoured place from which to bid. Certain trainers liked the anonymity the shaded doorway provided.

Bain was looking down on Graham Dent and his owners who were sitting together on the second row, their backs to him. Bain could view their faces in profile, but the Dent group would have to turn right around in their seats to pick out Ronnie and himself.

'I'm going for a wander,' Ronnie announced quietly in Bain's ear, 'I'd like to be a bit closer to the action, and I can watch Dent from that passageway down there.'

Bain considered her suggestion for a moment and decided it perhaps made sense to have two differing locations from which to keep an eye on the Dent contingent.

'Keep out of Hugo Dent's way,' warned Bain, 'Also, see if you can find the stud manager, Adrian Cooper. If you do, let me know. I've not laid eyes on him or Conor Moran yet.'

'Will do, boss,' Ronnie replied, touching her cap in the manner of a salute.

Bain grinned, 'Keep a low profile... and no bidding!'

Ronnie rolled her eyes at him as she got up off the bench. Bain dutifully swept his legs and feet aside to let her out. She grumbled something under her breath about him talking to her like she was a six-year-old and her being old enough to be his mother, and climbed the few steps to the top balcony. Bain screwed his head backwards to watch her depart and noticed the balcony behind him was now also thronged with potential bidders.

Returning his attention to the sales ring, Bain tried to spot who was trying to buy the latest two-year-old under the hammer. For the last half an hour he'd been testing himself by trying to pinpoint the bidders for each racehorse. It wasn't easy. A flick of a catalogue, nod of the head, or lifting of a single finger was enough for the auctioneer to accept a bid, but Bain reckoned he was on target more often than not. Mind you, just because someone bid, didn't mean they were buying the horse for themselves. He knew that half the horses sold today would be bought by trainers or agents who would sign for the horse on behalf of a third party, who in all likelihood, wasn't even at the sale. It made tracking the real buyers almost impossible until the horse was registered to race, and that could take months, or even years if immature young horses took time to become race-ready. Most racehorses didn't show up on any racing database until they'd been entered to run their first race. Owners rarely registered their ownership until just before their first run because, like everything else in horseracing, registering to race, and officially naming your horse, incurred Weatherby's fees.

Bain consoled himself with the knowledge that Dent was surrounded by the same trio of owners who had been at the breezing the day before. He expected Dent would bid, and if he was successful, the owner would sign for the horse.

Lot 22 reached fifteen thousand pounds. Bain was sure Dent wasn't involved in the bidding process for this particular horse. The trainer was in conversation with the lady wearing a faux fur coat to his left, and wasn't concentrating on this lot. He checked his notes, secreted in the pages of his catalogue and reminded himself that the lady's name was Miriam Blunt. She was the one who had been harangued by her ex-husband the day before.

Another lot went through quickly, only reaching fifteen thousand pounds. Then Lot 24 entered the sales room.

Bain noticed a marked change in Graham Dent, and also the middle-aged man to his right. Both were suddenly erect in their seats and as the auctioneer asked for twenty, ten, then five thousand to get him started, the two men shared a knowing sidelong glance and Dent made a flick of his catalogue. Interestingly, his son Hugo, sitting a couple of seats away from his father, also appeared to be at full alert.

'I have five thousand pounds as a starting bid, thank you, Sir. Do I hear six?' the auctioneer asked.

Bain studied the filly as she walked around the sales ring. She wasn't anything special to look at, and if anything, on the small side. Her pedigree was nice enough, but she'd looked backward and a little difficult to manage during her breeze. Based on the prices being paid up until now, and being by a cheap sire, Bain couldn't see her bringing anything more than twelve thousand, or fifteen at most.

As if wishing to prove him wrong, the bidding soon went through eight and up to fourteen thousand, rising in increments of one thousand pounds per bid. Dent's catalogue was kept busy, along with a number of nods of his head. Bain identified two bidders vying with Dent. One of the Westerly brothers, trainers based in Teesside, dropped out at ten, and an agent Bain recognised as an ex-jumps jockey went to sixteen, but Dent carried on, taking the price to seventeen thousand.

'Are we all done?' the auctioneer demanded, swinging his gavel from the right-hand side of the room over to the left. He consulted his bid spotters, two young women and a man placed strategically around the room, but it looked like Dent was about secure his first purchase of the day.

The auctioneer paused, gavel raised. Then in a quiet voice he said, 'Eighteen thousand. New bidder,' and pointed his gavel vaguely in the direction of the balcony to his left, opposite Bain's position.

Along with Bain, most of the onlookers in the seats lifted their eyes in an attempt to locate the late entrant to the bidding. To his annoyance, Bain was unable to pick anyone out. There had to be thirty people on the balcony rails looking down on the ring, any one of them could be signalling to the auctioneer.

The filly's price jumped forwards, rattling through twenty thousand and carried on through thirty thousand towards forty thousand, and still Bain couldn't identify the bidder. Furiously scanning the faces in the gallery for the umpteenth time, with bids raining in, Bain finally caught sight of a face he recognised. As the name Conor Moran entered his thoughts, Bain knew he had to be the bidder. His participation in this particular auction answered the question of why Moran had acknowledged Adrian Cooper at the breezing.

Moran was wearing a cap similar to his own, a shadow cast across his face, and with one hand on the balcony rail, his face was away from the ring, as if he was consulting with a third party. But every time his face turned towards the auctioneer, he blinked with both eyes… and the price of the filly rose.

Bain's pulse quickened. With Conor Moran's involvement confirmed, he was now sure there was something underhand going on. There was a small chance Moran was acting as an agent on behalf of a client wishing to purchase this particular horse, but Bain discarded the notion - Moran had to be bidding the price up on Cooper's behalf.

So where was Cooper? Bain asked himself. Surely he had to be playing some sort of role in this subterfuge. If nothing else, he had to be there just to oversee the sale of his horse. But three more scans of the room ended with no sign of the stud manager.

At forty-six thousand, Dent wavered for the first time, pausing before delivering a follow-up bid. Bain saw his owner, Paul Sanger, lean into his trainer. Hugo Dent joined them in a three-way whispered conversation, their heads almost touching. Presently, Dent lifted his chin to the auctioneer and registered another bid with a flick of his catalogue.

The auctioneer responded in a satisfied voice, 'I'm bid forty-eight thousand pounds for this fine filly out of a black type mare with winning siblings.'

He switched his focus to the gallery balcony and asked the question, 'One more, sir? It might be enough. Do I hear fifty thousand?'

Moran's hand dropped from the balcony rail and he turned away, disappearing behind a group of onlookers. The auctioneer's interest in his lost bidder dissolved immediately and he redirected his attention to Dent. With one more cursory sweep of the room, the filly was knocked down to Dent for forty-eight thousand pounds and the auctioneer offered him the best of luck with the filly.

Bain watched as a young woman clutching a clipboard made a beeline for Dent and Sanger, the latter signing for the filly with a triumphant smile. He's overpaid for her, Bain said to himself, and yet from the look on Sanger's face, the millionaire wasn't aware this was the case. That filly was nice enough, but small and underdeveloped. Her breeze had been nothing more than satisfactory. Bain was sure her real value was in the teens, not close to fifty-thousand. Between Dent and his son, plus Cooper, and of all people, Moran, they had fraudulently pushed the filly's price up to maximise profit, and he was sure all three of them would be sharing in the proceeds of their fraud.

Bain gave an involuntary shudder as his thoughts focused on Conor Moran. He'd had first-hand experience of Moran. His career in journalism had almost ended, thanks to that man's despicable scheming. And here he was again, involved in underhand dealing. The man was reprehensible and to Bain's mind, by association, so were Dent and Cooper. But how to prove it? To expose the men would require solid proof that Sanger had been made to pay three times the filly's expected sale value. And how would Bain do that? The men involved would certainly deny it, and would the auction house take his complaint seriously? After all, it wasn't the buyer complaining!

Even Sanger might not want to listen… would a self-made millionaire believe the bids from the balcony were fraudulent? Even if he listened to Bain's story, would he readily admit to being duped? It could be embarrassing for such a successful businessman.

And what did this double dealing have to do with Brooklyn Hartley's death? Apart from proving she had been working in a yard whose trainer was happy to defraud his owners, there was no evidence of a link to her death.

Deflated, Bain looked up to the gallery once more. Moran was nowhere to be seen, the crowd of onlookers at the balcony rails were now more concerned with the next lot, a colt whose sale was already underway.

Bain consoled himself with the knowledge that there were another three more lots from Cooper's stud due to go through the ring. Perhaps they would provide him with further proof of wrongdoing and possibly produce a lead for the Brooklyn Hartley murder.

Twenty-Seven

Gregory Blunt was rather pleased with himself. His late evening visit to the stud manager Cooper had gone better than he'd expected. The man's face had been a picture when he'd relayed the overheard conversation between him and his trainer friend, the younger Dent.

Blunt examined his breakfast bap and smirked. Cooper had been dumbfounded. And as a result, Miriam was in for the shock of her life.

In a state of euphoria and self-congratulatory fervour, Blunt was currently treating himself to an outrageously expensive hot bacon and egg bap and a cup of tea from the Goffs café, a sizeable tearoom and small bar that backed onto the salesroom. The sound of the auctioneer was being piped around the room via monitors dotted around the café displaying the lot and current bid details.

Blunt bit into his bacon and egg bap, allowing yoke to run down his chin, drip through his wispy beard and onto the table, missing his plate. He'd really enjoyed giving the young girl behind the counter a few choice words. Twelve quid for a bacon and egg bap and a cup of tea! It was daylight robbery, and he'd let her know about it in no uncertain terms.

He'd then paid for the meal with dozens of small coins instead of a note, systematically placing them, one by one, on her counter top, just to hack her off. A queue of customers had soon built up behind him, and he'd enjoyed forcing the increasingly irritable chap behind him to wait his turn. Yep, as far as days went, this one had already been memorable, and there was more to come!

Blunt glanced up at the nearest television screen. Lot 27 was being sold. He wouldn't have too long to wait, Cooper had confirmed it was Lot 56 that Miriam had chosen to buy. He turned the wafer thin pages of his catalogue to Lot 56 and viewed the pedigree of the Mehmas colt. The first and second dam information held therein was gobbledygook as far as he was concerned. However, everything was in place. He'd caught up with Cooper again at the colt's stable twenty minutes ago and been assured his instructions had been carried out; Cooper had confirmed he'd altered the ownership of the colt with Goffs that morning in order to keep Blunt from reporting him to the authorities. This meant that anything Miriam paid for the horse would now be his, and not

Cooper's. And he would endeavour to ensure Miriam paid through the nose for the colt. Right through the nose! And then he would rub her nose in it. He was really looking forward to that bit.

He munched happily on his breakfast, unaware that the girl he'd embarrassed at the checkout had ensured only the most fatty, gnarly pieces of bacon available in the kitchen had made it into Blunt's bap.

Twenty-Eight

Quickly bored of watching the endless parade of two-year-olds being led around the pre-sales ring, Ronnie had entered the sales ring itself and witnessed the sale of Lot 24 from a position close to where the horses exited, allowing her to place the stud manager, Cooper, in her sights throughout. He was sitting on his own, a few rows behind the Dents.

Watching Cooper as the bidding got underway, Ronnie swiftly came to the conclusion that to sell a horse you had delivered and raised for the best part of two years must be a fraught activity given that your profit, or loss, would be determined by only a few minutes of bidding, over which you had little control. Cooper had been nervous as the bidding had started, and even worse as it progressed. Ronnie felt a little sorry for him as the man seemed to be taking every bid as a punch to his stomach. The small, stout man whose face sagged, most noticeably from his eyes, had maintained a constant grimace.

Ronnie's heart went out to him. The man was obviously under pressure. But her perspective altered radically when the bidding reached forty-six thousand pounds. It had happened quickly, a simple movement of his hand making a quick, cutting motion across his throat. Blink and you'd have missed it. A few seconds later, Cooper had given himself away by looking up to the balcony where the underbidder was located.

Ronnie had known immediately what it meant. It had been a signal to cease bidding against Dent. Bain had been right!

This was why Ronnie had followed Miriam Blunt into the Goffs café and was in the process of introducing herself to the lady.

Twenty-Nine

Gregory Blunt was amazed at how much was being paid for some of the horses. He'd watched in amazement as lot 44, also owned by Cooper, had been signed for by a plainly dressed woman sitting beside Miriam in the second row whom the auctioneer had thanked and named as Mrs Poole. She'd been in a grump afterwards, her lined face coming to life only to share a bitter conversation with her trainer. Blunt assumed she was complaining about the price of the horse. At sixty-eight thousand pounds, Blunt agreed, and even admired her a little.

Miriam had disappeared in the direction of the café after Lot 44, and hadn't returned yet. Blunt was starting to worry she wasn't going to be back to bid on Lot 56, but then spotted her, although she didn't go over to join her trainer. No matter, it was the horse, Lot 56, that mattered. That was the horse she'd fallen for at Cooper's yard the other day. And it was now *his horse*!

With any luck, Miriam would be stupid enough to pay an even bigger sum for Lot 56. He would laugh in her face once the hammer had fallen. There wasn't long to wait now, just one lot. And he fully expected to be bidding against Miriam's trainer, currently being harangued by Mrs Poole whilst Lot 55 was being sold.

Standing in the chute opposite the auctioneer's raised desk, he and about thirty other onlookers watched in rapt silence as the numbers on the sales board leapt up in five thousand pound increments. As Lot 55 received a bid of one hundred thousand and started to climb higher in ten thousand pound jumps, Blunt's curiosity was pricked.

'This has to be the biggest waste of money I've ever come across. These people must be morons,' he muttered under his breath whilst studying Lot 55's page in the Goffs catalogue.

A man standing next to Blunt nodded at the auctioneer and the current bid increased by another ten thousand pounds. The bidder turned his head and stared belligerently at Blunt. Guessing the stranger had overheard his comment, Blunt coughed apologetically. Another rival bid caught the man's attention and he returned to the matter in hand.

Relieved, Blunt stared into his catalogue in the hope of divining a reason why the young racehorse being led around the central ring should be worth such an eyewatering sum. However, the breeding information may as well have been in another language. None of it meant anything to Blunt.

In a matter of seconds the bidding for the colt reached a hundred and eighty thousand pounds and Blunt found himself frowning. Intrigued to find out why a racehorse could be worth so much, he took out his phone. It must be the potential prizemoney. Win a few races, he reasoned, and you'd get your outlay, plus the racing costs back, plus profit.

Browsing to the Racing Post website, he scanned a few race results, his accountant's intuition telling him there had to be solid financial reasons for such huge sums to be spent on these animals. It didn't take long for him to work out that race prizemoney was so low it would never cover an owner's costs, except in exceptional cases.

Still befuddled by the bidding, Blunt watched as the colt's price reached two hundred thousand and kept on going. Now transfixed by the two bidders trying to own the colt, Blunt didn't realise he was being closely studied. Nor did he notice when his watcher began to push their way through the mass of people standing at the side of the sales ring. So involved in the excitement of the auction, Blunt didn't think anything of it when someone squeezed past, bumping him as they left the sales room. He aimed a scowl at the figure, but their face was turned away from him. However, the auctioneer's voice drew Blunt's attention back to the sale.

There was an air of expectancy in the sales room as the colt's price hit a quarter of a million pounds. Blunt was caught up in the theatre of the moment too. His heart began to pound in his chest as the auctioneer slowed, aware his bidders were reaching their limit.

Blunt found himself grinning. This was unexpectedly exciting! He was a man who knew the value of money and prided himself in the knowledge that he'd spent all his adult life ensuring every penny he and Miriam earned was well spent. But it was strangely exhilarating to be witness to someone else wasting a huge, life-changing lump of money on something that was nothing more than a frivolous gamble. And when the next lot entered the sales ring, he was about to experience what it felt like to bid thousands of pounds on each nod of his head or flap of his catalogue.

Blunt felt something bubble and groan inside his stomach. Then a moment of sharp discomfort made him rub the pot belly that poked over the top of his trousers. Perhaps it was nerves? Lot 56, Miriam's horse was about to go through the ring. The dark greyish colt was waiting in the gate only a few yards away from him. It was definitely nerves Blunt told himself. After all, he'd never done anything like this before. Come to think of it, he'd never blackmailed anyone, or spent a night sleeping in a campervan either. The growling in his stomach had to be nervous tension.

It came again, stronger this time, his stomach lurching as a wave of nausea swamped his senses. An image of his expensive breakfast bap swam before his eyes as a free-flowing sweat broke out across his forehead. His bottom lip began to swell and his tongue suddenly felt large in his mouth. It was then that Blunt realised he was wheezing. Simultaneously, he lost most of his sight through his right eye.

The nausea returned in a powerful way and Blunt could hold it no longer. He bent over and proceeded to deposit his breakfast onto the floor of the sales room.

With Lot 55's bidding stalled at two hundred and sixty thousand pounds, the auctioneer dropped his voice and advised the underbidder they had one last chance to own the colt. When no such undertaking was received, the hammer fell. As did Blunt. Without warning his legs went to jelly, his vision faltered, and Gregory Blunt collapsed.

Thirty

Lot 56, a sleek, angular son of Mehmas, winner of the July and Richmond Stakes, entered the sales ring. The auctioneer began to run through the youngster's pedigree and the hubbub of excited conversations that had broken out following the sale of the proceeding lot began to subside.

Bain wasn't concentrating on the horse now circling the sales ring, the Dents, or even Conor Moran. Utterly boggled by what he was witnessing, his attention was entirely focused on Ronnie and the fact that she had just entered the sales room alongside Miriam Blunt. The two of them were definitely together and were climbing the gallery steps on the opposite side of the sales room.

Rocking in his seat, Bain watched in disbelief as the two women reached the third row of seats and forcing several people to stand to let them through, seated themselves either side of a short, pale-faced man.

Adrian Cooper! Bain screamed inwardly. Ronnie was sitting… no, she'd started a conversation with the man responsible for selling lot 56! What on earth was she doing?

Bain had no answer to this question and it was soon forgotten as his attention, along with those of a good proportion of the people in the sales room, was wrenched from the colt in the sales ring and instead, focussed on a kerfuffle in the doorway. There was the sound of retching, a horrible, dry coughing and with immediate effect and considerable shuffling of feet, a space appeared. Someone was on the floor, a stricken figure who was on his knees, wobbling and retching, whilst trying to get up.

The auctioneer paused the bidding at seven thousand pounds and quipped, 'I believe we have a gentleman who is losing an argument with his breakfast. But no matter, we have our first aider on hand…'

To a man, the faces of those closest to the disturbance were screwed up in disgust. A few more had hands over their mouths.

Now on all fours in an expanding pool of his own vomit, Blunt lifted his head between the continuing convulses and stared bleary-eyed into the sales ring. His cheeks were a fiery red, his nose dripping sweat and snot, but worst of all were his eyes… He seemed to be suffering an allergic reaction, and the whites of one of his eyes had swollen up to comic book proportions. It occurred to Bain that every fibre of Blunt's being was pleading for whatever this was, to stop. He was finally lifted to his feet when a third man, an employee of the sales company, stepped in. Looking weak, washed out, pop-eyed, and burbling something about bidding for Lot 56, Gregory Blunt was half led, half carried out of the sales room on his way to the first aid room.

The auctioneer judiciously gave his audience thirty seconds to recover, during which time two more employees set about mopping up Blunt's breakfast and dousing the area around the doorway with water and antiseptic.

As the auction recommenced, Bain's gaze settled on Ronnie once again. She was still in conversation with both Miriam and Cooper, but this soon broke up. Cooper lifted his phone to his ear, whilst Miriam stood up and left the gallery in something of a flap, hurrying off after her ex-husband.

Bain stood up, determined to find out exactly what was going on by stalking around the balcony and dropping down to sit with Ronnie and Adrian Cooper on the other side of the salesroom. As he placed a foot on the balcony, Bain froze.

Standing rigid against the back wall, mobile pressed to his ear, was Conor Moran. His face wore an expression Bain could best describe as savage. Thankfully, Moran's attention was wholly focussed on the gallery on the opposite side of the room and specifically Cooper and the two women sitting at his side. It suddenly dawned on Bain that thanks to Ronnie's actions, especially with the apparent support of Miriam Blunt, Moran, Cooper, and the Dents were in disarray. They may have switched their seating positions to bid on this colt, but there was no way they'd factored a force like Ronnie into their plans.

Moran was still speaking vociferously into his phone whilst belligerently staring across the sales ring at an increasingly despondent Cooper. It struck Bain that Moran had to be on the phone with the stud manager. Unaware he was being monitored, and becoming louder as Moran's frustration increased, Bain picked up on a few phrases, sprinkled with bad language.

Moran was continuing to vent his fury into his phone when Ronnie raised her hand and bid for Lot 56.

'New bidder,' stated the auctioneer crisply, 'I have sixteen thousand pounds, looking for seventeen…'

Returning to his seat, Bain sat with his mouth open for the next two minutes as Ronnie, with a restraining hand on Cooper's leg, bid on Lot 56. It was impressive. Throwing determined scowls down a couple of rows to her left where Hugo and Graham Dent were sitting, and keeping a firm grip on Cooper, Lot 56 was successfully knocked down to Ronnie for twenty-eight-thousand pounds. Neither of the Dent's, nor Conor Moran or Cooper, placed a single bid.

Thirty-One

Bain caught up with Ronnie outside the salesroom, leaning up against the rails of the pre-sale ring. She beamed at him excitedly as he approached, maintaining her huge smile despite his somewhat grim expression.

'What were my last words to you?' he grumbled amiably, 'Holly is going to skin me alive.'

'Pish posh! Never mind that,' she countered with a flap of her wrist, 'Come on, we need to find Mimi.'

'Mimi?'

'I'll explain later. We need to give her the good news! Will you *come on!*'

Bain followed Ronnie as she navigated her way around the pre-sales ring, and through the half-dozen avenues of stables, eventually coming upon a dazed Gregory Blunt being cared for in a first aid room at the bottom end of the sales complex. Miriam, or rather, Mimi as she preferred to be called by her friends, was speaking with a nurse, but broke off to greet Ronnie and be introduced to Bain, immediately suggesting they left her ex-husband, and went out into the open air.

'It stinks of sick in there,' Mimi explained, wrinkling her nose.

'Is he okay?'

Mimi nodded, 'Once I saw his face I could tell he was having an allergic reaction. He may be a shrivelled up, mean old sod, but I couldn't ignore it. I always kept an adrenaline shot in my handbag just in case he had an episode. Lord knows why I'm still carrying it around, but he's flaming lucky I do.'

'So it could have been worse?' asked Bain.

'Uh huh. The whites of his eyes are the giveaway, they expand, and then his throat goes the same way, Mimi said, clutching a hand to her neck, 'He could have choked.'

Ronnie was frowning, 'What's he allergic to?'

Mimi's brow furrowed, 'Well that's the thing. It's dogs, or specifically, dog hair. Someone he was standing close to must have been covered in dog hairs and Gregory breathed them in. But that's the first time I've seen him throwing up like that.'

The sound of retching and a pitiful groan from inside the first aid room prompted all three of them to look through the open door at Blunt. He was sitting on the edge of a bed, his head almost between his knees, a small plastic bucket in his hands. Stripped to his waist, his face was still showing signs of being bloated, and there were angry red blotches down his neck and over his chest and back. But it was his eyes that drew Bain's stare. The whites had expanded, making Blunt's pupils small black dots within a bulging cauliflower of white. However, his looks were the last thing on Blunt's mind. Still fighting the urge to regurgitate, Blunt was more interested in complaining to the nurse that the receptacle between his knees was in danger over overflowing.

'He'll live,' Mimi sighed, adding, 'The stupid man has had the fright of his life. Can you believe he's just admitted he was trying to blackmail Adrian Cooper? He has this wild theory that he's been 'got at' in order to prevent him from bidding for Lot 56!'

Ronnie and Bain traded a sidelong glance.

'Would you mind if I have a word with… um, your ex…?'

'Gregory,' supplied Mimi, 'Yes, by all means. Come on, I'll introduce you both. Just a warning though, he's feeling pretty sorry for himself. After I got the adrenaline into him he… well, you'll find out for yourself. Quite how he got to know that Adrian Cooper and Hugo Dent were trying to dupe their owners, I don't know, but I gave Gregory a piece of my mind anyway.'

Ronnie grinned, 'We heard. I didn't knock on the door until you'd finished! And in my opinion, no less than he deserves, the little weasel!'

Mimi swelled with pride, smiling with pleasure, 'Actually, I rather enjoyed it,' she told them in a confidential tone, 'Like the song says, I think I've washed that man right out of my hair!'

'He treated her like a skivvy,' Ronnie told Bain with distain, 'In fact, I've a few choice words for him myself.'

Ronnie promptly marched into the first aid room and Bain set off after her, but Mimi caught his arm.

She whispered, 'Ronnie was good enough to tell me what was going on, you know, with the bidding for Cooper's horses? I'm ever so grateful... but I just wondered whether she's quite all there...?'

Bain held up a flat hand and said in a whisper, 'Ronnie is one-hundred-percent all there. Why, what did she say to worry you?'

'It wasn't anything she said,' Mimi offered with a small shrug, 'It's just... after we finished our sandwiches she tossed her plate, mug of tea, well... everything into the waste bin.'

'Ah! That one,' Bain said with a small chuckle, 'Yes, that's one of hers. Seriously, you don't need to worry. Ronnie has her quirks, but her mind is a trap. She's one of the sharpest people I know.'

'She can be brutally direct,' said Mimi, sounding impressed, 'I *really* like that!'

'She's also relentless when she thinks something is unfair,' added Bain as they stepped inside the first aid room, 'A trait that your ex-husband is no doubt discovering at this very moment.'

'...and if I hear of you perpetrating such nonsense against Mimi again, you'll have me to answer to!' Ronnie told Blunt with a wagging index finger as Bain and Mimi entered.

Bain stepped in and asked Blunt a number of questions. Satisfied they'd got as much information as they needed, all three of them left the medical room a few minutes later to allow the nurse to treat his rash and place drops in Blunt's bulbous eyes. They were walking past the dusty avenues of stables when Bain turned to Ronnie.

'Are you going to tell her, then?' he whispered, 'After all, you can't afford to keep him yourself, can you?'

Appearing a little downcast, Ronnie shook her head and admitted she couldn't. Bain looked around, smiled at Ronnie, then taking Mimi's hand, guided her over to stable B201. As they approached the box, the head of a slightly grey horse poked out. Mimi couldn't help herself, soon stroking the side of the colt's head and neck.

'Mimi, I have some good news for you,' Ronnie said brightly, 'Before we came to find you, I signed a receipt in your name for Lot 56!'

Miriam's eyes grew wide at this news, 'Really? You bid for me?'

'Yes, and this... is him,' said Ronnie, giving the colt's neck a pat.

Mimi cooed over the young horse, and Ronnie and Bain waited until her initial petting of Lot 56 subsided before broaching the subject of money.

'How much did Graham Dent say this lad would cost you?' Ronnie queried with a big grin, hardly able to contain her own growing excitement.

'Actually, it was Hugo who dealt with Cooper and his horses. Graham Dent said he'd bid on my behalf, but he said the choice of horse should be Hugo's and mine. Hugo told me I should expect to pay between sixty to seventy-thousand pounds, plus sales and transport costs,' said Miriam with a grimace.

Ronnie handed over a carbon copy of the sales receipt bearing Miriam's name. The woman made a strange giggling and squeaking sound as her eyes took in the contents of the receipt, and then threw her arms around Ronnie. Being a few inches taller than Miriam, Ronnie had to bend down to accommodate her. The two of them jiggled around on the spot for a few moments, squealing at each other like schoolgirls, before breaking apart.

'None of the Dent bunch dared bid,' Ronnie explained happily.

'So you were right, the Dents and Mr Cooper were trying to inflate the price of the horse?' Mimi asked, still a little breathless.

'Bain thought something smelled off!,' Ronnie admitted, 'I didn't know for sure until I saw Cooper signal to that bidder on the balcony to stop bidding against Dent for the filly Mr Sanger bought. I couldn't let you be cheated like that too. But I can't take all the credit, Bain here worked it out.'

To Bain's horror, Mimi stepped forward and threw her arms around him, squeezing hard. Standing stock still, not knowing where to put his hands, his face flushed red. Grinning manically, Ronnie fished out her phone from her bag and took a photo.

'One for the scrapbook!' she announced, giving Bain a hearty wink, 'Holly's going to love this.'

Thirty-Two

'What the hell did you two do to that poor man?' shrieked Cooper at Hugo Dent and Daniel Croft. The stud manager, smaller than both of them, agitatedly crossed his arms and glared angrily up at them, his eyes eventually coming to rest on Daniel.

'It was you, wasn't it?'

Hugo cast his gaze down to the grass, shrinking into the shadow of Cooper's towering articulated wagon. It was capable of transporting up to eight horses, and its tall sides were now helpfully shielding this impromptu meeting out in the horsebox car park.

Whilst Hugo chose to melt into the scenery, the vet stood his ground, a defiant scowl on his lips. Daniel had little time for Cooper, who he'd pigeon-holed as a small man with equally miniscule aspirations.

'You and Hugo didn't notice him listening to the two of you at your yard. So that was *your fault*. He tried to blackmail you, which was *your fault*. You asked for my help and I stopped him from bidding and alerting anyone what we had planned. What's your problem with me?' Daniel stated bluntly, glancing sharply between the two men, 'That's what Hugo asked me to do. So that's what I did.'

Moran looked on from a few yards away, sucking viciously on a cigarette. Hugo cut a nervous figure. Daniel knew him well enough though; Hugo would remain loyal to him. This ad-hoc meeting in the Goffs horsebox park, in the cold shade of Cooper's transport, well away from prying eyes or flapping ears, was Daniel's idea. The aim was to unite Moran and Cooper behind the same story. However, it was Cooper who was currently the centre of attention.

'You almost *killed* him, you moron,' Cooper ranted, spital flying from between his teeth, an accusatory finger pointed dangerously close to the vet's face.

Daniel flexed a nostril in disgust before grabbing Cooper's wrist. Gripping it in one hand, he pulled the man to him, leaned over and bent his head down so he was towering over Cooper.

'Murky work tends to get dirty,' he hissed into Cooper's face, 'I had to make sure I brought him down.'

Wrenching his hand away, Cooper stepped back, his eyes on fire.

'You're an animal.'

Daniel produced a pitying smile, 'I didn't see him bidding. Did you?'

'Okay, you two,' said Moran sounding tired, but businesslike, 'That's enough bickering. There's more important matters to discuss other than your would-be blackmailer. Our… work here has been compromised. I'm telling you all… no, I'm warning each of you… What happened here today goes no further. You don't speak of it, we don't contact each other. No emails or text messages.

Nothing. We don't know anything about causing allergic reactions and none of us know the identity of any mystery bidder inflating the prices of Cooper's horses.'

Daniel turned to take in Moran, who was once again, sucking on his cigarette, his eyes like slits as the smoke wafted into his face.

'You should leave,' Daniel advised, 'It's best we go our separate ways.'

Moran examined the end of his cigarette, 'What about my money from the first two lots?'

'You'll get paid if we get paid,' Daniel replied gruffly, 'But knowing that Blunt woman, Sangar and Mrs Poole will probably get to know they've been taken for an extra fifty grand between them. It's a case of damage limitation now.'

Moran flicked his cigarette onto the grass and sucked at his teeth for a moment, concentrating his gaze on the wisp of blue smoke still wafting up from the butt, 'The way I see it, if I keep quiet there is no evidence against any of you.'

He paused, slowly lifting his eyes to stare at Hugo, then Cooper, 'Between you two and this joke of a vet, you've screwed up. I did my job and I expect to get paid for the first two horses. Eight grand. If I don't get what's owed, you can kiss goodbye to your careers in racing.'

Baffled by this response, Cooper asked, 'Are you…? You can't be threatening us?'

'That's for you to decide,' Moran said with a twist of his wrist, indicating his boredom threshold had been reached.

He turned to leave, 'Of course, there's an easy way to find out. Try not paying me. You've got until the end of the month.'

The three men watched in stunned silence as Moran nonchalantly walked away without looking back.

Hugo was the first to speak.

'He's right. I've already met that old woman who bought the colt, the one with Miriam Blunt. She was at the yard yesterday with an even older bloke. Lara threw them off the yard in the end for wasting our time. If Moran tells her… I mean, shouldn't we pay him off, Daniel?'

Daniel wheeled around, clearly exasperated, 'What with, *Hugo*? Why do you think we were bumping up the price of these two-year-olds? Do you think I have money to burn? This was supposed to be a nice touch for all three of us!'

'Keep it down,' warned Cooper, screwing his neck around to make sure there wasn't anyone else in this far flung corner of the horsebox car park.

Daniel turned on him.

'Moran's right!' Daniel said savagely, if anything, becoming louder, 'If it wasn't for you, Coops, that Blunt woman wouldn't have known anything. You were speaking with the two of them in the sales ring. I bet you told them! Did you tell that friend of hers to bid on the colt?'

Cooper stared at Daniel, trembling, too angry to speak immediately. He swallowed hard, and in an oddly quiet voice said, 'I admitted nothing. She thinks Graham Dent organised it all.'

This brought a twitch of interest to Daniel's lips. Cooper frowned. These two young men were odd, and Moran was dangerous. If only he hadn't been so desperate…

'In that case, we're in the clear,' Daniel responded, staring at Cooper expectantly.

Cooper shook his head in disbelief, 'We're done. Like you said, we don't know each other. We don't have a business relationship. Don't call me, don't come to my yard. We're finished.'

'Once you get paid by Goffs, we want our share, and we will pay Moran,' warned Daniel, 'You heard him, he'll bring us all down if we don't. An invoice for our services will be with you by tomorrow.'

Cooper stared belligerently at Daniel for a long moment before stumping off between the sea of parked vehicles. Daniel watched him until he was lost among the horseboxes.

Hugo caught his friend's eye and shrugged a silent and

desperate, 'What now?'

Daniel allowed himself a small smile, but kept it to himself.

'It sounds like Miriam Blunt is blaming your father. He will defend himself and won't believe for a second that you're capable of such a crime. If anything, he'll think Cooper arranged it all, so you'll let him think that. I doubt he will ask Coops, but if he does, Coops won't talk because he's got too much to lose.'

'What about Miriam's ex-husband? He overheard me at Cooper's yard.'

Daniel comically rolled his eyes, 'No one is going to listen to that idiot ex-husband of hers. He can't admit to trying to blackmail her, can he? Besides, his deal was with Coops, so again, we're in the clear.'

A long moment passed as Hugo considered his friend's assertions. It certainly seemed that Daniel had thought of everything, and protected the two of them. But he was still unsure.

'You said this would be easy,' Hugo said despondently, his accusation half-hearted, 'You said there was no way our plan could be compromised. I was pretty nasty to Adrian at his yard and feel a bit guilty now.'

Daniel extended both his arms and took hold of Hugo, gently squeezing his shoulders as their eyes met. Hugo immediately felt a little better.

'Think about it like this,' said Daniel with a warm smile. Hugo melted, Daniel was so soothing, almost hypnotic at times like this, and he was only too happy to fall under his spell.

'We're in the clear, ' continued Daniel smoothly, 'See this hiccup as an opportunity! You've been trying to buy that filly, Morgan, off Miriam Blunt for months now. She's bound to be more receptive, now that she's fallen out with your father. Go and find her, maybe she wants to wash her hands of the Dent yard. This could be really good for us! Ask Miriam if she'll give up the filly. Tell her Morgan's still not responding to treatment and I've got someone who'll take the filly for a few hundred quid, as a riding horse.'

'You think Miriam will give her up?'

'It's got to be worth a try, Hugo,' Daniel breathed, 'We've worked too hard for too long, to just let this opportunity slip between our fingers. If we get paid for the two youngsters we bumped up today, and Morgan can be ours, we'll be right on track.'

'A place of our own,' said Hugo wistfully.

'A place of our own,' repeated Daniel, his gaze never leaving his young friend. He gave Hugo's shoulders a final squeeze and dropped his arms.

'Okay, I'll find Miriam,' Hugo agreed, 'I'll ask her about Morgan one more time.'

Daniel beamed at him and Hugo felt a warm buzzing in his stomach.

'Want one?' asked Daniel, producing a yellow and red coloured caramel wafer from the inside pocket of his jacket. Hugo declined, he found the biscuit too sweet for his taste. Daniel could easily eat two or three between meals.

As Daniel unwrapped his chocolate covered caramel biscuit, Hugo asked, 'What did you do to make that chap so ill?'

'Apomorphine Hydrochloride gave me the idea,' Croft snorted joyfully between masticating the wafer, 'It's an emetic injection for dogs who have eaten something poisonous like grapes, raisins, or a large amount of chocolate. It's particularly useful at Christmas because people leave mince pies and selection boxes around and the dogs binge on them, then get ill. We always make sure there's a supply in the practice around the holidays.'

Hugo was frowning.

'You injected him with a dog medicine… what did you call it?'

'An emetic. And no, of course not!' Croft scoffed, 'I gave

him a human emetic called Ipecac. But it produces the same result.'

Croft dug into the inside pocket of his coat and proudly dangled a small brown plastic bottle a few inches from Hugo's face.

'It makes the dog, or in this case, the creepy middle-aged man, throw up whatever's in their stomach. And I made it nice and strong so it worked within a few minutes.'

'So you injected him with it?' Hugo queried, sounding genuinely impressed.

Daniel returned him a self-satisfied smile, 'No, it's got to be swallowed. I squeezed it into his cup of tea as he was arguing with the serving staff. He didn't even notice.'

Hugo became thoughtful as the vet pocketed the brown bottle, 'So what about his face going red and swelling up?'

Daniel grinned, repulsing Hugo with the sight of chocolate and caramel gyrating around his mouth, 'Yeah, the poor dope is allergic to dogs! I read his emergency bracelet in the queue to pay. I treated a moulting Jack Russell before I left the surgery this morning and got covered in its hair, so I just collected a pinch.'

Daniel chuckled, 'I was worried the emetic wasn't going to work in time so I bumped into him as Lot 56 was going into the ring and flicked the hairs into his face. Did you see how quickly that rash came up? It was hilarious!'

Hugo found himself smiling back at his friend, maintaining it for a short while, then feeling uneasy, although he couldn't isolate the reason why.

Shortly afterwards the two men separated with a wave and a commitment from Hugo to go find Miriam Blunt. Daniel sauntered off to locate his car.

Two minutes later, a figure extricated himself from where he'd been hiding, hanging from the drive-shaft underneath Cooper's horsebox, and crawled out a little way. Satisfied there wasn't anyone close by, a swing of his legs from under the vehicle saw him leaping catlike to his feet in one fluid movement. He started to make off towards the sales ring but upon leaving the shadow of the horsebox he almost walked into a stable lass.

Good-natured apologies were swapped and they both continued on their way. For the next few paces the stable lass smiled to herself, wondering why someone would want a small exclamation mark tattooed on their neck, just below their ear. Her stride shortened and she looked back over her shoulder but the man was gone, lost among the vehicles scattered alongside the long white rails of the Doncaster Racecourse home straight.

Thirty-Three

It was mid-afternoon when Holly let herself into her mother's house in Northallerton. Hanging her bike helmet on the hatstand she checked her phone for missed calls. After listening to a message from Bain, excitedly explaining how he and Ronnie had thwarted a plot to defraud one of Graham Dent's owners, she rang back immediately, wanting more information. With no answer to her calls, either to her mother or Bain, she traipsed upstairs and took a shower, washing away the grime accumulated from her morning's work in Malton.

She had hoped to have a poke around the yard and speak with some more of the other lads and lasses, but the opportunity had never arisen. Instead, the work took over, and she'd laboured straight through until one o'clock, mucking out and freshening up the stables of five horses. Lara had turned up as her shift finished, inspected her stables, and judged them, 'Good enough, I suppose.'

Instructing Holly to be back at the yard the day after tomorrow for a six-thirty morning start, Lara had promised she would get to meet Graham Dent. Lara also mentioned that the assistant trainer, Hugo Dent, was likely to be around. The head lass had advised her to keep out of his way as much as possible. Holly had been left with the impression that both Lara and her mother held strikingly similar views of Hugo.

She was in her dressing gown, towel drying her hair when she heard the sound of someone on the stairs.

'Is that you Vladimir?'

She looked to her half open bedroom door, expecting a call up the stairs from the Widow Solanki, and Daisy to come shooting into her bedroom at a run, tail wagging furiously. Instead, there was a pause, then a baritone male voice drifted up from below.

'It's Robert. Robert Farley.'

I'm alone in the house with a man wanted for murder. The ramifications of this thought momentarily swirled around Holly's head like a swarm of angry gnats, but she shut them out by taking a second to stand stock still and concentrate on what she should do.

Heart pounding, Holly moved to the door and called out down the hallway, 'Robert? Please stay down there. It's Holly, I'll be down in a minute.'

Changing her mind, she added, 'Actually, no need to wait on the stairs, take a seat in the conservatory.'

She waited nervously for a reply, both hands gripping the top and bottom of her dressing gown tightly shut. After another pause the voice called out, 'I'll wait in the kitchen if you don't mind,' and there was the sound of footsteps leaving the stairs and crossing the hallway below.

Holly scampered around her bedroom, pulling on clean jeans and a t-shirt, her mind racing. Cursing herself for leaving her phone downstairs, she chose her running shoes over her other footwear options, pulled a comb through her hair, and ventured downstairs.

She found Robert in the kitchen, his back to her, busy making coffee. Noticing the door to the conservatory and garden were both ajar, she now knew how he'd gained entry. Her mother had forgotten to lock up again. He turned, spoon and coffee jar in hand, provided her with a broad smile and asked how she took her coffee and if she'd like a mug or cup. About to admonish him for breaking into the house and scaring her in the process, she answered his mundane query, her harsh words having gone clean out of her head. Robert Farley was a different man.

Gone were the army fatigues, backpack, and heavy duty boots. Instead, he wore a pair of camel chinos, a grey shirt and smart cotton jacket, admittedly a little crumpled, but with the addition of shiny black rider boots he carried off the look of an average working man with aplomb. Most striking was his clean-shaven face and short, neat hair. Only his eyes were still the same, holding a furtive nervousness that made it difficult for Holly to completely relax in his presence.

Robert noticed the confusion in Holly's face.

'The police are looking for an ex-forces professional and assume I'll be camping out, living rough, and staying away from people, and a razor,' he explained with a craggy smile, placing two mugs of coffee on the kitchen table, 'I've created the opposite look.'

Farley was certainly different to the mugshot the police had been circulating via the media for the last four days. The man in those photos looked haggard and middle-aged. This version of Farley was neat, many years younger, and eminently respectable. She could have walked past him in the street and not recognised him.

'Where are you…' she started, but trailed away and shook her head, 'Forget that, I don't need to know. Tell me why you've come back, Robert.'

'It was a risk,' he admitted, warming his hands on his mug, 'But I was desperate for an update.'

'Couldn't you phone, rather than breaking and entering?'

'No, ultra-risky,' he replied, ignoring her increasingly sharp tone, 'I expect all the communications in and out of this house will be being intercepted. And for the record, you really should get deadbolts for that conservatory, that way, each time you close the door it will automatically lock. Otherwise, anyone could walk in.'

'Quite,' Holly agreed, giving her uninvited guest a hard stare.

Farley's features crinkled up into a hurt expression laced with injustice. It was unexpectedly replaced by a flash of anger, a silent snarl that disappeared as quickly as it arrived. For a moment, Holly was reminded she was alone with Farley and tensed involuntarily.

He sighed deeply, 'I did knock.'

'Oh, well, I didn't…'

'I don't like creeping around in back gardens, you know,' he said earnestly, 'Until last week I was starting to get myself together again. I've spent the last thirty minutes in the bushes at the side of your house, waiting for Bainbridge or you to get home from Malton.'

'You knew I was in Malton?'

He nodded, 'I heard him telling your mother that you'd both get home at a similar time.'

'You *heard* him?' Holly said with a frown.

'At the Doncaster Sales, this morning,' replied Farley innocently. He swallowed a glug of his coffee but one look at Holly's incredulous face saw his expression darken.

'You were at the sales, the *horse sales,* with Bain this morning?'

'Not *with* him. I meant to catch him alone, but he was always with your mother and another woman. I was desperate for an update. That's why I'm here.'

'Were you driving a red mini?'

Farley shifted uncomfortably in his seat, seemingly embarrassed by the directness of her query. His slow nod confirmed he had been tailing Bain.

'Bain was convinced he was being followed, Robert. You scared him half to death!' Holly declared in an icy voice.

She took a sharp intake of breath. Hadn't that sounded

worryingly similar to the tone her mother used when she was unimpressed? Holly tried to ignore the comparison, confident she wasn't about to become her mother… or was it inevitable? God, what a depressing thought.

Farley took advantage of the pause in Holly's verbal assault to became apologetic again.

'I'm sorry. I guessed as much,' he shrugged, 'I backed off when he did a complete circuit of the Doncaster ring road.'

'And did sneaking around after Bain get you any information crucial to proving your innocence.'

Farley visibly crumpled a few inches in his seat.

'No,' he replied miserably, 'I'm sure something is going on in the Dent yard, but I'm damned if I can work out what it is. But I can't sleep for thinking about that poor girl and what 'snowdrop' meant to her.'

His downcast manner helped settle Holly's nerves. Her confidence in Farley returning, a feeling of compassion for her uninvited guest was growing within her.

'Robert, we really are doing everything we can to investigate Brooklyn's death,' she assured him, 'Bain is pursuing a direct route, like today at the sales, and I've been working at the Dent's yard in Malton today.'

Farley brightened somewhat, so she continued. Speaking in a measured voice Holly explained where she'd been that morning and her reasons for taking a job at the Beverley Hill stables. However, she was careful not to mention her conversations with the various members of Dent's team, or reveal the extent of the fraudulent activities Bain had uncovered at Doncaster sales.

'As long as Bain can keep investigating, and I'm able to poke around the stables and gain the trust of stable staff, I'm sure we'll turn over something,' Holly said in conclusion, 'Like you say, there is definitely something going on.'

Farley had listened attentively and the worry lines cut deep in his forehead and downward arc of his mouth now retained a semblance of hope.

'But you shouldn't be coming back here, or following either of us around. You increase your chances of being caught, you'll get in our way like you did this morning... and to be honest, Robert... it's a bit creepy. I jumped out of my skin when I heard you coming up the stairs.'

Shoulders hunched, head bowed, hands in his lap, Farley mumbled another heartfelt apology.

And then to Holly's surprise, he continued talking. He spoke uninterrupted, never lifting his head. Holly listened patiently at first, but was soon hanging on every word until the wanted man was spent, his story complete. The kitchen dropped silent, Holly dabbing at the tears welling up unbidden in the corner of her eyes.

'I'm sorry... for all of it,' she said in a small voice.

'It's not an excuse,' he sniffed, 'But it's probably why the police can't see beyond me as Brooklyn's killer.'

There was the sound of the front door being opened and voices. Three voices.

Farley's eyes widened and he froze, questioning her desperately with eyebrows high on his forehead. She held up a flat palm, then signalled to Farley by placing a finger to her closed lips.

'I'll go see,' Holly whispered.

Crossing the kitchen, desperately wiping her face with her sleeve to remove the evidence of her tears, she slipped into the hallway and made sure to close the kitchen door behind her. Bain and her mother were in conversation, busy hanging up hats and coats. Behind them another woman Holly couldn't quite place was asking questions about, of all things, the racehorse handicapping system. The woman looked up and smiled at Holly and the name Miriam came into her head.

Noticing Holly for the first time, Bain gave her a quick wave.

'Hiya,' he called out, 'Everything...?'

His voice trailed away as he took in her tear stained cheeks, worried eyes, and pursed lips.

'...okay?' he finished, half-heartedly.

Ronnie didn't look up, being consumed with pulling on her house slippers.

'Ah, hello darling! We have a visitor. Put the kettle on will you?'

Slippers applied, and without waiting for an answer, Ronnie hustled Miriam down the hallway towards her daughter.

Holly was momentarily lost for words. The most wanted man in Britain was in her kitchen and the force of nature that was her mother was bearing down on her, unaware she was about to introduce her new found friend to the prime suspect in a murder case. Miriam *had* to know who Farley was.

Determined to stop them, Holly stared meaningfully into her mother's eyes.

Ronnie blinked at her daughter, questioning her with a frown, then announced, 'You look a bit peaky, my love. Oh, by the way, this is Mimi. We met at the sales today.'

'Hello, Mimi,' said Holly, swerving past her mother and planting herself in front of the lady, shaking her hand. This effectively halted their progress into the kitchen.

'So nice to meet you,' Holly said quickly, pumping her hand up and down, then addressing Bain she added, 'Perhaps you'd all like to take your tea in the dining room?'

Mimi said that would be fine, but Ronnie was having none of it.

'What nonsense! It will be freezing in the dining room. What's wrong with the kitchen?' Ronnie adopted a low voice and asked with a comically raised eyebrow, 'You got a man in there?'

Alarm bells were now ringing in Bain's brain. Holly looked awful and was acting oddly. He was about to dodge around all three of the ladies, take a peek in the kitchen and discover what was causing Holly such upset, but Ronnie got there first. Striding forward, she flung the kitchen door open.

'Really Holly, allow Mimi to come in, will you? Oh!'

Holly followed her mother into the kitchen, fearing the worst. The room was empty.

'Oh darling, you haven't cleared the pots away from breakfast,' Ronnie scolded, 'Never mind, soon sorted!'

Ronnie took up the two mugs of half-drunk tea and proceeded to drop them onto the pedal bin in the corner of the room. She turned to Mimi and smiling broadly, asked what she would like to drink.

'Shut the conservatory door, will you, Holly?' Ronnie added, 'There's a draft.'

Relief flooding though her, Holly entered the conservatory and closed the door into the garden. There was no sign of Farley, but if you looked carefully you could see size twelve footmarks pressed into the soft spring turf. They plotted a course through the fruit trees and down to the bottom of the garden.

She became aware of someone behind her and was pleased when it turned out to be Bain. He stood beside her, looking out through the conservatory door. She pointed a finger at the grass and he examined the marks, murmuring, 'I see them,' after a few seconds.

'Sorry I wasn't here to help,' he added quietly, 'Farley?'

Still facing down the garden, Holly nodded, her eyes scanning the garden wall some fifty yards distant, imagining Farley vaulting over the six foot brick obstacle in his chinos, sports jacket, and shiny shoes.

'We uncovered a fraudulent business practice today, but we're no nearer to finding Brooklyn's killer,' reported Bain, 'Satisfying, but not what we were looking for. How about you?'

'It's still early days,' she told him.

Bain sensed a bitterness in Holly's words. It surfaced rarely, however, when it occurred he always looked upon it as a positive, rather than negative sign. It meant she was engaged. He'd no doubt find out why when Mimi wasn't around, but he did wonder what Farley had said to get Holly so wound up.

Without warning she spun around to face him.

'Farley shared something with me,' she said with steely determination, 'I don't care how long it takes. We're going to expose the Dents and find Brooklyn's killer. I'm in this for the long haul.'

'Good to hear,' said Bain, 'Because I have a job for you that will require an early start tomorrow.'

Thirty-Four

It was eight-thirty the day after the breeze-up sale when Bain walked into the Rous Stud in Malton and asked to see Adrian Cooper. As the stable lass rushed off, Bain used the time to cast a critical eye around the place.

By the time Cooper was striding towards him, he'd come to the conclusion that whatever extra profit had come the stud's way for inflating the price of his yearlings, it was going to take much more than that to reverse the years of neglect he saw around him.

'I know why you're here,' Cooper said as he approached, 'And I know who you are. Moran told us about you.'

Before Bain could reply, Cooper went on, 'Promise me you're not recording this and I'll tell you what I know.'

'I'm a sports journalist. I always record everything,' Bain said, removing his phone from his pocket and showing it to the stud manager, 'But only if I get permission.'

Bain tapped the stop icon and showed Cooper the recording program was no longer running. The stud manager sniffed his approval.

'I've told Dent I'm finished with him, ' Cooper said, his hands crossed defiantly over his chest, 'If my business fails due to me breeding bad racehorses, I'm okay with that. I don't want it to fail because I get sent to prison.'

'You won't be sent to prison, Mr Cooper,' Bain assured him, 'Ms Blunt won't be pursuing the matter any further and she's decided against informing the two owners affected by your fraudulent activities.'

Cooper stared at the cracked concrete floor and appeared to sag, his eyes becoming glassy for a moment.

'I'm relieved to hear that, and very, very grateful. I know it won't mean much to her, but please pass on my apologies to Miri… erm, Ms Blunt.'

'She's removing her original two-year-old from the Dent yard today, and the horse she bought from you yesterday was transported straight to the Thorne's training yard in Middleham.'

The stud manager pushed out his bottom lip and nodded.

'Mr Cooper, as far as I'm concerned the episode at the sales is concluded. I'm here to ask you whether you know anything at all about the accident, or the death of Brooklyn Hartley.'

Cooper's demeanour altered. He clearly hadn't expected this question. Uncrossing his arms, he stroked his chin for a few seconds before offering his answer.

'I don't know anything about the girl. Didn't they call her the Good Morning Girl on telly? I heard about the accident and then that dreadful stuff on the news, and that hunt for the maniac that killed her, but I have very little contact with the girls at the Dent yard.'

He considered a moment, 'I do know about Mrs Blunt's filly though. She was mine until Ms Blunt bought her at the yearling sales last August. Was a nice horse, but I understand she's had plenty of setbacks. The filly was fine when she was with me, but that's horses for you, fine one day and dead the next.'

'She's not dead, Mr Cooper.'

'Might as well be, if she can't do her job,' he retorted, 'In my world, a horse that can't do a job is costing me money I don't have.'

Spoken like a true horseman, thought Bain, remaining expressionless.

'I notice that lot 56 was sold under your name. I was led to believe Mr Blunt had taken ownership of that horse?'

With lips pursed, Cooper took a few seconds to answer, 'I didn't take his threat seriously. His argument was with his ex-wife, not me. Now, if that's all…'

'One last question,' Bain cut in, worried Cooper was trying to close the conversation down, 'Does the word 'Snowdrop' mean anything to you?'

Cooper thought for a moment, then shook his head.

'Perhaps a horse's stable name, or someone Brooklyn Hartley may have known in Malton?'

Another pause for thought eventually brought a shrug from Cooper.

The stud manager's reaction seemed genuine enough, so Bain didn't labour the point any further. He thanked Cooper and made to leave, but was unexpectedly halted a moment later.

'Listen, there's stuff that goes on in that yard of Dent's that isn't right,' Cooper said suddenly, his words heavy with bitterness, 'I happened to be there when that stable lass, Geena, left. If what she was saying is right… well then, the Dents are into far darker stuff than bidding up the price of a few horses at the sales.'

Nodding a curt farewell to Bain, Cooper turned on his heel.

Bain was reeling, and set off after him. Geena? Hadn't Holly mentioned that name before?

'What did this Geena say, Mr Cooper?'

Cooper waved a hand, indicating the interview was over, 'Not my problem, Geena can tell you. I'm finished with Dent, and his staff.'

'Geena who?'

'Coulter,' Cooper replied gruffly.

Bain tried again, but Cooper ignored the question, disappearing through a shed door and locking it behind him. Bain waited for a short while in the hope he might get more information, but soon gave up. He needed to spend some time looking into Geena Coulter. Perhaps Holly knew more about her, or could try quizzing her workmates at Dent's yard.

Cooper watched the journalist leave through a dusty window further up the shed. Unbidden, Geena's face on the night she was hounded out of the Dent's yard squirrelled its way into his mind. He winced. He shouldn't have mentioned her. Why did he? And to a journalist?

Cooper passed a hand over a brow that was slick with sweat. He knew the answer. In those moments of reflection and regret, it was that young girls' face that pricked his conscience. No one had seen or heard of her since that autumn night... and that was nearly six months ago.

Thirty-Five

He was a chip off the old block. Everyone said so. And Daniel Croft knew it to be true. He was a replica of his father, both in character and physical presence. With no mother to compare himself to, and grandparents his father had disowned, he only had one person, his father, Leslie Croft, a vet with a carefully manufactured unblemished reputation, to measure himself against.

From an early age Daniel recognised he was different to the other children. While they played, built lasting friendships, loved, and lost, he manipulated and milked relationships exclusively for his own benefit. He couldn't help it, after all, being dishonest and disingenuous were both fascinating and rewarding. He embraced this difference, emulating his father. Father and son were both good looking, charming, and endowed with an innate ability to get what they wanted. In short, they were able to manipulate, cheat, and lie with impunity.

Daniel never lost sleep worrying about anyone else. What was the point of that?

'Why should I fight it?' he'd asked the bespectacled female therapist who had been tasked with dealing with the troublesome fourteen-year-old who had been caught masterminding the practically industrial theft and re-selling of bicycles from all the schools within a thirty mile radius in his last year at middle school, 'Why be honest, when I'm so good at being dishonest?'

The therapist had removed her glasses and stared with bafflement into the young man's hard blue eyes.

'Daniel, doesn't it bother you that your actions upset the people around you?'

'Not really,' he admitted, 'I'm good like that.'

Daniel had eventually agreed to go away and think hard about honesty.

'I'll try. I'll consider how my actions affect others. I'll see things from your point of view,' he promised the therapist with the contrite puppy-dog gaze he saved for these conversations.

It took the therapist fifteen minutes to work out that Daniel had stolen her glasses from her desk whilst promising to reform. They were found by a third former whilst eating her lunch, having been pushed into her rice pudding when she wasn't looking.

The therapist's subsequent report categorised Daniel as a 'Successful Psychopath'. His father had laughed out loud upon reading this. It had really tickled him. Then his father had asked him whether he'd learned anything from the therapist. Daniel had thought hard and answered honestly. Only his father ever got an honest answer from Daniel.

'I learnt that I don't like getting caught.'

Pleased with his offspring, Leslie Croft had nodded sagely and offered his own advice, 'Always have a way out, an escape route, a back-up plan, an exit strategy. If you have an out, even when things go wrong, it makes you untouchable.'

With these words of wisdom stowed away in the young Daniel Croft's brain, he'd spent the remaining years of his education, as his father had done, successfully bribing, cheating, stealing, and blackmailing his way through university and veterinary school. At the age of twenty-five he'd joined his father's practice in Malton and immediately became his father's right-hand man – learning from the master.

Daniel knew he was no more than an adequate vet. That didn't matter. His focus wasn't on the animals he treated, his interest in his patients, and specifically, racehorses, was purely financial. As a result, Daniel was drawn to the racing yards dotted around the town. It was in these places he found his range of specialised abilities could be best utilised. And there was one yard in Malton that for various reasons stood out; the Graham Dent yard.

Daniel had come across Hugo Dent in his second week back in Malton, befriending the younger man and, yes, flirting a little. He soon discovered Hugo was complicated, intense, driven, and most importantly, naïve. He wanted to break away from his parents, to prove himself in his own way, to go it alone, rather than following the path his parents had mapped out for him. But that took money.

Daniel had taken Hugo under his wing, suggesting to the eager, green, and over-confident Hugo the ease with which one could extract profit from rich owners who, in most cases, were totally unaware of how the racing industry operated. When they had enough money set aside, they would set up on their own. A young trainer with a good racing pedigree, plus a young vet with a talent for treating racehorses; the perfect combination.

This was why Daniel had arrived at the Dent's yard nice and early today, much earlier than usual. Hugo had tracked Miriam Blunt down at the sales, but the lady had been insistent, her filly wasn't for sale and would be leaving Beverley Hill Stables for the David Thorne yard over in Middleham. A yard over which Daniel held no influence. That being the case, he had work to do on that filly. She couldn't be allowed to leave the yard, not without him being there.

It can't have been more than a few minutes past six o'clock when he reached the barn reserved for the fillies and mares. He was such a regular in the yard, no one would question his presence, even at this hour. In a yard of this size, there was always a horse that needed attention, and that provided him with a ready excuse. All the same, with sunrise still a few minutes away, the dim barn lights were a welcome aid, allowing him to silently slip along in the shadows of each stable until he reached the home of Morgan, Miriam Blunt's two-year-old filly.

Daniel checked up and down the barn's central corridor. He was alone. There was a chance Wendy or Graham Dent might be wandering the barns at this time, but the lads and lasses didn't start until six thirty. He had at least twenty minutes, and the injection he was about to administer would only take a few seconds. Unlocking the stable door he entered the filly's box and almost jumped out of his skin.

'Early start is it?' asked Holly from the shadows in the corner of the box, enjoying Daniel's reaction.

She moved forward, placing herself between the filly and Daniel and looked the young vet up and down, 'Can I help you?'

'What the hell?' gasped Daniel, a hand clamped to his chest.

'I'm sorry, did I frighten you?'

The vet glared at the woman. He didn't recognise her. She had to be new. But what on earth was she doing hiding in the shadows of the stable that contained the one horse he needed to… treat?

'I'm the stable vet. I need to see to this filly… erm,

what's your name?'

'Holly'

'Okay, Holly, I need you to leave please.'

Holly had been watching Daniel carefully from the recesses of the stable, having heard him approach. The way he'd slinked up the barn and checked for signs of other people had spoken volumes. She had to hand it to Bain, he'd been right to send her into the yard early to watch over Morgan once they knew Mimi was going to move the filly. And she wasn't about to allow this pipsqueak to get anywhere near the filly.

'I can't do that,' Holly replied.

Daniel smiled. Holly didn't reciprocate.

'If you run along and see Hugo, or Mr and Mrs Dent, they will confirm that I...'

'The owner of this filly, spoke to Mr Dent yesterday. The filly is leaving in a quarter of an hour and I'm getting her ready for the transport,' lied Holly.

'All the same, I should check...'

'Er... and Mrs Blunt also instructed Mr Dent that Morgan wasn't to be given any further medical treatment,' she added tersely.

This last instruction hadn't actually happened, but Holly was sure Mimi wouldn't want some small, slimy vet pawing over her filly before she left.

Daniel didn't move. He simply cocked his head to one side and looked at her with a mixture of curiosity and amusement. A bolt of vulnerability shot through Holly, making her shudder. For all she knew, they were the only people on the yard at this time in the morning.

'I only wanted to check her over before she left,' he said quietly, 'It's standard practice before a horse leaves one yard for another. Feel free to stay and watch... if you wish.'

In other circumstances Holly would have stepped aside. After all, it was a sensible thing for a vet to be doing, wasn't it? Yet it didn't feel right. All her journalistic senses told her so. Was Daniel Croft really here to inspection of the filly? Or was he here to do her harm? Perhaps she could find out…

'The new trainer is picking her up. If you're so worried about her, I'll tell him to get a full medical report on Morgan once she's reached Middleham. You satisfied with that?'

Daniel stared at Holly for a long moment, then gave a disgruntled sigh, 'As you wish. Tell them a full screening would be best. That's what I intended.'

'What the hell!' Holly screamed silently within herself. She stared back at the vet, desperately seeking an indication of scheming in his expression. He looked slightly irked, but nothing more.

'What's this? A mothers meeting?'

Holly and Daniel both jumped as Lara's face appeared between the bars of Morgan's stable, her eyes taking in the standoff between stable lass and vet.

After the initial shock of finding Lara's face pressed to the bars had worn off, Holly found herself quietly pleased to have her there. In contrast, Daniel looked irritated.

'Out. Both of you,' Lara ordered, 'Thornes transport has arrived. Morgan's leaving. I'll take her down. Holly, get on with your stables.'

Daniel, seizing this renewed opportunity, told Lara he needed time to examine the filly, but the head lass gave him short shrift, telling him she didn't have time to argue. The transport was waiting. Holly and Daniel were shooed out of the stable and watched as Lara led Morgan down the barn and to a new life.

'That's a sick horse,' Daniel commented with a sigh, 'I just wanted to make sure she was okay to travel.'

Holly gave him a prim smile and turned to walk away. She'd make herself busy in another barn for the next half an hour. It wouldn't do to have her cover blown if David or Mary Thorne were driving their horsebox and recognised her. But she would be phoning David after her shift finished to make sure that a full screening of Morgan was completed by an independent vet as soon as she arrived at their yard.

'I'm Daniel Croft,' the vet called after Holly, 'What's your full name?'

'Holly. It's just Holly.'

Standing stock still, Daniel watched the new stable lass retreat down the barn. The first weak rays of the new morning were lighting up the open end of the barn, providing him with a silhouette of her tall, athletic figure.

Once she had been enveloped by the barn door and he was alone, Daniel picked up his bag and allowed the smirk he'd been withholding to burst forth. That couldn't have gone any better!

Thirty-Six

May 17th

Despite Bain's best efforts, Geena Coulter was remaining annoyingly illusive. He'd spoken to dozens of people. He and Holly had tried everyone they considered a potential source of information to her whereabouts. While Holly probed the stable staff at Dent's yard, Bain had questioned DI Golden, Brooklyn's mother again, and even the people at the Doncaster Racing School. The story was always the same, after her time at the Dents, the trail went cold. Even Golden couldn't help, although she was able to supply an address for Geena's family, now living in London. Bain had got to speak with her father and discovered they hadn't heard from their daughter in over a year. Bain got the impression this was perfectly normal for their daughter, and her family weren't worried about her at all, despite the fact that to all intents and purposes, she had ceased to exist since last October.

Over the last three weeks, Bain had executed hundreds, if not thousands of internet and social media searches, all of which had ended in dead ends, and ultimately, failure. The girl's only online mention was in a Facebook page in her own name that hadn't been updated for seven months, the same time she'd left the Dent's yard.

The page was composed of a handful of photos, each with a single line of explanatory text. The images were taken at the Dent's yard, and always with a racehorse. According to her profile, she was twenty years old and still lived in Malton, which Bain had taken with a pinch of salt, but investigated nonetheless. He'd scoured every bulletin board, racing forum, horse lovers websites, and even dating sites for any mention of Malton, Geena, and Coulter. Then he'd done the same again, replacing Malton with Liverpool and Geena for Gina, then Gena, just in case. Every search provided a blank result. And despite Coulter being a popular surname in Liverpool, there wasn't a single Geena Coulter to be found.

He'd turned instead to trying to track down any previous employers, but that too led up a blind alley. He was left with a single known fact: Geena Coulter had vanished in late October and hadn't resurfaced since.

After several weeks of trying, Geena hadn't responded to any of the plethora of messages he'd left her via Facebook, urging her to get in touch. With a sense desperation and the threat of failure looming large, Bain drafted in Holly's help. Her internet skills had proved in the past to be far greater than his own, and yet following a week of intense searching, even she had to admit that bar the Facebook page, the girl's online presence was negligible and she had exhausted all Geena's online friends - none of them knew where she had gone. Bain was on the verge of giving up… it was almost like the girl was dead.

Holly's investigations in the yard over the last few weeks had provided similar results. Her few days at the yard had turned into weeks, as her investigations were moving at a slow pace. None of the stable staff knew why Geena had left so suddenly, or where she went, although her strong, somewhat fruity language and thick scouse accent had been mentioned by almost everyone. Holly had committed to another week of being a stable lass, but if she didn't get a breakthrough soon, she'd be leaving Beverley Hill Stables empty handed, apart from her minimum rate hourly pay.

Holly had even quizzed Hugo, Graham Dent, and Daniel Croft about both Geena and Brooklyn, casually dropping their names into conversation after mentioning the Farley manhunt. She had met a wall of silence from Daniel and in Graham Dent's case a complaint that Geena had left him short staffed by her sudden departure. Hugo's reaction was the most interesting, resorting to calling Geena annoying, accusing her of being work-shy, and storming off. Despite having touched a nerve, Holly had backed off, fearing further questioning might prompt Hugo to become suspicious of her motives.

She'd considered asking Lara if she knew where Geena had gone, but had eventually decided against it. Over the course of the last few weeks Holly had noticed that Lara's treatment of Hugo was carefully measured. Lara was protective of Hugo, despite the quite disgusting way he treated the other members of staff. Having joined the yard five years ago, Lara had quickly been promoted to head lass and she certainly knew how to play the Dents. Holly wondered whether Lara allowed Hugo some slack because she realised he was being groomed by his parents to take over the trainer's responsibilities in due course.

Lucy and Courtney, being the youngest, were regular targets for Hugo's curt management style. It was during one of Courtney's stand-up rows with him, over whether a particular stable had been prepared to the correct standard, that Holly had been witness to Lara breaking the argument up in a rather peculiar way.

Lara had sent Hugo away with nothing more than a sour look, then scolded Courtney for placing herself in a situation that allowed Hugo to criticise her. Lara had become aware that Holly was listening in the next stable and had advised her, 'Mark my words, prevention is better than the cure where Hugo is concerned.'

There was definitely something between Hugo and Lara, but Holly couldn't quite work out what it might be. As she'd told Bain, it certainly wasn't a romance, Hugo wasn't that sort of man. And she'd overheard Amber and Courtney making fun of Lara, the former claiming Lara had never had a partner because she never left work, rarely leaving the stables. Courtney had responded by saying that the whole town of Malton knew about Lara, but had never met her.

This declaration had elicited a fit of giggles from the two of them and dire warnings to, 'keep quiet about that' from Lucy and Mary, noting that Lara was currently helping herself to a biscuit at the other end of the tea hut. Puzzled by this conversation, some of the work riders had sought clarification from the girls. No explanation had been forthcoming, apart from being told to mind their own business.

Holly had long since given up on her surreptitious questioning of the current group of stable staff. Over the past few weeks she had asked all eight of them whether they knew anything about Brooklyn or her death, and apart from learning that it was a 'German' horse, that had given her the kick that almost killed her the first time, it had become clear that Geena was the most likely key to unlocking any hidden secrets. She'd even approached some of the professional jockeys that frequented the stables. Most of them knew Brooklyn's name because of the media coverage surrounding the ongoing manhunt, but hadn't known her well, and all of them had little or no knowledge of Geena.

Despite their combined hard work, Holly and Bain were no closer to finding Geena Coulter and asking her why she left so suddenly, and asking her who at Beverley Hill Stables might have a reason for killing Brooklyn.

The one lead that did help Holly, albeit to rule people out, rather than in, was the rota book. This dog-eared tome resided in the tea hut, pinned to a cork board by a length of string, and held the fortnightly shifts for everyone. Holly had gone back to October and the day Brooklyn was kicked and injured, to see who was working. She's also done the same for the day she was killed in York. However, this information was soon forgotten when Holly realised the rota wasn't updated when someone was sick, late in, or had swapped their shifts with someone else. The rota didn't prove anything. Any of the dozen or so employees of Graham and Wendy Dent could have travelled to York on the morning Brooklyn was murdered.

The one thing that became clear to Holly after only a few days as a stable lass, was who really ran the yard. And it certainly wasn't Graham Dent. As the figurehead, he was synonymous with the stables, and it was his name in the race listings and daily papers, but in reality it was Lara and to a greater extent, Graham's wife, Wendy, who made the place tick. The consummate horsewoman, Lara got the horses fit and ready, and managed the staff, while Wendy was always on the yard, keeping the ship straight and water-tight, managing everything on the racing side including entries, jockey bookings, and transport, as well as dealing with owners. Wendy also had a firm grip on the purse strings. Graham and Hugo flitted around the yard like butterflies, landing on something, or someone, every now and again, but to no lasting effect and wielding little in the way of real power.

It took a chance meeting with an apprentice jockey for Holly's big breakthrough to happen. She'd been called out into the main yard by Hugo. He was goading the small freelancer from the back of his own mare because the lad couldn't jump on a rather large mare's back from the ground. Holly was ordered to give the lad a leg up. The lad had been really light, and Holly had almost thrown him over the filly's back, but he'd seen the funny side and they'd had a quick conversation.

'By the way, is Geena back yet?' he'd asked Holly, just before they'd pulled out.

Her heart had leaped at the mention of Geena's name, but she'd tried to keep calm, and her voice low, in front of Hugo, Mary, Lara, and the other five mounted riders.

'No, she isn't here,' she replied.

The boy looked disappointed.

'Back from where?' queried Holly.

The boy had frowned down at her, 'France, of course.'

It had taken forty minutes of waiting around in the stables car park after her shift had finished for Holly to collar the apprentice and find out more before he shot off to Thirsk races. He'd been in France for the winter, riding on their All-Weather circuit and that's where he'd met Geena, leading up for an Anglo-French trainer. Recognising her from the Dent yard a few months earlier, he'd taken a shine to her. It seemed his interest was reciprocated as he'd spent a few hours with her at the Canne-sur-Mer racetrack. They'd got on well and the two of them had promised to meet up back in Britain. Yes, he had her mobile number and didn't have a problem sharing it with Holly.

And this was why Holly and Bain were currently up in their attic office sitting side by side and staring nervously at her laptop screen as the software tried to connect to a video call with Geena Coulter.

The call connected and a colourful image of a girl's face appeared with rolling grass hills in the background. The sun was shining so brightly behind the girl's head, it kept whiting out the image every few seconds.

'Sorry!' said the girl with a laugh, 'I'll turn around, I'm sun-blasting you.'

Bain slid Holly an encouraging look. The blonde, pixie-faced girl had a thick scouse accent. The image came back a third time to reveal a changed image, another grassy backdrop, but this time displaying a patchwork of paddocks inhabited by dozens of horses. Geena Coulter peered down into her phone at them.

'Hi Geena,' Holly said with a smile, 'Such a nice name.'

'Brookie! Where've you been? I've told you before, my mum loved that film, the one with Geena Davis and the car…'

The girl flicked a lock of her shoulder length hair out of her eyes with two fingers and squinted into her phone.

'Who is it? Is that you, Brookie?'

'No, Geena, I'm called Holly, and this is Bain… You don't know us, but…'

Geena cut in, 'Who are you? I've only ever given this phone number to...'

Worried she was about to hang up, Bain interrupted.

'We got your details from Finn Green, the apprentice jockey – I think he's friend of yours?

Geena shrugged, 'Yeah, Finn's… Hey, who are you again?'

'I'm Bain and this is Holly, we're investigative journalists. We've been trying to track you down for weeks. We need to speak to you about Brooklyn… er, I mean, Brookie…'

Geena's brow dived into a frown, and her expression filled with concern, 'What about her?'

Bain traded a look with Holly that asked, 'Who's best to tell her?' and she returned him the slightest of nods and silently mouthed, 'You.'

Bain swallowed hard, steeled himself, and as he spoke, witnessed the expectant eyes of the young woman crumple into a torrent of grief. It felt like hours, rather than minutes to explain the events that led from Brooklyn's accident to her subsequent death. When he'd finished and her questions had finally dried up, Bain waited for Geena to compose herself and then posed the question he'd wanted to ask since the call had begun.

'Geena, we could really do with your help to work out who killed Brookie. We've been focussing on the Beverley Hill Stables and we've already uncovered fraudulent business practices used by the Dents'. We wanted to know…'

'You know about doping?' Geena queried with surprise, her eyes glistening with more tears ready to trickle down her already streaked cheeks.

Bain was about to clarify when Holly's hand shot out under the desk and gripped Bain hard, digging her nails in just above his knee. A jolt of pain ran through him.

'Yes, Geena, we know,' Holly answered, 'Can you tell us how *you* know?'

'They said no one else would get to know,' Geena said bitterly, 'And that they would stop hurting the horse.'

'Stop what, exactly,' Holly pressed.

'Hugo and that evil little vet of his, Crofty,' Geena answered automatically, 'I caught them doing a tracheal wash of their vile stuff to one of the yearlings. I'd had enough. I was on my way to tell the owner on my bike but they caught up with me, offered to give me money and to relocate me over here in the sun… I love the sun…'

Geena looked away from her phone, 'I left Brookie… they said I wasn't to contact anyone...'

Her face disappeared from view, and the image became unfocussed.

'Geena? Geena…' called out Holly, 'Did Brookie know what Hugo and the vet were doing?'

The image swung around, turning from green to blue, then white.

Holly tried again, more urgent this time, 'This is important, Geena! Did Brooklyn know?'

The image solidified from a mass of green, into a small patch of grass. As Holly repeated her question again, the image swung and Geena's head and shoulders appeared. She was a shadow of the vibrant young girl who had answered their call minutes earlier. Her eyes were red, hair ruffled from where she'd been running her hands through it, and her face, now devoid of make-up in places thanks to her tears, displayed a number of deep wrinkles.

'Geena, did Brookie have evidence of what the Dents were doing?' Bain asked in a soft voice.

The girl stared back at them for a long moment. Sensing Bain was about to break into the silence, Holly strengthened her grip on his knee once more. Geena continued to eye the two of them, swaying slightly, weighing whether to answer or not. She spoke again, but looked away from the phone, as if embarrassed by her admission.

'Yes,' she whispered, 'I told her before I left the country.'

'Thank you,' Holly replied, wishing there was some way she could push through the screen and give the girl a reassuring hug.

Keen to push on, Bain asked, 'Geena, do you know what Brookie might have meant by Snowdrop?'

The girl's eyebrows leapt up her forehead and her mouth opened into a panic stricken, 'Oh'.

'You didn't know! You lied to me!' she exclaimed, fury in her eyes, 'You tricked me!'

Before Bain or Holly could react, Geena shouted, 'Don't call me again!' angrily at them and hung up the video call.

Holly and Bain stared at the blank screen.

'You did record that, didn't you?' she asked.

He nodded, his mind full of answers, and even more questions.

'There's more than sales fraud going on at the Beverley Hill Stables. We may have just found our motive for Brookies... er, Brooklyn's murder.'

'Let's watch it again,' suggested Holly, tingling with excitement.

'Fine,' he replied, biting his lip, 'But can you please stop digging your fingernails into my leg? I think you've broken the skin…'

Thirty-Seven

Daniel Croft had grown to hate working in the cellar. His father always made him do this part of the process because it was dusty and dirty. The oxygen mask was heavy and making his face sweat, and despite it covering both mouth and nose, it couldn't hide the fact that one or two of the chemicals he was handling smelled like rotten eggs. When he thought harder about it, all his tasks in the cellar required him to do menial, dirty, and repetitive work.

He dusted off the last batch, decanted them into a transparent plastic bag, weighed and sealed it, and put it with the rest. Tearing at the rubber straps around his head, he whipped off the mask and sucked in a welcome breath of real air. Leaning against one of the shiny steel benches, Daniel coughed, before filling his lungs again. The air tasted sweet, and when a few of the airborne specks of dust hit his lungs he received a small jolt that made him cough again.

'Finished?' called out his father.

Daniel just nodded, too tired to reply. It was three o'clock in the morning. It was okay for his father, he didn't do the grunt work, he just mixed ingredients. It had been exciting when he'd started doing this, aged fourteen, staying up until all hours, working with his father. That excitement had waned with the years. At twenty-six, Daniel no longer looked forward to playing a supporting role in the family business.

'How many pounds?' asked his father from the other side of the stark white basement. Already showered and changed, he was pulling on a sports jacket.

The corners of Daniel's mouth turned down, unable to hide the resentment building in his sleep-deprived mind. No doubt his father would be straight up the thin stone steps, the only way in and out of this sparkling white, windowless den. He'd be in bed and snoring a good two hours before him, Daniel thought bitterly.

'Almost fifty-one pounds,' he reported, pausing to

yawn, 'Over by twelve ounces.'

'Good. Always better to give the client a little extra,' his father responded, as he started up the steps. He noticed his son was silently mouthing his exact words.

'I'd prefer the product to be at the pick-up-point…'

'Tonight, yes, I know,' Daniel snapped, 'I'll take it, like I always do.'

Leslie Croft reversed down the stairs, covered the fifteen feet between him and his son in quick time, and landed a hard slap that saw Daniel's right-hand cheek immediately flare scarlet. His son didn't lift a hand, he didn't yell or scream. Daniel had known it would happen as soon as his father had turned around and he'd seen those eyes darken and become riven with malice.

'Wake up, do your job, and stop whingeing.'

His father made for the steps again, 'I've told you. The world owes you nothing. The only way the likes of me and you come out on top is through hard work and always being one step ahead of people who get in the way. There will come a time when you'll thank me for how I've shaped your life.'

Thirty-Eight

18th May

The incessant clicking was starting to get on Bain's nerves, so he was relieved when Vladimir suddenly piped up, 'For the love of God, Ronnie, will you please stop knitting!'

The four of them were in Bain and Holly's office on the top floor of the house in Northallerton, staring at Bain's wall-mounted whiteboard filled with photos and names. Even Ronnie, still busy clicking, was staring at the wall of suspects, somehow able to successfully clack away without looking down at what the needles were doing. Vladimir issued a pointed sigh in her direction and this time Ronnie's needles ceased their industrious clicking.

'I'll never get four Christmas jumpers finished for December at this rate,' she complained, dropping the half-finished jumper, wool, and needles onto her lap in disgust, 'We've been staring at that board for fifteen minutes now and it's mired in confusion. We still haven't any solid lead on who murdered Brooklyn!'

Daisy gave a little whine, padded over to Ronnie and sank her head onto her lap. Muzzle buried in a mess of wool, her tail wagging hopefully, Daisy swivelled her eyes up to meet Ronnie's gaze, only to recoil and sneeze a moment later, her nose tickled by the wool in the half-finished jumper.

'Keep on clicking those needles like that and you'll have another murder on your hands. I won't be able to help myself,' Vladimir muttered irritably, 'Even Daisy is unimpressed, and she thinks you're wonderful.'

'At least we'd know the reason for Ronnie's murder,' Holly offered miserably.

'Well that's just lovely!' trumpeted Ronnie, 'Make fun of murdering me, why don't you?'

'I spoke with Golden the other day,' said Bain, keen to reign in the discussion and get back on track, 'And by the way, she may call in later this morning.'

Leaning against the back wall, hands in jeans pockets, he'd moved around the room during Ronnie and Vladimir's spat, hoping a different angle on the whiteboard's contents might help solve the puzzle. It hadn't.

'I told Golden we'd exposed Graham and Hugo Dent to one of their owners as fraudulent dealers in racehorses,' he added without any conviction.

'Good!' declared Ronnie, 'So she's going to charge them with…?'

Bain grimaced, 'Nothing. As expected. Proving Conor Moran was acting as a rogue bidder is impossible without him admitting to it, and it's difficult to pin anything on Graham or Hugo Dent, or even Gregory Blunt for that matter.'

'Why not?' demanded Ronnie.

Bain scratched the back of his head and wrinkled his nose, 'If they all keep stum, there's no proof of any wrongdoing. And each one of them have good reasons to remain silent, so they don't implicate themselves.'

Ronnie picked up her needles and in a stew, began to knit angrily, soon losing her patience, throwing everything to the floor and harrumphing loudly.

'Did Cooper and the Dent's know Mr Blunt was allergic to dogs?' she asked testily, 'If they did, and purposefully brought it on, it was a pretty nasty trick. He could have died, but for Mimi's quick work.'

Vladimir stared blankly at Ronnie, his mouth hanging open, the conversation now completely lost on him.

'Possibly,' ventured Bain, 'Mimi did say that all the vomiting wasn't how his allergy usually played out. But we'll never know how Blunt came into contact with dog hairs.'

'You spoke with Adrian Cooper,' Holly said to Bain, 'What did he have to say about it?'

Bain shrugged, 'He was tight-lipped. Mind you, he was scathing about the Dents, particularly Hugo, and lumped Daniel Croft, the vet in there too. But in terms of working out who might have drugged or got at Blunt, it was a dead end. But I'm working on Geena Coulter, the stable lass he mentioned, and he definitely knows something murky about the Dents, but I couldn't get it out of him.'

There was a pause in the conversation that saw Vladimir shift his gaze from face to face until he finally reached Bain.

'Is anyone going to catch me up?' he asked, 'How can we manage to identify a whole bunch of roguish behaviour, but can't prove a thing against any of them?'

'I'll explain later,' Ronnie offered, flapping a hand at her neighbour, 'But on a lighter note, Mimi is very pleased with David Thorne, her new trainer. She's gone over to Middleham to visit her horses this morning, both the sick filly and the colt she bought at the breeze-up's, and been told that Morgan has been going well in the last couple of weeks.'

'That's great,' said Bain pointedly, 'But can we concentrate on the matter in hand? If Golden drops in to see us I want to sound as professional as possible. She's a valuable contact.'

Vladimir shared a pained look with Ronnie that pleaded with her not to make a comment. Bain's attraction to Golden was obvious. Vladimir was relieved when Ronnie rolled her eyes at him, but chose to remain silent.

It had been three weeks since the breeze-up sale, Robert Farley's unexpected visit to the house, and their conversation with Geena Coulter. While the images of people on Bain's whiteboard had quadrupled, they were no closer to finding Brooklyn's killer. Other fee-paying journalistic jobs, mostly football matches, were starting to crowd in on Bain's time. With Geena Coulter's information, they had evidence of further wrongdoing when it came to horse racing, but there had been a distinct lack of any progress on what really mattered, Brooklyn's murder.

An air of gloom had descended on the house over the intervening weeks as Holly and Bain examined every scrap of evidence over and over again, evaluated every possible motive, even the most outrageous ones, and yet, their efforts had yielded nothing of any substance. In addition, there was this face-to-face update on their investigations DI Golden had requested. Holly and Bain had discussed the policewoman's visit and felt sure that a story about underhanded price manipulation at the breeze-ups, a jealous ex-husband's cock-eyed attempt at blackmail, and a disgruntled ex-stable lass being bought off after discovering a doping offence, wasn't what the policewoman wanted to hear.

The manhunt for Farley was still a high-profile story, especially in the north, and there was an undercurrent of dissatisfaction with the police's handling of the situation beginning to surface in the media. They had reported Farley's visit to the house, but Holly had been adamant that they wait an hour before the call went in to Golden. It had puzzled Bain that instead of the anticipated policemen and dogs tramping through the garden, along with drones and helicopters buzzing over the house, forty minutes later Golden had turned up alone. She'd asked Holly a few questions, before being called away again. Her request for an update on their activities over in Malton had come three days later.

Bain had asked everyone up to the office on this wet Friday morning to see if, as a group, they could unravel the tangle of people involved with the Dent yard and determine a strong motive, and potentially link any murderous candidates before Golden arrived. It was a desperate throw of the dice that, so far, was proving entirely fruitless.

'Okay, Hol,' said Bain, once again desperate to move the conversation along, 'Can you run through the staff at Dent's yard again. I know you only did it recently with me, but Ronnie and Vladimir haven't heard it."

'Yep, why not,' she said with a sigh, moving over to stand in front of the whiteboard. Having spent four weeks working at the yard, she wasn't so sure there was anything going on other than a few dodgy business practices.

Bain smiled hopefully at Holly, but received little encouragement in return. She appeared uncharacteristically tired, grey rings visible below her eyes, her hair in need of a comb. However, she came forward willingly enough and began to run through the people of interest at the Malton yard.

'I've been at the Dent's yard four mornings each week, working from six-thirty in the morning until one in the afternoon,' she explained.

Running quickly through a rough hand-drawn map of the yard she noted the four barns, each with tack and wash rooms. Together, they housed a total of forty-two racehorses, although there were enough stables for twice that number. Each of the long, open-ended barns terminated at the large, circular courtyard.

Holly took a tired breath, 'There's a bunch of static caravans, one used as a tea hut and rest room, several are living accommodation for the on-site staff and then there are two or three that are used for storage. The Dents live in a four-bedroomed house on the edge of the courtyard where the morning lots congregate before heading out for their gallop work. There's plenty of paddocks, a menage, two walkers, three large turn-out fields, a couple are on the hill behind the yard, and there's a wood to the east of the property. It's more a forest to be honest, with lots of tall trees thick with brambles, and runs from behind the line of static caravans to the edge of the property which is bordered by a country lane.'

With no questions arising, she moved on to systematically list all the people that worked or visited the yard, spending a greater amount of time on those in management positions.

'There are ten stable staff in total, five of them part-time, seven women, and three men. The three lads are from India on work visas,' she said, pointing to the photos with the names Rajesh, Sajan, and Dilip written above, 'I haven't had a great deal to do with them as I'm stuck in the stables mucking out each shift and they ride out most lots, but from the few words I've had with them in the tea hut they seem friendly enough. All three of them share one of the trailers and religiously send money home to India each month.'

This information received patient nods but no questions, so Holly continued.

'Lucy, Amber, Courtney, and Mary are the stable lasses I tend to work with. There's also Trinny and Harriet, who do a lot of horsebox driving and leading up at the races. And then there's Lara, the head lass, in charge of all of us. The lads, plus Lucy and Courtney, get the chance to ride out every other day, the others are like me, stuck in the stables.'

'How old do you think they are?' asked Bain, 'Brooklyn was nineteen when she worked in the yard, so it might help to concentrate on the ones that were likely to be her friends.'

'Lara and Mary are older, mid to late-forties, the others, including the three lads, are anywhere between seventeen and twenty-three. All of them are single as far as I can make out. There's a lot of immature teasing goes on, and the younger girls have regular nights out together.'

'Why is there a small red cross above Amber's photo and the even smaller one against Lucy's?' asked Vladimir.

A weary smile pinned itself to Holly's face, and once again, Bain experienced a prickle of concern about her wellbeing.

'Amber was taken on only a month before Brooklyn's accident,' Holly replied, 'According to Mary, they suffer from a higher than average turnover of staff. Lara is quite intimidating and says they lose staff because of the high standards she demands, but I think it's more to do with most people's intolerance of Hugo. Amber says she didn't really know Brooklyn, and Lucy was on holiday when the murder took place. I checked, and she says she had a whale of a time in Greece. And from the stories she tells about the nightlife there, I believe her.'

'We can't rule either of them out completely, but it's less likely, hence the small cross beside their names,' explained Bain.

Regulars in the yard are the farrier, Roy Tattersall, the physio, Liz Williamson, and Daniel Croft, the vet.

'We met Tattersall and Croft,' noted Vladimir, 'Roy was a delight, he would have chatted with us all day about manipulating horse's backs if Hugo hadn't hurried us along. Daniel Croft was in a stable, treating a horse. He didn't say too much.'

'He was at the breeze-ups too,' added Ronnie.

'Really?' queried Bain,' Graham and Hugo Dent were there, along with Adrian Cooper and Conor Moran, but I didn't see anyone else I recognised, apart from the two stable lasses from Cooper's stud.'

Ronnie regarded Bain over her bifocals, 'I'm sure. The vet was sculking around the café when I was introducing myself to Mimi. Definitely him. He was wearing one of those awful grey cotton jumpers with a hood.'

'It's a hoodie,' Holly confirmed to the group, 'I've seen him in it. He wears it around the yard.'

'Well, I didn't like him. Anyone who chooses to spend time with that odious Hugo has to be a wrong 'un. He seemed as bent as a clothes peg to me,' declared Ronnie.

Bain stood, picked up a marker pen and made a small addition to the vet's name on the whiteboard to indicate he'd been present at the breeze-ups. Ronnie nodded her appreciation, not realising the Bain's 'B' stood for 'breeze-ups' rather than, 'Bent'.

'Hugo and the vet spend quite a bit of time together,' said Holly, 'I've come across them laughing and joking more than once. Daniel Croft is in the yard pretty much every day and I've seen the two of them going in and out of the static caravans and generally hanging around at the bottom of the yard. Being nineteen, Hugo has moved out of his parent's farmhouse and is living in one of them.'

'Are they the same age?' asked Bain.

Holly shook her head, 'I'd say Croft was mid to late twenties. I'm not sure their relationship extends beyond the confines of the yard.'

'I think we need to keep an eye on this Daniel Croft, given he was at the sales,' said Bain, 'He was also part of this potential doping. If Geena Coulter is to be believed, the vet was part of it with Hugo Dent.'

This received unanimous nods of approval.

'Okay, onto the Dent family,' said Holly, blinking to focus back on the whiteboard, 'As you know, Graham is the trainer, and Hugo, his son and assistant trainer. I'll come back to *him* in a minute. Graham's wife, Wendy Dent is a character. She has six dogs, all named after famous British painters.

Ronnie nodded appreciatively. Holly smiled at her

mother, but could feel her eyes wanting to close. She fought back against her tiredness and continued.

'Wendy knows her stuff when it comes to horses too. As well as breeding dachshunds, she has a few sheep, goats, and a couple of ponies. I caught her teaching Courtney how to calm one of the horses the other day by gripping its nose. She seems to float about as she pleases, keeping an eye on things, and I see more of her than I do her husband. Graham Dent always has a harassed look on his face and spends most of his time up the gallops, inside the farmhouse, or at the races. Wendy has a better idea of what's really going on inside the yard. If you want something doing, you go to Wendy and Lara, rather than Graham or Hugo.'

'Ah, yes! Hugo…' Ronnie chipped in, 'If I had to guess who was at the heart of anything illegal in that yard, he would be my first port of call! He's thoroughly disreputable, despicable, and a complete tw…'

'I think we can all agree on that, mother,' Holly broke in, hoping to be loud enough to drown her mother out, but failing.

'…twonk!' Ronnie announced with an impish smirk.

Holly aimed a warning glance at her mother, 'I've been keeping a close eye on Hugo and really wish I hadn't. His treatment of the staff is awful, and his mother and father are just as bad in my book because they both turn a blind eye to their son's behaviour.'

She continued, 'I don't think Hugo is all bad though. He seems to enjoy riding, but he's a self-obsessed teenager who doesn't know how to manage people. As a result, I think he compensates by being abrupt, rude, and tries too hard to appear to be confident.'

'We know he organised the fraud with Cooper. Then there's the accusation of him doping a horse. Could he be capable of something worse than that?' asked Bain.

Holly shook her head, 'I don't know him well enough yet. I need more time. I feel he's still working me out too. But there's been a few comments in the tea room.'

'Comments?' Ronnie queried.

'Lots complaining about him, but there was one that surprised me. I don't know if it's true, but Mary told me that Hugo was adopted by the Dents. Mary's been there for over twenty years, far more than Lara, the head lass, and isn't the gossiping type, so I tend to believe what she says.'

Vladimir sighed, 'Even so, that Hugo needs to learn a thing or two about good manners. How do the other girls in the yard cope with him?'

'I've seen Courtney and Amber get angry, but that only seems to encourage him. Hugo just laughs off criticism. Lucy and Mary put up with it, and Lara does her best to keep him in check, but she can't be everywhere in the yard at once. The only other person that spends any time with Hugo is…'

'Daniel,' Vladimir and Ronnie said in unison.

Holly smiled at them, took a ragged breath and continued, 'I've uncovered nothing new in the last fortnight. And apart from Hugo being a… *twonk* and trying to make himself some cash from a horse sale to a naïve new owner, I've found no evidence anyone at the yard was involved with Brooklyn's death.'

A heavy silence developed as Holly's words settled on the group. It was Bain who was the first to voice what both Ronnie and Vladimir were thinking.

'I wonder whether you should bother going back,' he said quietly to Holly, 'We've nothing to suggest anyone at the yard has been involved in Brooklyn's murder. Maybe we have to tell Golden that the Dents aren't to be trusted, but there's no evidence that links them or their staff to Brooklyn's murder.'

Holly didn't answer immediately. Pursing her lips, she considered the possibility of not making the journey to the yard again tomorrow morning and felt a weight lift, her dulled senses suddenly alive once more. But she was loathe to give up. She had a feeling there was something there, a key to Brooklyn's murder, lurking in the shadows. If only she could tease it out into the open.

'No,' she finally announced, 'I need to go back. At least for a few more days. Perhaps I could try getting to know the vet a bit better. So far, all I've done is catch him trying to check out Morgan before the filly left, and on reflection he was probably just doing his job. But with Geena calling him an evil weasel, and Ronnie seeing him at the breeze-ups, he's got to be worth a second look.'

She noticed Bain staring, or rather, studying her intently from across the room, 'What?'

He blinked and looked away self-consciously, 'I think... It's just, well... you don't look too well, Hol. I wondered whether you need a few days rest?'

It was true that she wasn't one hundred percent. Physically tired, and frustrated by the lack of progress, she supposed she should be pleased that Bain had noticed, but his observation had kindled self-doubt. She took a calming breath.

'I'm fine,' she replied firmly, her voice trembling ever-so slightly, 'I just need a good night's sleep. It's a long drive to and from the yard each day.'

In a breathy, depressed tone, Holly continued to brief Bain, Ronnie and Vladimir, revealing she'd found herself being shut down by most of the staff once she mentioned Brooklyn's name. Head lass, Lara had told her the Dent's didn't want the ongoing murder hunt reflecting badly on the yard, and so all talk of Brooklyn was frowned upon, whether it concerned her being accidentally kicked, or her subsequent murder months later.

'We were shocked, and every one of us grieved in our own way when we heard what happened to Brooklyn, but we have to put on a happy face for our owners and smile through the pain. What happens outside the yard, has to stay outside the yard,' were the only words the head lass wanted to say on the subject.

'The one interesting reaction recently was from Hugo,'

Holly told her select audience, 'Even though my query hadn't been aimed at him. It was yesterday, he overheard me speaking with Lucy in the next stable along as we did the morning mucking out.'

Holly paused and tried to concentrate in order to repeat the encounter verbatim.

'I asked Lucy if the name, 'Snowdrop' meant anything to her, explaining I'd heard it mentioned by one of the others in the tea hut. She asked me why I was bothered, and I told her I just liked the name and wondered if it was a yard nickname for one of the grey horses, or perhaps one of Wendy's dogs. Before our conversation could get any further, Hugo stormed into the stable I was working in and asked, 'Where?' and was searching the floor.'

'I was puzzled, and when I'd given him an innocent explanation for mentioning it, he got all defensive. He made an excuse to leave, but came back a minute later and demanded to know who had said 'Snowdrop' in the tea hut. I said I overheard it and might have got it wrong anyway. Since then though, I get the feeling Hugo's been keeping an eye on me.'

Vladimir said, 'I know you think you haven't found anything of use at the Dents, but that sounds interesting to me. Hugo's definitely the one to watch.'

'Absolutely,' agreed Ronnie, 'When I started bidding on the colt at the sales he was glaring at me like he wanted me dead!'

Bain was less enthusiastic.

'You… well, we all have to be *careful,*' he said, emphasising his point with open arms, 'I know you want to find any clue that leads to Brooklyn's murderer, but don't get overly involved. If there is a murderer in the Dent yard, we don't want to provoke him, or her, into another attack. Once you get any evidence, or a lead that will give Golden an excuse to get involved, you're out of there.'

Holly gave Bain a tired nod of agreement.

The doorbell rang out downstairs, prompting everyone to pause and look at each other.

'That'll be Golden,' Bain said with a grimace, 'I'll go get her.'

On his way down the three flights, the bell rang again, prompting Bain to descend a little quicker. He'd prefer a happy, smiling DI Golden. He did like her smile.

Swinging the door open, his own smile faltered as a flustered Mimi Blunt burst into the house. She was clutching a piece of paper and began waving it around, before thrusting it into Bain's hands.

'I've come straight here from the Thornes' yard. I had to. You'll know what to do. You won't *believe* what they've done to my horse!'

The blood drained from Bain's face. He had visions of something terrible having happened at the David Thorne yard. Bain and Holly had personally recommended the Middleham-based trainer to Mimi as being the best place for both her newly bought breeze-up colt, and Morgan, the filly suffering with the extended bouts of colic. The latter had arrived at the Thorne's the day after the breeze-ups, three weeks ago.

'What's wrong, Mimi?' Bain asked, trying to focus on the contents of the crumpled piece of paper. From the logo and address in the heading, it appeared to be a veterinary report.

As Mimi was catching her breath, Ronnie and Holly appeared on the landing above, and seeing Mimi in something of a state, Ronnie hurried down the stairs.

'Oh, Ronnie!' Mimi exclaimed in a flurry of discarded gloves, coat, hat, and scarf. Ronnie put an arm around her and guided Mimi down the hall and into a chair at the kitchen table, 'You won't believe it. I'm so angry.'

Ronnie took Mimi's hand and made soothing noises.

'I've come straight here from David's yard, added Mimi, 'It's Morgan, you know, my filly that was at the Dents?

The poor thing.'

'Is she okay?' asked Bain fearfully, still scanning the report. He turned it over, seeking out the comments at the end of what he now realised was a toxicology report.

'Oh, she's *fine!*' Mimi assured him with a bright smile no one had anticipated, 'At least, she's fine *now*.'

Bain's attention left the report, still unable to decipher it in any meaningful way, and he traded a bemused look with Holly.

'In fact, David's wife told me she's improving every single day that passes and is doing ever so well on the Middleham gallops. But it's that report. That's what has upset me. As soon as she arrived, David got his vet to do a full set of blood tests on Morgan, just to be sure the Dent's vet hadn't missed anything. The report makes no sense to me, but David says the reason Morgan's been so ill for the last four months is because she's been poisoned. She's been eating snowdrop bulbs.'

This drew a combined intake of breath around the kitchen, apart from Bain. He was gazing out into the back garden, his face a concentrated frown, the pages of the report limp between his forefinger and thumb.

'Let me have a look,' said Holly, sliding the pages from Bain's grasp. He didn't react.

It was Morgan, Bain realised. Mimi's filly, Morgan was the horse Geena Coulter had come across being given a snowdrop tracheal wash. The filly and the snowdrops! Why hadn't he put the two together?

Queries that had previously gone nowhere inside Bain's mind, began coalesce and connect. Geena had been on her way to inform Mimi when she was tracked down and bribed into working abroad, Bain realised. Hugo wasn't enhancing the horse's performance, he was purposefully making the filly sick… Mimi had said Hugo had offered to buy her out of Morgan on several occasions, the last time after the bidding debacle at the sales... which meant that Hugo was worried the filly would leave his yard and he would be found out. He'd made the filly ill, hoping Mimi would give her up at a vastly reduced price, or even free... Which made you think that the filly had to be something a bit special…

'Daniel Croft was at the yard when Morgan left,' said Holly.

She was staring blankly at Bain and he immediately understood from her expression that she was processing this new information and making the connections herself.

'I thought he was acting strangely,' she continued, 'He must have known, or been suspicious of what Hugo was up to. Perhaps that's why he wanted to examine her before she left.'

'Or there to muddy the waters… Didn't Geena say that she found Hugo and Daniel doing the doping together?'

'Erm… What?' said Mimi, looking from one face to another.

Vladimir and Ronnie shared a perplexed shrug with her and looked to Bain and Holly.

Holly blew a frustrated sigh through her nose and placing a hand to her forehead she began massaging her frown lines. It felt like every time they made a breakthrough on this case it immediately led to more complexity and confusion. But one thing was clear in her mind.

'I need to get to the bottom of the relationship between Hugo and Daniel,' announced Holly.

Thirty-Nine

'DI Golden?'

'Yes. What do you want Bainbridge?' said a scratchy voice down the telephone line.

Momentarily caught on the back foot, Bain paused before conjuring up a reply.

'Oh. Erm… you didn't come around to see us

yesterday?'

'No. Apologies. Busy.'

'Are you busy now by any chance?'

There was a short pause.

'You have two minutes.'

'We've… made a breakthrough, of sorts, on the Brooklyn Hartley case.'

Three seconds ticked by without a reply so Bain soldiered on.

'It turns out that not only are the Dent's adopting fraudulent practices at the sales, we have proof they are doping their horses.'

Golden asked, 'What, to make them win races?'

'No, quite the reverse. They are purposefully making them ill.'

Again, no reply. Bain could imagine Golden thinking hard about what this meant, although on second thoughts, she had sounded distracted up to this point. He forged on.

'We're certain they've fed a young, unraced horse with a substance that makes them appear sickly, so much so, the owners either give them up for free, or sell them to the yard for a fraction of their true value. I'm thinking the Dents must subsequently remove the poison from the horse's system, send them abroad, race them once or twice to show their true ability, then sell them on for a huge profit.'

Again, Golden said nothing for a long moment, but this time Bain waited, knowing what she would ask. If he knew her, she had to ask the one question he'd asked himself.

Golden cleared her throat and said, 'What does any of this have to do with Brooklyn's death?'

Bain grinned, caught himself, and continued.

'They used a compound called lycorine. It causes an upset stomach, griping, and mild colic, if given in small, regular doses. In larger doses it can kill.'

'You haven't explained…'

Bain winced, 'Oh! Okay, sorry… Snowdrops.'

'Snowdrops?'

'The plant,' Bain added, 'It was also Brooklyn's last word to Farley before she died.'

Silence on the line.

'She said, snowdrop,' said Bain, 'I thought we'd told you that? At the time I assumed it was the stable name of a horse.'

'And it isn't?'

'No,' Bain replied, taking a breath so he could speak the next sentence clearly, 'The compound lycorine is found in snowdrop bulbs.'

Bain and Golden spoke for another minute before the call ended abruptly with the detective being called away. However, she ended the call with a warning to do nothing with this new information until she contacted him again.

Tapping the end call button on his phone's loudspeaker option, Bain looked around the kitchen table, 'I get the impression that either I didn't explain myself too well, or Golden is really busy with another case at the moment. What do you think?'

'It's the same few people that keep cropping up,' said Vladamir, 'Graham and Hugo Dent, Adrian Cooper, and that vet, Daniel Croft.'

'Yes, but what do you *all think*?' repeated Bain.

Ronnie clapped her hands together, making Holly jump, 'I think we nail the poisoning little beggars!'

'Golden told us to sit tight,' Bain reminded her.

'And when did you last give up the chance of a big story because someone told you to sit tight?' inquired Holly.

She still looked tired, but her eyes were currently dancing with brightness as they darted around, reading the other people sat around the kitchen table.

Bain knitted his fingers together and stretched his arms above his head, his headache fading, 'Right then, Hol. Time to construct one of our plans!'

Vladimir tapped the table with his index finger until he

had everyone's attention.

'Can I gently remind everyone that the last time Bain constructed a plan, nothing happened the way it should. And I was required to render someone unconscious through the use of a jam pan.'

'And what fun we had!' Ronnie chipped in.

Forty

May 20th

Holly's phone rang late afternoon and she pounced on it, only to discover it was her mother. Ronnie was out for the day with Vladimir, visiting a garden centre near Bingley that boasted birds, fish, and even a vintage amusement arcade, as well as the usual plants and gardening equipment. Ronnie had been attracted by the promise of cheap squirrel food and talking parrots.

'We've had an invite to the races on Friday!' Ronnie announced as soon as Holly answered the phone, 'Mimi Blunt has asked whether all four of us would like to come along to the races. Her filly, Morgan, you know, the one that was made ill from the snowdrops?'

'Yes, mother. I know.'

'Well it's apparently fit, well, and having its first race on Friday at… York, or Redcar. No, it's Wetherby… or maybe Darlington?'

'Ripon, Ronnie. Mimi said it was Ripon,' Holly heard Vladimir say in the background.

'Ripon? Yes, I told her it was Ripon. Why are you telling me Redcar?' Ronnie snapped at her friend.

'Anyway, Mimi said our tickets will be on the door and we are to meet her in the Owners and Trainers lounge. Shall I tell her we'll all be there?'

Holly called over the office to Bain, sitting staring

blankly at his laptop screen, 'Hey! Fancy the races on Friday afternoon? Morgan is running.'

Bain blinked himself out of his doze, checked his calendar, and stuck his thumb up. Any excuse to cease writing the requested two hundred words about a local amateur football team's loss of their changing room due to flooding.

'Yep, Bain's in,' Holly related back into her phone, 'Tell Mimi we'll be there... at Ripon.'

'Ripon? I thought it was Redcar?'

After a short pause, during which Holly tried hard not to roll her eyes, she added, 'Tell you what, mother, I know you're incredibly busy at the moment. I'll call Mimi myself to save you the bother.'

Forty-One

May 23rd

Holly had been following Hugo and Daniel around the yard for almost a week now. It had become something of an obsession after finding out the two of them had poisoned a horse with the snowdrop compound Brooklyn had thought important enough to be her last words. Wherever they went, especially if they were together, she would construct a reason for being close to them, or an excuse to walk past the stable they were in, listening to conversations when she could, trying to read their body language when she couldn't.

That was why she'd hung around after her shift finished. There was something going on between the two men. She could feel it. Something in the way they met each other's eyes this morning had signalled a change, an uneasiness between them that either meant something was about to happen, or their relationship had reached a critical stage. There was a palpable electricity arcing between them, and Holly needed to be there to see what happened.

It was early afternoon and the yard was quiet. She should have left for home forty minutes ago, indeed, only Lara, Wendy, and Hugo remained at the yard to her knowledge, the rest had either left for the races at Redcar, or gone home after their shift. It was when Daniel arrived, looking serious, heavy thoughts apparently occupying his mind, that Holly decided it would be worth hanging around. The vet had made a beeline for Hugo's caravan and after only a few seconds the two of them, along with Daniel's veterinary case, had headed off to a group of stables at the back of the yard, generally reserved for horses out of training, many of whom were recuperating following minor injuries. Holly followed them at a safe distance.

***

Daniel had sensed it coming a few days ago. A gradual cooling of Hugo's interest in him, so he had to act quickly to rectify the situation. The loss of Morgan to the David Thorne yard, and the debacle around the breeze-ups had left their relationship in a rocky place. He'd worked too long for his plans to falter now. It was essential to have Hugo present and willing to participate in what he was about to do. This act would would ensure Hugo was forever his.

In a small and very private holding paddock surrounded by a wall of ten foot high Leylandii at the back of the Dent's property, Daniel knelt and removed the necessary equipment from his veterinary case. Behind him, the colt shook its head to dislodge a fly and Hugo fidgeted with his lead rein, watching the vet nervously.

After preparing everything, Daniel returned to a standing position and turned, taking the three-year-old colt's lead rein and nodded at the syringe lying on his euthanasia kit. Hugo was about to administer a fatal injection into the colt's bloodstream.

The colt was a bleeder, a condition discovered in the

last run of his two-year-old season. It meant his lungs would rupture during his races. Blood would flood into the bottom of the colt's lungs due to the stresses and strains placed upon them in a horse race. In effect, the poor animal would slowly lose the ability to breathe, slowly drowning in blood each time he was asked to race, making it impossible for him to reach his potential as a racehorse. Costing hundreds of thousands of pounds as a two-year-old, being a bleeder, the colt known as 'Jack' in the yard was now worth no more than a few hundred pounds.

Both Daniel and Hugo knew the condition didn't stop the young horse enjoying a full and active life in another sphere of equine sport. A loving owner and a less arduous discipline could see this fine animal live out a long, happy life. However, this horse was heavily insured.

After carefully establishing that the owner valued money above the future, or indeed the life of his horse, Daniel had found it straightforward enough to involve Hugo and extract a promise of a substantial fee for his services. He'd ensured Hugo was involved. Always have an out... and Hugo would be his.

In order for the owner to collect the six-figure insurance sum the horse had to break down with a fatal injury, for example, a badly fractured bone. Bleeding was a *retirement* condition, not one that demanded euthanasia, and thus no insurance payout would be due. So they would inject the racehorse, snap its leg in the right place, and then write up the death certificate to claim the colt had injured itself whilst in the paddock. Just one of those things, a terrible accident. Hugo would be the co-signatory and claim to have found the colt in distress and in need of immediate euthanasia. It would be the easiest twenty thousand pounds Daniel and Hugo would earn this year. More importantly, it would ensure Hugo would forever be under his control.

Hugo's eyes widened as Daniel took control of the colt.

'I thought you... were going to do it?'

Daniel shook his head.

'We're a team, Hugo,' he breathed, 'We have to do this together.'

Daniel inspected his co-conspirator and didn't like what he saw. Hugo was clearly perturbed. It was a sunny, but still a cool afternoon with a sharp breeze, and yet the lad was sweating profusely. And then Hugo spoke the words Daniel had half-expected, but was hoping not to hear.

'I've changed my mind. I don't want to do this, Daniel,' Hugo told him in a low, yet determined voice, moving between the vet and the colt, 'It's… not right. He's a fine horse and could live for another fifteen or twenty years. This is a… a step too far.'

Daniel reminded his young charge of their agreement with the owner. He referred to the payment Hugo would receive and how he might spend his windfall. Becoming agitated when Hugo refused once again, Daniel manufactured a raging anger and played on the strength of their friendship. All to no avail. The lad wouldn't budge. And then, real anger got the better of him. Daniel resorted to threats.

To Daniel's horror, his threat was unsuccessful. If anything, Hugo became even more intransigent. Hugo stood firm and steadfastly refused to allow him to administer the fatal dose when he grabbed the syringe himself. With the argument having reached an impasse where further negotiations were impossible, Daniel watched Hugo lead the horse away, out of the paddock, back to his stable, and a long and bleed-free life.

Daniel cursed himself for pushing the trainer's son too far. He should have been patient and played him for longer. There was a streak of sentimentality in Hugo, a spark of goodness he'd seen before, but hoped to subjugate.

The vet packed up his euthanasia kit. By the time he'd reached his car, Daniel had already decided what he had to do. It was time to invoke his exit strategy. It was time to get out.

***

Holly had watched Daniel and Hugo's argument. Thanks to the stiff breeze masking their words, she hadn't been close enough to work out the exact details, but it seemed to concern the vet's preferred treatment for Jack. Hugo had become genuinely angry and upset. There had been tears in his eyes when he'd hurried past her hiding place, behind the line of Leylandii bordering the small turnout paddock reserved for horses recovering from injury. Strangely, the entire conversation between the two men had been conducted in low growls and urgent whispers.

Holly was now certain there was something about this relationship that didn't ring true. She had witnessed a bust up between them, but couldn't be sure what it was about.

She waited until Daniel, in a foul mood, had packed up his kit and left before emerging from her hiding place. Holly stopped dead. Lara, the Head Lass, and her boss, emerged from the same line of trees, no more than a few feet in front of her.

Lara was brushing herself down when she became aware of Holly. The two of them silently stared at each other, Holly with her mouth open, Lara looking glum, but with a rouge tinge to her usually pale cheeks.

Lara reacted first, swallowing, narrowing her eyes and asking, not unkindly, 'What are you doing here?'

Holly squeezed her eyes shut, kicking herself for not checking for anyone else before leaving the cover of the evergreen trees. There was no use denying that she too had been hiding in the trees, like Lara, she had small green pieces of Leylandii bush attached to her jumper.

'I'm sorry, Lara. I wanted to see how Daniel treated Jack, you know, the three-year-old colt.'

This was entirely true. However, her explanation was about to divert from the truth.

'I've been working in Jack's stable this week and become a bit attached to him. I… just wanted to make sure he was… okay. I saw Hugo lead him away to this paddock and was a bit worried.'

Holly shifted her stare to the dirt track and tried to appear suitably regretful.

'Look at me,' Lara said, taking a step closer, 'Did you see what they did to Jack?'

Holly was surprised. The question was a *request* for information rather than a demand. There was just a hint of desperation about Lara that threw Holly for a moment. Buying time, she slowly lifted her chin and met Lara's gaze.

There seemed little point in not telling the truth, her spying on the two men had been a bust. It might just save her job if she was straight with her.

'They actually… did nothing. They didn't do anything to the colt that I could see,' she admitted with a shrug.

Lara nodded slowly, as if this made sense. She regarded Holly with arms crossed, biting the inside of her mouth in contemplation. To Holly's amazement, Lara dropped her arms to her side and sagged, all tension gone from her stance and her stern Yorkshire stare crumbled into a look of genuine relief. Confused, Holly waited.

'I like you. You work hard, you're sensible, and you don't complain. You understand horses and although you need more experience in the saddle, you'll made a decent work rider in time.'

Holly blinked, but didn't reply immediately. This felt more like a friendly chat than a dressing down. This was puzzling.

'Erm… thank you, Lara. I like working here. I didn't mean to be nosey, I was…'

Lara waved her apology away, 'That's okay. You're allowed to feel compassion for the horses. No need to sneak around though, eh?'

Holly chanced a little smile, and was pleased when Lara

returned it, indicating the matter had been dealt with.

Lara turned to leave and Holly went to follow. However, the head lass drew to a halt after only a couple of steps, her back still to Holly. Lara spun around and eyeballed her employee. It seemed to Holly something was playing on her bosses mind. Lara took a deep breath.

'You'll find out soon enough. One of the others will mention it eventually, so I might as well tell you myself,' she began, her eyes having dropped to focus on the few yards of dirt track between them, 'You might have been wondering why I treat Hugo... well, the way I do.'

Holly didn't know how to react. This was out of character for Lara, a little *too* intimate.

'It's because he's Graham Dent's son,' Lara blurted.

She shot Holly a quick look to gauge her reaction.

Holly frowned, 'Yes, I... know.'

'Listen, Grant erm... *Holly*. Hugo will be taking over this yard soon enough, and so my job depends on him. Daniel Croft has a strange relationship with Hugo I'm not too happy about. If you hear anything, or see anything untoward concerning either of them, I'd appreciate you letting me know. Hugo's quite an impressionable lad and I don't want him getting into any more trouble.'

'Of course,' Holly committed with an affirmative nod.

'Okay. Good,' said Lara with palpable relief, 'So... let's get on.'

As Lara strode away, Holly hung back for a few seconds before following her at a more sedate pace. It was as she left the edge of the paddock that it struck her. Lara hadn't asked if she'd *heard* anything of Hugo and Daniel's argument. Lara had known this because she'd not heard anything whilst secretly watching from the safety of the Leylandii A shiver rippled down Holly's neck and across her back as the pieces fell into place. And she'd said any *more* trouble. Holly picked up her pace and managed to catch up with Lara at the entrance to one of the barns.

'Lara, I think you're right about Daniel,' she said, lowering her voice to a whisper as she drew nearer, 'I've seen the two of them disappearing into Hugo's trailer. Daniel is all smiles on the outside, but I get this chill when he's around. There's more to him, isn't there?'

Lara pinched the bridge of her nose as if in pain.

Holly asked, 'Was Daniel close to Brooklyn Hartley?'

As soon as the words had left her mouth, Holly knew she'd shown too much of her hand. Her query was met with a hard stare. It proved enough to make Lara shut down and state quietly, but firmly, 'No.'

Lara pointed down the barn, 'No more tittle-tattling. Get on with your work.'

Knowing she'd over-stepped the mark, Holly left, hoping she hadn't blown her chances of digging deeper. When she passed the stable belonging to Jack the colt, she noted Hugo was in there with him, speaking to the horse in a hushed tone, brushing him down.

Forty-Two

May 25th

Starting work in the dark sucks, Holly grumbled to herself as she pushed a wheelbarrow with a large plastic bucket and a rake poking out of it across the expansive courtyard in front of the Dent's barns. The rain continued to beat down, hard and relentless, as it had for the past hour. Holly wasn't bothered by it being wet and ignored the raindrops plinking onto the brim of her baseball cap. However, she scurried across the empty courtyard anyway, keen to miss the half dozen horses and riders that were about to gather for the first lot of the day.

She'd been up since five o'clock and wasn't concentrating on her barrow, instead ruminating about these early mornings. Holly had never needed to be up so early in her life, at least, not on such a regular basis. And she had reached the conclusion it was this change to her lifestyle that was playing havoc with her sleeping patterns.

Holly hadn't bothered her mother or Bain with her problem, assuming it would solve itself, given time. Her body would adapt... eventually. But now in her sixth week of being a Graham Dent employee, despite it being only four days a week, she'd reached the conclusion that her biorhythms were shot to pieces. She couldn't sleep, spending hours every evening fighting insomnia, then being dog-tired each morning and lying zombie-like on her bed for an hour when she got home at two-thirty in the afternoon.

Surviving off three or four broken hours of sleep each night was starting to take its toll on Holly, both physically and mentally. Even part-time, this job was a killer. She shuddered, remembering her loss of concentration experienced on her motorbike that morning on her way to Malton. Mind you, the adrenaline rush after wrestling the bike back onto the road at speed had kept her wide awake for the final few miles. That hedge… and the mature tree growing in its centre! The experience had scared the life out of her. Mounting a grass verge after having slipped into a sleepy stupor had left her sweating and panting at the roadside. The tree had rushed at her so quickly…

Holly gripped the handles of the barrow harder and pushed the memory of her two wheeled dice with death to the back of her mind. She needed to be mentally sharp. She and Bain had agreed; one way or another, they had to get some hard evidence on Hugo.

It was a quarter to seven on Saturday morning and amid the sound of horses' hooves milling around the yard, banter between the riders, and the strains of the dawn chorus she entered the older horses' barn and headed for her first stable of her day. The cacophony of bird song and equine feet on concrete was immediately drowned out by the sound of the rain hitting the steel roof as she entered the barn, so loud Holly's head was soon ringing.

Shaking her head, Holly told herself to get a grip. Today was the day she would try and get to the heart of the Hugo and Daniel relationship. The two of them had been distant since that day with Jack, the colt and that argument. And her subsequent run-in with Lara had added some urgency to that situation. She could kick herself for mentioning Brooklyn. But today, with luck, she could perhaps unearth the evidence they needed to get Golden involved with the yard. Holly was going undercover!

She threw open the first of her five boxes allocated to her for mucking out that morning and set to work, keeping a keen eye on her watch. If her calculations were right, and it was like every other Saturday, Daniel Croft would be here at eight o'clock for his standard sweep of all the horses. If Lara went for her usual cup of tea in the house with Wendy at seven twenty, it meant she would have the best part of twenty minutes to roam freely around the yard once the first lot had departed.

'Morning, Holly. I'm in position,' said a male voice in her right ear, 'I can see Dent's first lot collecting in the courtyard. I'll let you know when they reach the bridleway.'

Holly went rigid. She'd almost forgotten she had a virtually invisible ear-bud communicator pressed into her ear. She paused in her work, breathing deeply, then moved to the stable door and glanced up and down the central walkway between the two lines of boxes. Lucy was working on a stable opposite, but at the other end of the barn, at least ten boxes distant. She wouldn't overhear anything from there.

Retiring to the back wall of the stable Holly leaned on her rake and pushed a finger onto the bud in her ear.

She said in a hushed voice, 'Okay, Bain. I hear you.'

'Good stuff,' he replied, 'You in position yet?'

'No. I told you! I have to wait until they are up the gallops and Lara's done her early morning rounds.'

'Understood. Erm... remind me again, his car?'

Holly rolled her eyes, 'Look out for his silver Volvo estate. It has the CVS logo on the doors and the boot.'

'Erm... CVS?'

'Croft Veterinary Services! Crikey Bain, what's wrong with you?'

There was silence for a few seconds. Holly couldn't be sure but could have sworn she'd heard Bain yawn.

'Ah! Yes. Sorry, not a morning person,' he said sleepily, 'Will let you know as soon as I see Croft.'

You and me both, Holly thought ruefully.

'No mobile phones,' said a female voice from between the steel bars of the stable.

Startled, Holly swung round and met the gaze of the head lass standing outside the stable, looking in. Lara's eyes narrowed when she didn't find a phone in Holly's hands.

'Just talking to myself,' said Holly, pasting an embarrassed smile onto her face, 'I wasn't... phoning anyone...'

Lara sniffed and cast her gaze around the stable suspiciously. She returned to eye Holly up and down again before finally accepting her answer.

'I'd keep your thoughts to yourself. You never know who's listening,' Lara advised, 'And that bed will need new shavings, but reuse as much as you can. Only half a bale per stable, understand? We're not made of money.'

Over the sound of her heart thumping, Holly confirmed the instructions back to her and Lara moved off, apparently satisfied. Holly moved to the front of the stable to watch through the bars as Lara strode down the barn to check on Lucy. Busying herself in case Lara doubled back, she cleared some of the mess and added new bedding. Lara didn't return. That meant she'd now be on her way back to the house, via the third barn, to share a cup of tea with Wendy, the two of them putting the world to rights over the kitchen table for the next twenty minutes. Graham, Hugo, and the six horses and riders that made up the first lot would return from the gallops about forty minutes later to find Lara ready and waiting to hose down, dry off, and take the horses to warm down on the walkers. The second lot would be ready for saddling, and off the riders would go… rinse and repeat.

Over the past few weeks Holly had discovered Lara was a creature of habit, adopting a similar routine every morning. The head lass made sure the yard operated smoothly, despite the chronic lack of staff. Lara liked to think she ruled her dominium with an iron rod, but Holly found her accommodating, as long as you treated the horses well and were willing to put in a proper shift each day.

Holly checked her watch. She should have about fifteen minutes of search time. Fifteen minutes to find the evidence they needed against Hugo...

Once the first lot reached the bridleway to the gallops, she could go. Wendy and Lara would be drinking breakfast tea, Lucy and Mary would be hard at work, and no one else, like the farrier, physio, and most importantly, the vet would be on the yard this early in the morning. The key to not getting caught would be to remain unseen and be back in her stable, rake in hand, before the first lot returned.

From his vantage point four hundred yards away, half-way up a hillside dotted with sheep behind the Dent's stable, Bain watched through binoculars as one by one, the first lot turned onto the bridlepath.

'The horses have cleared the walkway. They're on their way up the bridlepath to the gallops,' reported Bain, 'Dent and his son are following them in a battered old Vauxhall.'

'Okay,' breathed Holly, 'I'm on my way.'

Slipping out of her stable, she walked to the open mouth of the older horses barn, thankful the rain on the roof was masking any sound her feet might be making. From there, she skirted around the courtyard, keeping as much distance between her and the Dent's farmhouse as possible, and finally, she dodged behind the tea hut and into the long grass behind the line of mostly cream and blue coloured static caravans. This ten yard strip of land had been forgotten once the trailers had been set in place. Holly imagined it would have been somewhere horses might once have enjoyed a pick of grass after returning from the gallops. It was now busy being reclaimed by nature. Only a few yards away from each trailer the grass merged into dense woodland dominated by mature sycamore and hazel trees. The wood was made virtually impenetrable due to masses of brambles growing unhindered around its fringes, slowly eating into the grassy space and in places, reaching the stabilising legs of the trailers. It made a perfect, hidden avenue for her to check some of the living quarters on her way to Hugo's trailer.

Holly picked up her speed, nimbly racing over the uneven ground, hurdling the mounds of last year's dead grass growth that had been rolled over into straw-like waves by the winter winds. Her feet squelched as she ran, here and there sinking ankle deep in a mixture of mud, grass, and standing water.

Holly passed the end of the second trailer that served as a tack room, and slowed as she reached the third trailer. This was the washroom and general dumping ground for worn out or broken equipment. It had once been the management's racing office, so there were old racing programme books, magazines and even a few aging takeaway boxes stacked on a cupboard. She'd only been in there twice, and it didn't hold anything of interest. The memory of the smell she'd encountered on her most recent visit, when dumping a threadbare rug, was enough to make her nose wrinkle.

A set of blinds blocked the view into the next caravan belonging to the a few of the male work riders. She passed the end of the trailer and found herself marvelling at how three men could live so happily cheek to jowl.

The next trailer was different to the others, this was a white, windowless steel box, a shipping container that held all the heavy equipment, from lawn mowers to fencing posts;

everything required to keep the yard functioning. It was a handyman's dream. Holly paid it no attention.

The next was Lara's caravan. Holly took a peek inside at the living area and was found it tidy, and if anything, a little lacking in character. There was no evidence of personal belongings, nothing adorned the walls. It was a neat, clean room that was merely functional; a long way from being homely. Holly wondered for a moment, but Lara struck Holly as a bluff sort of woman, it was perhaps fitting that she lived like this. She moved on through the wet grass and onto the final two caravans in the line, furthest from the centre of the yard. This was where Hugo spent most of his time.

Forty-Three

Holly looked back along the row of caravans. She'd reached the eighth trailer, Hugo's caravan. She'd often watched him quietly slip away up the lane to his caravan during particularly busy mornings. Daniel would tend to join him, but only after spending time with the lads and lasses in the tea hut for a break. He seemed to get a kick from listening to their gossip.

She was at least a hundred yards away from the courtyard now and the barns and farmhouse were out of sight. Rain splashed with tinny regularity against the aluminium roof on Hugo's caravan as Holly moved to look in on his life through the large window at the back of the trailer. It was almost entirely blocked out by curtains, however a two inch gap in the middle allowed her to achieve a vertical letterbox-sized view inside.

It was pleasant. There were no other words to describe the inside of Hugo's trailer. On first look it was... fairly normal. Peering down the length of the trailer, Holly saw a bed, made up with a flowery bedspread, the small kitchen was neat and tidy, pots and pans hanging from a rack on the wall. Holly was a little taken aback. She could believe it of Lara, but could Hugo really be this houseproud?

Closer to her, the living area had been altered. A dining or occasional table should have sat around a horseshoe sofa, but instead the space was occupied by an alternative piece of furniture.

'Bain?'

'I hear you. What you seeing?'

'What do you call a table an architect or a painter might use?'

After a few seconds thought, Bain replied, 'An easel? Or maybe a drafting table?'

'Drafting table sounds right. Well that's what I'm looking at in Hugo's caravan. It seems like he's a bit of an artist… Oh my word!'

'What?'

'I think we may have underestimated the depth of Hugo and Daniel's relationship,' whispered Holly, 'I'm assuming these must be Hugo's drawings. I'm looking at some of the work he's done, and they're… stunning.'

'What's that got to do with Daniel Croft?'

It was only when she stood on tip-toes and put her eye right to the wet glass that Holly could take in a couple more of the unframed sketches. They adorned a particular wall of the trailer, the one side of the caravan impossible to view unless you were either inside, or happened to be at the back window, stood in long, wet grass, and peering between a small gap in the curtains.

'He works in pencil and charcoal,' said Holly, 'And he does portraits of men… exclusively. In fact, all the pictures are of one man. Daniel.'

'The vet, Daniel? Are you sure?'

'The half-finished portrait I'm looking at is *definitely* Daniel, the vet,' Holly confirmed.

'So that's it? Hugo is a closet artist?'

Holly bit her lip as she considered the art. There could

be little doubt. The pictures were incredibly expressive, so full of… yearning.

'I think he could be a closet something else too.'

'Eh?'

'The portrait of the vet on his drafting table is stunning. It's eerily accurate. I'm no art critic, but the others look a bit fanciful to me. But he's got Daniel's character spot on in his latest portrait.'

'Do you think they're in a relationship?'

'Mmm. Could be, can't be sure. Unrequited love is probably more likely. Saying that, the others are idolising Daniel, you know, all smiles, whereas the latest one shows Daniel's face, flaws and all. It's a bit creepy if I'm honest.'

Bain took a moment to reply, taking this new information in whilst trying to ignore the rain thumping onto his jacket hood.

'That puts a rather different perspective on things.'

'It would explain why up until their argument over Jack, Hugo followed the vet around the yard like a puppy dog and why he was so desperate to please him.'

'I'm moving on,' Holly added quickly when Bain didn't answer, 'There's nothing else to see here and to be honest, I feel like I'm a bit of a voyeur.'

'Okay. Understood. Quick, check out the last trailer and get back to the stables. You've got…. Five to six minutes left.'

Before moving on, Holly took out her camera and snapped a series of photos through the gap in the curtain. Thirty seconds later, she quietly announced she was at the last caravan in the line.

Bain's voice came straight back at her through her ear-bud.

'Good. See anything?'

'Not yet, it's different to the rest. Older for a start. And fewer windows. Each window looks to be blocked out. I may not have enough time to see inside this one.'

'I chose my pitch really carefully,' Bain reassured her,

'No one will get any more than ten yards down that line of trailers without me seeing them coming. That'll give you plenty of time to hide. Keep cool, Hol. Four minutes left.'

'Can't help but be cool, Bain,' Holly complained, a little prickly, 'I'm soaked to the skin.'

The final trailer in the line was in serious danger of being reclaimed by the forest. Holly was standing under a particularly large sycamore tree whose branches were shading half of the caravan's roof. She'd had to be careful approaching the back of the trailer as thick spears of freshly budding bramble had made the last few yards perilous. Their barbed stems seemed to be reaching over the grass like tentacles, intent on eventually ensnaring the trailer and claiming it for the forest. This trailer had seen better days, its sides were pitted, paint peeling away to reveal rust covered steel. There was only a single window on its side, and the aluminium flashing surrounding the pane of glass had long since lost its lustre. It looked far more utilitarian than the others and as Holly battled through the bramble stalks she remembered a coffee break conversation about this trailer. At one point, it had been the *original* tea hut.

Holly was careful not to touch the green algae starting to take hold on the sides of the caravan, ensuring she made no imprint. However, there was evidence that someone had recently been busy down the side of the caravan, as the grass was trampled and two gas bottles were neatly stacked just below the caravan sill, presumably spent.

Holly inspected the back window and swore under her breath. She'd dodged down the line of caravans a couple of times recently to check out each unit from the lane side, but never chanced going around the back. That had been remiss of her, she could have done with some tools.

'What is it?' asked Bain a moment later.

'The big window at the back. It's all boarded up behind the glass. There's no way I'm getting a look in from here. Even if I can get the window open, I'll never get through the boards, they're solid wood.'

Bain didn't reply, his silence speaking volumes. The windows on these aging caravans were a sneak thief's friend, easy to jemmy open. Bain had reckoned the back window was Holly's best way into the caravan, rather than trying to force the lock on the door.

'Who boards up an old caravan?' Bain asked himself out loud.

Venturing around the side of the caravan Holly found another two boarded-up windows. About to slip around the caravan to check the final side on the dirt track that included the door, Holly steadied herself by placing a hand on the aluminium strip that ran around one of the small windows. She froze. The square strip with rounded edges had moved. Not just a little, it had come away from its housing. Bringing her other hand up she carefully pushed and with little effort the entire aluminium window frame came away with a tinny pop. She pushed gently on the window and its hinges squeaked. Pulling on the sill, the window pivoted an inch on her first tug, then another couple of inches, providing a gap big enough for her fingers to enter the trailer. Holly flattened her hand and pushed on the brown board on the inside. It stayed put, but bowed slightly, feeling flimsy to her touch. It wasn't like the wooden planks at the back window, this was a thin piece of hardboard, a half-hearted attempt to block the window off.

Looking furtively around, Holly took a moment to breathe, having realised she was taking smaller and smaller quick breaths and her lungs were fit to burst. The patter of rain on the trailer roof masked the sound as she inhaled. She held her breath, then slowly exhaled, bringing her breathing, and her heartrate, back under control. She found herself wondering whether burglars felt the same rush of endorphins when they were breaking and entering.

Covering the last few yards to the front of the trailer, Holly bobbed her head around the corner of the caravan and checked the dirt track lane that led down the line of trailers, willing there to be no one there. The track was empty. She cursed herself for being so silly, of *course* it was empty - Bain would have told her if someone was coming! As she dodged the worst of the wet grass on her way back to the window she told herself to get a grip.

'I may have found a way to look into the last trailer,' she told Bain as she inspected the half-open window, encrusted with dirt, algae, and at least three dead spiders, 'I've managed to get a window open. It's not massive, but I think I can move the board and take a look in.'

The downpour got heavier and the wind was picking up, directing the rain into Bain's binoculars. As he wiped the drops of water from the glass he noticed the sheep that had been grazing around him had migrated down the field. They were now grouped together in small hollow at the bottom, close to a thick green hedge. He, on the other hand, was open to the worst of the elements. Rain splattering his binoculars wasn't the worst of it, the hood of his wax jacket was being pelted and the sound was deafening, added to which his handkerchief was now so damp he was smearing, rather than drying the lenses.

Out in the open hillside the rain was beating down at an angle and because he was craning his neck to peer through his binoculars, every now and again a fat raindrop would plink onto them and splash back in his face.

However, his discomfort was of no relevance to Holly, so he didn't mention it. After checking the bridlepath was still clear of horses, he moved downwards to concentrate his gaze on the last trailer and the dirt track lane, keeping watch for any movement.

'That's great. Make it so!' he replied to Holly, glancing down to check his watch, 'Also, make it quick. You've got between two and three minutes. I'll let you know when the first lot appears at the end of the bridlepath.'

'Thanks,'

'Remember, as soon as the horses enter the walkway back to the yard you'll only have two minutes to hightail it back to your barn.'

'Understood.'

Once again, everything blurred through the binoculars and giving the lenses a quick wipe with his handkerchief Bain continued his vigil.

Feeling the weight of her increasingly limited time pushing down on her, Holly threw caution to the wind. Pulling from its base, she wrenched the window in the side of the trailer up and open, grimacing as it squeaked on its ancient hinges. Holding the almost horizontal window with one hand, she pushed on the centre of the board behind with a flat hand. It bowed, but annoyingly, remained fast. Grunting with the effort, Holly balanced the window on her head, steadied herself, and thrust both hands at the top of the board. Screws pinged and the board flopped over with a satisfying waft of dust.

Holly stuck her head through the window and looked around the inside of the trailer. It was dark, smelled of rotting wood, and rather disappointingly, it was virtually empty, save for a few bits of old furniture. She took a couple of photos through the window with the flash enabled on her phone, and did her best to pull the board back up into place.

'Holly?' whispered Bain. There was a nervous uplift of urgency in his voice that immediately made her frown.

'The vet is…'

A loud knock on the trailer next door made Holly freeze and look around, wide-eyed. Standing between the two trailers she felt like a startled rabbit, not knowing which way to run.

'Hugo? Are you in there?' said a man's voice.

Bain swore under his breath. He'd had the perfect position, he could see the front of the caravan, the lane running up to the courtyard and beyond the stable buildings he could see about a hundred yards of the bridlepath the horses used to get to the gallops. How had someone got right down that track without him noticing?

'Sorry, Holly. Abort. Get back to the stables.'

'Can't,' she said softly.

'Holly, get back to the...'

She waited, hardly moving for several long seconds, but Bain's remark was left unfinished.

Daniel Croft came around the corner of Hugo's trailer and almost walked straight into Holly, halting only inches away from her. For a moment she could smell him. It was a nose-piercing whiff of male deodorant.

Holly gave out a sharp howl of fright and automatically thrust out a flat hand that met the vet's chest.

'What the hell?' the hooded man exclaimed, stumbling backwards, palms held up at chest height to placate her.

Daniel took a long look at her from under his hood and dropped his hands, 'Crikey, you scared the crap out of me!'

Holly couldn't speak. Her heart felt like it was about to burst out of her chest. She stared at the vet, frightened to take her eyes off him. A hand went to her heart and she could feel it beating double time. Trying to breathe and get her heartrate down wasn't being aided by a knot of anger biting at her insides. He'd been too close, far too close. His eyes, just visible below the hood were large and dark, almost black. And now he was studying her like... like she was prey. Holly shivered.

'What are you doing?' she heard herself mutter, her words spaced by short, hot pants to get her breath.

'I could ask the same of you,' Daniel smiled back. He was annoyingly relaxed and straightened as he spoke, his eyes disappeared under the rim of his hood, so only the smiling lips and his chin remained visible.

Bain's voice bumped Holly out of her funk, 'Hol! This is important. Do as I tell you. Tell him you have to go. Move forward onto the track so I can see you. The first lot is back and I want the people in the courtyard to see both of you.'

'It's... okay... um, Mr Croft, I need to get back to work,'

said Holly, edging sideways towards the track, carefully maintaining the same four yards between her and Daniel, and always facing him. He turned with her, cocking his head sideways at one stage, his smug half-smile in evidence throughout. Looking beyond Croft she could see movement at the entrance to the dirt track. Horses and people.

'Please. It's Daniel, you don't need to call me Mr Croft,' the vet said with a smile, moving to stand directly between her and her exit up the dirt track. She considered racing past him, but the track was glistening with moisture and was now more of a mud track than dirt. She would have to be careful if she ran.

'So what are you up to around here?' he asked.

'Tell him you were looking for some riding waterproofs in the tack room, but couldn't find them, so thought you'd try some of the other caravans,' ordered Bain.

Regaining a little confidence, Holly regurgitated Bain's words, although she added, 'I heard you knock. You must be looking for Hugo?'

'Yes, he mustn't be back from the gallops yet,' replied Daniel, his gaze leaving her just for a moment to look down the side of the last caravan.

'I think he's back,' Holly said quickly, pointing over the vet's shoulder to where a small figure was now standing, hands on hips, staring down the track from the courtyard a hundred yards distant.

'It's Holly isn't it?'

She nodded, rain dripping from her nose.

'You're wet through,' he added with a smile that bordered on a smirk, 'Didn't find any waterproofs, huh?'

Holly didn't answer immediately. She was standing in the heavy rain wearing jeans, polo shirt and a thin gilet, her clothes sticking to her body, her hair plastered to her head.

Daniel sniffed, 'Well, you best be off. Apologies for bumping into you like that. I'll wait here for Hugo.'

He moved to stand side on, adopting a position that

meant Holly had to sidle past him and be assaulted by his smell for a second time. Once past, she had to control herself so as not to look back, and not break into a run. Looking up, Hugo had gone, but she recognised Lara waiting for her at the top of the track, no doubt ready to discover why she'd been out the back of the yard and not doing her job. Holly didn't care. She needed to be among people and horses - and as far away as possible from Daniel Croft.

***

'Daniel Croft definitely knew what you were doing,' were Bain's first words when Holly bent her six foot frame into the passenger seat of her mother's Fiat 500 after her shift had finished.

Bain continued, 'Because when I first saw him, he was watching you from the corner of Hugo's caravan. It was afterwards that he went to knock on the door.'

'What? He saw me then...'

'...watched you for a few seconds, went back to the door of Hugo's trailer, knocked, and then purposefully walked around the corner of the caravan. He was *aiming* to walk into you.'

Head in her hands, Holly replayed the entire conversation with Daniel and a feeling of dread slowly entered her. The vet had played her!

'It was a perfect strategy when you think about it,' Bain added, sounding impressed, 'He wanted you on the back foot to question you, but with a good excuse for himself being down there that early in the morning.'

Holly settled into the passenger seat and without thinking, hugged herself to make herself feel better. She was aware of Bain looking over at her as he drove, but wasn't in the mood to say anything to him. Not yet. With three hours to replay the incident in her mind whilst finishing her shift, she'd come to the conclusion that she didn't want to return to the Dent's yard. What's more, there was something about the vet that made her stomach tighten and heart quicken. And not in any positive sort of way.

Feeling the silence in the car had become oppressive, Bain started to speak, 'I'm sorry. I missed him… my binoculars got wet, then they steamed up… I know, it's a poor excuse, but…'

'I'm not angry. At least, not with you,' said Holly.

Bain waited for her to continue. It took another excruciating two miles during which he was desperate to discuss the case, but forced himself to remain silent. She looked desperately tired, with dark rings under her eyes. Holly spent the entire time flicking between the handful of photos she'd taken through the window of the last caravan down the track. She turned her phone and zoomed in on certain areas, giving disgruntled groans every now and then. When she eventually said something, Bain was left in no doubt of her intentions.

'There's something funny about that trailer, Bain. The last one. For a caravan that's hardly ever used, there's a lot of footprints on the dust on the floor. Something's in there that Daniel didn't want me to see. He was nervous about it. It has something to do with Morgan and her being poisoned with snowdrop bulbs. I'm sure of it. I have to go back and get inside. And I think…'

Holly had to stop speaking. Whether it was excitement, or her mind being awash with possibilities, she was running out of breath. She took a moment to fill her lungs and let it out slowly, suddenly aware of the exhaustion washing over her. Meanwhile, Bain gave her an impatient half-smile.

'…I think I need to get inside that trailer, and as soon as possible,' she finished with conviction.

'You have remembered we're going to the races tomorrow?'

Holly swore. Of course, it was Mimi's horse, Morgan, racing at Ripon. It was her first run. All four of them were supposed to be going. Still, this was her job. Fighting the sleepiness trying to swamp her, but determined to know the truth, she made her decision. She picked up her phone and dialled a number. It was picked up after only one ring.

'Lara? It's Holly. I can work tomorrow now. Yeah, my plans fell through. Do you still need me at the yard?'

Forty-Four

The ship's deck was starting to take shape, but Gregory Blunt had yet to experience any sense of accomplishment. And that wasn't right.

It was Friday afternoon and it was wet outside. The house resonated to the sound of raindrops plinking onto windows and long greasy rivulets were running down the panes of glass, giving them an inadequate, and overdue washing. A broken gutter at the back of the house was spilling a constant rush of water onto his patio, the splashing adding to the drumming of rain on tiles coming from the kitchen roof. But Blunt wasn't listening, or even aware of the action of the rain.

The house was dark. Sitting at his dining room table, Blunt's desk lamp shone ninety watts of light onto his face, neck, and shoulders. He was consumed with his model, adding match after match in the correct order, all cut to the correct length and glued with microscopic accuracy.

Blunt had started creating matchstick models when he was a child. He'd never been happier than when he was up in his bedroom, patiently building scale models at his tiny desk, the combined smell of wood and glue softly comforting him. And as each model took shape, he would revel in the growing sense of achievement it gave him. Every match taking him closer to that ultimate moment of completion. And once the glue on that final match had set, for a few moments Blunt would be filled with accomplishment, and a soporific warmth would percolate through him. Oh, how he loved that feeling!

The Mary Rose should have been finished by now. But it was taking longer than it should. It was Miriam. He couldn't concentrate. His thoughts kept returning to his ex-wife. His failed attempt to rob her of tens of thousands of pounds at the Doncaster sales. His emasculating embarrassment at having to be rescued by her from his allergic reaction, and worst of all, his subsequent argument with her. Her words in that first aid room, with nurses, sales staff, and those awful people she now associated with… all of them, laughing behind their hands at him. Poking fun at his inability to deal with something as benign as a dog hair! The horror of that moment kept returning, swamping his thoughts. Until he was left with an image of his father, bearing down on him.

Blunt shivered. The image faded. He looked down at the deck of the Mary Rose. It was covered in a long, syrupy trail of wood glue that had already begun to set, ruining the four hours of work he'd put into the ship that day. He made a half-hearted attempt to mop up the damage, but the tissue stuck and only made the mess worse.

Getting to his feet he walked the length of the living room to the front window and glumly stared out. He studied the motorhome, sitting on his drive. He noticed the rust around the door sills, as if seeing them for the first time. It didn't drive well, and was uncomfortable and smelled of damp. It now seemed like a colossal waste of money.

He closed his eyes and grimaced. Perhaps Miriam had been right. What was it she'd said? 'He was wound too tight, he was a control freak, solely obsessed with his own miniscule world.'

She'd told him to, 'Find something he loved doing. Then he might discover someone who made him happy. It was no longer her. It would never be her again.'

Blunt sighed, and walked back through into the dining room and around the table. Looking out the back window he noticed there was standing water on his tiny lawn in the garden. That meant there was a chance of flooding. Living this close to the river made it a constant threat.

He turned and leaned on the table, inspecting his matchstick boat. It was perfectly illuminated by his desk lamp. It looked deformed, the deck was warped, the prow uneven and incorrect. Glue seemed to be bulging from every joint. It was a monstrosity.

Taking the corners of the plastic sheeting the model was sat upon, Blunt carefully pulled them together and tied them tight. He carried the bundle to the back door and out into the rain, where he smashed it against the wall of the house several times before depositing what was left of the model into the dustbin.

Time for a change, he thought, lifting his chin until the rain started to patter down onto his cheeks and rush through his beard. To do something he loved... that would be the key. He would take Miriam's advice. No more small-minded plans, he had to think big. He still had half his life to live. And Blunt knew what would make him happy. It had brought him joy before, and would do so again.

Once back inside the house Blunt fired up his ancient laptop he'd recovered from the loft after quitting his job and waited what felt like an eternity for a browser window to appear. Typing in the search terms, 'cheapest way to sell a house,' he'd listed his house for sale within a few hours with an execution-only web-based firm. He spent the rest of the day perusing travel websites and researching the best way for a single man to traverse the world. Then, he googled Miriam's name and intrigued, followed a link to the Racing Post website.

Forty-Five

Bain phoned DI Golden the moment they got back to Northallerton but was forced to leave a message. Every time their phone rang that night Bain and Holly rushed to answer, hoping it would be the policewoman, but by nine o'clock in the evening there was still no contact. They tried her a few more times, but their calls and messages went unanswered.

Perusal of Bain's news scanning software revealed the most likely reason. There were reports that police were acting on a reported sighting of Robert Farley on the outskirts of Stamford Bridge, about ten miles away from Malton.

It was a warm evening, so after a light dinner, Bain, Holly, and Ronnie decamped to the conservatory to discuss the Brooklyn Hartley case. They assumed Golden had to be in Stamford Bridge, and in Farley tracking mode; far too busy to discuss an inconsequential matter such as the poisoning of a racehorse and a possible plot to cover it up.

Bain was desperate to speak with Golden. Anything to stop Holly going back to the Dent yard, and specifically, that trailer - especially on her own. She'd got it into her head that she was going to do some breaking and entering at the Dent's yard the next morning and try as he might, he couldn't dissuade her. It didn't help his argument that Holly had done her homework.

'Lara told me that she's desperate for me to work because Graham and Hugo Dent will be heading off to Ripon tomorrow morning with the yard's four runners. What's more, Daniel Croft will also be at the races because he and his father are the racecourse vets at Ripon. There will be hardly anyone around the yard by late morning, so I can search the trailer knowing all our suspects have to be miles away,'

'And what is it you're hoping to find?' asked Bain. He already knew the answer, but wanted to make Holly say it.

Having picked up on Bain's resignation, Holly felt like grinning in triumph, but managed to remain poker-faced.

'I'm looking for evidence of the manufacture of a compound, of one sort or another, based on snowdrop bulbs. If I find it, I'll collect both photographic and physical evidence, and then leave the yard immediately. I've seen

Hugo and Daniel Croft hanging around the trailer. It has to be where they are either hiding or manufacturing their poison.'

'And if you don't find anything?'

'I'll still leave the yard,' promised Holly.

Up until now, Ronnie had remained silent, sitting in her favourite chair, her elbows on the armrests, fingertips touching to create a contemplative steeple. Her eyes had been closed, but they now popped open.

'I'll send the Widow Solanki with you.'

'No, mother,' Holly said, wagging an index finger, 'There's no need for that.'

'Tosh!' Ronnie replied in a tone that indicated it was already decided, 'I'm not having my daughter enter a den of criminals with no backup.'

'It's hardly a den, mother. I've been working there for the past six weeks.'

A grin slowly spread across Bain's face, 'Actually, That's not such a bad idea. Will Vlad be okay with missing Morgan's first run?'

'He will be,' Ronnie replied with a cold certainty.

'No, really, I'll be fine on my own,' Holly insisted, 'I'll go to work as normal and once they've all left for the races I'll head straight down to that last trailer, crack the lock open and see what I find inside.'

'You'll be breaking the law.'

'What? Who will care if I take a quick look in an empty old trailer at the forgotten back end of a racing yard?' challenged Holly.

Ronnie's eyebrows climbed her forehead, 'Oh, I don't know… how about a murderer with a short-bladed knife who is hell bent on making sure their victim's death remains unsolved?'

Holly opened her mouth to utter a rebuttal but after a moments reflection found her mother had effectively removed the wind from her sails.

'It's still breaking and entering, Hol,' Bain pointed out,

'The caravan is all boarded up and there's a hefty lock on the door. It makes sense to have someone there as backup, and Vlad is reliable. I'd come myself, but given the animosity between the Dents and Mimi…'

Holly cut him short by waving her hand as if she was holding a white flag.

'You have to go racing at Ripon with my mother,' she said, her shoulders slumping in defeat, 'I'll take Vladimir with me and we'll use the ear-buds. He can keep watch. He can't be any worse than you were!'

Bain's initially triumphant smile soon dissolved. He'd not been aware of the redness of Holly's eyes until now. And this tiredness was exaggerated further as she pushed herself gingerly to her feet and announced she was getting an early night. The long drive each morning, combined with the stable work and the pressure of the murder case was taking its toll.

'Whatever happens, tomorrow is your last day at the Dents,' he called out to her as she left the conservatory.

'We'll see,' she replied, 'We'll see what happens.'

Forty-Six

'You've delivered the product?'

'Yes.'

'Good. Any issues?'

'None,' Daniel replied, with a small twitch of his cheek muscle.

Leslie Croft muted the huge wall-mounted television and swung his legs off the expansive leather sofa.

'None?'

'That's what I said,' Daniel confirmed, heading to the fridge in the open-plan kitchen and selecting an ice-cold can of Pepsi, 'Don't you think I'd tell you if there was a problem?'

'So the collection point is secure?'

'What the hell? Yes, everything is fine. Everything is

just fine, dad. How many times?

He popped the tab on the can and took a swig of the cold bubbles.

'Everything is just fine.'

***

The centre of Stamford Bridge was finally free of flashing blue lights. DI Golden waved off the last of the search team at a little past midnight and climbed into her car. She sank into her drivers' seat and just sat there, exhausted. Happy to be comfortable and alone, she closed her eyes and emptied her mind of everything apart from the prospect of a hot shower and a soft bed when she got home.

The last six hours had been a complete waste of time and money. Several reported sightings of Robert Farley buying groceries from a small supermarket in the town's centre had led to an exhaustive search of the area right down and along the river bank. The endeavours of twenty officers, four dogs, two drones, and for the initial hour, a helicopter, had eventually rewarded them with their prize, a Robert Farley lookalike.

The unfortunate, middle-aged, bearded white male who had been tracked down to a boat moored on the river turned out to be a rather chunky bin man from Rotherham.

Golden had been required to calm the man and his wife down once the case of mistaken identity had been confirmed, although their twelve-year-old son had taken the experience in his stride. She was pretty sure that the North Yorkshire constabulary had provided the youngster with the highlight of his family's week-long cruise down the Derwent. After being bundled off their boat they had been pinned to the river bank by armed officers shouting commands at them and large dogs growled menacingly. Whilst the adults had needed to be treated for shock, their son had been treated to a friendly chat with the armed response team. Profuse apologies and red faces had been the order of the day.

It occurred to her that she hadn't checked her personal phone for hours. She examined the device, sat in its cradle, tempting her. She tapped it, but scowled when fourteen missed calls, twenty-three messages and numerous alerts blinked into life. She ran a tired eye down the caller and senders list and decided there was nothing that couldn't wait until the morning. She was too tired. The morning would have to do.

She started her car, and pointing it in the direction her Satnav decided was the best route back to Northallerton, realised that it was past midnight. It would be late morning before she saw to those messages.

Forty-Seven

June 5th – Ripon Races

'What's up with you?' asked Leslie Croft, watching his son half-heartedly chase cornflakes around his breakfast bowl.

'Nothing.'

'You're nervous. What's wrong?'

Daniel sighed and rolled his eyes, 'Seriously. Nothing.'

Leslie Croft knew his son. He lost his appetite when something was on his mind, and there was that thing with his face. Leaning over the breakfast bar, he examined Daniel's profile once more. There it was again, that tiny twitch of the cheek that told him that his son was nervy. And he didn't need him to be nervous today.

'You want me to do the pick-up?'

Daniel shook his head vigorously whilst scraping his unfinished breakfast into the bin. He looked up at his father and sighed with irritation.

'No! Will you stop it?' he demanded with both arms raised, 'You're the one who's nervous. You haven't shut up about me doing the pick-up since you got out of bed.'

Leslie sucked on his teeth, his gaze still set on his son. It was probably one of the side deals his son had going. Daniel had told him about the couple of small money-making projects he'd been undertaking at the Dent yard. He'd actively encouraged them, it was good for the lad to be taking the initiative. They were harmless enough.

'Okay. Let me know when it's done,' said Leslie, 'On the burner phone. And I'll meet you at Ripon at around eleven, after you've done your morning calls. Don't forget we're the on-call racecourse vets today.'

'I won't forget. How could I? You keep reminding me every…'

'Daniel!' interrupted his father in a bark, 'What is it with you today?'

Daniel threw his cereal bowl into the dishwasher and slamming it shut, shot his father an irritated glance, 'Nothing. Absolutely nothing. God forbid you show any belief in my abilities!'

Counting out on his fingers, Daniel continued, 'I'll do my morning calls, then I'll do the pick-up, then I'll travel to Ripon. By the end of the day everything will be wrapped up neat and tight!'

Forty-Eight

Beverley Hill Stables had been such a hive of activity all morning, Holly had hardly had the chance to finish one stable before she was being called to help out with this, take that over to whoever, or get on with something else. It was a relief to see the three horses due to run at Ripon that afternoon clamber onto their transport along with Amber, Lucy, and the travelling lasses. They were followed out of the yard by a separate car containing Graham and Hugo Dent.

Holly watched them leave and checked the time. It was

a quarter to eleven. Leaning her shovel up against the stable wall she was currently mucking out, she made her way to the tea hut to take the break she should have enjoyed two hours ago.

Stepping up into the tea hut caravan she was surprised to discover Lara in deep conversation. What was more shocking was that she was in discussion with Daniel Croft. Lara was a regular in the tea hut, but Daniel rarely joined the staff on their breaks, always preferring Hugo's company. So he shouldn't have been here. Not today, and certainly not at this time of day.

He was lounging back on a sofa while Lara was sitting on the edge of a kitchen chair, leaning towards him, her clenched fist grinding into her palm, trying to make a point. Croft didn't appear fazed by Lara's forceful delivery. Holly couldn't catch what was being said, as they both became mute once she arrived in the open caravan doorway.

Their conversation was of little interest to Holly. It was the sight of Daniel that had her sweating under the collar of her polo shirt. The vet hadn't been around all morning, which she'd taken as a good sign, given the awkward nature of their near-collision the day before. The fact remained that Daniel was supposed to be over at Ripon races with his father. If the vet was sticking around here it would put a serious crimp in her plan to investigate that mystery trailer. Lara looked up at Holly expectantly.

'I haven't had my break yet,' she volunteered warily, 'But... I can go...?'

Lara shook her head, 'No, you get a cuppa. Been a busy morning. I'm finished here.'

Lara got up and was through the caravan door without another word to Daniel. He also rose to his feet, but was languorous about it, yawning and stretching. Instead of leaving, he crossed over to the kitchenette and Holly tensed, aware of her vulnerability, now Lara had left.

'I'm glad I've run into you,' he told Holly, placing his

used mug into the sink but remaining there, inches from her as she reached for her own mug. Holly backed away, and left her mug on the shelf. She had no wish to brush against him.

'Allow me to make your tea for you. I'm feeling pretty guilty for giving you that shock yesterday.'

Holly flicked the kettle on and whipped round to face him. She didn't fancy keeping Daniel behind her and out of her line of sight for too long.

'I'm fine. It was nothing,' Holly replied, forcing a thin-lipped smile.

'Really, go sit down. I'll bring you your tea. I know how you take it, milk and one sugar isn't it?'

'No, really. I'm fine…'

'Oh come on, please?' he insisted, holding her gaze and placing his hands together close to his chest, as if he were about to pray, 'I'd like to apologise properly. And I'd love to get the chance to know you little bit better.'

'Aren't you supposed to be racing today?'

The vets lips pouted and one eyebrow moved slightly upwards, as if he was impressed.

'You're well informed,' he told her with a hint of arrogance, 'For a stable lass.'

Holly stared at him, her feeling of vulnerability returning.

An urgent shout of, 'Daniel!' made them both look to the open door of the tea hut. When it came again, closer and louder this time, the shout was easily identifiable as having come from Lara. They both barrelled outside and met her, running up from the paddocks.

'Bring your bag of tricks,' she ordered Daniel between gasps for breath, 'I've a gelding with a deep cut down his thigh.'

Daniel doubled back to his car for his bag, but managed to catch up with the two women by the time they'd reached the gelding's paddock. Holly recognised the horse immediately. He was a three-year-old called Freddie, a decent sort, although he could be a bit of a handful at times. He was standing, knees locked, in the corner of a two acre grass paddock looking sorry for himself. A five inch slice of flesh was peeled back from a gash of a similar size on his rump.

Holly guessed the injury was at least an hour old as there were several streams of dried blood running down his legs and back. Small crescent shaped pools of blood had filled a number of the gelding's hoofprints in the soft earth and was already coagulating. As Holly picked her way across the paddock she noticed crimson splashes on the blades of grass, presumably the result of the gelding's initial panic, although he seemed relaxed now. Freddie turned his head and regarding the approaching trio with a sullen acceptance.

'I've warned Graham about those old wooden fence bars,' growled Lara as the three of them made their final approach to the gelding.

'Freddie's cracked a wooden spar and then impaled himself on the shard,' she said, indicating the offending fence bar, 'They should have been replaced years ago.'

Lara stepped forward and managed to get a head collar onto the poor animal. Freddie made no move and seemed only too happy to be the centre of attention and under human control.

'He's gone mental and run around after he's done it,' remarked Lara, 'There's blood everywhere. But his testosterone levels must have dipped now. We should be safe enough.'

Daniel took a look at the injury, then ran his hands over the gelding's legs and spine, flipping effortlessly into professional vet mode. He ordered the gelding to be walked straight, and then in a circle.

'It's only a flesh wound. A nasty one, but it shouldn't have any lasting effect on his ability as a racehorse. The muscle will take time to mesh together, but he's walking fine. Let's get him back into his box. I'll get the wound cleaned and we'll stitch him back up.'

The sun was high in the sky by the time Holly and Daniel walked out of the shade of the barn. Lara had gone off to the house to make a call to give Graham and Hugo, and then Freddie's owner, the bad, but ultimately, good news. The yard was quiet, and yet Holly realised she hadn't thought twice about being left alone with Daniel. Both of them had been concentrated solely on putting Freddie back together again. For the last thirty minutes, she'd ensured the gelding remained quiet and content while Daniel worked on him. The result of Daniel's attention had been impressive. His intricate needlework on the cut meant that Freddie would be left with a scar, but not, as Holly had assumed, a misshapen backside. Daniel had been careful to ensure the contours of the geldings rump remained sleek and natural. If, as she and Bain suspected, Daniel was involved in doping Morgan, he was certainly a man of contradictions.

Daniel allowed his large, square veterinary case to drop and leaning up against the side of the barn he closed his eyes and turned his face to the sky, allowing the sun to warm his skin.

'I'm going to be late getting to Ripon. I won't get there until after the first race at this rate.'

Holly consulted her watch and her mouth dropped open. It was past one o'clock. Thank goodness Vladimir hadn't been able to make it today, he would have been expecting her to contact him a long time ago.

She hadn't told her mother or Bain about Vladimir being called away down south on a family emergency. She couldn't face all the hassle of them whining about her being at the yard alone. It was probably just as well, as her reason for being at the yard today - the trailer at the bottom of the dirt track - had gone right out of her head once they'd discovered the injured gelding.

'What time were you due at Ripon today?' asked Holly, hoping she could chivvy Daniel along and get him to leave for the racecourse, 'If you set off now, you'll just about make it in time for the first race.'

'My father is the head vet,' he said without opening his eyes, 'As always, I'm just his assistant. If I miss a race, he'll moan at me, but he'll cope.'

Daniel's irritation with this state of affairs caught Holly by surprise. It was the first time he'd spoken about himself, or his father, in any way other than complete confidence. Usually he was with Hugo, stroking the younger man's ego, joking with him, and making scurrilous remarks about the stable girls.

This was an unexpected opportunity. Had she the time, Holly could easily scrape away at this animosity toward his father. Something was bubbling away in Daniel's family life, perhaps surfacing because of their shared experience with Freddie. Her thoughts returned to investigating that mystery trailer at the end of the lane... she couldn't afford to engage with Daniel. How she wished he'd get on his way to Ripon!

She was considering suggesting she had to leave herself, when Daniel's eyes blinked open. His lopsided smile sent an involuntary shiver down Holly's back. Daniel had a calculating gleam to his eyes.

He bent down, flipped open his case and produced a small thermos flask from one of the compartments.

'We never did get that cup of tea I promised you,' he said, unscrewing the flask's cap and producing two small plastic cups. He poured two milky-looking measures and offered her one.

'Milk and one sugar,' he said, holding the cup out to her.

Holly hesitated, but took the cup with a tight smile, offered her thanks and again reminded him he was running late. If she could satisfy his request to share a cup of tea with him, he would surely leave. As she took her first mouthful of the sweet, weak tea, her gaze followed Daniel as he placed the flask on top of his case. It had always been facing away from her in Freddie's paddock, but now she could see all the compartments lined up in what amounted to a transportable apothecary. Her reaction to seeing a small bladed knife, lying in one of the open compartments, similar in every way to the one Robert Farley had handed over all those weeks ago, was to remind herself of Golden's words, that the knives were ubiquitous, used by everyone. It was when the image of Brooklyn's blood-soaked body rested in Holly's head that she shivered again.

Daniel closed his case, straightened, and smiling at her, lifted his plastic cup in a silent toast. He must have seen something in her face, as before the cup reached his lips Daniel's smile altered, and he adopted, for him, an unusually thoughtful pose.

'Would you be interested to see what's in that last trailer?' he asked in a quiet voice.

Holly choked on her tea, prompting Daniel to produce a grin that bordered on sinister, 'You know, that caravan you were hanging around yesterday when you should have been working?'

Coughing to buy herself some time to come to terms with this surprising turn of events, Holly decided playing dumb was her best option.

But Daniel didn't wait for an answer. He emptied his untouched drink down a nearby drain, then pointed his cup at Holly and narrowed his eyes.

'I know who you are,' he said, wagging the white plastic cup at her.

With the hairs on the back of her neck leaping to attention, Holly did her best to remain calm. She gave the vet a sceptical frown she hoped didn't reveal her rising concern.

'Holly Grant,' said Daniel, enunciating her name in a gleefully staccato fashion, pausing a moment to judge her response, 'You work with that investigative journalist who was at the Doncaster sales.'

'That's my name, but you've got the wrong Holly…'

'I'm serious,' he interrupted, cocking his head to one

side to stare belligerently at her, 'If you *are* Holly Grant the journalist, you'll want me to show you what's in that trailer. It will be the biggest story of your career…'

They traded a stare for what felt like an eternity, Holly desperately trying to read Daniels intentions. All manner of thoughts ran through her mind, not least the conundrum of why Daniel would be making such an offer. What would he stand to gain by showing her evidence of Hugo's misdeeds? After all, he knew who she was. He had to know she would act upon any unequivocal evidence. Quite apart from his offer, there was the question of whether she should trust Daniel. Was he dangerous? Should she shout out for Lara and Wendy in the house? They'd definitely hear her…

'Just the two of us,' he said, reading her mind, 'What I can show you will ruin someone's career prospects, but your career…,' he grinned, '…will go from strength to strength.'

Holly continued to weigh up her options. Meanwhile, Daniel waited impatiently for her response, tapping the palm of his hand with the base of his empty plastic cup, as if he was the second hand on a clock. He *was* acting strangely… yet that last comment had awoken an even deeper curiosity in her, not because of his promise of improved career prospects, but because Daniel must have thought long and hard about this moment. He'd assumed career advancement was the strongest reason he could use to make her go with him. Whatever was in that trailer, he was desperate she should see it for herself.

She rubbed her chin, buying herself further thinking time. He didn't seem to be dangerous - she didn't feel threatened in any way. But he was making her more certain that he was either aware of, or involved in something underhand with Hugo, whether it was the fraud at the sales, or the poisoning of Mimi's filly. Yet he wanted to show her something, *knowing* she was a journalist. And she *really* wanted to know what that something was…

Any thoughts of calling out for Lara, or not accompanying Daniel receded when he spoke again. His arrogant, gleeful air from earlier had dissolved, and maintaining a steady gaze the vet made his request once more.

'Holly, please…' he pleaded, 'Please, let me show you something…? You'll be saving my life...'

Forty-Nine

Ronnie and Bain entered the racecourse and after a short wander around the Club Stand enclosure, found themselves at the rails beside the winning post. Turning their backs on the final furlong of the track they admired the grandstand. A fine old three tier structure, a riot of flowers cascaded from the first balcony and underneath in four foot white letters the grandstand was emblazoned with the words, 'Ripon Races – Yorkshires Garden Racecourse.'

'It's a good job Holly checked with Mimi,' Bain pointed out to Ronnie playfully, 'Otherwise we could be standing in a car park in Redcar wondering why no-one was there.'

'I *told* her it was Ripon,' said Ronnie with a mildly contemptuous shake of her head, 'I do wish the two of you would listen. And you can stop being so cheeky!'

Bain responded with a chuckle, then suggested they head for the Owners and Trainers lounge as despite Mimi's horse being in the opening race, they had forty-five minutes to spare.

They found Mimi upstairs in the Owner's Bar holding court at a small round table with her young trainer, David Thorne, and his wife, Mary. Invited to join them, the five of them ate a few sandwiches together and discussed the filly's chances until the husband and wife team excused themselves to prepare Morgan for her race.

This prompted Ronnie to dive into her handbag and pluck out the full colour race card she'd been given when they'd entered the racecourse. Bain guided her to the correct page for the 2.10pm, the first race, and the only heat dedicated to two-year-olds on Ripon's seven-race card.

'So where's Morgan?' Ronnie piped up as she ran a fingertip down the list of runners.

She was keen to know the colours Mimi's jockey would be wearing, as she was looking forward to meeting the rider in the parade ring. Ronnie was no stranger to racing and had recently stood in the parade ring at York as an owner. However, on that occasion she'd been a shade embarrassed when the jockeys had entered the parade ring, not being sure who was who. This time she was determined to spot the rider early and know his name.

'It's actually a lady jockey,' Mimi announced proudly, 'She's called Chelsea Brooks. I met her at the stables the other day.'

Bain consulted his own race card and bit his lip, his eyebrows bunching up.

'What's wrong?' Ronnie asked in a whisper loud enough to carry to the next table, 'Isn't she any good?'

'No, it's not that. She's one of the best professional riders around,' replied Bain, giving Mimi an assuring smile.

In a lower voice he said to Ronnie, 'It's Morgan… I *assumed* 'Morgan' was the horse's name.'

This sent Ronnie scrambling for her race card again. Adjusting her bifocals, she found the list of fourteen runners for the 2.10pm and ran her eye down the names. None of them mentioned Morgan. She looked up at Bain.

'I can't find her,' she said, 'Isn't she running?'

Bain wasn't listening.

'He's away with the fairies,' Ronnie groused to herself, making a disgruntled tutting sound.

Bain continued to stare blindly up and out of the second floor window at the cloudless blue sky. She could see he'd taken himself off to somewhere inside himself, and Ronnie, being the restrained, mature woman she was… at least in public… stopped herself from barking at him.

Shaking her head, Ronnie tried her racecard again, this

time looking for Mimi's name in the smaller, italicised print beneath the bold of the horse's names. And then she saw it. Horse number eight in the first race was a two-year-old filly owned by Miriam Blunt and trained by David Thorne, carrying 9st 4lbs in a fillies-only Maiden over six furlongs.

'You called your filly, Guten Morgen?' blurted Ronnie.

Mimi frowned for a moment, but then smiled generously, 'Yes. I thought it was rather clever!'

'The filly's stable name was Morgan, but not the German spelling?' asked Bain, his attention back in the room.

Mimi nodded, 'Yes, the stable lasses at the Dent's called her that when I told them I was naming her Guten Morgen.'

Warming to her subject, Mimi continued, 'Morgan's father is a horse called Mehmas, which means 'Good Host' and her mother was a German filly called 'Stürmischer Morgen', or in English, Stormy Morning. Do you see what I did? I put the two names together. I thought it worked quite nicely.'

With only a quick breath, she added, 'There is another reason I liked 'Good Morning' as a name, but that's a bit personal...'

An uneven silence fell upon the table.

Mimi, suddenly aware the temperature around her had dropped to zero degrees, asked, 'What is it? Don't you like her name?'

'Of course we do!' Ronnie assured her.

'When did you name the filly?'

Mimi's smile faltered a little as she met Bain's ever-so earnest gaze.

Girding herself she replied, 'I decided on the name the day after I bought her at the yearling sales last August. She's got a German mother, so I thought something in her mother tongue would suit her.'

Bain nodded sagely, 'So the stable lasses at the yard knew this back in summer last year, which is why they gave her a *stable name* of Morgan.'

It was Mimi's turn to nod, her smile long gone, replaced with a puzzled frown, 'Is there a problem?'

'It's just…' Bain started.

'It's just er… We want to have a bet on her, and had to make sure we get the right horse!' Ronnie interjected sharply, simultaneously pulling Bain to his feet by his elbow, 'We'll catch up with you in a few minutes, Mimi. Bain and I are off for a cheeky little bet on… Good Morning.. er…Morgan!'

Bain was thankful to be in the fresh air. He and Ronnie walked away from the Owners and Trainers building and went to lean on the parade ring rails. It was getting busier, and in the background a band struck up with a brass version of Blaydon races. Standing shoulder to shoulder in the late spring sunshine, or rather, Ronnie's shoulder to his head, they stared at the perfect grass oval of the parade ring shaded by mature maple trees and bordered with spring flowers. Ronnie waited patiently for Bain to speak. Presently, he turned his head towards and up at her.

Holly said that the lasses in the yard referred to the horse that kicked Brooklyn as the 'German Horse', didn't she?

Ronnie nodded imperceptibly.

'Mimi doesn't know, does she?'

'No, she doesn't,' warned Ronnie, 'And there's no need for her to know that it was Morgan that kicked Brooklyn.'

'I know. I just can't get that image out of my head of Brooklyn smiling on that television programme,' complained Bain, 'There she was, calling out, 'Good morning' to everyone she met in York. And all that time she was calling out the name of the doped-up horse that almost killed her. The media actually called Brooklyn the 'Good Morning' girl for heaven's sake!'

He stared at his feet, cursing himself for not working out the link between Brooklyn's accident and Mimi's horse.

'It makes me wonder… Whether there was something inside Brooklyn's damaged brain that was desperate to get out. Some nugget of information it couldn't quite release.

Robert Farley was lucky that he was with her when she managed tell him, 'snowdrop'. That led us to the Dents...'

'We can't know that Brooklyn was trying to send everyone a message,' said Ronnie, 'She may have just been pleased to see people.'

Bain squeezed his eyes shut, reacting to a cold shiver that had just run down his spine.

'David Thorne told me confidentially that the filly would have been in constant pain from that snowdrop compound. He said the Dents must have given her a regular dose, not enough to cause any lasting damage, but enough to make the filly appear to be going slowly downhill and be worthless as a racehorse.'

Bain bit his lip, 'David said the filly wouldn't have been herself, liable to be anxious, temperamental, depressive, and possibly violent… and Brooklyn was in Morgan's stable, mucking her out when the accident happened…'

'But she must have *known* about the snowdrop compound,' reasoned Ronnie, 'That's why she told Robert Farley. Why would Brooklyn go into a stable with a horse she knew was potentially dangerous because it was doped up?'

Bain shook his head, 'Geena said she'd phoned Brooklyn *before* she left Britain. As far as Brooklyn was concerned, Lara had assured Geena that Hugo had stopped poisoning the filly…'

Ronnie looked to Bain. His lips were pressed shut so hard he was trembling. She placed a hand gently onto his shoulder, 'What is it?'

'They didn't stop, did they? Hugo Dent kept on… Oh, dear god… Brooklyn was kicked by a horse who was doped up and dangerous. And for what? To pretend Morgan was a lost cause, and so Hugo and probably that vet, Daniel, could sell her for a profit. And here we are here at Ripon to watch Morgan, a horse that almost killed Brooklyn, run its first race and…' Bain swallowed hard, '…and to cheer her on!'

Bain took Ronnie's hand in his, fighting to remain calm.

The thought of Brooklyn entering a stable with a filly liable to turn nasty made him feel queasy… And when Brooklyn started to recover, did Hugo decide to make sure she wouldn't talk?

Bain leaned back against the parade ring rails and tried to collect himself.

'Do you think the Dents realise they are responsible for Brooklyn's accident?' asked Ronnie.

'According to Holly, she thinks Graham Dent doesn't know what's going on in his yard half the time,' Bain said with a shake of his head, 'But Hugo and that vet Daniel... they're a different proposition…'

Ronnie was struck by a sudden change in Bain's expression. His face had gone slack and grey, his eyes were no longer on her. She twisted around, followed his gaze and took in the sight of Graham and Hugo Dent walking side by side. Father and son were heading for the Owners and Trainers building. Both dressed in tailored suits, they appeared calm and professional. They passed within ten yards of Bain and Ronnie without a glance in their direction from either of them. With the confidence of those who know they belong, both men breezed past the Owners and Trainers doorman without acknowledging him, entered the building and went straight up the steps to the café-cum-lounge.

'I feel sick to my core,' Ronnie griped, her upper lip bent sideways.

Suddenly angry, she said, 'Why on earth hasn't Golden arrested them? Surely she has enough on them, what with the goings on at the sales and that vet's report on Morgan?'

Bain had his nose in his race card once more, 'Golden's still not been in touch…. At least, I haven't spoken with her. All I got was a text message saying she was busy on another case and would call as soon as she could.'

'That girl is far too busy for her own good. I'm surprised she can solve anything the way she buzzes around. And always in such a bad mood!'

'I don't know. I think she's pretty impressive, given the job she's got,' replied Bain absently, still flicking through his race card.

Ronnie eyed him, her tongue stuck into her cheek, but Bain didn't notice.

'Ah, here you go…' he said, 'The Dents have three runners today, but nothing in Mimi's race, thank goodness. I wouldn't fancy standing beside them in the parade ring.'

Ronnie nodded her agreement.

They stayed at the parade ring rails for another few minutes, not speaking, both of them contemplating the damage Hugo Dent had inflicted. The course was starting to fill up and there was a healthy crowd, three deep in places, watching the horses for the first race enter the pre-parade ring.

Ronnie became restless, and pinched Bain's race card closed to get his attention.

'I'm going to get Mimi. We don't talk about Brooklyn, agreed?'

'Agreed,' Bain echoed.

He watched Ronnie hare off, dodging between racegoers as she made her way back into the Owners and Trainers building.

Ronnie returned a few minutes later with Mimi in tow, smiling with a wide-eyed, gleeful zeal. She winked at a beaming Mimi, the two of them almost skipping the last few yards over to Bain.

'You two are full of the joys of spring,' he commented.

His wary look amused Ronnie enough for her to giggle loudly. This set Mimi off. Bain sighed. The two of them were behaving like a pair of naughty schoolgirls. This always meant Ronnie was up to something.

'What have you done, Ronnie?' he said with mock dread in his voice.

'What hasn't she done!' Mimi exclaimed with an amused roll of her eyes, 'We met the Dents upstairs in the Owners and Trainers Bar.'

'I simply pointed out to pretty boy Hugo and that boring plank of a father of his that they both deserved to be flogged for what they did to Morgan and to Mimi,' Ronnie explained airily.

'You should have seen their faces!' exclaimed Mimi, 'It was priceless.'

Bain asked, 'Did they say anything in reply?'

'Hugo just looked stunned,' reported Mimi, 'Graham turned his back on us. But Ronnie was brilliant!'

Close by, a filly whinnied and there was a louder squeal from a horse in the saddling boxes that made everyone turn their attention to the pre-parade ring. The saddling area was now a hive of activity with the young fillies being readied by their stable staff.

Bain consulted his watch. A quarter to two. The runners would be crossing over into the parade ring in a few minutes. He had time. Time for the one question he'd been burning to ask since learning of Morgan's racing name.

'Guten Morgen... It's a really lovely name, Mimi. You said there were *two* reasons you chose that name for this filly. The names of her sire and mare was one, what was the other?'

Ronnie gave Bain a hard stare as they crossed over to the pre-parade ring. He returned an innocent smile.

Mimi compressed her lips and her cheeks flushed a little, 'It was Gregory, actually. You know, my ex-husband?'

'Really?' questioned Bain, nodding encouragingly.

'After we were married I got into the habit of making us both breakfast on Sunday mornings, bringing it back to bed so we'd eat together. You know, just some toast and coffee and a cuddle. Gregory loved it, he always was a creature of habit. When I brought the tray in I'd say, 'Good morning!' and he would reply, 'Ah, it's my good morning girl!' It was one of those daft things that stuck, like a pet name.'

Mimi smiled faintly at the memory. It faded almost immediately.

'It happened without me really noticing. I sleepwalked

into becoming his downtrodden maid, rather than his wife. I'd slave over a frying pan and deliver his full English on his lap at exactly half-past eight every Sunday, or face a whole day of snide comments. For the last twenty years I left him to eat his breakfast alone. I put up with him because I didn't have any other option, until the lottery money came along.'

Mimi paused, a regretful sigh issuing between her lips, 'I grew to hate those three words… which is why I had to reclaim them for myself.'

'So your name for the filly is…'

'My way of sticking two fingers up at my ex,' Mimi said with a shrug.

Ronnie held up two fingers and flicked them skyward, 'Good morning to you Gregory! Ha ha, I love it!'

'I suppose you could look at it that way,' Mimi said thoughtfully as several horses passed by on the other side of the railings. She took a big breath and let it out slowly.

'I've named my first horse 'Guten Morgen' to help me be at peace. To make those words into something I'll remember fondly, not something to loathe every time I hear them. And it's also a warning to myself. It's a warning to never put up with that sort of treatment from anyone ever again.'

'Good for you,' said Ronnie firmly whilst tenderly touching Mimi's arm, 'Hey, here she comes now.'

As Guten Morgen was led around the pre-parade ring by a smiling Mary Thorne, the trio's attention was fixed on the good-looking filly and her handler. Bain was the first to unlock his gaze, taking the opportunity to sneak a side-long look at Ronnie. To his surprise, like him, she wasn't following the two-year-old around the pre-parade ring. Instead, Ronnie was gazing fixedly at something, or rather, someone in the crowd.

Fifty

Daniel led Holly down the dirt track beside the line of static caravans. It was well on the way to drying out. Apart from the odd dark spot of mud, the first properly hot, sunny morning of the year was making the usually dull sides of the caravans shine. She was following a few paces behind, in case she needed to bolt, sure she could beat the vet in a straight running race up to the Dent's house.

They passed Lara's caravan, and Hugo's, which she'd half-expected to be their destination. Daniel didn't give the padlocked door to the final trailer in the line a second look, and to Holly's surprise, continued around to the opposite side of the caravan. This side faced into the woods, constantly in shade, thanks to the encroaching sycamore tree. This was the side of the trailer she had ignored because it was a blank apart from one tiny, boarded up window where she had imagined the toilet may once have been located.

'Give me a few seconds,' Daniel said, lifting a hinged two inch square metal cover in the side of the caravan that was virtually invisible if you didn't know it was there. The metal plate revealed a padlock beneath.

Rolling the spindles until the padlock clicked open, he inserted a few fingers, and with a flat palm placed further down the caravan's side, pushed, then pulled. To Holly's surprise, Daniel proceeded to easily swing a four foot by three foot hinged piece of aluminium siding out from the caravan, leaving a dark rectangular hole in its side.

'No need to climb through a window,' he told her with a cocky smirk before getting down to his knees and crawling through the hole.

Moments later, Daniel's face appeared in the secret entrance in the caravan's side, 'You coming?'

Holly fought off her reservations. She'd come this far, she had to go inside. For the first time that morning, she regretted not having Vladimir watching over her. She bent over and crawled in after Daniel.

It was the smell that hit Holly first, a mixture of rodent urine and rotting… she wanted to say manure, but it didn't have that rich odour of a mature compost heap. This was more like rotten fruit, vegetables, or a fungus; a confused smell of decay infused with ammonia.

'Let me see your phone,' ordered Daniel as soon as she got to her feet, 'You're a journalist. I'd be disappointed if you didn't have it recording me.'

In semi-darkness, Daniel had pulled the secret door to the caravan closed and was now standing in the corner of the trailer. The only reason she could pick him out was because of a sliver of sunlight that cut across his shoulder. Its source was the window she'd tried to open the day before, the board was still pushed back where she'd forced it, trying to get a few photos.

'I've not got anything, just my phone,' she said, holding it up so he could see its illuminated face, 'And it's not recording. Stop messing around Daniel, why have you brought me in here?'

Daniel raised his hand and she flinched, only to discover he was actually reaching for a large plastic block on the wall. He clicked the switch down. Strip lights pinked into life along the roof of the caravan, four out of the five eventually managing to reach full illumination, the fifth annoying continued to flash on and off, bestowing uncertainly upon the bottom end of the caravan.

The trailer wasn't as empty as her grainy photos had led her to believe. A rusty old fridge was set against the left-hand wall and a long trestle table stretched down the opposite wall, covered in scraps of racing newspapers, magazines, and a layer of dust deep enough to run a finger through. However, as she had pointed out to Bain, there were a large number of shoeprints on the floor of the caravan. She counted at least three different sizes and tread patterns - several people visited this trailer.

To her left was a doorless freestanding wardrobe, empty as far as she could make out. The only other piece of furniture was a tattered old sofa that filled the back wall, the lucky recipient of the flashing strip light. It lent an ominous feel to the piece of furniture it probably didn't deserve. A thin layer of lino with a repeating square pattern, ripped and possibly eaten in several places, served as a floor covering. Otherwise, the caravan was bare.

'Impressive, isn't it?' Daniel joked in a poor attempt at humour.

Smirking at the lack of any reaction from Holly, he nodded at her pockets, 'Your phone holding charge and got a signal?'

He approached her, his hand held out, 'Let me see.'

Holly rolled her eyes, 'I'm not giving you anything, and get any closer to me and…'

He snorted derisively and shook his head, 'Hah! You've no idea have you?'

Daniel leaned forward, demanding attention, his face only two inches from Holly's. The flashing strip light was distorting the shadows on his face, making him appear to alternate between a snarl and a leer, 'You're going to need the phone… to call for help.'

Holly's reaction was automatic, visceral, and to her horror, extremely effective. Without thinking, she rocked back on her heels, locked her arm and thrust her whole body into a flat palm that went straight into Daniel's face, striking him forcefully with the heal of her hand. He yelped in pain.

His nose stood little chance, exploding with a sickening crack of cartilage that made Holly wince. With wide, shocked eyes, the sheer force of the blow took Daniel off his feet and he landed on the floor of the caravan, backside first.

Holly stared down at him, her arm still extended, astonished and pleased, then wracked with worry over how the vet might react. The last thing she wanted was a fist fight inside this filthy tin box. An image of the small, sharp knife in

Daniel's case leapt into her mind and she looked around the caravan for any sort of weapon but came up blank. God, she wished Vladimir was with her, she should have listened to Bain.

Her worry was soon replaced with puzzlement. Daniel seemed to think it was funny. He remained on the linoleum, carefully handling his nose and to Holly's amazement, chuckled as he inspected the blood on his fingers. But as quickly as it had arrived, his levity disappeared, to be replaced with sadness.

'I can't help it,' he said, head down, morosely rubbing the blood between finger and thumb, 'I've been raised by a monster, to be a monster. A chip off the old block…'

'Daniel?' Holly asked quietly, 'What are you talking about? I don't understand. This concerns snowdrop bulbs and poisoning Mrs Blunt's horse, doesn't it?'

Daniel snorted in amusement, then winced from the pain that immediately flowered from his broken nose.

'You've no idea what Hugo's involved in. He's the lynchpin in this operation. I've the proof down there,' he replied, indicating the end of the caravan where the sofa was being sporadically lit by the malfunctioning strip light, 'You need to see what's in the floor.'

Feeling she was safe to move down the caravan, Holly backed away from Daniel, nonetheless keeping a close eye on him. She edged backwards until she couldn't go any further. He remained on the floor, consumed with his attempt to stem the flow of blood from his nose.

The sofa was in a dire state and almost certainly had something like mice or rats living inside its frame, based on the amount of gnawed fabric and shredded foam littering the floor.

Having never been a fan of small rodents, Holly shivered, and satisfied she'd covered the entire floorspace and found nothing, she was about to call up the caravan to Daniel when something caught her eye.

She would have missed it if it wasn't for the bits of yellowing foam that had all been swept to one side about a yard from the sofa. This part of the caravan floor was covered with a ragged square of dirty mint green carpet and someone had rolled one edge of it back, collecting the foam bits in a yard-long wave. Either that, or someone had swept the pieces up, then inexplicably left them in a line.

'Found the box yet?' Daniel called out.

Holly jumped at the sound of his voice, swinging round. Daniel was sitting up, legs akimbo on the lino where she'd left him. This was very unlike him… she couldn't work it out. It was almost as if he was *enjoying* his broken nose and the game of hide and seek.

'There's something wrong here,' she said, grasping the edge of the carpet and tugging at it. It came away easily.

'That's it, you've got it,' he smiled.

Holly didn't like that smile. It was the sort of smile a cat gave a budgie before it extends its claws and whips the unsuspecting bird off its perch. She shivered and tried to concentrate. She was staring down at a steel plate, measuring one by four feet, hinged on the long side. Kneeling down, she lifted the plate up and back, resting it against the sofa. Underneath was a large plastic box, the sort for storing garden equipment. Its lid was level with the floor of the trailer but the box itself extended below and into the void beneath the caravan.

'What's in the box?' she called back to Daniel, reaching down to grasp the black plastic lid with both hands. Spring loaded, it lifted easily. She paused after a couple of inches, waiting for an answer. He was a vet after all, she shuddered to think what sort of horrors he might have squirrelled away in secret boxes beneath a decaying trailer. Maybe that's what this was all about, Daniel's idea of a sick joke.

'Take a look,' Daniel said with a shrug.

Holly pulled the lid upwards, hoping she would be faced with snowdrop bulbs, equine syringes, or tracheal washes filled with the same compound that had rendered Morgan so ill for so long. The lid settled on its hinges, almost vertical, and Holly peered in.

'Oh, fudge.'

Daniel snorted a laugh, which was swiftly followed by another cry of, 'Owww!' as he tenderly held his nose in his hands once more.

'My thoughts exactly,' Holly replied grimly whilst studying the contents of the box, 'Daniel? What on earth has Hugo got himself into?'

Fifty-One

Robert Farley hadn't had too much to grin about since swapping his comfortable bed and breakfast for squatting on the top floor of an unoccupied set of offices. However, the sight of Daniel Croft having his nose broken had been both unexpected, and enjoyable.

He'd been following Holly Grant's progress at the stables on and off for a few weeks. Since he'd visited her at her house in Northallerton it had only seemed right to be on hand in Malton, where the evidence and their investigation had brought Grant and Bainbridge. He'd been impressed; she was a hard worker and wasn't too bad at surveillance either.

He'd been witness to a number of cleverly manufactured instances that had allowed her to study the young vet and his sidekick, Hugo, up close. He'd surveyed all of this from afar, ensuring he was well hidden. However today was different. He'd been forced to break cover and get close enough to this trailer to overhear what was being said – close enough to satisfy himself that the young woman wasn't going to come to any harm.

So far, he was more than satisfied. In fact, the source of his first genuine smile of the day had come when he'd spied her planting the vet onto the seat of his pants from a small crack between the rotting floorboards and the aluminium side of the caravan.

She'd found something under the caravan, he didn't know what, but it had spurred the vet to launch into a speech that, if true, was nothing less than startling

Farley saw no need to intervene. At least, not yet. Instead, he would continue to listen.

Fifty-Two

'Penny for 'em?'

'Umm, what?' Ronnie replied distantly.

Bain gave her a questioning smile, 'Something has got your brain working overtime. You've got that look you get when one of the Yorkshire Post crossword clue answers is playing hard to get.'

'Mmm. We mustn't let her see him,' Ronnie said out of the side of her mouth, checking to make sure Mimi was still over at the pre-parade ring rails, watching Mary Thorne lead up her filly.

'Okay, see who?' Bain asked impatiently.

Ronnie bent her head down to Bain and in a loud whisper said, 'Over there, standing on those steps overlooking the parade ring. Beside the woman in the white dress and flamingo pink hat.'

Bain was relieved Mimi wasn't in the immediate vicinity. Ronnie couldn't have been more obvious about imparting her secret. She may as well have hollered and waved. At least three racegoers close to them had heard her and were nosey enough to be following his gaze. However, looking over at the woman in the pink hat, Bain was immediately drawn to a figure in a grey raincoat next to her. The nose and his close-set eyes gave him away. It was Gregory Blunt.

He was standing on the lower step closest to the parade

ring rails, hands in the pockets of his coat, grimly watching the first of the two-year-old fillies transfer from the pre-parade into the parade ring.

'Oh, great,' Bain moaned, 'I'm assuming Mimi didn't invite him?'

'Definitely not,' Ronnie confirmed with a shake of her head, 'She told me he'd sent her a letter apologising for Doncaster and saying she wouldn't be hearing from him again because he was selling up and moving abroad. She was over the moon.'

Bain took a moment to take another, longer appraisal of Blunt. From the look on his face, Bain reckoned Blunt wasn't here at Ripon for the horses, nor the convivial atmosphere. A terrible, gut wrenching thought travelled across Bain's mind. He turned to face Ronnie and took her hand in his, demanding her full attention.

'Whereabouts did Mimi live before she won the lottery?'

Ronnie blinked, trying hard to dredge up the information, 'York. Yes, I'm sure it was York.'

'Anywhere near the river?'

Ronnie's frown turned into a wide-eyed stare, 'Yes, she told me she used to watch from her back garden as the pupils from St. Peter's school rowed past on the river. How did you know?'

'A wild stab in the dark,' he replied, immediately regretting his chosen turn of phrase.

He squeezed Ronnie's hand tight, 'I think he could be Brooklyn's killer.'

Fifty-Three

Hugo nursed a half pint of lager at the Owners and Trainers Bar as he watched his father do the rounds of the tables to meet and greet other trainers, horsemen, and his owners with runners later in the afternoon. Thankfully, the news of them running up the prices at the Doncaster sales hadn't gone any further. They'd even got the money off Cooper and been able to pay off Conor Moran. So there was little chance of embarrassment on that score. However, it had been a shock to have Miriam Blunt and her mouthy friend accost them as soon as they entered the bar. The encounter had served to remind him that Miriam's filly was racing today, a situation that had left his father in a foul mood.

Given the conversation he'd had with his father during their journey to the racecourse, facing Miriam Blunt's anger had been troublesome, but expected. Being dressed down by Miriam's friend she'd called 'Ronnie' had been more challenging. He'd been left with the distinct impression he'd met that lady before, but couldn't place her.

Hugo had told his adoptive father everything in the hope that he might understand and help extricate himself from the huge mess he'd created.

Being completely alone with his father for the eighty minute ride to Ripon had offered him the perfect opportunity. It had felt good to unburden himself, just as it had been when at the age of fifteen he'd revealed his homosexuality to his family and received unequivocal support.

He'd explained to his father how he'd fallen for Daniel, and how the older, more experienced vet had started visiting the yard on a daily basis, often with no reason other than to spend time with him. He'd spoken about poisoning Morgan, and how they had intended to sell the promising young filly for profit once Miriam Blunt had given up on her.

Throughout his fifteen minute speech, his father hadn't said anything. He'd driven the car, his eyes fixed on the road ahead, with nothing more than a purse of his lips, or a small sigh. His father's face had turned red when he recalled how he and Daniel had argued about euthanising the colt for the insurance money, but he hadn't blown up as Hugo had expected. When Hugo had finished, his father had pulled the car over into a layby. He'd switched the engine off and they'd sat in silence for the best part of a minute, his father simply staring out of the windscreen at the oncoming traffic.

'Making a living from being a racehorse trainer is tough. You know that, Hugo,' his father had eventually said, 'We do it because it's a way of life we choose for ourselves. But poisoning horses, and to contemplate killing a horse for profit… as a man who has spent his life caring for horses, it makes me sick to my bones.'

His father had gone quiet, staring blankly through the windscreen and into the distance for a couple of miles. Without warning, and still staring ahead, his father had asked whether anyone else was involved. He'd replied no.

Were there other schemes Daniel was running in the yard? No, he'd answered, not to his knowledge.

Was the relationship with the vet over?

He answered yes. Daniel asking him to kill the colt had made him realise what a mistake he'd made in trusting such a man.

Then his father had asked a question Hugo hadn't expected. He had answered truthfully, and his father's lengthy reply had been so liberating it had filled his heart with renewed hope.

Taking another sip of his somewhat bitter tasting drink, Hugo leaned against the Owners and Trainers Bar, waiting patiently for his father to return to his side. He wasn't interested in the alcohol, it wasn't needed to give him a kick. His adoptive father had already given him that.

Fifty-Four

'One hundred and seventy-five thousand pounds in used notes,' Daniel smirked, 'That's about the size of what Hugo's into.'

Holly's mouth had gone dry and she was finding it

difficult to prise her gaze from the contents of the garden hamper. Fifty pound note bundles filled the box, each held together with a number of elastic bands, lengthways or in a roll. Still on her knees, she leaned forward and picked up one of the bundles. It was heavier than she expected and flicking through the wad of cash she began a quick calculation. Daniel was way ahead of her.

'Fifty notes in each, two and a half grand per bundle. A hundred and ten bundles makes one-hundred and seventy-five thousand pounds,' commented Daniel from behind her.

Holly stared into the box again. She'd been expecting… What had she been expecting? Snowdrop bulbs? The sheer volume of cash piled below her was boggling, and yet, the mountain of money was strangely beautiful at the same time.

She blinked twice to clear her head. That much cash was beguiling her. She tried to concentrate on Daniel. What exactly was he up to? Why would so much money be lying here? What did he have to gain by leading her to it? These and many more questions began cramming her brain so full of possible answers and counter arguments she became befuddled. A sudden, overpowering urge to speak with Bain washed over her. She needed to make sense of this nonsensical pile of money, or at least receive a response that was honest, something she was sure Daniel was incapable of providing. Her free hand unconsciously went to the jeans pocket that held her mobile phone.

Still sitting on the floor of the caravan, Daniel watched for another couple of seconds, trying not to smile. So far, he was pleased with Holly's reaction to his grand reveal, and judged it was the right time to discover whether this girl really was as squeaky clean as she made out. He got to his feet and returned to stand at the opposite end of the caravan.

'It's amazing the effect that money can have on some people. Being presented with that much… possibility, sends all sorts of thoughts through your head, doesn't it?'

Daniel allowed his words to settle, studying Holly as

she continued to kneel over the mound of money in the floor. Standing in the corner of the caravan, the bar of sunlight from the window was slicing down one side of his face and glinting off the brass buckle on his belt. If he directed the reflections in a certain way, flashes of silver bounced off the banknotes and sparkled onto the roof of the caravan. Those sparkles partially illuminated Holly's features.

Presently, Daniel asked, 'How long would it take you to earn that sort of money?'

Years, Holly thought, ten at least, probably more… Wow, with that sort of money she could…

Her self-loathing hit hard when it kicked in, but Holly accepted it gladly. She slammed her eyes shut for a second. How had she been so easily tempted?

Telling herself to get a grip, and not dwell on what had happened over the last few seconds, Holly took a couple of ragged breaths. It was the speed at which the temptation and greed had crept over her. The promise of wealth had covered her in a warm, selfish blanket.

Holly shuddered. Whatever this was, wherever the money had come from, and whatever game Daniel was playing, she knew she wanted none of it.

With the spell the money had cast swiftly dissolved, Holly's fascination with the hoard turned into a heady mixture of guilt and revulsion. Realising with disgust she was still holding onto one of the wads of money, she threw the bundle back into the sunken box, spun round to face Daniel, and sprang to her feet in one easy movement.

'What is this?' she demanded of Daniel in a low voice, her eyes fixed and unwavering.

'This?' Daniel repeated airily, indicating the trailer with a glance around and a shrug, '…is my father's drop-off and pick-up point. He believes in separation of manufacture from distribution.'

'Stop talking in riddles, Daniel.'

'Oh, come, come, Holly. You're the journalist,' said

Daniel with a forced chuckle that left an ugly twist on his lips, 'Can't you work it out?'

For a fleeting moment, Holly considered smashing her hand into his face again in order to wipe away the arrogant smirk and force him to speak plainly. She was taller, had a longer reach, and it would be *so satisfying*. Images of the sickly filly, Robert Farley, and the bloodied body of Brooklyn flashed across her mind. Daniel's arrogance could be quashed later. Instead, Holly concentrated, running Daniel's words through her mind again. Manufacture and distribution…'

'You're… all of this is…' she started, but froze, poised ready to launch herself at Daniel when he unexpectedly dug a hand into his jacket's inside pocket.

Pausing with his fingertips just inside his jacket, Daniel lifted his free hand into a calming palm.

'Whoaa! Cool your jets, detective!'

He slowly removed a transparent plastic bag, holding it out at arms-length between finger and thumb, offering it to Holly. She snatched it from him, stepped back, and examined the diamond-shaped blue pills, each with an 'E' stamped into them.

'For the last six years, my father has been the primary supplier of high-grade ecstasy to drug gangs based right across Yorkshire,' said Daniel in a dead, monotone voice, 'I'm his bloody assistant, and Hugo, bless him, is my father's get out of jail free card.'

Holly stared at him. If Daniel was acting, his performance had just improved immeasurably. He stared back at her, his face striped with the single bar of sunlight, otherwise pale and sullen.

'But your father is a vet. He's a *racecourse* vet for heaven's sake,' Holly said, shaking her head, 'You're saying this place is used to drop off… what? Payments?'

'In exchange for the product,' Daniel said with a heavy sigh, gesturing to the sunken box, 'I drop the tablets in there. Hundreds of thousands of them. Hugo makes sure no-one tampers with this trailer. We text the client on a burner phone. They pick up the shipment and leave the payment behind. When Hugo calls, I have to collect the cash the next morning… it offers anonymity for both buyer and seller. That's why I was around here yesterday morning when I bumped into you. I was supposed to pick up the money but couldn't because you were hanging around. This trailer is the perfect place because it's always locked and therefore private, hardly ever used, easy to access through the woods via a public country road and if anything was ever discovered, there's no link back to my father.'

Holly noted that Daniel's mood had shifted. His amusement had been replaced with a weary frustration. She tossed the packet of pills onto the sofa, not wanting to touch them, and watched Daniel as he began pacing from one side of the caravan to the other, head bent forward, staring at the dirty lino, still talking.

'Poisoning the filly was my father's idea. I blame myself. I'd heard from Hugo that she was tearing up the gallops after only a week or two in full training and mentioned it to him in passing. He convinced Hugo we could clear a couple of hundred thousand if we could convince Miriam Blunt that Morgan would never be capable of racing, offer to find the filly a good home, then ship her abroad, bring her off the snowdrop bulb mouthwashes to win a couple of races and sell her on. But then Geena found out… she told Brooklyn and…'

His voice trailed away.

'And what, Daniel? What did your father do?' Holly demanded sharply. She was beginning to lose patience with him.

'I want out,' he shouted back at her, 'I'm tired of being his whipping boy, his drugs mule. I don't want the money, the constant worry, or to be forced to do the things… the terrible things he makes me…'

Daniel was shaking a fist at Holly but the effort of

shouting seemed to have emptied him of all his energy. His chin dropped to his chest, and with shoulders sagging and with arms limp by his side he slowly shook his head.

'I've no friends because of him,' he murmured, 'Like Hugo. I've lost him. My father told me to…'

Daniel winced, 'Never mind, it was awful. I just want to be *normal*. You're a journalist. You were putting everything together, the snowdrops, the filly, Geena and Brooklyn. I saw an opportunity. My father is an evil, manipulating liar who pedals misery in the shape of blue pills. I want you to tell everyone my story, even if it means I end up in prison. At least I'll be free of him.'

He emitted a shuddering sigh and fell silent.

'Where does your father manufacture these pills?'

Daniel inhaled another deep breath and said, 'Under the veterinary surgery,' as he exhaled.

'It used to be a coaching inn. He cooks up the ingredients in the cellar.'

Holly took out her mobile phone, woke it up, and tapped it a few times. Daniel seemed unaware, too busy gazing at the open chest of cash. The call connected and she walked to the other end of the caravan and turned her back on Daniel to grant herself a little privacy as she waited for DI Golden to pick up.

'Don't go anywhere,' she called over her shoulder.

Fifty-Five

'Is something wrong, you two?' enquired Mimi, her mouth puckering with concern.

Bain offered her a reassuring smile, 'No, nothing at all. You know what Ronnie's like!'

Mimi didn't look convinced. She rather liked her friend's odd behaviour, but this was beyond anything she'd encountered to date.

'Just soaking up the atmosphere, my dear,' Ronnie declared with a smile so intense it made Mimi recoil a little and knit her brows together.

Ripon's parade ring was a thing of beauty. In Bain's opinion, the best in the north, and certainly the most floral. From the shade of one of the three mature trees allowed to cast their shadows onto the finely clipped turf inside the egg-shaped ring, Bain and Ronnie had made a point of keeping Mimi closely quartered. Annoyingly, Blunt had vanished from his position beside the ring. Between scouring the crowd for any sign of Gregory Blunt and keeping Mimi under close guard, they'd achieved both, but failed to hide their intentions from the one person who mattered most.

Ronnie in particular was acting out of character, which was a stretch for her. She'd already squealed three times, believing she'd seen Blunt, only for it to be a false alarm.

'It's just that you seem a bit… distracted, the two of you,' Mimi persevered.

'Oh, here comes your jockey with David,' Bain announced with more than a little relief, pointing over Mimi's shoulder.

Dressed in bright orange with white checks, Chelsea appeared young. Really, very young. Ronnie couldn't believe that a fourteen year old could be allowed to ride, and found herself telling the girl so.

'I'm nineteen,' the girl assured her with a grin, 'I get that a lot. I don't wear make-up when I ride, and the helmet makes every jockey look younger. You wouldn't recognise me out in Leeds on a Friday night!'

For a couple of minutes the possibility of Gregory Blunt being the 'Good Morning' girl killer was set to one side as they engaged with David and Chelsea. All too quickly, the call of 'Jockeys, please mount,' came over the public address system and the focus of the crowd altered as the riders did as instructed, and filed out onto the racecourse to begin hacking down to the six furlong start.

'We need to tell her what we know,' Bain said to Ronnie as they watched Chelsea and Morgan exit the chute and kick off into a trot down the track and disappear behind the grandstand, 'We don't know where he is, and we can't protect her with so many people around.'

'Right. Come on, I've had enough of this. Spill the beans,' said a voice from over Bain's shoulder.

When they turned to face Mimi she eyed the two of them expectantly, hands on hips, waiting for her answer.

'We think Gregory may have killed Brooklyn Hartley,' said Ronnie baldly.

Bain winced.

Mimi's expression didn't alter. She switched from Ronnie's weak smile to Bain's embarrassed, but grimly serious stare, and back again.

'That poor young girl? But that chap they're after…'

Ronnie's smile went tight and she shook her head.

'You called your horse, Good Morning. It wasn't just your nickname, it was Brooklyn's. She was the 'Good Morning' girl. She used to pass the back of your house every day on her daily dog walk. Gregory lives within half a mile of where she was killed. You said he was angry around that time in October because you'd left him. Maybe when the local TV station did that interview it tipped him over the edge…?'

Mimi shook her head, 'No. Gregory was a horrible husband, but he never hit me or hurt me.'

'You said he used to smash things?' suggested Ronnie.

'Well, yes. He could be downright vindictive. He once slashed a photo of my mother because… well, you don't need to know why, it was over an old pair of trousers… but he never actually *hurt* me.'

Bain said, 'He's here today, Mimi.'

The fifty-five year old appeared to age a decade in a matter of seconds, making Bain wish he'd kept this last nugget of information to himself. Ronnie, who always seemed attuned to these things, put an arm around Mimi and gave her a squeeze.

'He told me he was selling up and leaving to live abroad,' Mimi told them with a dazed expression.

'I suppose that could be true,' Ronnie replied uncertainly, 'But we've seen him today. It's definitely Gregory, although he seems a bit... different. Do you think there's any way we could be right? Could Gregory have killed Brooklyn, the 'Good Morning' girl out of... I don't know... frustration or a twisted revenge?'

Mimi paused a moment in contemplation, before replying with a resounding, 'No!'

She brushed Ronnie's hand off her arm and collecting herself, began to march across the freshly deserted parade ring and towards the entrance to the grandstand.

'I'm going to watch my filly run in her first race, and to hell with Gregory. If he comes anywhere near me, he'll get a whack across the face!'

Ronnie chuckled and Bain rolled his eyes. Before Mimi could lose herself in the crowd, they hurried after her.

Fifty-Six

Golden had received the call from Holly twenty-five minutes ago and that's how long she'd been cursing and slamming her hands onto her car's steering wheel. Why hadn't she seen it? The 'Doctor' who had supplied most of the northern organised crime gangs with ecstasy for the last few years was a flaming *animal* doctor. Suddenly, so many otherwise meaningless leads, snippets of information from along the network of pushers and informants about the location, distribution, and manufacturing volume of the tablets made sense. It *all* made sense!

Leslie Croft and his son. Now *that* also made perfect sense. A search of the police database had revealed the father had grown up on a tough estate in Sheffield and been involved with a number of known villains as a teenager. Shoplifting, a couple of misdemeanours and a short prison sentence for supply of a small quantity of cocaine, and then he'd fallen off the radar. For the last twenty years Leslie Croft hadn't troubled anyone. He'd paid his taxes, built a thriving business, was respected in the community, and to anyone on the outside, appeared to be living an understated, upstanding rural life.

A check of his veterinary qualifications saw him having qualified abroad. Not standard for a British National, but nevertheless, acceptable. Further checks had seen Leslie Croft's name popping up as a director of several companies based offshore. Now that had been of interest. Of even greater interest were his past known associates… in particular a co-conspirator in his youth who was now heavily involved in organised crime rings in north and south Yorkshire.

Golden turned onto Old Maltgate and grimaced as she approached the Croft Veterinary Practice. She'd been here only ten days ago. She'd walked past the surgery and ignored it…

***

Golden's instruction to stay put hadn't sat well with Holly at the time of her call, and it wasn't working out to her liking. Given the yard's location, Golden had promised police back-up would be at the yard in twenty minutes. That was ten minutes ago, and she was feeling terrible. Daniel had offered her another drink from his thermos, which she'd gratefully taken, so now she and the vet were at opposite ends of the trailer, waiting. Her head was throbbing, her vision blurring and it didn't help that Daniel kept asking her how she felt every minute.

She'd tried calling Bain, but he hadn't picked up. A check of the time had given her the reason why; Morgan's race was about to start. Typing out a text message to him had made her dizzy, and she was now sitting, almost doubled up on the filthy sofa at the back of the trailer, trying to keep her eyes open.

Her stomach growled angrily at her and the band of pain across her forehead increased from a thump to an assault. What was wrong with her? She'd been feeling weary for days, if not weeks, so this had been coming, but why now? She didn't know the answer, she couldn't concentrate. That blasted flickering strip light! Every flash was sending a dagger of hot white pain through her head.

Holly bent further forward, cradling her head in her hands. She watched with a fevered fascination as the grubby rug on the floor of the caravan began to dance and flicker a number of different colours, as if viewed through a kaleidoscope. She had to stay awake! Blinking her eyes open took a huge effort, but she managed it, only for another burst of pain to encompass her entire head. She was grateful when the lights went out.

At the other end of the caravan, Daniel watched intently as Holly's agony increased. He voiced his opinion that, 'She really didn't look well at all,' for the last time and watched the investigative journalist flop onto the floor.

Daniel took out a phone and sent a short text message.

***

Leslie Croft waited patiently at his favourite pitch, a few yards beyond the winning post, for the first race of the day to go off. Being a racecourse vet was generally an enjoyable day, and having Daniel with him usually meant he did the minimum amount of work and enjoyed the maximum amount of hospitality. With his son missing, and no answers to any of his attempted communications, Croft was in a suitably bad mood.

Just before the off, one of his phones buzzed against his chest. It was a device he only used for certain personal messages. Private and untraceable. And when he read the contents, Leslie Croft knew he had to initiate his exit strategy. He typed out a short message, took a moment to check it was correct, and as the racecourse commentator announced the race was off, Leslie Croft sent a coded message that would bring about the obliteration of his business and most likely, the next few years of his life.

***

In the cellar beneath the Croft Veterinary Practice a hidden device clicked into life. On the opposite wall a circuit box crackled as an ignition took place. It would take a few minutes for the surrounding plastic to melt, but once it met the solvent drenched plasterboard Leslie Croft had carefully installed around the socket, the fire would take on a life of its own.

***

On the rails, almost level with the winning post, Bain and Ronnie stood alongside Mimi, looking back at the sea of faces. While Mimi concentrated on the huge screen that adorned the old information building in the centre of the racecourse, they were busy scanning the crowd for one face.

'This is impossible,' Ronnie complained, 'Blunt could be anywhere.'

'Keep on looking,' Bain replied above the sound of the race commentary booming from the public address system, 'Mimi may not be taking this threat seriously, but the more I think about it, and having met the man, I'm not willing to take the risk that Gregory Blunt doesn't hate his ex-wife enough to hurt her. A race meeting offers every opportunity for him to creep through the crowd and... well, you get the picture. We know he's here, and besides, who on earth wears a raincoat on a day like this?'

Ronnie considered this for a moment.

'I don't think you can brand a man a killer for wearing a raincoat on a fine day.'

'Just keep your eyes peeled,' he shot back a shade defensively.

As the race unfolded on the straight course behind him, Bain paid it little attention. Sweeping his gaze from left to right, he tried to pick out the movements of one person among several thousand. As he scanned, slowly but surely, an un-scratchable itch developed in his mind. Something he was missing. A nagging note of caution was vying for brain space with his need to keep a constant vigil. Something in the recesses of his mind had started a fire. It only smouldered, but it was enough of a distraction for Bain to miss Gregory Blunt, standing on the raised hump of grass just beyond the winning post. Blunt was watching too. His eyes were on Miriam.

***

At least I was only twenty or thirty minutes away, thought Golden as she pulled into the vets' surgery, drew to a squealing halt outside the automatic front doors and ran inside. She was soon back out again, having received confirmation from the receptionist that neither Leslie Croft, or his son, Daniel, were on the premises.

Of course they aren't, Golden said to herself. Holly had told her all of this! Daniel was with her at the Dent's yard and Croft senior should be at Ripon races. But it was good policy to check. She didn't want any nasty surprises...

The surgery was built around the remains of a nineteenth century coaching inn, although little of the original architectural features remained. The back of the property still boasted stables and a small amount of turnout, but it was a modern, flat-roofed building that Golden had to run around before reaching a set of padlocked gates that led into a small cobbled courtyard behind the original inn.

Scaling the gate wasn't a problem, although her arrival into the courtyard was met with the howl of at least two dogs and the continued barking from another. Thankfully, they were all contained in their own private cages.

'Cellar... looking for a... cellar' muttered Golden to herself.

She'd expected a pair of heavy wooden doors to be set into the cobbles, through which pubs across the country accepted their casks of beer. No such entrance existed here. Golden hunted around, eventually returning to a metal grate she had originally discarded as a sewage manhole cover. Bobbing down onto her haunches, she could see the cover was standing slightly proud on one edge, she slipped her fingertips under the edge and yanked. It flipped up, much lighter and thinner than she had anticipated. Underneath was the oak boarding she was looking for. An open padlock lay on the boards. Golden tossed it aside. However, it still took a full two minutes of frenzied pulling and pushing for her to get one of the three boards to move, and then lift away. She was rewarded with a set of stone steps leading into darkness.

What she hadn't anticipated, was a sucking of air into the cellar below and an almighty whump of smoke and sparks as the cellar, feeding on the new source of oxygen, exploded into life. Golden was sent sprawling backwards onto the cobbles as the remaining two wooden boards were blown several yards into the perfectly blue, cloudless sky. One of them landed with a clank on the flat roofed extension and set the dogs barking again.

Ears singing with the blast, Golden got to her feet and after checking herself for lost digits and limbs, was happy to scrabble back to the hole in the ground and carefully peer inside.

A mixture of grey and black, oily smoke was twirling its way up and out of the two foot by four foot square hole and it soon forced Golden to pull back and take a deep breath of fresh air, but she'd seen enough. There was a decision to be made. It looked like a laboratory down there. Either she got the evidence she needed now, or she waited for help, and hoped the cellar wouldn't become a melted wreck, incapable of producing any evidence of the drugs it had once illicitly produced.

Golden stabbed at her phone and barked a torrent of commands into it. Then she set it to camera mode and returned to the smoking hole in the ground. She peered at the thin stone steps for a moment and took a deep breath. The fire brigade were on their way, the staff and clients in the surgery had been warned to exit the building… and she was going in.

***

Chelsea Brooks screamed at the rider to her left whose filly had come across her as the stalls opened. Morgan threw her head up and half-bucked for a stride before settling a length off the back of the field, and five lengths away from the front rank.

'Brilliant', Chelsea complained to herself ruefully, 'I get one ride for the day, and I've already lost a couple of lengths.'

But if her one ride on Morgan up the Middleham gallops was anything to go by, she was on a horse with a decent turn of foot.

It took until after the first furlong pole had slid by for her to cool the filly down and get the youngster to use herself properly. Once travelling, a gap appeared in front of her and she let out a little rein to allow Guten Morgen to move forward so the filly was sharing last position, a competitor on both sides.

David Thorne's words returned to her as the duo of horses alongside her and another to her far right were asked to quicken by their pilots, their hands punching vigorously up the necks of their two-year-olds.

'Don't start riding a finish until she's gone through the undulations two out. Let her find her feet first.'

As the three pole spun past to her left, the filly went up a small rise and then grabbed for the ground on the downward side. Tempted to correct her and start pushing, Chelsea crouched lower in the saddle but fought the urge to start asking the filly for more, and waited. Morgan changed her legs and surged forward on the rising ground, making up four positions in the same amount of strides.

Surprised to suddenly find herself in third position with just over a furlong to run, and with the undulations behind her, Chelsea pushed. Third on debut would be a good result for the filly, given the start she'd got. Concentrating on keeping Morgan balanced should ensure she maintained that position. Yet judging exactly where she lay in the field was impossible. To her left the leader was on the grandstand rails, Morgan had edged into the centre of the course, and the second placed runner, to whom she was now drawing to its quarters, had veered to the far, inside rail. These were all green, inexperienced fillies… perhaps she had a chance of second place…

A slap down the filly's neck was all that was needed to keep her straight and claim second place from the unruly competitor to her right. And what had appeared an impossibility only a moment before, now sent a new surge of belief rippling through Chelsea's veins… this filly was learning quick, and she could race! The horse and rider on her right soon vanished from view, and the leader was so far to her left she couldn't make out exactly where they were… she kept it simple, focused straight ahead and pushed. Morgan responded.

The red ring of the finishing post shone in the foreground, vivid on a canvas of blue sky and trees in full leaf. Two strides remained. The grandstand had already rushed past in her peripheral vision, and so Chelsea urged Morgan on in one final effort to pass their remaining rival. There would be no use of the whip today, not on the filly's first outing. With her ears flat to her head, nose dipping, Morgan stretched out. Together, they cut through the photographic beam on the winning line as one, both stretching every sinew.

Chelsea lowered her reins onto Morgan's withers, then chanced a sharp look to her left before the track cut away to the right. Her breath escaped in a sigh as their opponent rounded the bottom end of the course ahead of them.

***

Her eyes wouldn't open. Even a fractional movement of her head made the interior of the caravan become more distant. Holly tried not to panic. She breathed. She concentrated on nothing else. Slowly, like the ebb and flow of the tide working its way up a beach, the sounds from the caravan returned.

The panel door opening. Scuffling and a scraping close by, and bags being dragged, moved. A sweet smell that quickly became pungent. No chat, no conversation. Holly could feel the floor of the caravan swaying slightly as the weight of one… or was it two… people moved around. Another scraping sound, a set of muttering. Goodbyes? Holly sensed someone approaching the end of the caravan, footsteps almost on top of her.

A shout. From outside this time. Asking a question.

The feet beside her scraped as they turned. Perhaps this was a good time for her to groggily wake up?

The decision was immediately stripped from Holly's thoughts when something hard slammed viciously into the back of her head.

***

Golden was three-quarters of the way down the stone steps into the cellar before realising she may have bitten off more than she could chew. The cellar was a swirling fog of acrid smoke, flames had just broken out on the wall opposite and the heat was intensifying every second.

Clicking photos on her phone, she started to cough, wishing she'd thought of covering her mouth and nose with some sort of cloth or gauze before venturing into this hell hole. She could see two sacks at the bottom of the stairs, and on a nearby bench a stainless steel cauldron. Other laboratory-style items swam tantalisingly into view, but disappeared just as quickly as the smoke rushed around, trying to find an exit.

Two more steps down, a few quick photos, then out, she thought. Golden could feel the heat singeing the hairs on her neck, but perhaps being just a yard closer would allow her to have proof of what this place was dedicated to manufacturing. She sucked in what she hoped would be a clean breath and stepped down.

Smoke immediately filled her lungs and she coughed violently, lost her balance and fell forwards into a fog of dirty, thick smoke. Landing heavily on the sacks at the foot of the steps, all the remaining air in Golden's lungs was expelled, and she immediately gasped, tears now streaming from her stinging eyes… and yet she still held her phone up in her right hand.

For a moment, the smell of the burning and smoke was replaced with a musty, almost sweet odour and as Golden pushed herself up she tipped one of the hessian sacks and found herself being covered in a cascade of little white bulbs.

Close to the cool floor of the cellar, the air was still poor, but at least when she took a pair of ragged breaths, it didn't illicit another coughing fit. She gratefully took a third breath, deeper than the others, and squinted up the steps leading to a small oblong of daylight that indicated where that final breath needed to take her. She *had* to climb the steps and get out.

Screw this, she told herself, I'll be beggared if I'm going to die down here.

She stuck her phone back in her trouser pocket, pushed herself to her feet and shielding her face with her arm, set off upwards. Breath held, slitted eyes stinging, and clothes so hot they felt like any part of her could spontaneously catch fire, Golden was forced to use arms and legs staggering on all fours up the stone steps and into ever-thickening smoke.

Head down, hands feeling their way up the steps, Golden made progress. After what felt like an interminable number of steps she chanced a look up. The square of light had become larger. It had to be only a few steps further until she could take another breath. Suddenly excited by the prospect of being able to breathe again, she scrabbled up the next two steps, misjudged one with her right foot, and slipped. Her forehead smacked into the edge of a step, soon followed by both knees. Dazed, she slipped down two, perhaps three stone steps and lay uncomfortably on her stomach. But only for moment. She had to move, time was her enemy. Golden tried to push herself back up. Pain ripped through her legs. Automatically inhaling a breath, the black smoke coated her mouth, stung her throat, and her lungs fizzed angrily in protest. Overcome with the heat, smoke, pain, fear now filled her. Becoming woozy, the fear and pain receded and Golden felt oblivion beckoning.

A set of strong, rough hands grasped Golden's wrists and pulled. She could feel herself traveling, no, *bumping* over the steps. Was she going up or down? She couldn't be sure. Suddenly, her eyes were flinching from the light. She was being dragged over cobbles, then laid against someone. Someone breathing hard. She couldn't see who, she was still blind, tears streaming down her cheeks, and sporadically coughing up all sorts of gunk from her lungs.

He was saying something, asking, no telling… telling her to breathe. To breathe evenly… slowly.

Spinning over onto all fours, retching and coughing, Golden took the offered advice and the weariness began to fade. After a few more seconds of life-affirming fresh air, she tried to open her eyes. A man's smiling face, covered in smuts, swam into view. It was a face she recognised.

Golden coughed once again, turned over and sat on the

cobbles of the surgery courtyard, her legs out straight and wide, hands flat to the floor, keeping herself upright. She tried to speak, but her mouth was too dry. She ran her tongue around, swallowed, and tried again.

'You're…' she gasped, 'Under arrest.'

Robert Farley grinned and flashed an amused eyebrow at her.

***

'Photograph, photograph.'

The judge's voice reverberated around Ripon racecourse and the crowd, still bubbling with excitement, turned their attention to the television screens, desperate to see a replay and determine the result.

'The photograph is between horse number one, Gordon's Goal, and number six, Guten Morgan,' the disembodied voice added.

Mimi turned around from the rails where she'd been jumping up and down in the closing stages of the race, her fists punching the air, and launched herself towards Ronnie.

Having long since given up trying to locate Blunt, in favour of watching the closing stages of the race, Ronnie welcomed Mimi into her arms and the two fifty-somethings danced around awkwardly for a few seconds, bouncing off each other, whooping and squealing with excitement.

'Did she win?' Ronnie asked, holding onto Mimi's arms to try and calm the dance.

With eyes sparkling, Mimi replied, 'I don't know! I don't care! She just ran so well!'

Bain followed their celebration with one eye, the other still scanning the local area. Torn between congratulating Mimi and keeping Blunt away from her, he kept reminding himself that coincidences did happen, but rarely. Blunt was here at the races for the debut of a horse named expressly to… rile him up. Here was a man who had already tried to defraud his wife at the sales, and not only failed, but been humiliated. He had been in York when Brooklyn was murdered, his house being only a matter of a few hundred yards away from where she was found. In the past, he'd been happy to smash, break, and slash things when Mimi had incurred his wrath…

A figure caught Bain's eye on a raised knoll a little way behind the chute that led to the track, and a thought occurred to Bain.

'Mimi, you need to tell me, what did he use to slash that photo of your mother?'

Slightly calmer, but now waiting nervously for the result of the photograph, Mimi frowned back at him.

I might as well be speaking a foreign language, thought Bain.

'Please, Mimi,' he implored her, cocking his head to one side to look around at her, 'It could be important.'

She grimaced, but to Bain's relief, closed her eyes and screwed her face up as she dedicated her thoughts to that particularly dark memory.

'It was his modelling knife. That's right, he'd been building one of his matchstick models. It was a liner, the Titanic, I think.'

'What, like a scalpel or a Stanley knife?'

She shook her head, 'No, it's a small thing with a wooden handle,' she said, raising her hands and holding them about five inches apart, 'Really sharp. He was forever slicing into his fingers with the blasted thing and bleeding everywhere. Now, tell me why a thing like that could be of such importance!'

Bain compressed his lips.

'Because Gregory is standing behind you. He's wearing a raincoat despite it being a clear day, and he hasn't taken his hands out of the pockets for the last minute. He's got a face like thunder and has been glaring at you and Ronnie ever since the photograph was called.'

Mimi and Ronnie immediately swung round.

'I'm also a little perturbed by the fact that he seems to have given up shaving and washing his hair.'

'Good God, Bain,' Mimi gasped, 'If I'm not mistaken, he also appears to be wearing his pyjama bottoms. I recognise the stripes – I bought them two years ago in the John Lewis sale.'

'Nice,' said Ronnie absently, her gaze still on Blunt.

The three of them continued to stare the fifty yards across the heads of racegoers at Blunt on the higher ground, who glared back.

'Is it just me, or does he look like he might explode at any moment?' commented Ronnie lightly.

'Oh, my!' Mimi exclaimed, 'You don't think he wants to blow us up...'

'Not his style,' Bain quickly assured her as they continued the stared standoff, 'You said it yourself, he's never touched you. He's purposely upset you, belittled you, and even tried to defraud you of some of your lottery winnings, but never physically assaulted you.'

On something of a roll, and with the words coming easily to Bain, he continued, 'He's been trying to control you with mental torture, by hurting the things you love. Like the photo of your mother.'

Mimi only had a fleeting moment to consider Bain's conjecture before the loudspeakers attached to the grandstand made a popping sound, three notes played, and the hub-bub in the crowds on both sides of the racecourse fell to almost nothing. Into the silence, the brass band's rendition of 'On Ilkley Moor' could now be heard coming from behind the grandstand.

'Here is the result of the photograph for first place.'

This was met with a collective intake of breath as the announcer paused.

'There is a dead-heat...'

The announcer continued, but was almost drowned out by cheers and groans in equal measure, then general discussion.

Smiling as Ronnie and Mimi embraced again, Bain checked on Blunt who remained a static figure with his hands in his pockets. If anything, the man's glare had become even more intense.

'You go,' Bain told the two women, 'Go and enjoy your win, Mimi. I'll keep an eye on Blunt. He's not moved, so maybe he's just come to glare at us.'

Mimi didn't need telling again. She and Ronnie scuttled off toward the grandstand gate. Blunt was still standing motionless. On the racecourse, the runners were starting to return to their lads and lasses, the unplaced horses being relieved of their jockey and tack. Among them, Bain could see Chelsea and Guten Morgen being led through the melee by Mary Thorne, a huge smile on the assistant trainer's face.

Bain tore his gaze from Guten Morgen and Mary to contemplate Blunt once again. Mimi's ex-husband's glare had altered direction. He was following Ronnie and Mimi as they headed for the winner's enclosure.

Bain started to move towards Blunt, a sick feeling in his stomach. His own words from a few moments before the announcement of the result replayed in his head and Bain found himself saying, 'He doesn't hurt Mimi, he hurts the things Mimi loves.'

If that's true… the one thing Mimi is loving at the moment, jumping and dancing happily with was…'

'…Ronnie!' Bain said out loud.

And she's just about to walk with her back to Blunt as she heads to the winners enclosure, Bain finished in his head as he began sprinting for the grandstand gate.

Shimmying past people at a half run, Bain skipped through the grandstand gate, bumped someone, apologised over his shoulder but kept on going. Blunt was still there, on the other side of the chute, still glaring from his knoll, although now he was closer, Bain could see the corners of Blunt's mouth were slightly upturned, as if stuck. His hateful glare frozen as it turned into a manic grin.

Bain thought about shouting a warning to Ronnie. However, he was only a matter of yards away from Blunt now, albeit the two sets of rails that made up the chute divided them. He decided against it, Blunt still hadn't moved and with three of four horses now coming off the course, he could end up causing chaos among the returning riders for no good reason.

He reached the walkway chute rails and couldn't go any further. There was a gateway across the chute fifteen yards to his left, but it would soon be closed to allow the horses to come in from the course. Locking eyes with Blunt he shook his head at him and mouthed, 'No', but still refrained from shouting.

Very slowly, Blunt's rictus grin transformed into a full-blooded snarl. If Bain had needed any confirmation that Blunt wasn't in his right mind, the state of Blunt's eyes were enough to convince him. Watery and desperate, Gregory Blunt looked to be in pain.

Without warning, Blunt pulled a pair of empty hands from his pockets and he darted forward, dodging between a couple of racegoers, as he headed straight for the chute rails, arms and legs pumping to produce a sudden burst of speed.

Caught off-guard, a puzzled Bain watched as Blunt reached the white plastic chute rail, jumped, and scrambled over the five foot high barrier. Where was he going? Ronnie and Mimi were heading in the opposite direction? He mounted the rails on his side and slid over to join Blunt in the chute.

Blunt growled an angry, 'Get out of my way!'

A terrible thought hit Bain.

'Blunt would ruin things Mimi *loved*… but she hadn't loved Brooklyn, had she? Was the fact the media named Brooklyn the 'Good Morning Girl' enough for Blunt to kill her?'

The walkway chute was busy. Unplaced jockeys were

returning from the course, lads and lasses passing each other on their way to the weighing room, or to the stables, and the first of four horses home in the race had just entered the top end of the chute on their way to the winners' enclosure. One or two people were now looking guardedly at Blunt and Bain as the two of them took up a classical confrontational stance, a few yards apart.

'I can't let you do it,' said Bain.

Blunt frowned and asked in an exasperated tone, 'What is your problem?'

Up close, Bain could see that Blunt's glare was more glassy than it had appeared from over thirty yards away. Also, the man didn't look so much angry, than in pain. As if to confirm this, he squeezed his eyes shut and rubbed. The answer to Bain's query over the bloodshot eyes and red marks across Blunt's cheeks was answered.

'Bloody dog hairs,' Blunt complained, 'I must have bumped into a dog owner. At least I'm not throwing up this time.'

Blunt dipped into his raincoat and removed an inhaler. After shaking it, he sucked in a deep breath.

'This should keep the symptoms at bay,' he told Bain as he exhaled.

Bain's aggressive posturing relaxed as Blunt showed him the red plastic box that held his back-up medication, the same one Mimi had produced from her bag at the Doncaster sales.

'Just in case,' said Blunt, 'I guess I relied too much on Miriam and didn't appreciate...'

Blunt trailed off, a mixture of emotions stunting his ability to speak. Unless Bain was badly mistaken, this wasn't a man about to conduct a heinous act. Although his attire still needed some explaining.

'What are you doing here, Mr Blunt?' Bain asked as one of the placed horses passed between them. He waited for the animal and its lass to pass before adding, 'You know you've given Mim... er, Miriam a fright.'

'Really? Oh blast it. I suppose my eyes looking like this hasn't helped… my allergy has flared up a bit.'

He blinked hard several times, grimacing on each occasion. Bain found himself wincing in response and he realised he'd mistaken the onset of Blunt's allergy for the bug-eyed stare of a madman. His eyes really did look sore.

'I had this idea that I would lead her horse in,' Blunt said, wiping gunk from the corner of one eye, 'You can do that can't you – lead the winning horse in? I thought she'd like me to do that. You know, to show there's no hard feelings before I head off abroad. I saw the name of her horse on that racing website and it made me think…'

He blinked at Bain again and shrugged, 'I wanted to make a grand gesture.'

Opening his raincoat, Blunt revealed he was wearing a complete set of stripey pyjamas.

'I thought she might think it was funny?' he said hopefully, 'There was a time when she laughed a lot. I used to call her my Good Morning girl.'

Bain took in the pyjamaed Blunt and wrinkled his nose. As he did, two more horses were led past, one of them with a grinning Chelsea on board. Bain waited until horse and rider had gone by.

'Well Gregory, she erm… Miriam *might* see the funny side,' Bain said doubtfully.

Blunt hesitated, reading the uncertainty in Bain's expression, then gave a sharp shake of his head.

'No. I can see this was a mistake. I thought it would be a good way to say a final goodbye to her, but I've misjudged it. This being big-hearted is harder than I imagined. Besides, I'm getting a few strange looks in this get-up. It was ill-judged.'

Blunt looked over to where Miriam and Ronnie were waiting for the arrival of Guten Morgen and Chelsea.

'Tell her I'm delighted for her... in all sorts of ways.'

Bain agreed he would.

'I've got a brand new camper van outside. Got rid of the old one. I'll be in France by tomorrow,' he said with a smile and some excitement, but then his face became grave and he shocked Bain by reaching out and taking his hand in both of his.

'Tell her…' he bowed his head, as if unable to squeeze the last couple of words out, '…tell her I'm sorry.'

With that, Blunt thanked Bain and headed for the exit. He never looked back. Bain watched Blunt until he was outside the racecourse, striding into the car park, then he bolted for the winners' enclosure.

He found Ronnie and Mimi in raptures over their winning horse and jockey, with lots of hugs and photos being taken. This was only increased when he gave them a potted version of his encounter with Blunt. Next to them, the stable lad with the joint winner looked on bemused, with no connections present for the highflying stud that owned Gordon's Goal.

David and Mary Thorne had winning grins filling their faces, in stark contrast to Hugo and Graham Dent. For some reason the duo had parked themselves on the steps of the weighing room, behind one of the columns that gave the building a temple vibe. Standing a little to the side of Morgan, the Dents were looking down on the celebrations with grim amusement. With some relief, Bain realised neither Mimi or Ronnie had noticed they were there… yet.

After a good amount of hand shaking and kissing, Bain backed up to the weighing room steps and pushed his way between the Dents.

Bain leaned in on Graham Dent, 'Given the circumstances, do you think it is sensible for you to be here?'

Dent cogitated for a second and looked sideways at his son before speaking.

'I knew nothing about the debacle at the sales or what my son was doing to this filly. I'm here to support him in case it gets ugly. The boy has something he wants to say to Mrs

Blunt.'

Hugo caught Bain's eye and held his gaze. A smidgeon of the arrogant young man was still there, buried deep, but Bain got an overarching sense of contrition.

'Don't tell me, tell her,' Bain said, motioning towards Mimi, 'She's an understanding woman, she'll listen.'

The lad nodded and with a final glance at his father, he jogged down the weighing room steps, tapped on Mimi's shoulder and started to speak with her.

Bain and Dent followed the conversation without knowing what was said, and after a rocky start, Mimi's expression softened and she listened.

During an announcement over the public address system asking for the racecourse vet to attend the stables, an insistent vibration in Bain's pocket had him diving for his phone. Holly! He'd almost forgotten. She must have news on what was inside that trailer!

With so much to tell her, he answered the call without checking the caller ID and was shocked to be cut off within two seconds of launching into his greeting. It was Golden.

Between coughs, she imparted the bones of what had happened over at the Dent's yard and in Malton at the Croft Veterinary practice. Bain said a few words, then hung up the call.

Taking a deep breath, Bain dropped down the weighing room steps. Landing softly onto the turf of the winners enclosure, he waited impatiently for the racecourse photographer to finish taking photos of Ronnie and Mimi accepting a prize of a glass vase etched with the word, 'Winner'. Bain instantly approached Ronnie, pulled her to one side, and with a stoney face told her that they needed to leave the racecourse immediately for York General Hospital.

Fifty-Seven

June 4th - three days later

Daniel Croft woke to the sound of his mobile phone loudly announcing a call from his bedside table. Taking a moment to rub his eyes with the heels of his hands, he swung his legs out of bed, grasped the phone and peered blearily at the caller. It was unknown.

It was ten-thirty. He'd slept in. A shot of panic suddenly coursed through him. He'd missed opening the surgery, he had visits to… His pulse slowed as reality hit. The surgery was closed, all his appointments were cancelled. The business had been shut down, at least for the next few days until the fire damage was assessed, the building was certified safe, and more importantly, the police forensic team had finished their work.

He tapped his phone, 'Daniel Cr…'

'Hello, Daniel.'

He'd been expecting it, but hearing his father's voice still sent a shot of electricity around his nervous system. He took a breath and held it for several seconds and wondered why his father, just the sound of his voice, held such a grip on him. After all, he'd won. He opened his mouth to reply, but his father was already speaking.

'How would you like to play this, son?'

'What do you mean?'

'Should we pretend you didn't sell me out and talk about the trial, prison visits, and how we can make things work? Or would you prefer we discuss your plan to usurp me?'

His mouth dry, Daniel paused to run his tongue around his lips before he answered.

'You treated me like a slave. What I've achieved proves I'm your equal… and more.'

A chuckle vibrated its way into Daniel's ear.

'You know something, Daniel? I'm almost proud of you,' Leslie Croft said airily, before his tone darkened, 'Almost. You always rush at things headlong. You don't think things through. You end up making what could have been very simple, terribly complex. I assume you had help?'

'What makes you say that?'

Again, that chuckle. Daniel could feel his patience beginning to flatten out.

'I *know* you Daniel. I brought you up. I crafted you into what you are today. I know you weren't ready for this sort of project. I blame myself, I gave you too much rope… and you've hanged yourself. And I know you had help. Who was it? That Hugo boy you're so keen on?'

'I didn't have any help, father,' responded Daniel in a steely, uncompromising tone he was pleased with, 'I took you and your business down. I did. On my own. You'll go to prison and I'll…'

'Run the business?' his father interrupted with a laugh composed of condescension, but no mirth.

'I've already found where you stashed all my equipment. Did you really think I wouldn't know about your storage units?'

Daniel almost cut the call. He paused, staring down at the unknown number on his phone's screen, knowing his father was speaking on a mobile smuggled into the prison expressly for his use. He pursed his lips and sucked up some courage.

'You haven't told the police?'

'Why would I? It doesn't concern them.'

'Have you taken the equipment, the chemicals?'

'What would be the point?'

'So why…'

'That's your problem, Daniel. You don't cover the bases. What did I always teach you, Daniel? What is the rule that guides everything we do?' his father asked.

Daniel knew the answer. God, did he know that

answer! But he no longer *needed to answer,* not to Leslie Croft.

'Always have an out, son.'

Daniel was pretty sure he heard his father sigh before he rang off. It was the sigh that bothered him most about the conversation. He stared at the phone screen for one, maybe two minutes, eventually tapping it several times to block further calls from his father's number.

Fifty-Eight

June 19th - four weeks later.

Bain adjusted the oxygen mask on Holly's unconscious face, stared for the umpteenth time at her vital statistics displayed on the monitor above her bed, and sat back down on the chair that had become his second home over the course of her laboured recovery. He noted with satisfaction that her face had a pinprick of colour to it today, but she was still a long way away from being... Holly.

He consoled himself with the knowledge that at the very least, the numbers on the screen had settled into something approaching normality over the course of the last week. Those first few days had been tortuous, her extended period in critical care, that moment on the second night when the alarms had rung and she'd been rushed back into an emergency theatre and Ronnie had clung to Vladimir like a rag doll, her body somehow smaller, her face pale and drawn from the combination of shock and heartache. It was an image Bain wasn't keen on recalling as it always sent a shiver through him, usually the preamble to a cold sweat.

That was enough, Bain told himself. He got up, walked around the bed and leaning a hand on the windowsill, brushed the curtain aside to allow the last of the late evening sun to enter Holly's private room. He looked out over the hospital car park to the line of trees in the distance behind which a long terrace of Victorian houses was hidden in shadow. He could recall this view perfectly. Another image that would live with him for some time as a result of his experiences over the last few weeks.

It had been his fault. Bain didn't care what Ronnie, Vladimir, Golden, or any of the well-meaning nurses said. He was to blame. He'd allowed her to go back into the Dent's yard without back-up. Vladimir had called him and he'd never listened to the message. If he had, he'd have insisted Holly didn't go to the yard alone.

She'd never woken up. The bleed caused by that blow to her head had placed a critical pressure on her brain not once, but twice. There was every chance she would have lasting neurological issues, or… worse. Holly was confined to a hospital bed because he'd been too busy. He'd seen the messages, but ignored them, too focused on what was happening at Ripon. It was the worst of decisions. And no one, not least of all the parade of consultants who had pored over the brain scans could be sure whether she would ever…

'Penny for 'em,' said a small, dry voice.

Bain swung round and almost lost his balance, his heart missing several beats. A pair of drowsy blue eyes met his and Holly sarcastically raised one corner of her mouth just a fraction before the effort became too much and she fell back into another deep sleep.

***

June 25th

'Someone came into the caravan. I could hear bags being scraped across the floor, and… a shout from outside. That's all I can remember,' Holly said with a shrug, 'I don't…'

'Just rest, dear, It's not your fault. You're worn out!' Ronnie said sharply, although she then shot Golden and Bain a hard stare to make both of them aware she was unimpressed with their relentless questioning.

As neither of them replied or moved, Ronnie weighed in with a more direct approach, 'You've both been grilling her for too long! Leave her be! It's only been a few days and she gets tired so quickly. I'll get that nice consultant, Mr Gupta, in here and he'll tell you…'

'I am *here*, mother,' Holly said breathily from her bed whilst waving a hand at Ronnie, 'Don't I get a say?'

'Maybe it's best you rest, Holly,' Vladimir called out above the rustle of his newspaper.

From his chair set against the wall opposite Holly, he added, 'Listen to your mother. From my experience, rushing things won't help. Both the professional and amateur sleuths here could do with a lesson in patient etiquette.'

Bain groaned in frustration. Golden made an irritated click with her mouth and gave Holly a tight-lipped smile; her way of admitting defeat. She got to her feet.

'Good to see you sitting up. You're looking and sounding much better. I'll be back later in the week if that's okay with you?'

Holly nodded a thank you at the detective, who gave her hand a squeeze before she went to the door of her recovery room. The patient and her family then watched with amused smiles as Bain followed Golden out of her room. As soon as the door into the corridor clicked shut, Ronnie was busying herself smoothing out errant bits of Holly's covers and tucking them into the base of her bed. Holly was soon pinned in so tight she couldn't move from the chest down.

'Leave my bedclothes alone, mother!'

'Just straightening you up.'

'I don't need any straightening. I'm completely and utterly straight, okay?'

'It's your mother's latest thing,' Vladimir rumbled from behind his newspaper, 'She's become obsessed with ironing. I've tried telling her. Maybe you can get through to her. That ironing board of yours has been getting a hammering since you've been in here.'

'Nonsense,' declared Ronnie, pulling the top sheet so tight Holly felt as if her torso was being shrink-wrapped.

Vladimir bent the top corner of his Yorkshire Post over and eyed Ronnie keenly, 'Yesterday, I caught you pressing the Sunday Times from last weekend because you'd run out of things to iron! You've even ironed the dog's collar and lead!'

'Steamed!' she retaliated, 'I steamed the dog's things.'

'I had to stop you from steaming poor Daisy,' muttered Vladimir.

'The Widow Solanki seems to be forgetting that I've also ironed his entire wardrobe!' Ronnie said indignantly, turning her back on Vladimir.

'Your mother seems to forget that I didn't ask her to break into my house and flatten all my clothes,' Vladimir rebuffed in a calm tone, 'My dickie bow will never be the same again.'

'The door was open.'

'Only after you'd used the spare key!'

'My head hurts,' Holly announced, struggling, and eventually failing to extract an arm from her mother's handiwork with her sheets.

Ronnie and Vladimir jumped, and were immediately at opposite sides of the bed, both of them glancing worriedly at the monitor for evidence of swiftly rising or falling key indicators. There were none.

'I meant the two of you are giving me a headache from all your bickering,' Holly said in an exasperated voice whilst supplying her mother with an impish smile and Vladimir with a wink. They glumly returned to their seats, somewhat chastised.

Outside in the corridor, Bain and Golden had stopped to listen as the elevated voices penetrated the thin wall. They now resumed their walk down the long ward corridor.

'Hmm. That explains why Daisy's been giving Ronnie a wide berth the last few days,' Bain commented, 'And why my jeans have developed creases down the front.'

Golden stepped back to regard Bain's trousers from a couple of angles and gave a thoughtful sniff.

'Not a great look. But I wouldn't worry,' she said with a mischievous grin, 'The lines make you look taller.'

Bain shot her a silly smile, 'Thanks for that. I'll have your number on speed dial for the next time I need an ego boost.'

'No problem. Here to serve,' Golden said with a small chuckle, enjoying the light-hearted nature of the conversation. It made a welcome change from the last few weeks spent grilling interviewees.

'Seriously though, I'd keep an eye on Ronnie,' she added, 'The last thing Holly needs is to come home to another kitchen burnt to the ground because her mother's forgotten to switch the iron off and left it face down on the ironing board all night.'

'Don't worry. Between the Widow Sol... I mean Vladimir and myself, we're making sure she's not left alone, and every appliance is unplugged before we leave the house.'

Golden nodded her approval.

They soon reached the end of the corridor and from the way Golden was fidgeting with the pockets of her jacket, Bain assumed she was keen to be away. So her next suggestion was unexpected.

'Er... could I interest you a coffee or something?' Golden asked a little awkwardly.

Bain frowned, then raised his eyebrows. Not wishing to appear shocked, he immediately frowned again. Aware he'd not answered for a second or two, he opened his mouth, but was cut off.

'It's okay if you want to get back to Holly.'

'No!' Bain replied, a little too stridently than he'd anticipated, 'I mean, no, I don't need to get back to Holly and yes, a coffee would be great. The hospital café?'

Golden smiled and if he wasn't mistaken, looked a little

relieved.

'Actually, I'm pulling together all the facts of the case for our feature in the Sunday Times and wanted to check a few things with you, if that's okay?' said Bain.

'Sure,' Golden replied without hesitation.

They set off together down another corridor at no more than an amble.

Fifty-Nine

Golden was more than happy to delay her return to the York office for a couple of reasons. As ever, she had a mountain of paperwork to complete regarding the Brooklyn-Croft case. However the other reason was a more serious one. She had reservations. She'd tried to talk it through with her colleagues in the office and been largely ignored. It would be good to get another view. She'd gone through that day so many times, with so many people.

Leslie Croft had left Ripon by the time her officers had reached the racecourse, however, he was subsequently picked up at an airfield in Berkshire, trying to charter a small plane to take him to France. Brought back to Yorkshire, Croft provided Golden with a comprehensive 'no comment' set of interviews. It was his son, Daniel Croft, who had helped her to sew together the various locations, movements, people, and deduce their motives.

Following the cellar fire, Golden had interviewed Daniel Croft for almost three straight days, for the first few hours stinking of smoke and sporting bruises. He'd been such a veritable font of information it meant his father's input hadn't been required for her to charge Leslie Croft with not only the manufacture and wholesale supply of Class A drugs, but also the murder of Brooklyn Hartley.

Brought up as his father's prodigy and involved on the fringes of his father's business, Daniel had eventually rebelled,

Brooklyn's murder being the final straw. Daniel had described how his father had started to manufacture and supply ecstasy tablets almost a decade ago, thanks to his boyhood contacts within the criminal world. His veterinary business had been lucrative, but not enough to satisfy the single-minded Leslie Croft. He had wanted more, and digging through his personal accounts led Golden's team to discover a string of properties dotted around the world, all funded by illicit activity.

It had been a relatively simple set-up. Croft would manufacture the drugs in bulk and deposit them somewhere that represented a safe, clean location that provided easy access for himself and his customers. The customers collected their order on a quarterly basis, leaving payment behind for Croft to pick up at his leisure. It meant there was a level of anonymity between the parties and should the drugs or the cash be discovered, they were on premises that were practically impossible to link back to Croft or his customers.

It had amazed Golden that the transaction was completed on a trust basis, but then she imagined if either party had defaulted, the consequences for anyone trying to upset the equilibrium, as it was for Brooklyn, would be dire.

Daniel Croft had also been most forthcoming about Hugo Dent's involvement, and as a result the teenager had been interviewed at length. This was what Golden wanted to discuss with Bain.

It was almost eight o'clock when Bain and Golden reached Ellerby's restaurant on the ground floor of the hospital. With the end to visiting time fast approaching, and the restaurant already closed for hot food, only a smattering of customers were dotted around the vast number of tables. Bain indicated a coffee machine he knew well from his numerous visits to Holly over the last few weeks, and clutching their plastic cups containing steaming lattes, they sat down opposite each other at the end of a long bench.

'So how can I help you and Holly become the next publishing phenomenon?' joked Golden, piercing him with an amused stare.

Bain choked for a moment. He pretended it was his coffee, but it wasn't. For the first time in years, Bain had looked across at a woman and understood he wanted something more than to be just an acquaintance. He made an excuse for his cough and told himself it was the wrong time to be asking a policewoman out on a date. He was busy, she was busy…

'I know you can't tell me what happened in the interviews with Daniel and Leslie Croft,' started Bain, 'The same with Hugo and Graham Dent, not until they've been to court…'

Golden shook her head, 'It's doubtful Graham Dent will be charged with anything. Being unaware of a drugs trading location on their property isn't a crime, and proving they purposefully poisoned a horse in their care isn't something we're too interested in pursuing.'

'What about the BHA?'

Golden gave a wry smile, 'You won't be publishing any of this until after any trial?'

Bain nodded, 'We're thinking we will just write a book first, then see if the Sunday papers will serialise it. We did it the other way round last time and it didn't work in our favour.'

'Okay. Well I can tell you that the Dent's misdemeanours will be looked into by… other authorities that may, or may not be a three letter acronym.'

Bain smiled, 'And the Crofts?'

Golden took a sly look over her shoulder. The nearest other customer was a large bald man with a red face two tables away, yet she still bowed her head over the table towards Bain. It made a stray lock of hair fall across her face and he had to restrain the urge to reach forward and tuck it back behind her ear for her.

'Daniel Croft has turned out to be our star witness,' she said in a quietly sceptical tone, 'He is claiming Holly as the catalyst. When he realised she was an investigative journalist, he decided it was the opportunity he'd been waiting for to expose his father. And what he told us does stack up perfectly with what Holly is saying.'

'You still sound unsure,' Bain noted, 'Why are you wary of Daniel Croft?'

Golden shot him a penetrating glance, 'Leslie Croft wasn't just a drug manufacturer, he's been grooming his son since he was born. In my view, Daniel is broken. It's just a question of how much.'

Golden encouraged Bain to lean closer and she proceeded to recount the highlights of her investigation in a low voice.

'It turns out that Leslie Croft wasn't satisfied with the profits from his drug manufacturing business, and so searched for other ways to supplement his income. The local racing industry was a prime target because of the huge sums that could be paid for well-bred or proven racehorses. He sought out a natural way to feign a non-specific equine sickness and after exploring many other options, turned to snowdrop bulbs. A moderately ingested quantity could kill, but Croft produced a carefully calibrated liquid that could be given, masquerading as a tracheal wash. It wouldn't kill, but with a regular, steady dosage, the compound produces an ongoing sickness that makes the animal slow and lethargic.'

Golden lowered her voice even further, 'Most importantly, Daniel Croft pointed out that once the substance was removed from the horse's diet, it would return the horse to full health within days with no side effects.'

'So offering to take the animal off the owner's hands for a pittance, especially when it's the vet doing the offering, seems the perfect solution,' chipped in Bain.

'And this is where Hugo Dent enters the scene,' added Golden with a wonky half-smile.

Bain loved the way her mouth adopted that crooked, sceptical smile. He nodded encouragingly for her to continue, in the hope it might return for him to enjoy sometime soon.

'According to Daniel, Hugo was Leslie Croft's primary contact inside the yard. He said Hugo was not only doping the horses, he'd been taking a cut from every ecstasy drop that went through that trailer on the Dent's premises. We checked, and there have been two significant deposits made in cash into Hugo's bank account in the last six months. We also found a number of cash bundles hidden in his caravan, alongside enough ecstasy tablets to charge him with intent to supply a Class A drug...'

Golden cut her story off and she glared at Bain, 'What is it?' she demanded in a voice loud enough to carry across the cafeteria.

Bain had been leaning an elbow on the table, his hand cupping his chin, and with a disgruntled grimace playing on his face. He dropped his hand immediately, and a hurt look momentarily washed across his features before being replaced with the same grimace.

'I wasn't aware I was telegraphing my thoughts to you so vividly,' he said, looking around the café to see if Golden's raised voice had aroused any interest. A dozen people were scattered across the café but there wasn't a single set of eyes studying them. Apparently sudden outbursts were normal in a hospital cafeteria.

'I heard you had Hugo in custody. I'm just not too sure…'

'I know!' Golden said energetically, 'I've got my drug manufacturer, I have his man on the inside, and I have a talkative witness and a wealth of evidence… the thing is, I've got a problem.'

'You mean you haven't tracked down who whacked Holly on the head and who killed Brooklyn?'

'Okay, I've got two, or even three problems,' Golden restated with a roll of her eyes, 'Although my first problem does have some bearing on the second and third.'

'Which is?' Bain queried, leaning in another inch.

Golden held Bain's gaze. Not for the first time she had to ignore the way his eyes somehow drew her in.

'It's Daniel Croft. He has an answer for everything. According to Daniel, Hugo is responsible for the fraudulent activities at the Doncaster Sales, the doping of a talented racehorse, and hosting an extremely lucrative drugs handover location. Daniel also told us his father killed Brooklyn, not because of any doping with snowdrops, but because she'd followed Hugo and discovered the drugs waiting to be collected in the trailer at the bottom of the yard. That does work out. I couldn't tell you at the time, but our forensics found a hair embedded in the hilt of that knife you got from Farley. It didn't match anyone at the yard, or any of Brooklyn's friends we interviewed, but...'

Golden paused and raised both eyebrows.

'Not Leslie Croft?' Bain whispered with incredulity.

Golden nodded, 'What are the chances, eh?'

'It's almost too good to be true,' said Bain, his frown deepening, 'And what about Holly's attacker?'

'Daniel claims he was incredibly worried about Holly. He says she'd passed out due to the stress of the situation. But I'm not buying that... although Holly did say she'd been feeling weary at the time.'

'I can vouch for that,' Bain murmured, 'I'm probably responsible for wearing her out.'

'Anyway, Daniel reckons he left the caravan to get help when she started to, in his words, go a bit funny,' Golden continued, 'My officers did find him outside the farmhouse in a bit of a state and then discovered Holly in the caravan being nursed by the head lass, Lara, and the cash gone. Daniel reckons a member of the gang who left the payment must have heard about his father's business going up in smoke, and decided to retrieve the money they'd deposited there the night before. Daniel reckons they must have gone into the trailer when he left, and Holly got in the way.'

Golden paused and gave a sigh, a sour expression

ruining what, in Bain's opinion, was otherwise a pretty face.

'So here's the thing…' she stated in a conspiratorial whisper,' I don't believe a single word that has come out of Daniel Croft's mouth.'

She waited for Bain to react. As his brow rippled into a frown she broke eye contact, leaned back and with elbows out and hands on her cheeks, slumped in her seat. Bain's reaction had been similar to her work colleagues. Her suggestion that Daniel Croft, their star witness, might be lying, had been received with little in the way of support.

'Do the paperwork and move on,' had been the advice from her boss, Sayers, 'A major ecstasy supply route busted and the 'Good Morning' girl murder solved… not a bad day's work. Don't complicate things.'

Bain straightened. He maintained his focus on Golden and when she chanced a glance up, to her surprise, his perplexed look had dissolved.

'You should keep investigating,' he said, his eyes now wide and excited, 'Holly and I agree with you. There's something we're all missing. There's too many loose ends.'

Golden's face brightened, 'Go on.'

Sixty

'Leslie Croft was manufacturing ecstasy. I assume you have evidence?'

Golden paused a moment, wondering whether she should be sharing such knowledge with Bain. What the hell, no-one else had time for her view of Daniel Croft's evidence.

'Daniel has confirmed the manufacturing plant was in the cellar, although the fire was so intense, all we found afterwards were lumps of melted metal. The pictures I took on my phone during the fire aren't great, but I managed to snap a couple of pieces of chemical equipment you would expect to find in an ecstasy manufacturing plant, as well as the sacks of snowdrop bulbs.'

'How convenient,' noted Bain.

Golden brightened, 'I know!'

She continued afresh, 'We also found a sophisticated exhaust system built into the cellar that was syphoning the fumes into the sewage pipes. It was a clever set up. Very expensive, very professional... Croft must have been clearing at least half a million kilograms of ecstasy a year, and probably more, if his property portfolio is anything to go by.'

'So if Leslie Croft was onto such a good thing, why would he risk it all by travelling to York with a small, farriers knife and murder a stable lass in broad daylight?'

'I asked him that very question. He just smirked and said, 'No comment.'

Bain reached out across the table top and laid his palm gently over Golden's right hand and patted it. Feeling a small buzz of excitement, she brought her left hand over and cupped his hand in hers. If felt dry and warm. Looking up, she immediately knew she'd made a mistake. Bain was holding an index finger to his lips. He'd been warning her to stop talking. She released his hand. A moment later a casually dressed young man sidled past their table. He was a wiry sort with a pinched, wary face and a small blue exclamation mark tattooed under his right ear. He eyed the two of them closely as he passed.

'That was a bit weird,' noted Bain.

Golden assumed he meant her holding onto his hand, but soon realised he was referring to the man as Bain was craning his neck to follow the chap out of the café.

'He was sitting over there,' he said, indicating a table to their far left, 'But he chose to walk twice as far, right around the café. It was as if he planned to come past us,' he observed.

'Daniel Croft is out on bail,' said Golden, keen to move the conversation on, 'I'm not happy about it, but we didn't have a reason to hold him once our time limits had elapsed. We've no evidence he was actively involved in his father's illicit business, and he claims he's only known about it for a couple of months.'

'And you'll need him to testify against his father.'

Golden gave him a rueful nod, 'So why am I wracking my brains and losing sleep thinking there has to be more to all of this?'

'Because it's too neat, and Daniel Croft screams liar to you…?' offered Bain.

A fleeting smile graced Goldens face, 'So what am I missing?'

'Well, I can believe Leslie Croft was making and selling ecstasy. But like you, I'm struggling with his motive for murdering Brooklyn. She was saying the horse's name, 'Good Morning' to everyone she met, and told Robert Farley 'snowdrop' before she died, which had to refer to the poison. She concentrated all her efforts on the horse's wellbeing, there was no mention of ecstasy. Also, why would Croft, a career criminal, make such a bodge of killing Brooklyn? It's the same reason you and I cast doubt on Robert Farley being the killer… Why be so amateurish, and why leave the knife behind with a hair attached, conveniently placing him at the scene?'

'You know Robert pulled me out of the cellar?'

Bain pursed his lips and inclined his head slightly in silent confirmation.

'I have apologised to him… and thanked him,' she added.

'Once you'd arrested and questioned him.'

Golden lifted her eyes to the hospital ceiling, 'I guess you've spoken to him.'

Bain grinned, 'Of course. He's been to visit Holly three or four times. He's a good guy. And super resilient. Considering how he was treated in the services, it's a miracle he's so centred.'

'I read his file,' agreed Golden, 'I should have known he would be in Malton all along. He'd been watching the Dent yard, and was at that Doncaster sale you attended. He's been following Hugo around for weeks thinking he must be responsible because he's such an ass to everyone he meets.'

'I know. Robert was sure Hugo and Daniel were deeply involved in some sort of plot. I did sort of tell you at the time… in a roundabout way.'

'Mmm… If I remember rightly, you chose to inform me at moments when I was incredibly busy.'

'I wouldn't know anything about that,' Bain said with an amused shrug.

'Talking of loose ends, whatever happened with that chap you wanted me to test for a DNA match to the knife that killed Brooklyn Hartley? Blunt wasn't it?'

'Oh that,' Bain replied with a desultory wave of his wrist, 'No, I… um… got him all wrong.'

He wondered whether to mention to Golden that Blunt had taught him a valuable lesson in not assuming strangeness was an indication of guilt, but decided against giving her chapter and verse.

'It turned out Blunt was a little odd, and took his wife for granted, but nothing more.'

She pursed her lips, 'Mmm… it's the odd ones that get in the way of finding the real culprits.'

'Like Robert Farley?'

Golden gave him a sharp look.

'I mean your boss, Sayer isn't it?' Bain modified quickly, 'He was convinced Farley killed Brooklyn and stopped you from pursuing other leads? I'd say that Farley's background caused Sayer to rule out other options.'

Golden wrinkled her nose, 'Honestly… I'd just received a tip off, a strong lead on a drugs case and I wanted to follow it. I'm not proud of that, especially with Holly lying in a bed upstairs because of my decision. I was being pretty single-minded and on reflection, a tad selfish. With another two detectives working on Farley, I wrongly assumed I could be best used elsewhere. I gave you and Holly the green light to investigate the Dents because I thought…'

Golden winced, 'I thought it wouldn't lead anywhere. I had no idea both crimes would end up being linked.'

Bain didn't reply, but didn't take his eyes off her, watching the policewoman's embarrassment mount the longer his silence lasted. Eventually he capitulated.

'So, the man you'd written off as a murderer…'

'Pulled me out of a burning building and probably saved my life,' Golden finished for him.

'The irony isn't lost on me,' she added miserably.

Bain couldn't keep his face straight any longer and allowed a grin to develop, 'That's priceless,' he said, stifling a small laugh.

Golden looked up from her cup of coffee and found Bain gazing at her, a warm smile lighting his face. His irises appeared bigger than normal and she couldn't help but smile back.

Twenty minutes later, Golden looked into her plastic cup again and discovered there was still an inch of coffee. She picked it up and was about to take a sip, but the brown liquid wasn't warm to the touch. She'd been speaking with Bain for so long it had gone cold.

'You know what really bugs me about this case?' asked Bain.

Golden smiled and shook her head, 'Wow me, Bain.'

He responded with a grin.

'Holly is up there, in a hospital bed, unable to remember what happened in that caravan. She knows Daniel was there, but can't tell us anything about who hit her. We have his account, but you and I both know he's only telling his side of the story.'

Golden feigned a yawn, 'Get to the punchline. I'm a long way from being wowed.'

Bain didn't respond. His eyes were directed over her shoulder and he'd gone rigid.

'What?' Golden asked, turning in her seat to follow his

gaze.

'He's back.'

The wiry young man walked up to Golden, a strangely embarrassed half-smile playing on his lips. He ignored Bain and came to a halt in front of the still seated policewoman.

'You're that detective,' he said in a heavy Yorkshire accent, 'You were on telly today weren't you? Talkin' about that girl who got stabbed by the river?'

Golden got to her feet, 'Yes, that was me.'

'Yeah, thought so. Saw you upstairs. Got a mate in the same ward, like. He said that lass you were talking about who got bashed on the head was in the next room.'

'Yes, well I can't discuss…'

'One thing,' said the man, waving his index finger around by the side of his head, 'It's 'bin bothering me.'

'Oh, yes?' inquired Golden, crossing her arms. She was expecting some homespun amateur detective drivel. It happened all the time. As soon as anyone worked out what she did for a living people couldn't help themselves.

'That bloke, Croft. He's a wrong 'un, right?'

'Absolutely.'

'An' he stabbed this lass the day after that TV show about her bein' all smiley was shown. So, how'd he manage that then?'

Golden stared at the man, trying hard not to lose her patience and send him away with a flea in his ear.

'It's like this,' the man continued, now on a bit of a roll, 'I'm a supermarket delivery driver, and I know that chap. I deliver his order every Thursday morning, Malton, nine-oh-nine prompt, like… lives above the vets.'

'Right,' Golden replied, slightly more engaged with her amateur sleuth.

'So tell me. How did Croft get from Malton to York to kill that poor lass in ten minutes? An' before you ask, I just went out to check my logs. He was definitely there. I saw him that day, on March 5th, in his flat above the vets place, large as life. Still in his dressing gown he was.'

'You're definite about that?'

'Been doin' the round for seven years. You don't forget your reg'lars.'

Golden hurriedly took the man's details, thanking him profusely for coming forward and promising to have a police officer call on him to take a full statement the next day.

'Can do,' he replied, 'But I came back 'ere to give you a heads up, like.'

'What do you mean?' asked Bain.

'Well it means the murderer is still out there, don' it. An' last time there was news on the telly about someone recovering enough to remember stuff, that lass got killed.'

'Yes?'

'Well I've just gone back up to my mates room. Left my glasses behind you see,' he said, brandishing a pair of spectacles, 'Saw a right bruiser going into your young lasses room next to his, I did.'

Bain shot a worried look at Golden. The smile fell from the detective's face and her skin turned grey.

'Kirsty? Are you...'

'I briefed the press today to tell them that Holly was over the worst and was expected to make a full recovery,' she said in a faraway voice. She got to her feet, her gaze now fixed on the restaurant exit. She started walking, soon breaking into a trot. Bain swiftly followed, leaving their witness to stare after them, stoney faced.

'Brooklyn's TV appearance was the prompt for the murderer to strike the first time...' said Golden, now in a jog 'And if Leslie Croft isn't the killer, they're still out there.'

'The man he saw going into Holly's room,' said Bain, picking up the pace, 'You don't think...'

As one, Golden and Bain broke into a run.

Sixty-One

It had gone so quiet in her room once Ronnie and Vladimir had left for Northallerton, Holly had almost nodded off. Perhaps there was something to be said for her mother's excessive tucking in? If it wasn't for the burble of the television on the far wall, she probably would have slept. Instead, she was lying with her eyes closed, half listening to a conversation between two characters injecting a much needed dollop of humour into a dismal episode of Coronation Street.

When the door to her private room opened, she assumed it would be Bain returning to wish her goodnight, or if she was up to it, challenge her to a game of chess. The nursing staff knew Bain so well by now, they tended to allow him to stay beyond the normal visiting hours. He was usually with her until she fell asleep, and more often than not, sitting beside her bed when she woke. He'd been incredible… something her mother kept reminding her of whenever Bain wasn't in her room.

Far too sleepy for a game of chess, Holly decided to keep her eyes closed and feign sleep; it would release Bain from any duty he felt he owed her and if he left now he'd be back in Northallerton before ten o'clock.

Once the door had creaked and juddered its way open, Holly knew for certain it wasn't Bain. The sound was all wrong. Bain knew the door squeaked and always made an effort to only open it a crack and slip in quietly if she was resting.

'Oh, hello, my dear,' said a kindly voice Holly half recognised, but had initial difficulty in placing.

Holly opened her eyes, expecting to see a nurse.

'Hello, Wendy!' replied Holly in surprise as she flapped around with her elbows, struggling with her mother's tight bedclothes, trying to sit up. A combination of her weak body and Ronnie's excessive tucking regime put paid to any thought of her sitting up properly and she admitted defeat and lay back.

'This is… a surprise.'

'Don't get up for me,' Wendy said, shaking a bouquet of flowers at Holly, 'I'm only on a flying visit. I heard on the local news you were doing better and thought it was time I popped in to see you, my love!'

Holly laid back into her pillows and turned her head to watch Wendy cross the room, 'Well, that's lovely, but you shouldn't have.'

'Not a fuss, dear girl. Not a fuss,' Wendy said, bustling around the room in search of a vase, her tote bag emblazoned with 'Beverley Winning Owner', as always, hanging from her shoulder. Only this time, the bag was full… and was moving. Wriggling to be exact. A dachshund's pointed nose poked out and sniffed the air.

'Erm… Wendy, are you allowed dogs in a hospital?

'Don't fuss dear. Hogarth will be fine!' Wendy assured her, 'He's ever so well behaved. I take him everywhere.'

Wendy found a vase with some perfectly fine blooms in it, and without hesitation, removed them, shaking the water off the stems. Dropping the dripping flowers into a bin reserved for medical waste, Wendy haphazardly bunged her rather dreary offering of half a dozen pink carnations into the vase and stepped back, hands on hips, reviewing her artistry.

'Carnations. They last such a long time,' she remarked absently, 'They truly are the Northern Dancer of flowers.'

She turned around to face Holly and provided her with a pleasant smile. Holly returned the smile, but as Wendy removed her tote bag from her shoulder and settled herself in the chair beside her bed with the little dog on her knees, still in the bag, she had the strangest feeling that something felt wrong. No, something was *different* about Wendy. Then it struck her; Wendy's jet black hair was tied back, scraped over her head and all bunched tightly together down her back.

'I do like your new look. You suit it with your hair back, Wendy,' Holly commented generously.

Wendy seemed a little taken aback. Her expression flipped through a variety of reactions, including what Holly read as disbelief, until eventually, she thanked Holly with a genuine smile whilst running the tips of her fingers over her hair, drawn tight to her skull.

'I hope you made the most of your twenties, my dear,' Wendy advised with a regretful sigh, 'Once you reach your thirties no man gives you a second glance.'

Holly had been ready to gently suggest this wasn't the case, but found herself remaining silent. There it was again, that feeling that something wasn't quite right about Wendy tonight. She couldn't put her finger on it. Perhaps it was Wendy's last remark having been delivered with such a degree of heartfelt bitterness.

'Is everyone at the yard okay?' she asked in the hope it would take the conversation in a more positive direction.

Wendy's eyes dropped to the floor and she didn't answer. With the woman's head relaxed and tilted downwards, Holly noticed a thick application of make-up around her eyes and cheeks. Even with this extra help, Wendy looked gaunt.

'Are you okay, Wendy?'

'I'm *always* okay. I have to be,' she replied somewhat sarcastically, peeling back the sides of her tote bag up, thus allowing Hogarth to leap out and onto her lap. She leaned over, only a few inches from Holly's head on the pillow.

'Haven't you noticed? I'm the one that keeps the yard going, dearie.'

And Holly was suddenly transported. Wendy's smell. The smell of dog. Both odours connected a synapse somewhere in her brain and awakened a memory. She was suddenly back in the trailer, the odour of decay and rodents suffused with that particularly pungent smell... of ripe dachshund urine.

'Lara and Graham flap about the yard thinking they run the place and meanwhile, I do all the work,' Wendy continued, her voice crackling with suppressed anger, 'And Hugo is bloody useless! He's a little runt… a little *bastard*.'

At that moment, Holly was mightily pleased that her visitor wasn't looking up at her monitoring equipment. Otherwise, Wendy would certainly have noticed her heartrate and blood pressure figures soaring. She imagined her vital signs were now bouncing all over the readouts and the last thing she needed was an alarm going off in her room. She wondered whether the alarms were ringing at the nurses station down at the end of the corridor fifty yards away. Holly *really* hoped they were.

Wendy felt settled. She sighed contentedly as she took in Holly's tightly packed limbs in a single sweeping glance of her bed. An over-officious nurse had made her job easier. The rails on the bed had been lowered and the investigative journalist who had tried to infiltrate her business was effectively pinned down. What's more, the girl looked tired. A tired body… and yet the girl's eyes were wide with terror.

'You remember, don't you?' she said calmly, staring down at her trapped victim.

Wendy disappeared from Holly's view as she leaned over and carefully dropped Hogarth to the floor. She was back upright in her seat in a trice. Wendy staring at her, patiently waiting for a reply. Holly noticed the woman's hand had crept inside her tote bag and was fumbling around, searching for something.

'I'm not sure what you mean, Wendy,' Holly replied, only the slightest quaver in her voice and presenting her ex-employer with a blank look. She needed to concentrate, consider her options. The nurses desk was too far away for shouting or screaming, besides, it would only make Wendy act sooner. She could hardly move, thanks to her mother's tucking fetish and her weak body, and the buzzer to call for help was hanging down beside the bed, out of immediate reach. Could she extract one arm and reach the alarm button?

Holly told herself that although she was nowhere near

recovered, she'd been feeling much better the last few days. She might just make it. But fending off a middle-aged woman when she was pinned down would be a tall order. And despite her shape, Wendy was fit. She was always buzzing around the yard...

'I spoke with Brooklyn,' Wendy said with a sad smile, 'You know, before I, or rather, she...'

Wendy's voice trailed off for a moment, but then she cleared her throat with some purpose.

'Dearie me, that girl just wouldn't see sense. Why couldn't she be more like Geena?' Wendy asked, shaking her head, 'Brooklyn couldn't talk of course, but I could see it in her eyes. She'd already remembered. She knew it was Daniel and I who were forcing Hugo to poison Morgan. Then she accused me of dealing in drugs too... well, I couldn't have that, my dear. That silly little girl had a soft spot for Hugo, Lord knows why, and she'd followed me down to the trailer with Daniel and seen the drugs. I think she'd remembered I was in the stable with Morgan and I was the one to hit her. She was just turning when I brought my...'

Holly gaped at Wendy, hardly able to believe what she was hearing. Guten Morgen's hoof hadn't been the weapon that had hit Brooklyn... it had been Wendy... but why?

Wendy fell silent, with not so much a regretful, but rather, a thoughtful look. Holly's glare hardened.

'And you're a journalist,' she continued, 'So we couldn't rely on *you* to keep quiet. I did tell Daniel. I said it was dangerous allowing you into the yard, but he wouldn't listen... I discussed it with her of course...'

Wendy eyes glazed over for a moment.

'I sometimes wish I'd never listened...' she said in a low rumble, 'And Brooklyn would still be alive, but when it comes to direct action, well, Daniel needs to grow a pair, and I'm far better at it.'

She shivered, blinked, and was suddenly alert, emerging from her moment of reflection.

'It would have worked too,' Wendy said with a sad smile, 'If Daniel had put you to sleep like he was supposed to.'

'Put me to sleep?' echoed Holly, unable to take her eyes off Wendy, her hands clenched tightly into fists under her sheets.

Wendy produced a small, coy grin, 'Oh, surely you must know, my dear! Daniel and I have been drip feeding you a sedative for weeks, the same one he uses to sedate horses. We didn't want you poking around without us knowing, so a little Xylazine in your coffee each break time, and the odd one I brought you in the yard, was enough to keep you nicely dulled. Xylazine also has an interesting effect, giving you a high, making you talkative for a short time, so I'd always know where you were in the yard. The high dives into a sudden bout of tiredness. Daniel was worried you might fall off that motorbike of yours on your way home! We couldn't have that happening before Leslie's drugs drop happened, we had to arrange for you to find the cash in the trailer.'

Holly gawked at the older woman. Wendy was Brooklyn's killer. She was working with Daniel. But for what possible reason?

Wendy cocked her head to one side and gave Holly a pitying smile, 'But… you were still half awake when I came into the trailer, and I couldn't chance you knowing Daniel and I were working together, so I gave you that tap on the head. I was all ready to give you another when the police turned up. I heard her shout, and had to hurry to get back out of the trailer and back to the farmhouse. You're a *very* lucky girl.'

'Wendy, you don't have to…' Holly started, but her plea was cut short by the older woman shushing her.

'…Yes, Daniel thought you'd be perfect. What better way to implicate his father and in the process, rid me of that devil spawn, Hugo, by having a journalist write about their shortcomings. But just like Brooklyn, it all got a bit messy.'

'But Hugo is your…'

'That brat is not my son!' Wendy interrupted fiercely,

for the first time allowing anger to bubble up. On the floor, Hogarth stopped sniffing at the bin and turned his head to regard his mistress. He recognised that tone in her voice and scurried under her chair.

'Twenty-two years I've cared for that despicable wretch, putting up with his rotten moods and whining, and for what? He's pathetic as a horseman, and worse than useless around the yard. And there won't be any grandchildren coming my way any time soon!'

Wendy's arm was now lost in her tote bag, her hand rummaging around at the bottom like a fevered rat.

'Then I discover that I've been lied to for all those years!' she spat, 'It turns out that Hugo, my adopted son, is the result of a roll in the hay between my husband and a stable lass!'

Holly reckoned Wendy must have been pleased with her stunned reaction to this revelation, as she rocked back in her seat, 'Yes, my dear! It turns out my husband is a lying, two-timing pig!'

Holly nodded, her eyes fixed on Wendy. At the same time she used these few extra seconds to think hard.

'Who told you Hugo was Graham's boy?' asked Holly, adopting a conciliatory tone, desperate to keep Wendy talking, 'Was it Daniel?'

Wendy didn't respond for a long moment, regarding Holly with a growing sadness in her eyes. When she did eventually speak, it was sudden and she was back to being calm and collected.

'Did I ever tell you that I used to be brilliant at rounders, my dear.'

Holly screamed, 'What?' inside her head. Dear old Wendy wasn't making any sense. Holly winced; the pain in the back of her head had returned. All she wanted to do was close her eyes and sleep, but instead she watched nervously as, yet again, Wendy delved into her tote bag, pushing items to one side, then the other, searching for something.

'We won't be needing this,' she told Holly happily, pulling out a whittling knife, exactly the same type of short, sharp knife used to stab Brooklyn over a dozen times. It was unceremoniously dropped back into the tote bag.

'Here we go,' Wendy declared in a singsong voice, digging deep for a final time and pulling out a short wooden baton of about a sixteen inches long.

So that's what lay at the bottom of that dreadful bag, thought Holly. A rounders bat. But a rounders bat with a major modification. A steel horseshoe had been contorted out of shape in order to bend it around the bat's base and up the shaft. The holes in the shoe that would normally host nails that were hammered into the horse's hoof, now sported small cross-headed screws that held the out-of-shape steel shoe fast to the rounders bat.

Wendy held the bat out so she could admire it at eye level for a moment, inches away from Holly's face, the silvery horseshoe snaking around its base standing slightly proud. Holly examined the bat closely and wished she hadn't. A cold shiver of disgust shook her and the pain in her head thumped quicker, in tune with her quickening heartbeats. There was blood. Dark red, clotted blood dotted with hairs. Brooklyn's hair, or perhaps her own? The sickening bloody mixture filled the ridges in the horseshoe and was smeared up the bat's shank. For a second Holly's vision swam. Slamming her eyes shut, she breathed and tried to concentrate, telling herself not to lose control. She was alone, weak, and would need every ounce of her energy.

Wendy stood up and hefted the bat from hand to hand, feeling its weight. She looked over at Holly, grinned, and holding the bat in her right hand she slapped it twice into her left. Bat readied for use, she leaned over Holly's bed, raised her arm and smiled down at her victim. Holly boggled at her, it was as if Wendy was about to tell her a bedtime story!

'Don't fuss. This won't take long, dear. You'll be out like a light.'

Sixty-Two

'You take the lift, I'll do the stairs,' Golden shouted at Bain as they dashed down the ground level corridor, the main artery of York General. The chances were that their informant in the café had made an awful mistake, and Holly would be asleep, Bain told himself. They would burst in and find her safe and sound…

Bain had settled a long time ago for being a gatherer. An uncoordinated runner, he lolloped rather than ran. Conversely, Golden was like Holly, a hunter. Already many yards ahead of him, Bain watched her disappear around a right-angled corner of the corridor he wouldn't reach for several seconds. He imagined her leaping up the stairs three at a time, in awe of her catlike flexibility. She was gone when he rounded the corner, but he could hear her feet pattering up the stairs above him.

The lift opened at the touch of the button and he spent the fifteen seconds it took to rise to the fourth floor bent over wheezing and trying to refill his lungs without panting too loudly. When the doors opened, Golden was nowhere to be seen, neither was the nurse who usually sat behind the curved desk at the small reception at the end of the corridor.

A soft, muffled scream echoed down the blue and black tiled corridor. Bain recognised that scream. He'd only heard it once before, but he was unlikely to forget it.

The scream had the effect of a starting pistol. Taking a large breath and ignoring the pain in his legs, Bain charged down the corridor, cursing his inadequate physique. A shout of his name and the immediate padding of running feet close behind signalled Golden had made it up the stairs and was catching up with him.

***

It had taken most of Wendy's conversation for Holly to

slowly push at the bedclothes and work enough room to extricate her right arm.

Withdrawing the arm in one jerky movement, Holly half grunted, half screamed with the effort required to fling her closed fist upwards at Wendy as she leaned over the bed with her rounders bat raised.

Holly didn't have any formal self-defence training, but had read somewhere that a strike to the throat was more effective than a punch to the face. Quite where she had dredged that thought up from, she didn't know, but was glad of the effect when her knuckles struck Wendy's larynx. Shock registered on the woman's face first, then she staggered backwards, making a terrifying choking sound that Holly was at first pleased about, then slightly concerned, as Wendy began to recover with a couple of good, long breaths.

Before she could worry too much about Wendy's angry response, Holly needed the room to stop spinning. The sudden jolt had disoriented her. Her foe was a blurry mess and her head was exploding with a pain that started at the base of her skull and washed over her eyes, down her neck and into her shoulders and spine. With eyes slammed shut and gritted teeth Holly slid her body as far to the right-hand side of the bed as she could go, until the tight sheets wouldn't allow her any further, then in one, final, supreme effort, she rolled all her weight to the edge of the bed and prayed that her mother had been as fastidious with her tucking as Vladimir had made out.

Her forehead thumped as she transferred her weight beyond the edge of the bed and slowly at first, the other side of the mattress lifted. A couple of course coughs and growled curses signalled she didn't have much time; Wendy was recovering. Hanging off the edge of the bed, her entire brain singing out in pain, Holly bounced in her self-made chrysalis of bedclothes and sensed the left-hand edge of the thin, national health mattress rise. Bracing herself, she waited for the inevitable thump and potential crack of bone the four foot drop to the unforgiving tiled floor would be bound to deliver.

As she fell, Holly filled her lungs and let out a scream.

***

The corridor had to be fifty yards long, and to his horror, as he set off, a figure emerged from a door at the end of the corridor, glanced his way, then immediately hurried away in the opposite direction. Holly's unknown visitor vanished through a door at the end of the corridor.

Golden passed Bain like he was standing still. She sprinted down the corridor, her sensible rubber-soled work shoes squeaking on the slick square tiles and complaining bitterly as she screeched to a sliding halt outside Holly's room. She burst through the door and found chaos. A chair was on its side, discoloured water streaked the floor where a vase of carnations had smashed, and the bed where Holly had lain only twenty minutes ago was stripped to its carcass.

The bed's mattress was laid haphazardly on the floor, ripped and torn, bits of foam and white stuffing ringed the area. Slimy, congealing trails of blood emanated from under the bedding, some soaking into the sheets, others smeared across the floor, either by hands or feet. It was a scene of wild, animalistic destruction.

'Holly?' Golden called out, half in hope than in expectation.

The mattress quivered and a small voice from beneath called out a weak, unintelligible reply. Golden rushed forward, taking no time to pull the mattress and sheets aside. Underneath, Holly lay face down, a bloodied mess of puncture wounds, shivering in her backless hospital gown. She instantly whipped over, her hands clasped to her chest, ready to punch, scratch, and claw, her eyes wide and scared, her body tensed in expectation of fending off a final assault.

'Holly, its… Kirsty,' said Golden tenderly, lost for words for a moment as the enormity of Holly's injuries registered. Recognising the voice more than the blurred shape kneeling over her, Holly's chest compressed, then rose as she let out her held breath. Golden grasped Holly's hands and squeezed them together to offer reassurance but only succeeded in making her friend wince.

Her chest still heaving from her sprint up the stairs, Golden took a couple of short breaths, straightened and called out for help at the top of her voice. She didn't attempt to move or cradle Holly any further - there was pain enough, without her creating any more. There were simply too many wounds and each cut was oozing life from her friend's tortured body.

A shadow fell across Holly and Golden swung around, fists ready to punch, feet ready to kick, only to find an out of breath, heavily sweating, Bain standing behind her. He stared down at the two women, his lungs burning, anger rising in him.

Holly blinked twice at the heavily blurred outline of Bain and instinctively knew it was him. Closing her eyes, she concentrated, flicking her tongue around her dry mouth to say the one word she knew Bain was desperate to hear.

'Wen… dy.'

'Look after her. Don't you *dare* let her die,' Bain barked at Golden before turning on his heel. Entering the corridor he screamed for a nurse only to find there were already two hurrying towards Holly's room. Satisfied, he turned his back on them and ran to the same door from which he'd seen the distant figure exit.

Golden got out her phone and started to gabble instructions into the device, clamping it between her head and her shoulder whilst balling up a sheet and gently pressing it to what she judged to be the worst of Holly's wounds.

'Wendy?'

The word bounced around Golden's mind. Holly had said 'Wendy'?

Holly's eyes fluttered opened and she met Golden's gaze. The fear in that look struck Golden cold, and she tried to assure her injured friend, but almost immediately she was met with a glazed expression. Holly's eyes travelled up into her head and she went limp. Golden screamed for help and didn't stop screaming until the nurses arrived at a run.

Bain was in a small anti-room filled with cleaning equipment. Five yards distant a fire door with a push bar was ajar. He hurried over and thrust it open, gasping as the night air rushed at him, the breeze whipping his hair.

Finding his bearings in an instant, Bain determined this was a steel fire escape pinned to the side of the six story building. In front of him was a small, square, railed landing with a latticed steel floor. He stepped out. It felt solid enough, although being able to look down through the holes in the steelwork gave him a swirling sense of vertigo, so he settled himself by grabbing onto the landing rail and staring out at the city horizon for a moment and swallowing hard to settle himself. He had to get a grip! For Holly. For his best friend.

More latticed steel steps led in a zig-zag pattern to the next floor, repeating the same sequence all the way down seventy yards or more to the ground. There were six or seven levels in total, the base of the stairway leading to a paved dead end filled with a line of large steel refuse bins.

Swallowing hard again, Bain went to the edge of the first step and looked down. It wasn't easy by any means, but the gaps in the latticed steps allowed a view of sorts down the levels of the fire escape.

It took several seconds before a shadow crossed beneath him. Movement, two landings below. With the image of Holly's bloodied body freshly burnt into his mind, Bain started down the steps at speed, using the rail to whip himself around when the steps doubled back on themselves.

***

As Wendy faced another flight of steel steps she cursed Holly and hoped with all her heart that trixie little madam was dead.

She was proud of her modified rounders bat. Landing that first blow had been so straightforward. Wendy had realised then how easy it was to kill. Brooklyn had turned her back, and *pow*! But using the knife had been so… she winced at the thought… it had been messy! Far bloodier than she had imagined as she'd waited in the bushes with her dogs, down by the River Ouse. But Daniel had told her to use it… and leave it there. Quite why, she never fathomed… something to do with that forensic stuff the police did.

That's why the rounders bat had been her weapon of choice this time. In her mind's eye, she'd seen herself striking Holly as she slept; a single blow that saw her heart monitor immediately flatline. It had been useless once the girl flipped herself out of bed, and held her mattress over herself. The knife had to come out again. It made everything… difficult and messy.

Rounding yet another switchback, Wendy reached a landing. Looking over the edge of the rail, her vision swam a little at the two flights remaining. She paused, took a breath and gave Hogarth a reassuring pat inside her tote bag. She was worn out, frustrated at how messy things had become, and was looking forward to getting back to Malton. This entire outing… come to think of it, the last few months had turned into a *proper mess*. And Daniel had made his plan to get what they both wanted sound *so simple* all those months ago.

Getting Graham barred from training for running up prices at the sales, and implicating Hugo in poisoning a horse; both had failed at the cost of two members of her staff. So, they'd tried the euthanising insurance scam, and the boy had walked away. Trust Hugo to finally find some scruples when you least expected it! They'd been reduced to implicating both Graham and Hugo in dealing in Daniel's father's drugs… which had worked… to a degree. She hadn't been so happy with that. Making cash deposits in Graham's name, then Hugo's, had been time consuming and was a dirty business.

She'd hadn't minded her yard being used as a staging post by her vet for the last ten years… it meant completely free veterinary care she could charge on at whatever rates she wanted.

She had the yard now, but it was annoying that Graham and Hugo weren't under lock and key. Of course, Daniel had got what he wanted; his father's business. She, on the other hand had been required to tie up the loose ends. It seemed there was an abundance of loose ends and she was the one who had to do all the tying.

Holly Grant had been the last loose end. That interview with the police lady… it had been just like that Look North report. If Holly remembered who had been in that trailer, administering that blow to the head... so she had to be dealt with. Beverley Hill stables would be her yard, with *Wendy Dent* as the trainer… no weak, cheating, lying husband or illegitimate son around to get in her way.

'Come on Hogarth,' she called out to the little dog in her tote bag, 'Not far now.'

Her thoughts went back to Holly. She couldn't be certain she was dead, but she had finally gone still for those last few seconds before she'd heard footsteps coming down the corridor.

Wendy set off down yet another flight of steel steps, growling to herself in frustration. She hated doubt. You would think a good blow to the head would be enough, but no…

A sound from above. That had been a clang of feet on one of the steel landings. She froze for a moment, wondering what to do. She was still two floors from the bottom, but once she was back at ground level and away from this building, there were dozens of routes that would allow her to lose her pursuer.

Hogarth popped his head out of the tote bag and licked one of her fingers holding the strap. She regarded his bug eyes and cute little whiskers and smiled at him. He was weighing her down. It would be much easier to scoot down these stairs if he was running with her…

***

Wendy. He'd only seen her in the photos Holly had stuck on their information whiteboard, but the broad, doughy face that had looked up at him from twenty yards below was definitely...

'Wendy Dent!' Bain shouted as he careered down the steel steps and down onto the next level.

'It's pointless running Wendy! I know who you are. You may as well stop right now.'

Wendy had started down the dozen or so steel steps leading to the next landing, but stopped. The young man was right. She lifted her eyes and watched in dismay as he flung himself around the switchbacks until he was only a floor above her. Perhaps it was best to simply wait for him to come to her.

Trying to ignore the muscle-wrenching agony going on in the bottom half of his legs, Bain jumped down the last few steps and onto the third floor landing. He turned to rush down the next flight and was shocked to be met by the dominating figure of Wendy Dent filling the stairway just below him, blocking his path. Down at her feet was a small black and tan dog that immediately started to yap at him, it's tail thwacking against his mistresses ankle.

She smiled up at Bain, climbing one more step to stand a few steps below him, level with his midriff.

'Nice to meet you,' she grinned, and held out her hand as if she was about to shake his. Instead, Wendy lunged forward and plunged her knife into what was in front of her, which was one of his legs.

'Oww!' gasped Bain at the first pinch of pain, recoiling across the landing to lean awkwardly against the railings. His right hand automatically went to the small hole in his jeans, a few inches above his left knee. A short moment passed before a nerve-jangling shot of pain permeated his nervous system and he let out a moan.

'Oh, come on, dearie. Don't fuss! It's only a small knife,' Wendy scolded, her hand dipping into her tote bag.

Bain glanced down. Blood oozed between his fingers, blackening a patch on his jeans. How could he have been so stupid? He should have checked where she was. And what she had in her hand!

This thought became moot as Wendy stomped up the last steel step and onto the landing. Now level with her, Bain could just make out in the twilight what the woman was withdrawing from her bag. His heart sank. It was a short wooden bat. Wendy brandished it in hitting mode above her shoulder, and surged forward.

At that moment the sensors on the fire escape lights decided it was now dark enough for them to illuminate. On each landing a steel encased external light powered up and a stark three hundred watt bulb flicked on, casting a glare onto the steel.

Wendy, stopped mid-surge and blinked to remove the blazes of silver bouncing off the steel fire escape that had momentarily clouded her vision. With this unexpected reprieve gifted to him, Bain's immediate thought was to dash back up the stairs to his right, however his injured leg gave him pause for thought. It was a pause that would prove fatal.

'Well dear, that almost put a cat amongst the pigeons, didn't it?' Wendy said with a toothless grin.

'Wendy!' Bain pleaded with one hand raised, the other supporting his leg, 'Think about this. You won't get away with...'

Wendy had heard enough.

'Fuss, fuss, fuss... People just need to get on with things!'

She surged forward once more, bat raised and ready, the warped horseshoe making the end of her weapon sparkle, just like Wendy's own eyes as she fixed her vicious glare onto

Bain.

This meant she wasn't looking down. And Hogarth wasn't looking up. Wendy tripped over the dachshund and Hogarth gave out a yelp. She stumbled a step and then toppled towards Bain, unbalanced, but still trying to land her killer blow. Bain slid to the floor to avoid the woman's tumbling frame and watched dumbstruck as a combination of Wendy's momentum and her desperation to land a blow on any part of him she could reach, sent her cleanly over the fire escape rail.

She grunted as the rail took her breath from her and once he'd realised she'd gone, Bain squeezed his eyes shut. A dull clang sounded two seconds later as Wendy reached her destination with the minimum of fuss, her flailing body slamming onto one of the steel refuse bins at the base of the building.

Bain didn't move for some time. Holding his hand to his stab wound, he winced while catching his breath. He dropped his chin and peered downwards between the steel mesh. He could see Wendy's contorted body sprawled across the crumpled lid of a steel bin, her lifeless eyes open, staring blindly back at him.

Presently, Hogarth gave a little whine. The little dog trotted over to Bain and gave the hand he was holding to his wounded leg a hopeful lick.

Sixty-Three

It was testament to Holly's good health and mental resilience that she was capable of leaving hospital only three weeks after Wendy Dent's late evening visit. Conversely, she only lasted three days at home in Northallerton, primarily under Ronnie's care, before she was begging Bain to allow her to return to work. He finally took pity on Holly in the second week of her confinement in Northallerton after witnessing an egregious argument that had resulted from Ronnie's attempt to give her daughter an unsanctioned bed bath. Bain was mightily relieved his own stab wound had only required cleaning up and a few stitches.

Holly returned to work, but hadn't been herself for the next fortnight, although having her in the office had some benefits; Bain had someone to bounce ideas off, he could keep a close eye on her, and it kept Ronnie in abeyance. At first, Ronnie would pop her head around the door of the office every half hour to check up on Holly, but her mother's overzealous mothering gradually petered out. By the start of week four, Holly had returned to being his quick-witted, sharp-tongued partner and Ronnie was back to throwing crockery in the bin because it had been used, ironing anything that resembled cloth until it was flat, and every room in the house reeked of Pledge.

The many small stab punctures Wendy had inflicted on Holly's back, arms and neck through the thin, yet thankfully, resilient National Health mattress soon healed. However, she was still prone to dizziness. Holly often found herself leaning, or walking sideways, even though her brain was telling her she should be perfectly balanced.

While the visible wounds had faded, Holly's head injury was a different matter. Even Bain, who was constantly playing it down, or poking harmless fun at her new-found penchant for bumping into the furniture, insisted she never climbed the stairs alone. Holly had been flabbergasted with Bain's reaction when she'd been discovered ignoring this rule.

She'd been trying to navigate the third-floor stairs on her own after a visit to the bathroom, and Bain had found her halfway up the flight of stairs, two hands clamped to the banister as she battled with a bout of dizziness. He'd lost his temper. And Bain *never* lost his temper. She was the one who lost her temper. She'd never seen him like that. After berating her, he'd insisted on carrying her up the remaining steps. Whilst embarrassing and a little shocked he actually managed to lift her, on reflection, Holly had thought it rather sweet of him. Since then, she'd never attempted the stairs, or any steps without a helper. And as far as Holly was concerned, Daisy qualified as a suitable accomplice when no-one else was available.

It had been in the fifth week of her recovery when she'd started to remember. It had been the last week in August and she'd been wandering around at the bottom of the garden. Without warning, a rain shower came across and as the big, fat raindrops struck her scalp, people, places and conversations popped into her head.

'It was as if the rain was playing a tune on my head and shoulders,' she told Bain, 'Finally, all the right notes fell into place in the correct order…'

After being captivated by what Holly had to say, Bain asked questions. Once he'd listened to her answers, Bain told her in an excited voice that she was amazing, and for the first time in many months, Holly had blushed.

Following another short conversation, they took their whiteboard downstairs and subjected Ronnie and Vladimir to a thirty minute presentation. With the royal thumbs up having been received, they called Golden and repeated the presentation later that evening to an audience of one.

Sixty-Four

September 3rd, 3-00pm.

His father's Range Rover felt gloriously impenetrable as he rolled it around the country roads. With the veterinary business back up and running, the police accepting, albeit grudgingly, his version of events, and Wendy having taken herself out of the picture, Daniel was feeling confident. It had been a master stroke to shift all the ingredients and equipment out of the cellar and store them on the morning of the fire.

Knowing the number of his father's burner phone meant the police could locate, and then track the text message that sparked the fire in his father's drugs den.

Daniel allowed himself a triumphant grin as he recalled what Deputy Chief Constable Sayers had told him; the police needed him… he was their star witness, the son who turned his back on his father's wrongdoing and did the right thing!

The resulting court case would see him testify against his father and once things had calmed down, get on with running the all-new operation. He'd be moving the ecstasy equipment out of his lock-up, to a new location for manufacturing. He was returning from Leeds, after coming to an amicable agreement with his father's old clients, and was enjoying the freedom to operate as he wished.

He was taking the longer, prettier way home, as it suited his buoyant mood. As he climbed the brute of a car to the top of the East Yorkshire Wolds the sun emerged from behind a cloud and drenched him in sunlight. Daniel smiled. Didn't they say that the sun shines on the righteous? The plan had worked, perhaps not *perfectly*, but it had worked.

Sixty-Five

September 3rd, 4-00pm

Today was Holly's first venture out into the world, bar a couple of return visits to the hospital for follow-up brain scans. She was doing well, the bruising had receded, she was free of clots, and the dark areas of her scans the doctors had initially been worried about, had dissolved. However, the dizzy spells remained.

Which was why Holly grasped Kirsty Golden's proffered arm in order to lift herself tentatively out of the backseat of the policewoman's car. She took a moment to stand and sway slightly, checking her balance. It was a weird sensation, feeling yourself falling to your right, and land on the left, and she was determined that today's visit wouldn't come to that. Grounding herself gave her time to survey the Dent's yard with Bain and Kirsty at her side. On first look, very little had changed.

Just over two months had passed since she'd left Beverley Hill Stables in an air ambulance - not that Holly had known anything about it at the time, she'd been asleep for another couple of weeks. She was wondering where the helicopter would have landed when Hugo and Graham Dent appeared from the gloom of one of the barns. Holly broke into a beaming smile as Lara emerged at the same time from a second barn entrance. She'd learned that the head lass had played a large part in ensuring her survival and whilst Golden and Bain shook hands with Hugo and Graham, Holly encouraged Lara to embrace her, which she did without hesitation.

Although the yard had appeared unchanged, walking through the two-year-olds' barn, over the courtyard and towards the farmhouse, Holly detected a significant number of empty boxes and a distinct lack of staff. It seemed the Dent's employees and owners, having digested the recent bad press the yard had attracted, had voted with their feet. A quiver of guilt vibrated inside Holly for a moment, but was soon vanquished when she reminded herself of the knowledge she was holding close to her heart.

Once the visiting delegation was inside the farmhouse, Lara organised cups of tea and they each took a seat around the kitchen table. As soon as everyone was settled, Golden took charge.

'Many thanks for agreeing to this discussion, Mr Dent, Ms Bailey and of course you, Hugo,' Golden said, catching the eye of each person as she said their names.

'I think we're all fine with first names,' said Graham Dent. Lara nodded her agreement.

'Thank you, Graham, Lara,' Golden responded, placing

a leatherbound pad on the table, lining it up with her fingertips and laying down an expensive looking pen beside it.

'I wouldn't normally pursue a meeting of this kind,' Golden continued, 'But I wanted to update all three of you with the progress of my investigation. I wanted to do so in less formal surroundings, rather than our interview rooms. I'm sure you've all had quite enough of trekking into York to be interviewed. And you never know, by being together we may also learn something new.'

Golden shot her audience a quick smile, opened her pad, and proceeded to systematically flick through until she landed on a page thick with handwritten notes. Satisfied she'd found where she needed to be, Golden slowly smoothed out the crease in the centre of the pad. Picking up her pen, she clicked the end of the ballpoint and hovering over the pad, began to run her eyes down her notes. Halfway down the page she hesitated, and her gaze wandered off the page.

'You know what,' she said, clicking her ballpoint and placing the pen in the central fold of her pad, 'I'll let Holly and Bain speak first. After all, they're the reason we're here today.'

Hugo had been on tenterhooks since sitting down at the kitchen table and he now leaned across the table and addressed Golden directly.

'Why isn't Daniel Croft here?' he demanded, 'Surely his evidence is critical? I'm still on bail after you found that money and pills in my caravan!'

'I did ask him to attend today, but he refused,' Golden replied smoothly, 'I can understand your frustration, as I share it. However, Daniel Croft is still a person of interest in our inquiries.'

Golden's gaze remained on Hugo, but having said what was on his mind, he shrank back in his seat.

'Right. Holly, Bain?'

They shared a quick look and Bain, knowing it was he who had to speak, took a breath. He and Holly had rehearsed their little double act until they were sick of hearing their voices saying the same phrases over and over, but now they were here, dutiful audience in front of them, and even scarier, Golden waiting patiently… he couldn't remember his opening words.

Holly gave him an urgent stare. That only made his mouth go dry. Then she spoke five words that jolted his memory into gear.

'On the face of it…' prompted Holly.

'Er… yes,' Bain blustered, 'On the face of it, this case is messy and confusing.'

A sharp intake of breath followed, before he added, 'The mis-identification of Robert Farley as Brooklyn's killer, and the involvement of Miriam Blunt's husband at the sales, and also Holly coming to work here, only served to cloud what we believe is a far simpler scenario.'

He glanced at Holly.

'That's right,' Holly agreed, 'We think that my arrival here in March delayed the plot.'

Graham murmured, 'You mean my wife's plot?'

'Not at all,' Holly fired straight back, 'Wendy spoke with me at the hospital. We talked for several minutes. It's taken me a while to remember, and even longer to make sense of it, but with Bain's help, we got there. Although Wendy didn't realise it at the time, our short chat was incredibly helpful.'

Even before Holly had finished speaking, Golden was watching Graham, Hugo and Lara with hawklike intensity for any indication of a squirm in a seat, or any indication of a guilty conscience. All three of them remained annoyingly steadfast.

Bain picked up from where Holly had left off.

'I've a few questions for the three of you, if I may?' he asked without pausing for their permission, 'Graham, would you agree that your relationship with your wife began to sour in or around August last year?'

Somewhat abashed, Graham crossed his arms tight across his chest.

'It's evidence we collected from Lara, Courtney, Mary, Amber…'

'Yes, alright. That sounds about right,' Graham muttered.

'And Hugo, it was around the same time that you started a relationship with Daniel.'

Hugo's eyes grew wide and his mouth dropped open.

'I'll take that as a yes,' said Bain smartly, 'And Lara, was it around the same time that you moved into the farmhouse?'

Lara bit her lip and looked thoughtful, 'I guess. Er… what has any of this to do with… um, anything?'

'I'm establishing a timeline.'

'A timeline for what?'

Bain considered for a moment.

'For revenge… actually, for retribution.'

Sixty-Six

September 3rd, 4-00pm

Daniel's Range Rover swept around a right-handed corner and stepping on the accelerator, he switched lanes and breezed past a tractor. Recognising the farmer in the cab, he lifted a hand to acknowledge him. The old boy cast a set of watery blue eyes on him and didn't return his wave. Instead, the veteran farmer flicked a 'V' sign at him. It could take some time to rebuild the reputation of the veterinary practice, Daniel thought as he watched the farmer become nothing more than a dot in his rearview mirror.

The village of Wetwang flew past without him noticing and within a minute he was on the B1248, heading north across the Wolds. Another shallow right-handed turn and he saw the roundabout, and smiled to himself. It was where it all started; where Geena lost control of her motorbike, where they caught up with her and brokered a deal to keep her silent.

That night he'd finally understood why his father had chosen the Dent's yard as his trading post, and Wendy Dent as its overseer. By god, she'd been a tough, single-minded old bird! She'd managed the deposit and collection of his father's product for over a decade because she knew what was required and didn't hesitate to make it happen… and Daniel had known that if he played her right, she would be his foot soldier. All it had taken was to slowly pour the poison in her ear, and down her throat, and gently point her in the right direction.

It was a straight three-quarter mile road that led to the roundabout. Daniel pressed on, getting a thrill from the surge of power under his command. The road was clear and he was making excellent time. Everything was going his way.

Sixty-Seven

September 3rd, 4-10pm

'What happened the day Geena left?' Bain asked.

Hugo made to start explaining, only to be halted by Bain.

'I'd like Lara to answer this one,' he told him, 'Geena has told us about being chased on her motorbike. I'd like to know what happened afterwards.'

Lara blinked several times and looked surprised, 'I… um, wasn't involved.'

'So who was involved in the pursuit of Ms Coulter on her motorbike?'

'Just Daniel and myself,' Hugo replied, 'Geena overheard us talking as we gave the filly the snowdrop compound. She didn't do anything immediately, but came back to the yard at night, banged on my caravan door and started shouting accusations. Daniel and I came to calm her down and she started arguing with both of us. We set off after her when she threatened to drive over to Mrs Blunt's place in Beverley and tell her what we were doing to her filly.'

'Was anyone else involved?'

Hugo shook his head, 'I didn't mean her to crash her motorbike. It had been raining and the road was greasy.'

'Daniel told me something similar,' Golden confirmed.

Holly was frowning, 'But Geena says she spoke with a woman?'

'Er… that *was* me,' said Lara, raising her hand.

'Oh?' Bain asked expectantly.

'Yes, Daniel called me. He was with Hugo. He said Geena was leaving immediately for personal reasons and ideally, she wanted to work abroad. I'd been in France for ten years, working in racing and he asked whether I still had a few contacts.'

'So you gave him your contacts?'

Lara paused a moment, then nodded.

'You gave Hugo and Daniel the information directly, ' he repeated, 'And you didn't question why she was leaving so suddenly?'

Lara shook her head, 'Stable lasses come and go all the time. Besides, Geena had always been a bit flighty.'

Bain wrote something in his notebook.

'Okay!' Bain pronounced, looking up and smiling at Lara, 'That's all I needed.'

Bain gave Holly the tiniest of nods.

'I noticed a few days ago that the name Lara Bailey has been registered with the BHA as the official trainer here at the Beverley Hill Stables,' remarked Holly, 'That would be you, Lara?'

Bain noted that Lara greeted this news with little more than a sarcastic raising of one eyebrow at Graham Dent.

'Yes, that's me. With all the bad press the yard has been getting, we've lost about forty percent of our horses. So to try and stop the rot, I have become the trainer,' Lara confirmed.

Beside her, Dent bit the inside of his lip a little too viciously, and made himself wince.

'Yeah,' Golden said, stretching the word out with a sigh, 'I think that's sensible. Someone needs to take a grip on what happens inside this business.'

Hugo took a sidelong glance at both his father, and Lara, the beginnings of a grin on his face. Graham continued furiously chewing on his lip, but remained mute.

Bain traded another look with Holly.

'Now then Hugo,' Holly said after a considered pause, 'I understand that the BHA are still considering action against you for the poisoning…'

'It won't matter. I'm leaving racing,' he cut in, 'I've decided the sport isn't for me… none of this is my future.'

'I wasn't enquiring about your employment prospects,' Holly said pointedly, 'There's still the matter of the ecstasy and sum of twenty-five thousand pounds in cash found in your caravan.'

'I've told DI Golden, it's not mine…'

Golden held up a hand, 'I can tell you that the charges against you concerning possession and the intention to supply class A drugs have been dropped.'

Holly waited to allow time for this to register with the teenager. Hugo's jaw silently opened and closed and his hitherto pale cheeks suddenly flushed.

Golden continued, her eyes locked on him, 'Of course those charges could be reinstated if new evidence points to your involvement.'

'That's great news, and about time!' said Lara, reaching out to place her hand over Hugo's. She turned to Golden, 'So you've found solid proof that Leslie Croft was controlling everything?'

Golden provided her with a quick smile that Lara took

as confirmation.

Holly rejoined the conversation, 'You probably know that Wendy tried to kill me.'

There were muttered acknowledgements around the table.

'Before she attacked me, we spoke. At length,' she added, 'But it's taken until recently for me to piece together everything and make sense of what she was telling me.'

Bain felt the atmosphere in the kitchen tighten. Even Golden, whose bottom lip he noticed was bent over her teeth, was held within Holly's spell.

'Wendy was quite effusive when it came to her views on Daniel Croft,' replied Holly, 'She'd realised Daniel had used your infidelity, Mr Dent, to ignite a powerful need in her to exact vengeance. The poisoning, the debacle in the sales ring, and... planning to euthanise a colt for the insurance...'

'That wasn't me! That was Daniel!' Hugo spluttered, 'He had some sort of deal with the owner, a cut of the insurance claim. The filly, the sales, and the colt... Daniel said he was going to use the money so we could go away and...'

Hugo's voice faltered. He took a glassy-eyed moment to compose himself before adding, 'He lied.'

'It doesn't exactly paint you in a good light, son,' muttered Graham, 'We're lucky the BHA haven't got the evidence to push ahead with any charges for what you did at Goffs, or to that poor filly. You have to accept it. You...'

'That's your answer to everything,' Hugo retorted, rounding on his father, his words spiked with anger, 'That's why mum did all those awful things. Why didn't you tell her from the start? Why didn't you tell her who I was? Why didn't you tell her you'd adopted your *own son*!'

The teenager shrank back from the table, his hurt, pained expression bending his good looks into an ugly mask. Graham Dent's lips opened, closed, and opened again, without shaping a suitable reply.

Holly pressed her palms to the table, took a breath

through her nose and continued. She'd played this conversation, around this table, through her mind countless times in the last few days. She was primed and ready. She *had this*.

'I'm certain Wendy and Daniel were working together,' Holly said to Hugo softly, 'I also think that all of those acts were stage managed, but for various reasons, went wrong.'

'What do you mean?' queried Hugo.

'The poisoning of Morgan almost worked. Daniel made sure you, rather than himself, administered each dose of the snowdrop compound. Miriam Blunt was asked separately by both you, and your father whether she would sell Morgan for a pittance, or give the filly away. I think Daniel or Wendy pushed the two of you to make those approaches.'

Holly paused, she could see both men were casting their minds back, recalling requests and conversations.

Holly continued, 'Those acts implicated both of you. A telephone call to the BHA would have seen both of you warned off for poisoning and malpractice. But Geena first, and then Brooklyn got in the way… So Wendy and Daniel moved on to the deception at the sales. Again, it failed. This time thanks to Mr Blunt, Bain, and my mother's involvement. The insurance fraud was next…'

'I refused to do it…' Hugo said in a faraway voice.

Holly pointed a finger at Hugo and then his father, 'Daniel and Wendy were trying to implicate you in crimes that would force both of you to leave racing, allowing Wendy to take over the yard.'

Dent shook his head, a troubled expression contorting his features. Bain couldn't decide whether he was agreeing or disagreeing with Holly, but it soon became clear Dent was having difficulty comprehending his wife's actions.

'Wendy did change this past year,' Dent admitted, 'She became cold towards me. The communication stopped. She started doing things around the yard without telling me... But if she knew about Hugo being really mine, why keep it to herself? Why not just confront me? My Wendy wasn't… so calculating, and certainly wouldn't… I mean, I still can't believe my one lie was the reason she ended up killing Brooklyn!'

Golden had been quiet for some time. She now leaned forward, resting her elbows on the table and steepled her fingers, 'As you would expect, given the circumstances of your wife's passing, we performed a postmortem on Wendy. Would it surprise you to learn that your wife was a user of amphetamines?'

A look of confusion creased Dent's face

'Wendy never… I mean, she wouldn't even know how…'

Dent pinched the bridge of his nose and screwed his eyes shut, 'It's not her! None of this is… Wendy!'

Holly waited a few seconds before she spoke her next few words.

'I agree, Mr Dent,'

Every set of eyes in the kitchen tracked onto Holly.

'From what Wendy said to me at the hospital, I believe there was something far more sinister happening here.'

Sixty-Eight

September 3rd, 5-03pm

He slowed the car as he approached a near ninety degree left-hand bend in the road, the smile still playing on Daniel's lips as he started to turn in.

A flash of sunlight from a car appearing suddenly on his left, and there was a loud bang. Glass shattered and the grinding sound of metal on metal saw the Range Rover shunted onto the grass verge, slide down a ditch, and come to a stop up leaning up against a dry stone wall. He took his foot off the brake and gritted his teeth. Virtually every icon on the dashboard was blinking at him. Whoever had run him off the road was going to pay for this.

Taking a series of calming breaths, Daniel checked himself over. His neck was aching, and he had flying glass cuts on his cheek, but otherwise he was fine. Unable to open his driver's door due to the proximity of the wall, he looked over to the left-hand side of his Range Rover, now a tangled mess of plastic and bent aluminium. Framed by the jagged hole where the window once fitted, was a head and shoulders.

Daniel stared into the hard blue eyes of a man wearing a black balaclava and a mottled green jumper. The balaclava reached just below his chin, allowing a two inch gap before his jumper started. Daniel was drawn to an exclamation mark tattooed on the left-hand side of the man's neck, just below his ear.

'Hello, Daniel.'

Daniel frowned, still somewhat confused and rattled from the crash, 'You're going to pay for this. What the hell…'

'I work for your father,' interrupted the man, leaning his left arm on the window sill, keeping his other out of view.

Daniel's mouth fell open, his heart suddenly thumping alarmingly in his chest. He found his voice again and started to jibber nonsensical half-questions. The man slowly shook his head and placed his index finger to his lips. Daniel fell silent.

'I've been following your progress closely these last few months, Daniel. Not that you've noticed me,' said the man in a conversational tone, 'Your father is disappointed. You've not only let him down, you've made some serious mistakes.'

'Well he's not here, and he won't be for a long time, thanks to me,' Daniel spat back.

'No, he isn't. I'm here,' the man replied smoothly, 'See me as you father's right hand. I take his instruction and I do his bidding. Just as I did at York Hospital. It was your father who made sure that Holly Grant wasn't murdered by Wendy Dent. He guessed you'd try that, and couldn't let it happen. He's sure she and that Bainbridge character will help reduce his sentence.'

The man paused, taking time to read Daniel's reaction, before adding, 'You should have killed her in the trailer.'

'How do you…'

'I was there,' interrupted the man, 'I was at the Doncaster sales too. Now that *was* embarrassing.'

'What the hell do you want?' demanded Daniel, allowing his temper to flare up.

'It's not what I want. It's what your father wants,' replied the man softly, 'And he wants to know your out.'

Daniel gawked at the man, 'What?'

'What's your out?' the man repeated with a shrug, 'It's a simple enough question.'

Daniel pushed his head back into his headrest and snorted a half-laugh.

'What's your out?' demanded the hooded man again, this time slowing the words, his fierce blue eyes consumed with Daniel's response.

'You can't be serious?'

'Have you ever known your father be anything other than serious? What's. Your. Out,' the man restated, making an effort to pronounce each word with clear diction, 'What. Is. Your… Out?'

The man inclined his head slightly, his eyes widening with a quality Daniel read as… expectancy.

Opening his mouth as if to reply, buying himself a few precious seconds, Daniel concentrated, processing the man's words. A sudden jolt of stark realisation, and of possible consequence, shot through him. He glanced back at the man at his passenger-side window and the eyes told him he was right. He had no doubt his father would kill him. Even so, he was unable to conjure up a suitable reply.

When he didn't receive an immediate answer, the man cocked his head to one side and waited. Time dragged as another few seconds of silence elapsed. Daniel's brain kicked into gear, aware he had to produce an answer. The right answer!

Still the man waited. Daniel's eyes strafed the inside of the car for an answer. His frantic search saw his attention drawn to three bright red and yellow coloured oblong biscuits lying on the passenger seat. Had he tasted his last Tunnock's caramel wafer? Another long second ticked by and Daniel, devoid of ideas, turned his head to stare forlornly at the man, now leaning on the frame of his passenger-side window.

The look of sheer terror on Daniel's face was enough to answer the man's question. His wait was over.

'Didn't your father teach you to *always have an out?'*

Dumbstruck, Daniel nodded.

'He instructed me to wait. To give you every chance. Your father wanted you to produce your out, your own back-up plan that would extricate you from this mess,' the man told Daniel as he began to raise his hitherto unseen right hand, 'But as you haven't produced one, this… is his out.'

Sixty-Nine

September 3rd, 5-14pm

'What did Wendy say?'

Holly met Lara's gaze and smiled sharply, 'She said I have *you* to thank for ensuring I wasn't killed in that caravan.'

Lara returned her smile.

'I remembered who shouted. It was you. You shouted. If you hadn't been there to shout out for me, Wendy would have had time to finish me off. Instead, she and Daniel fled.'

'You're welcome. It was nothing,' replied Lara, producing a smile that gave way into a humble shrug.

'Seriously, it *really* was nothing,' she insisted, 'The police had arrived in the courtyard and I'd guessed you were in the tea hut, so I came out of the farmhouse and called out for your help. I had no idea what was going on in that trailer.'

Holly gave a nod of acceptance, 'Well, it saved my life, for which I'm grateful... not just for saving my life, but because it meant I got to speak with Wendy. And she said something... peculiar. It's been playing on my mind ever since that night at the hospital.'

Holly smiled at Hugo, 'Your mum spoke with me about you,' said Holly quietly.

Hugo stiffened.

'Wendy loved you and your dad,' said Holly, her gaze never leaving Hugo, 'I'm sure of it. That's why she felt so betrayed when she discovered your father's lie. It hurt her deeply. I think she'd suspected for some time because of your resemblance to your father. That only made it worse. Yet I'm sure she regretted the course of action she took. But she was compelled to act. The lie had been allowed to grow and fester.'

Holly paused a moment, aware she was the centre of attention. She took a breath and continued.

'Wendy told me something I couldn't make sense of at first. She was talking about Brooklyn, and the day she went to York, hid in the bushes and then attacked her...'

'Wendy said she wished *she'd never listened to her.*'

Holly paused again, allowing the weight of those words to settle on her audience.

'It didn't seem to mean anything, after all, Wendy was about to murder me... but it should have been *him.* She was working with Daniel, she should have said *listening to him,* unless...'

Swinging in their seats, Holly and Bain both turned their attention away from Hugo.

'Remind me again, Lara, when did you move into the farmhouse?'

She blinked twice, a little taken aback.

'I noticed your caravan has hardly been used in the last few months,' explained Holly, 'I also know that you never go racing and hardly ever leave the yard. So when was it?'

Lara stared blankly back at Holly.

'I told you before. Last August,' said Graham, frowning at Lara's inability to provide an answer, 'Her caravan had an infestation of ants and... well, it seemed to work quite well with Lara in the house, she was a good house guest and Wendy seemed happier, so she stayed.'

Bain committed this to his notebook. Holly waited for him to finish writing before continuing.

'I'm certain someone was quietly dripping their own evil into Wendy's mind, and into her body,' said Holly, 'A regular user of amphetamines, or in this case, speed, can expect to experience an increase in energy, but also increasing amounts of anxiety and paranoia. Some people can become highly aggressive. I don't think Wendy was taking it herself, or even knew she was being fed speed, but the evidence was there for everyone to see. She certainly exhibited the signs of heightened awareness and frenetic activity each morning around the yard. I saw it myself. And whoever did this to Wendy, kept going until she couldn't see anything except anger and revenge... her love for her family was subverted, crafted, and bent until it was so out of shape even murder was an acceptable reaction. To my mind, whoever corrupted Wendy was the real criminal here.'

'And what does Daniel say about all of this?' interjected Lara.

Golden spoke up.

'As you would expect, he blames Hugo. The way Daniel tells it, he had no relationship with Wendy, and he was simply a bystander and all of those misdeeds with the horses were Hugo's idea.'

'But Daniel's lying, isn't he Lara?' pressed Holly.

For a split second, Lara pierced Holly with a withering stare, before catching herself and relaxing into something far less aggressive.

'I'm sorry? I don't understand,' she said, her eyes now soft and seeking clarity.

Holly delivered the line she had been rehearsing for the

last three days. She and Bain had worked together, then brought Golden in, and she had confirmed their suspicions.

'You know Daniel is lying, Lara. A mother always knows when *her son* is lying.'

Seventy

September 3rd, 5-15pm

Lara remained motionless in her kitchen chair, her unflinching gaze fixed on Holly.

'You've engineered this from the start,' Holly said, staring back stoney-faced at the newly promoted trainer, 'None of this is about racehorses, or even drugs. Like Bain said earlier, this is all about revenge.'

Lara broke into a nervy smile, 'I don't know what you're talking about.'

'Perhaps, I can help fill in the blanks,' offered Golden.

'Yes, please do,' Dent requested. Both he and Hugo were wearing expressions of utter confusion.

'Holly and Bain came to me three days ago and expressed their suspicions. It sounded fantastical, but as I started to pull at the threads of their story and back it up with investigations of my own, a pattern emerged.'

Golden turned the page on her pad, her eyes flitting across her handwritten notes.

'You are Lara Bailey,' she said. Without waiting for an answer she added, 'And you were known as Laura Beaumont when you worked in several racing yards in the south of France. You were there for the best part of eighteen years. Before that, you were known as Lauren Croft, married to Leslie Croft, the local vet, and mother of Daniel Croft. Care to comment?'

Lara crossed her arms, smiled at Golden and said nothing.

'You came back to Malton five years ago,' said Bain, taking up the story, 'And made a beeline for this yard, starting as a stable lass and rider and soon becoming head lass. We're guessing you knew it was being used as a staging post for the sale of drugs manufactured by your ex-husband and he had to have someone on the inside, namely Wendy Dent. You used your maiden name of Bailey, stayed away from Leslie Croft, and worked your way up and at some point in the last eighteen months, made yourself known to Daniel, your son.'

Holly took up the commentary.

'When I worked here I noticed you always went easy on Hugo. With all the attention you lavished on Hugo, I actually thought you and Mr Dent might be his parents,' Holly explained, 'And when I discovered you weren't living in your caravan, I still didn't suspect foul play, after all, your private lives are your own… It was only when Wendy let slip she discussed her situation with a woman that I started to question who within the house might have counselled her.'

Holly waited in anticipation of a rebuttal. Lara gave a small sigh, re-crossed her arms and remained resolutely silent.

Golden cleared her throat, 'Your marriage to Leslie Croft was turbulent to say the least. We have reports of Malton police being called out to deal with domestic arguments and aggressive behaviour from both of you at the family address. I imagine your husband wasn't thrilled with the boys in blue turning up at your flat when he was hiding a drugs manufacturing operation in his cellar. And at some point I'm sure the police will be interested in hearing the reason you left Leslie for a life in France.'

Golden didn't so much smile over at Lara, it was more of a threatening grin. Lara, to her credit, smiled wanly back, maintaining a silence that suggested this would be her stance on this matter, and probably everything else.

'Poisons,' said Holly, 'Let's talk about poisons. Both equine and human. They pop up around here with disconcerting regularity and always administered without permission. Morgan was being slowly poisoned with snowdrop extract, Wendy was on regular doses of speed, and she also told me I was given something by Daniel to slow me down and dull my senses when I worked here. I remembered Daniel sharing his flask of tea with me on the day I was attacked in the caravan, after which I could hardly keep my eyes open.'

'The thing is Lara, neither Wendy nor Daniel had the opportunity to drug me on a regular basis,' continued Holly, 'But you did. Always in the tea room, offering to make my cup of tea at our breaks, even bringing me a mug to the stables when we were really busy…'

'Lara, would you agree that as Lara Bailey you hold a first class honours degree in toxicology from Birmingham University?' asked Golden.

Lara examined the wall behind Golden and didn't reply.

'Makes me begin to wonder who, between you and your ex-husband, was the one who came up with the idea of creating an amphetamine factory in the cellar,' Golden stated baldly.

A stunned duo of Dents were staring wide-eyed at Lara.

'So what do you say?' pressed Golden.

'I have nothing to say, apart from good luck trying to pin any of this on me…'

'Oh, don't worry,' Golden hissed, 'There's plenty more.'

Lara placed her hands flat to the kitchen table and pushed herself up to her feet.

'If that's everything, I need to get on,' she said calmly, 'It'll be evening stables soon and the horses are due their feed.'

Everyone watched her stride over to the kitchen door, swing it open and quietly click it closed behind her.'

Hugo stared incredulously at Golden, 'Aren't you going to do anyth…'

Golden held up a silencing hand and mouthed, 'Wait.'

Lara pulled on the front door to the farmhouse and

found two tall, solemn constables waiting for her. They immediately began the process of arresting her.

Allowing herself a small, satisfied smile, Golden and everyone else listened to her constable's words through the kitchen window.

When asked if she had anything to say, Lara shook her head, but as she was led away she shouted, 'You've got no evidence, Golden. Nothing. And you'll not get it. My son loves me too much, and my dim-witted husband can't do anything from behind bars.'

Golden waited until the sound of footsteps on the courtyard had faded away before addressing Holly and Bain.

'Well done you two. Nicely executed. I'd Best go though, I've an interview to conduct with Ms Bailey that I'm sure will contain far too many, 'no comments'. I'll be in touch.'

'She's right, isn't she,' stated Holly, 'You haven't enough to make any of this stick.'

Golden paused at the kitchen door and over her shoulder, produced what she hoped qualified as an enigmatic smile. She replied, 'No comment,' and was gone.

Bain and Holly exchanged a despondent shrug. They'd hoped Lara might break down and admit to being the architect behind this whole mess. Most of their work had been supposition as hard evidence that proved the depth of her involvement was in short supply. Golden's interrogation was going to be challenging, especially if Daniel kept to his story.

Seventy-One

September 3rd, 5-15pm

'I'm waiting,' said the masked man with the small exclamation mark tattoo on his neck, 'Last chance.'

His right hand lifted a pistol into view, poked it through the car window and levelled it to Daniel's head.

'*Always* have an out,' said the man.

'My mother!' screamed Daniel, 'My mother! I'll give my father… my mother.'

The tattooed man lifted an eyebrow, 'Your mother?'

Daniel spoke for a full minute without a pause for breath. By the time he'd finished, ribbons of frustrated tears were flowing freely down both sides of his face and coalescing under his chin. Panting, he began pleading with the man to tell his father what he'd said.

The tattooed man withdrew his pistol and spoke quietly to his colleague. When he returned to the window Daniel could sense the man was grinning behind his balaclava; his eyes said it all. In his rearview mirror the gunman's colleague was speaking into a phone. Presently, he lifted a hand and made a thumb's up gesture to the man at his window.

'Congratulations Daniel. Your father has accepted your out,' said the man, 'He'll be in touch with you to organise what you tell the police.'

The man promptly disappeared from view. Straining to peer over his shoulder, Daniel watched the man stalk away, only to draw to a halt ten yards from his car. A new shiver of fear shook Daniel. But the man didn't turn, instead he nipped at the tattoo on his neck… and peeled it off. Seconds later, a vehicle sped past Daniel, leaving him alone, collapsed at the wheel, his battered, disabled car leaning at an angle into the ditch at the side of the deserted roundabout.

It didn't take long for Daniel to recover some sense of normality. When it arrived, he began wondering whether he'd made the right decision. Had he used the right *out*?

Daniel screamed again, long and hard. This time, in frustration. He'd made the wrong choice... He'd let her down and began trembling at the thought of incurring his mother's wrath. The memory of her reaction to both the failed poisoning and Doncaster sales fiasco filled him with dread. It was the fortuitous arrival of Holly Grant that had saved him that time, and it had worked perfectly… well, almost perfectly. He hadn't counted on the speed-addled Wendy deciding to kill her; he'd had to wrestle the woman out of the caravan once he heard his mother's warning calls.

The Range Rover's communication system suddenly sparked into life, it's jarring digital beeping making Daniel's heart jump into double-time once again. He groaned when Kirsty Golden's name appeared as the caller name. He didn't have the strength left in him. Feeling like crying again, he allowed the call to go unanswered.

I should never have come between my mother and father, he told himself mournfully. I shouldn't have listened to Lara, my newly found mother, and been swept along with what she had planned. I could have gone straight to my father and ignored the promise of running both the veterinary and ecstasy production businesses. But his mother had been right. She had got what she wanted; to be the trainer at Beverley Hill Stables, and for a fleeting moment, he had become his own boss, his father had been behind bars… and he'd been happy, truly happy, for the first time in his adult life.

Half laughing, half crying, Daniel Croft wryly wondered whether he should have chosen to say nothing to the tattooed man. Right now, a bullet to his head seemed a viable alternative.

Seventy-Two

November 29th

Ronnie crunched her way angrily down her gravel drive, her ankle length skirt flapping like a kite in the autumnal wind. She reached the kerb and with hands firmly set on her hips, stared fiercely up the road. She stayed there, chin set, lips pursed, before the icy breeze got the better of her. Hugging herself, she stomped back down her drive.

'She better come back in one piece! I'm blaming you if

she ends up under a bus!' she squawked as she passed Bain on her way back to the warmth of the house.

Bain didn't bother replying, to have done so would have been counter-productive. Ronnie had heard the engine of Holly's motorbike depart down the drive, so there was no point denying her daughter was taking her first solo bike ride since Wendy had tried to kill her.

Bain went to the end of the drive and shoving his hands into the pockets of his newly re-waxed jacket, leaned back against the gatepost. A minute later the buzz of a bike engine made him straighten and venture onto the pavement. He could see Holly in the distance. Smiling, he hurried back down the drive and waited by the open doors of the garage.

Holly swept into the drive and came to a sideways sliding stop just in front of Bain, sending a shower of driveway pebbles onto the concrete base of the garage.

'That was sooo good!' she exclaimed, revving the bike's engine, 'I have to do it again!'

'No, you don't,' replied Bain, 'Twice around the block is enough fun for you today. I'm surprised Ronnie isn't out here, clamping you and the bike to the garage wall.'

'She knows?'

The slam of the front door announced Ronnie's imminent arrival and moments later she went nuclear.

***

The Widow Solanki's face appearing through the shrubbery bordering the two houses raised a smile from Holly. She was sitting uncomfortably in one of the creaking wicker seats in the conservatory, still in her bike leathers and helmet. He entered via the door to the garden and took a seat beside her. Bain looked up from the small sofa opposite and greeted him.

'Welcome to the madhouse.'

From the kitchen, Ronnie was still in berating mode,

although from the sound of clinking crockery, Vladimir reckoned she had calmed somewhat.

'I heard her explode and decided to wait until she was only at the volcanic stage before venturing through the hedge,' he explained to Holly, 'I assume you've been out for a ride?'

'The whole street knows she's been out for a ride, Vlad,' said Bain, 'Where've you been for the last ten minutes?'

Vladimir grinned, 'I was listening to your podcast.'

Holly sat up, 'What did you think?'

'Exceptional. I heard Ronnie – that woman's voice carries like a sonic boom, by the way – but had to listen to the last five minutes before I came over. Very enjoyable. And I see it's had plenty of plays.'

Ronnie bustled into the conservatory carrying a tea tray loaded with a teapot, cups, saucers and a small pile of traditional biscuits.

'Helmet off, if you please!' she barked at Holly.

Holly groaned, but did as she was told.

'No sign of dizziness then?' Vladimir inquired.

'None at all. I'm A-Okay.'

'She's been unnecessarily reckless and should have waited for the consultant to…'

'He did! I told you he did,' sighed Holly.

Ronnie swung around, 'You can be so vexing! You didn't tell me she'd given you permission to drive.'

Bain, knowing this would only set off the two of them on another bout of ranting at each other, swiftly interjected.

'The podcast was Ronnie's idea, Vlad. She discovered them a few weeks ago and suggested we give it a go. The feature for the Sunday Times helped us get noticed and it's actually turning into a fairly lucrative little sideline.'

Ronnie straightened from pouring a tea for Holly and beamed at Bain before nodding at Vladimir.

'My idea,' she echoed proudly, all trace of her argument with Holly forgotten.

'It helps that you've a really interesting story to tell,' Vladimir added, 'And it's good to know that all three of the Crofts will be getting their comeuppance.'

Bain became thoughtful for a second, 'It's a bit of a head-scratcher to be honest. I don't know what changed Daniel's mind, but thanks to his interviews with Golden, Lara is facing charges as well as Daniel and his father.'

'Golden reckons he's been leant on by someone, almost certainly his father, but Daniel's remained tight-lipped,' said Holly.

'That reason for his change of mind is about the only thing he hasn't blabbed about,' noted Ronnie as she planted herself in her favourite seat in the conservatory. She picked up her knitting from a side table and was soon clicking away, only to pause her ferocious needle jousting after receiving a meaningful stare from Vladimir.

'I don't care. I have to finish this,' she told him, 'It was blumming cold out there today and Hogarth needs a coat before winter sets in.'

'Hogarth?' frowned Vladimir.

Bain gave a whistle, then called out, 'Daisy? Farley?'

There was a scrabbling sound as claws made contact with the kitchen floor. Daisy bounded into the conservatory and made a beeline for Bain, standing on her back legs to aim a lick at his hand. Two seconds later, a dachshund lolloped over the threshold of the conservatory, tied itself in rings around Bain's, then Ronnie's ankles, and finally headed for Holly.

'The latest member of the team,' Holly announced, bending over to fondle the little dog's velvety ears between finger and thumb, 'He arrived last week.'

'Golden told me that Graham Dent was rehoming Wendy's dogs,' explained Bain, 'I sort of bonded with this little chap at the hospital, and he gets on great with Daisy.'

'Wasn't he the dog that Wendy Dent took with her when she...?' Vladimir asked sceptically.

'Which is why we've given him a new name,' Holly cut in, ' He's called Farley now, after Robert Farley. Both of them have witnessed some horrible things and gone through enough recently, but are now in better places.'

'Really? Where's Robert?'

'Golden recommended him. He's got a fulltime job as a fireman.'

Vladimir smiled, 'Sounds appropriate. Mind you, I don't know if Farley here is in the right place.'

'What do you mean?' asked Holly.

'Well, the two of you find trouble even when you're not looking for it. Actually, make that the three of you – Ronnie's just as bad. This young pup is going to see more action before long, you mark my words.'

'Talking of action,' Ronnie chimed in, 'That reminds me. You got a call on the house phone, Bain.'

Bain looked over at Ronnie expectantly.

'Mmm... it was your father. I do wish you'd give him your mobile number. Anyway, you need to call him back.'

Grumbling, Bain got to his feet, pulled his mobile from his pocket and made his way into the house, not wishing his friends to overhear any argument. Recent conversations with his father had followed a familiar pattern, involving money and demands for him to return to London and embrace the family business.

Two minutes later he was back at the entrance to the conservatory where he hovered, as if uncertain whether he should enter. Holly saw him first, white as a sheet, he was staring vacantly at his phone's screen.

'What is it?' she asked, worried Bain's father was making even greater erroneous demands of his son.

'It's my brother,' said Bain in a hollow voice, 'He was involved in a traffic accident...'

Bain lifted his eyes to meet Holly's gaze, 'He's dead. I've got to go to London.'

Enjoying the Grant Bainbridge Series?

I do hope you have enjoyed reading this story. If you have, I'd *really* appreciate it if you would visit the Amazon website and leave a rating and perhaps a short review. Your ratings and reviews help more readers find my books, which in turn means I can dedicate more time to writing.

Simply visit **www.amazon.co.uk** and search for 'Richard Laws'.

You can also register for my book alert emails and news on upcoming books at **www.thesyndicatemanager.co.uk**

Many thanks,

Richard Laws
July 2024

Printed in Great Britain
by Amazon

47322840R00199